PEARLY GATES

a novel

BONNIE SOLOMON

Published by Bonsol Press

This is a work of fiction.
Names, characters, places, and incidents are
either the product of the author's imagination or
used fictitiously. Any resemblance to actual persons,
living or dead, or actual events is purely coincidental.

ISBN: 979-8-9926133-0-8
Cover design by Ryan Mulford
Printed in the United States of America
First Edition

For Mom, and for Gungie

ONE

To bling or not to bling? Normally, it wouldn't be a question. Pearly Gates likes to shine. But tonight isn't about Pearly. She's not the one who's been awarded Employee of the Year. It's Thunder's moment, and he should get the spotlight – even if he's not the spotlight-seeking type. That's always been Pearly's thing, long before her last life as a drag queen. But she wants to look good for him. She wants to look like she deserves him. Maybe that's why she's standing in front of the mirror with a furrowed brow, manifesting her seventeenth look – a sequined chessboard gown with a heart-shaped Elizabethan collar. The white lace of the ruffles matches her white glitter eyeliner, and her fuchsia updo is fashioned into a queen's chess piece. *Too much?*

"What are you wearing?" she calls out.

Thunder steps into the bedroom, and Pearly's heart skips a beat – even after all this time. He's dressed in a sleek black suit, leather boots with a silver toe cap, and the thunderbolt cufflinks Pearly got him for their 200th anniversary. You wouldn't guess from his lumberjack build or the tats on his arms, but he's a big softie. He works as an ICU nurse caring for newborn souls. In the spirit world and in all their lives together – switching between different gender identities and sexual orientations – Thunder's been the nurturer. And Pearly's been...what? The mess?

"You look beautiful," he says, coming up behind her and wrapping his arms around her waist. His aura glows a brilliant blue while hers is still mostly green – a painful reminder he's evolved more than she has over their dozens of incarnations. Maybe that's why she went for the bling. If she's going to be his arm candy all night, she might as well try to match his inner glow with a little razzle-dazzle in the costume department.

"I don't know..." She experiments with different lip colors as he nuzzles her neck — fuchsia — aquamarine — crimson — appearing and disappearing in accordance with her thoughts. "Should I just start over from scratch? Maybe go Gladiator Chic?"

She feels him stiffen in her arms. "Pearly," he sighs, "we're already running late—"

"I know, I'm sorry, you're totally right." Pastel purple. Neon yellow. "These events are just so vanilla. I always feel like a disco ball at a prayer circle." Back to fuchsia.

He laughs, a deep baritone that makes her tingle in all the places. "I wouldn't have it any other way," he says. "You make a room come alive. You always have."

She smiles, but it feels painted on. She knows him better than anyone, and lately his support has felt a little...distant. He wouldn't have gotten this award without the overtime, but she wonders if he's avoiding her. Maybe she's just imagining things. She hates the vulnerability in her eyes, so she turns away from the mirror and into his embrace. The golden thread pulses between them, and Pearly relaxes. Just like the silver cord that tethers each soul to its body, there's an energetic bond between soulmates, an agreement to keep growing together from life to life. For lifetimes, it's been the one thing Pearly could count on. Her anchor, her touchstone, her armor against the mysterious will of the Higher-Ups.

"Thunder?" she says.

"Yeah?"

"I'm proud of you." She lifts her head from his shoulder, meets his gaze. "You really deserve this."

"Thanks, babe." He kisses her forehead. "But you know, it doesn't mean anything."

And that's the difference between them. To Pearly, it would mean everything.

※

The banquet hall of the Eternity Inn is packed. Thunder and Pearly walk hand-in-hand into a crowd of his colleagues, mingling over drinks and hors d'ouevres. Souls are formless and have no gender, but they can appear however they like. Pearly spots a couple of musical notes and a furry 4-dimensional cube, but most, like her, prefer the familiarity of the human form. She's still hanging onto aspects of her last incarnation – long legs, full figure, big hair. Pearly isn't a "woman" – that's a human thing – but she feels most comfortable as a "she." For now, anyway.

As she and Thunder weave through the swarm of suits and togas, she can't help comparing herself to them. A trio of White Robes – guides for souls in human bodies on Earth – nod as they pass, flaunting their indigo glow. The one feature a soul can't change is their aura, a public indication of their spiritual progress. Red for the newbies, up to violet for the most advanced. There's not supposed to be any judgement – it's beneficial for souls at all levels to interact and learn from one another on their journey toward Enlightenment. But there still is. Of course, there still is. A twinge of jealousy ripples through Pearly's gown, taking away a bit of the sparkle. *Come on, Miss Thing. Keep. Your shit. Together.*

A server comes by with a tray of fizzy drinks. "Champagne supernova?"

"Oh hell yes." Pearly takes a glass. Thunder doesn't. She raises an eyebrow.

"Gotta be sharp for my speech," he shrugs.

There it is again – that twinge. Pearly holds up her glass. Shades of pink, violet, and midnight blue swirl around the starry bubbles like rotating galaxies. "Well, cheers," she says, and takes a big sip. It's not champagne in the earthly sense. It's the idea of champagne – but it has the same effect. Warmth. Optimism. A softening of edges. Pearly's jaw unclenches. Maybe tonight won't be so bad.

"Thunder!"

They turn to see a couple approaching in matching suits and yellow auras. The male-presenting one has pointy ears and a Cro-Magnon skull. The female-presenting one has a pregnant belly, which Pearly considers an interesting choice. Souls don't have babies.

"Hey bud," smiles Thunder, addressing the male. "Glad you made it."

"You kidding? I heard they're raffling off a soul glow package at that spa in Elysium."

"And a day pass to the Department of Dreams!" says the female, flashing an array of ultraviolet teeth. "I've always wanted to take that tram tour."

"Well, good," says Thunder. "At least that takes the pressure off my speech." He turns to Pearly. "This is Sen-Sen," he says, gesturing to the male. "And that's Aditi. They've recently been assigned to work in the Nursery with me."

"And what an honor it is!" says Sen-Sen. "Thunder's a genius with the newborns."

"Total genius," says Aditi. "I asked him once for his secret, and you know what he said? 'Nothing special, I just love them.' Personally, I'm convinced he's a Higher-Up masquerading as one of us mid-levels."

"Oh, please," chuckles Thunder. "The real magic's by my side. This is my soulmate, Pearly Gates."

"Pleasure," says Sen-Sen, extending a hairy hand.

"And what do you do, Pearly?" Aditi asks, giving her aura the once-over.

Pearly flushes. "Oh, you know," she stammers. "This and that." She sips her champagne, stalling. But they just smile, waiting for more. She glances at Thunder, who gives her an encouraging nod. "I, uh – I work in waste management," she says.

Their smiles falter, just a little. Pearly shifts her weight, feeling the walls of the room press in.

"Oh," says Sen-Sen. "How...lovely."

Aditi throws him a look, tries to salvage the situation. "And what does that entail, exactly?"

Pearly cringes, wishing she was powerful enough to disappear into another dimension.

"Pearly's job is very important," says Thunder, seeing her hesitate. "She transports hazardous debris from the Tunnels to the recycling plant." When the body dies, the soul travels through a Tunnel to reach the spirit world. The Tunnel strips the good energy from the bad, and the latter gets sucked down vacuum chutes into hermetically-sealed drums. It's like taking a shower after a long, dirty life – it doesn't rid a soul of their karma, but it gives them a little boost to prepare for the next phase of their journey.

"Fascinating," says Aditi. "I didn't even know we had a waste management department."

Neither did Pearly, not until she got assigned to it after her last incarnation. "It's just temporary," she says. "I wanted to broaden my horizons. To really grasp the nuts and bolts of the cosmic order from the bottom up."

Thunder raises an eyebrow. The stream of bullshit spewing from her mouth freezes midair as they're approached by one of the White Robes they passed earlier, a willowy blue-skinned soul. Their vibration is so delicate, Pearly feels like a bull in a china shop. They're stunning in that sexy alien sort of way, the kind of soul you can't look away from, even if they're not your type.

"We beg your pardon," they say in three voices at once, casting long-lashed eyes at Pearly, "might we steal your soulmate for a moment?"

She smiles, lifts her chin. "By all means. Just keep the tags on if you're gonna return him."

The White Robe forces a laugh, each of the three voices less authentic than the last.

Thunder squeezes her hand, then leaves with the hoity-toity Smurf. Pearly fights a sense of disorientation, suddenly un-tethered. *It's fine*, she tells herself. *You're fine.* But she keeps sneaking glances at her soulmate and the White Robe while his coworkers continue to ply her with questions.

"Why do you wear a hazmat suit?" says Aditi.

"To stop the negative energy from leaking in," she says. "And the smell that comes with it."

"Ghastly!" Sen-Sen's eyes gleam. "What does it smell like?"

"Like a masturbation gym sock sprayed with wet dog and cheap perfume."

They blink at her, and Pearly flushes. Apparently, this is not the same crowd as a drag show. But it does shut them up long enough for her to finish her champagne and signal the server. This time, she takes two glasses.

"Are you sure?" the server frowns. "I've been told they brewed these strong."

"Pffft." Pearly can hold her liquor. She waves them off. As she takes a sip, an otherworldly bell chimes in her mind, signaling for attention.

"Welcome, friends and colleagues," says a melodious voice.

Pearly glances to the front of the room to find a luminous cloud shaped like a pair of cradling hands. This must be Lucina, Thunder's boss and the cause of all that overtime. "It's so nice to see how many of you showed up for our guest of honor," she says. "Please join me as I kick things off with a few words of appreciation."

The crowd heads to the stage. Pearly sees Thunder front and center and elbows her way through until she's standing next to him. He grins, resting a hand on the small of her back as he turns to Lucina.

"Many of us know Thunder," says Lucina, "as the soul whisperer. Even the fussiest of newborns calms in his embrace. And I assure you, those little bundles of starlight can be quite a handful! We like to say you haven't really lived until you've had a baby soul spit up a swirl of cosmic dust all over your scrubs."

Everyone oohs and ahhs as Lucina's form shifts, spiraling into a strand of DNA. Pearly looks down at her own dress. It's starting to feel less couture than chintzy.

"Thunder has been a superstar in the Nursery from his humble beginnings as Assistant Caregiver to his current position as

Head Nurse. Tonight, we're going to hear from two souls who've been greatly impacted by his actions. Sen-Sen, would you please come to the stage?"

Pearly claps with a distinct lack of enthusiasm as she polishes off another glass of champagne.

Sen-Sen clears his throat, pulls out some note cards. "When I first met Thunder, I was a wreck – barely able to hold my form. I'd been sent to the Sanctuary for restoration, and my healer took me to visit the Nursery. Thunder gave me a newborn soul to hold, and it mended something inside me that had been broken for many lives. He took me under his wing, training me as a caregiver, and blah, blah, blah..."

Pearly tunes out the speech. Her eyes wander over the crowd toward a table near the stage. Sitting on top is a glorious seven-level cake painstakingly decorated to represent the Cosmic Womb. Its tiers evoke the astral nebulae from which new souls are formed, and a sugar-spun cradle sits on the top layer, housing a glowing orb that pulses with life. Someone sure put a lot of energy into manifesting it.

"Thank you, Sen-Sen," says Lucina, whose dress transforms into a butterfly's cocoon. "That was so moving. And now we're going to hear from Thunder's former guide, Elethel-3."

The attractive White Robe takes the stage. They find Thunder in the crowd, give him a wink. Pearly's face tightens. She takes Thunder's arm.

"It is a truth well-known that Thunder is the gentlest soul we know." Elethel-3's voice ripples through the banquet hall. "Yet have you ever wondered — how did such a gentle soul receive so fearsome a name? We must confess, dear friends and colleagues — it was not always so. Indeed, our Thunder lived many lives as a warrior, and he took many lives before he learned to nurture life instead. We all make mistakes in our journey to Enlightenment.

But Thunder chose to become the soul he is today — a shining example of every soul's potential to overcome the obstacles of the material world. We know, we know. Guides are not meant to play favorites. But there could be no other more deserving of this award. We love you, Thunder, with all our hearts." A tear falls from Thunder's eye. He bows in gratitude.

Pearly forces herself to take a breath as she swills more champagne and follows Thunder to the wings of the stage. She's a little off-balance and needs to grab his suit jacket for support.

"And now," says Lucina, holding up a crystalline statuette with a personalized plaque at its base, "please join me in giving a warm round of applause to our Employee of the Year – Thunder!"

Pearly follows him past the cake table, up the stairs, and onto the stage. "Wait!" she says, as he's about to accept the award. "I'm Thunder's soulmate, and I have something to say too!"

All eyes turn to her. She squints in the spotlight at the sea of souls. They sway like waves, in and out of focus. "Thunder, my love..." She turns to him, raises her half-empty glass. He smiles politely, brow furrowed. "You are the kind of soul we all aspire to be. I should know. I've been with you more lifetimes than there are stars in the sky. I mean, not really, but it sounds romantic, doesn't it?" She pauses for a laugh that never comes. "Anyway. Lots of lives. You've been my lover, my sister and my brother, my parent, my child, my friend, my enemy – but always my rock. My glue. My...glue-boo."

She burps, emitting a puff of bubbles that sends her into a giggling fit. But no one else seems to think it's funny. Obviously, she needs to go farther.

"And yeah," she says, "you're good. Really good. Kind and competent and always *there* for everyone. It's nice to see a soul rewarded for their hard work and dedication. Because, let me tell you, being good at your job doesn't always get you the recognition you deserve!"

She gestures for emphasis, sweeping her hand in a wide arc that spills the rest of her champagne. Thunder moves closer, opens his mouth to say something.

"I'm not finished!" she slurs. "I'm not finished, glue-boo, just a wait a sec, OK? Look, I know we're not supposed to question our superiors, but maybe if the Higher-Ups got their heads out of their asses, they'd realize there's something wrong with their system. Do they even have heads? Or asses?" She pauses, reflects. "I mean, that's just it, right? They never bother to show themselves. They just hole up in Sector One patting themselves on the back, having headless, assless orgies and God knows what else? Oh Lordy, don't even get me started on God—"

"Pearly." Thunder takes her by arm. "That's enough." He leads her toward the stairs.

"I got it," she wobbles. "I got it!"

But she doesn't. As she wrenches herself out of Thunder's grasp, she trips over her feet and careens down the stairs, arms outstretched. She tries to slam on the brakes, but she's a runaway train on stilettos, headed straight for the cake. All she can do is grit her teeth and brace for impact. The next thing she knows, she's sprawled on the floor covered in shame and spun sugar. Holographic fireworks explode from the orb, spelling out a message as they form a halo around Pearly's cake-covered head.

"Congratulations, Thunder!"

Two

Pearly Gates barrels through the lobby of Cosmic Cinemas, bracing for chaos. "Excuse me, folks!" she shouts through her hazmat suit. "I'm gonna need you to clear the space."

A handful of heads swivel in her direction – two students from the local soul school, an off-duty reaper, a White Robe and one of their recently deceased charges, and a ticket-taker cherub hovering mid-air.

"But," says one of the students, "the movie's about to start."

They're taking in Pearly's sanitation uniform and her bedazzled homemade cape with what she's sure is thinly-veiled scorn, pity at best. But she's got a job to do. Even if it's the worst job in the afterlife, she's still getting it done, hangover be damned.

"Sorry," she says. "But we've got a Hostile Energy Leak and I've got to lock it down—"

The popcorn machine explodes from the shelf to punctuate her request, sending buttery kernels ricocheting off walls and patrons alike. Customers and staff clamor out the rear entrance, grumbling as they go. Working in Waste Management, Pearly's used to complaints. The important thing is the leak. She chased the damn thing on foot from the Tunnel, and she's not about to let it go now. She narrows her eyes, zeroing in on her target. The escaped energy oozes and pulses behind the concession stand, a phlegmy gray blob glistening with the regret of all those unchecked items on someone's bucket-list.

Never climbed Everest, it wails. *Never had a threesome...*

A telepathic communique marked "urgent" bypasses her mental inbox and blares into her mind, exacerbating her throbbing headache. "Gates!" It's her boss, Mr. Mustard. "What in tarnation's goin' on?"

99% of the time, Pearly's job is simple and boring – pick up the barrels of bad energy and take them to the recycling plant. But that 1% requires action and ingenuity, and she's not quite at the top of her game. Why did that 1% have to be today?

She crouches low, the rubbery suit squeaking as she army crawls down the carpet. "Code Marigold in Sector 74."

"Shit on a biscuit." Sector 74 is an infamous drop-off for the spiritually toxic – politicians, talent agents, serial killers, mimes. "Do you need backup?"

"No, sir. Situation's under control." Pearly springs up and leaps at the entity, arms flailing as she wrestles for control. The swirling cloud of negativity bucks her like a bronco. Windows shatter. Framed movie posters fall off the walls. She grits her teeth and digs her heels in, wishing she'd worn the thigh-high stilettos.

"I hope you're not fudgin' the facts on me," says Mustard. "There's gonna be a real hullabaloo if we don't get that contained."

"Yes, sir. I'm on it, sir." The entity throws her across the room and into the soda fountain, spraying Astral Cola everywhere and soaking Pearly's cape.

"Alright, Gates. Get her done and just..." he sighs, and she imagines him pulling on that oily handlebar moustache, "try not to cause too much of a ruckus."

The telepathic link fizzles out as the entity catapults upward, bouncing off the ceiling and walls like some spastic ping-pong ball, sliming everything in its path with the stench of negativity. It's hard to get off, no matter how many times Pearly washes her uniform.

"Hey Frankenstink," she warns, "you better pause with that attitude."

The entity emits a nails-on-the-chalkboard screech, spewing noxious aether-particles that stick to the walls, to the register, to Pearly's hazmat suit. "Now that is downright nasty!" She knows what that shriek means. Creatures like this love some light bullying. It gives Pearly an idea – if she keeps throwing shade, she might attract it with negativity and get it to stop bouncing around. "Does your ass ever get jealous of all the shit coming out of your mouth?"

The entity wriggles in some kind of masochistic glee, oozing toward Pearly. Good, the plan seems to be working. Ever so slowly, she reaches toward her Handbag – a purse-shaped containment unit with 5-D lining, stoned with glittery gems for extra pizazz.

"Damn, bitch," she says, "you make a space whale's booger look cuddly. No wonder you couldn't score that threesome."

The entity shudders, expands. It creeps even closer, then it rears up to make itself as big as possible and emits another horrifying screech. It wants to consume Pearly, absorb her into its innards and keep spreading its stench across the Sector. Before the Higher-Ups came up with Waste Management, negative energy stagnated and coalesced in the spirit world. These dirty little pockets comprised what humans like to call Hell.

Nowadays, thanks to the efficiency of the department, there is no such thing. That is, if Pearly does her job.

She unclasps the Handbag's luscious red lips. Truth is, she's only had to contain a leak twice before, and both were much smaller than this. Her hands tremble, but she's determined to nail this. Maybe then she'll get a damn award, or at least make up for last night's performance.

Right as it lunges towards her, Pearly holds out the Handbag. Brilliant light shines from the interior, piercing the shadows that cling to the malevolent beastie and sucking it into the trap. Tendrils of dark energy recoil and squeal, trying to escape the Handbag – but its pull is too strong, like trying to break free of cartoon quicksand.

Never wrote that novel, it cries. *Never told Samantha I loved her...*

The air buzzes with a high-frequency vibration, the friction creating sparks that crackle and fizz. Pearly grits her teeth and firms her grip, refusing to let go. With one final grunt, she sucks in the last wisps of negativity and clasps the Handbag shut.

It's over. The entity settles down, stops bucking. She carries it back to her pink dump truck, Seraphina – Pearly's emotional support vehicle in the afterlife. Seraphina welcomes her owner with a gentle honk, turning on her own radio to play "We Are the Champions." Pearly slides to the ground with a sigh of relief and a sense of accomplishment. She takes off her helmet, setting it next to the smoking Handbag. Given the circumstances, she feels surprisingly good – even her headache has gone away. Maybe her afterlife isn't so terrible. After all, she has a soulmate. And not just any soulmate, but the best soul.

Enough dawdling – it's time to get home. Thunder's almost done with his shift, and she's got a pot roast to manifest.

***

Pearly speeds down the astral highway, passing all manner of souls. Some travel as winged beings or balls of light, while others use sentient vehicles like Pearly. A holographic billboard hangs in the air, showing a cross-section of the cosmos with a dot marked "You Are Here." Sector 74 is part of an interdimensional honeycomb comprised of independent but interconnected sectors that souls can travel between freely – depending on their level of advancement. The higher your vibration, the greater your access, and the closer to God, sequestered in Sector Zero at the center of the honeycomb. At least that's the theory.

She's so amped up that she almost misses her exit. Fortunately, Seraphina knows where they're going and lights up her own turn signal.

"Good girl," Pearly says, and Seraphina rumbles a mechanical purr.

They descend onto Lightbody Lane – Pearly's home in the spirit world. The neighborhood is modest, none of that fancy archangel shit with the interdimensional closets and the infinity pool. But she loves the casual, cozy vibe. As she guides Seraphina into the driveway, Pearly's shoulders drop, and her jaw unclenches. She and Thunder didn't talk much this morning, but she can't wait to tell him about her heroics. He's sure to get a kick out of it. As Pearly glances at the house – at the afterlife they've created over so many lifetimes – her eyes glaze over and she retreats into memory, to the first time she saw her home...

***

"Don't peek." Thunder's warm hands cover Pearly's eyes as he guides her across a stretch of gravel.

"I'm not peeking!" She is, though. He's been promising a surprise and the curiosity is killing her."You can't bullshit me, Pearly Gates. I know all your tricks."

It's true. Nobody knows Pearly like Thunder. Even back in soul school, he was the only one who knew when she was up to something. And she was always up to something.

"Okay, fine," she sighs. "I'll play your stupid game."

They take a few more steps. Thunder turns Pearly by the waist and takes away his hands. "Happy anniversary, babe."

Pearly blinks. The house sits all Happily Ever After on a small patch of lawn. It's a mash-up of their best lives together – part Victorian, part log cabin, part seaside cottage. There's even a Zen rock garden in the yard from their stint in the monastery, and a patch of tulips from the garden in Amsterdam.

"How did you..." Pearly swallows a lump in her throat. She hasn't reached a high enough vibration to earn her own apartment, much less a house. But Thunder's been working hard for many lives, taking every opportunity to evolve. He probably could've gotten something in a fancier neighborhood, if it hadn't been for her.

She wants to thank him, but the words don't come. She's overwhelmed by his generosity – by the evidence of his love. She's afraid that she doesn't deserve him, that this has all been some elaborate dream, that she's just hallucinating while she dies in whatever life was the real one. So she just kisses him and leads him into their new bedroom.

***

Pearly shakes off the reverie and hops out of the truck. She checks her reflection in the rearview, hoping she doesn't look too much of a wreck. After the incident, she doesn't have the energy to magic away the smudged mascara and the stinky aether particles clinging to her suit. At least she has a moment to regroup before Thunder gets home. Or so she thinks — until she opens the garage door and sees his winged motorcycle leaning on its kickstand.

"What the whaaat...?"

He must've requested to get off early. Pearly wouldn't be surprised to find a romantic dinner waiting for her, even though it was supposed to be her turn to be domestic. Maybe he knows how shitty she feels about last night, and he's trying to cheer her up. That's Thunder for you.

"Ooh girl, someone's getting lucky tonight." She imagines a decadent bubble bath, maybe some role play in the bedroom. Seraphina flash-winks a headlight and gives an encouraging honk. Pearly grins, then shimmies out of the garage and into the house.

The first thing she notices after removing her work boots is the suitcase by the door. A tingle runs up her spine.

"What is this?" Pearly glances at Thunder, sitting cross-legged on the living room sofa. He takes a sip of tea from his favorite mug, the one they got on that vacation to Sector 12, when they attended the space opera and got kinky in a black hole. Thunder always drinks tea when he's looking for comfort.

"It's my suitcase," he says. "I'm...I'm leaving."

He's in his riding gear, that sexy getup with the motorcycle jacket, leather pants, and spurs. She'd like to jump his astral bones right there — but the air feels charged with tension.

"What, you mean like for a trip or something?" A last, desperate hope.

"I'm sorry, but I just—I can't—" His voice cracks. The tears start flowing. "I can't do this anymore."

She takes a step back, her hazmat suit crinkling against the bannister. "Why?" Okay, sure, she's got some things to work on. But their relationship made sense – Thunder grounded Pearly, and Pearly brought Thunder to life...didn't she?

He reaches across the sofa for a tissue. "C'mon Pearly. You know why."

"Is this about last night? I told you I was sorry."

"Pearly—"

"I know, I know, I had a little too much to drink. I was just nervous." She tries to smooth down her hair. "I don't think your co-workers like me very much."

"Well now they don't..."

"Come on, it wasn't that bad."

He just stares at her.

"OK, fine, alright," she says, "I'll see that couples' therapist—"

"It's too late. I'm tired of the excuses." He blows his nose, crumples up the tissue. "You're stuck, Pearly, but you're not willing to do anything about it. I want a partner I can grow with, and you're...not."

She feels the heat rising in her chest and makes an effort not to lash out. "It's not my fault I got assigned a shit job," she mumbles. Even though it kind of was.

"You could reincarnate," says Thunder, "increase your chance for a transfer."

"Ugh." Pearly pulls a face. Part of her wants to hide out here forever, never reincarnate again. Her most recent life as a Chicago drag queen had its moments. It was one of her favorite lives, actually. But it was also hard. Life on Earth is always hard. Besides, she knows what this is really about. "You're ashamed of me."

His eyebrows arch. "What? No —"

"Lies! Liiies-a Minnelli!" She crosses her arms, glancing down at a recreation of the Berber carpet from their life in Morocco. Life was hard then too. "Look, I know you could do better than a garbage collector. I see the way other souls look at you. Even the White Robes—"

"You're not hearing me, Pearly!" Thunder puts his head in his hands. "It's not the job. It's you. You're stagnant. Something's holding you back, and until you figure out what it is, you're going to keep making things miserable for yourself and everyone around you. I love you — I'll always love you — but I can't be your enabler anymore."

She swallows, but her throat is still dry. "Okay, yeah, so I fucked up. But are you really going to cut the cord over one stupid mistake?"

"The party was just the last straw." She watches his face, imagines him playing a slideshow of all her worst moments — all the times she dragged him down to her level. There are a lot of slides. "Look," he says, "I know our last life didn't exactly end the way you wanted. But you've got to make the best of it. Let it go. Move on. There's a lesson in everything — even in this. I know it may not feel like it, but this is what's best. For both of us."

Pearly's face goes numb. This is real. Her worst nightmare, coming to life. Thunder, her rock, her foundation — the one soul she could always count on — is abandoning her. Could what he's saying be true? Did she take him for granted, drive him away? After so many lives together, did she forget how to love? She blinks back tears and tries to stand tall, but her knees buckle. Rather than collapse, she sits precariously on the sofa.

"Where are you..." She swallows, starts again. "What are you gonna do?"

"I don't know." He reaches over, rests a hand on her leg. "But I'm sure whatever happens, it'll be for the greatest good. I trust the Higher-Ups."

She rolls her eyes. "You would."

"What does that mean?"

"They love you," she sighs. "You're like the poster child for self-actualization. If God has photos on the fridge, you're probably sandwiched in between Buddha and whoever invented corn dogs."

He chuckles in that sexy baritone, and it hurts. "Pearly..."

"Don't soften it," she says. "Not unless you're going to stay."

He looks down, clenches the wadded up tissue. "I can't."

They sit in the finality of the thing, listening to the neighbor Earl fire up his lawnmower next door. He could have gotten an Eternalawn, but he likes the earthly reminder of impermanence. Everything fades away in the world of form – the only constant is love. That's what they teach you in soul school. But as Thunder reaches over for a parting hug, Pearly's pretty sure the only constant is pain. Call it weakness, or habit, or the will of the Higher-Ups, she allows her lips to meet his one last time.

The cord between them shimmers. They're not just kissing their ten-thousandth kiss on the living room sofa. From the cosmic perspective, everything happens all at once. They're also kissing their first kiss at the Astral Overlook and their eighty-sixth kiss in that tent in the desert and their nine-hundred thirty second kiss in that hospital in Buenos Aires. For one timeless moment, Pearly rests in the comfort of her soulmate's embrace – of a universe that bears her no ill will. And then she feels it – the cord severs. When she opens her eyes, Thunder and his stupid suitcase are gone.

THREE

P early pulls up to The Crooked Harp and smooths the wrinkles in her outfit. After what happened with Thunder, she couldn't just sit at home. The silence was deafening, and everything reminded her of him, of the afterlife that he just flushed down the toilet. If she thinks about it too much, she's going to crack. Better to avoid, distract – and what better way to fill the hole in her heart than with libations from the sector's seediest dive bar?

"Girl, you look fierce," she says, trying to psych herself up. It's not a lie. She's changed out of her hazmat suit and into an iridescent sequined leotard, gold glitter lipstick, and winged stiletto sandals – accented by a teased-to-the-max pink bouffant. Her perfectly pointed eyebrows match her claw-tipped nails, and her aura glows with energetic padding purchased on the black market. The padding is more a fashion statement than anything else, and it doesn't hold up to scrutiny. But it gives her a temporary boost.

Hopping out of the truck cab, she gives Seraphina a friendly pat. "So what if the glitter stripe makes your wheels look fat?"

she says. "Big is beautiful, baby. It's all about confidence. Don't let anyone give you shit."

Seraphina revs her engine, and Pearly heads for the bar's green door trimmed in flaking gold paint. Above it, a chalkboard sign reads "LATE NITE HAPPY HOUR" and "2 for 1 Flaming Swords." Another sign advertises a smoking patio – mainly for the aforementioned shots.

Pearly swings the door open and steps into the dim interior. String lights line the ceiling, illuminating an L-shaped bar, a pool table, a couple of vintage pinball machines, and a self-playing harp in the corner. The harp has its own agenda – it waits 'til you're good and drunk, then swindles you into trading your valuables for a song. This place used to be legitimately seedy until its seediness made it a tourist trap for White Robes and other older, more advanced souls. Now it's somewhere between seedy and touristy, a pub in purgatory, a barroom bardo. The joint is hopping tonight. Pearly has to squeeze past a drunken Viking demi-god, a bouncing ball of light, and a party of lost souls, just to take a seat at the only open stool.

"Hey Pearly," says Diesel, flipping his long hair as he polishes a glass. He used to be Jesus, in a past life – that is, if you believe the rumor mill. "The usual?"

"No," she sighs. "Make it a Genesis – neat." Diesel raises an eyebrow, then unlocks a cabinet and pulls out a slim opaque bottle. Pearly settles in, placing her rhinestone purse on a hook under the bar. To her right is a pair of googly-eyed Twin Flames, downing shots and sucking face to celebrate their reunion. To her left, a White Robe nurses a pint of Nirvana Lite, scrolling on his scroll. It's not an actual scroll, of course — nothing so low-tech. It's a personal holographic device meant to evoke that ancient aesthetic.

Diesel hands her a glass of crackling rainbow fizz and Pearly knocks it back. For a few precious moments, the bar fades – along with her problems – as her chest explodes with the ecstatic energy of Creation, causing the tips of her bouffant to stand on end. She relaxes, letting the shockwave run through her. Amateurs clench and end up blowing out a chakra, but Pearly's been around the block a few times.

"Tough day, huh?" says the White Robe, looking up from his scroll. "TGIF."

Pearly tilts her head. She tends to be judgmental of these cookie-cutter types – the ones who look like they jumped out of a da Vinci painting, with their flowing locks and their gleaming halos and their manicured wings. This turkey isn't fooling Pearly – he has bags under his brilliant blue eyes, and no amount of frankincense can cover up the faint smell of defeat emanating from him.

She shrugs. "Nothing a stiff drink can't turn around." Or a stiff...something else. She doesn't say this out loud. The guy's not exactly a booger, even if he is a dime a dozen. But sex in the afterlife is different from sex on Earth. You're not just merging with a body. You're merging with a soul and all its past lives, emotions, and memories. That shit can get messy. And anyway, Pearly doesn't believe the cure for getting over someone is getting under someone else – at least, not this soon.

"Preachin' to the choir." The White Robe lifts his drink. "Wanna talk about it?"

A lump forms in her throat. She forces it down. She doesn't want to talk about Thunder, not to some random White Robe. That would just make the breakup feel real, and Pearly wants to live in denial as long as possible.

"Sorry," says the White Robe, clearly reading her face. He drains the last of his pint. "I didn't mean to pry."

"It's okay." She waves it off. "No use crying over spilled glitter."

The White Robe erupts in a stupid snort-laugh and Pearly can't help but smile. He doesn't seem that bad, actually. She realizes her earlier judgments may have been a tad...cunty.

"What about you, Tipsy McWasted?" she says. "You look a little busted. Do *you* wanna talk about it?"

He blinks at her. Pearly imagines it's been a minute since anyone's asked him that. After all, White Robes are supposed to be close to Enlightenment. Closer than everyone else, anyway.

His cheeks are flushed from the booze, and Pearly watches a bead of sweat drip down his perfect forehead. "I shouldn't complain," he says, pushing a coaster around the bar-top. "I know a lot of souls would kill for my job."

Now that's an option she hadn't considered. She'd love to be where he is – to skip the pain and suffering of reincarnation and get straight to the part where she's got the fancy scroll. But killing for it, well – that wouldn't be very enlightened.

"Thing is," he says, "the red tape's out of control. And we're egregiously understaffed. The Higher-Ups changed the recruitment process to require dozens of interviews and several centuries worth of research into candidates' past lives. Our department hasn't had a new hire in decades, and we've all had to double and triple-up on cases. My last day off was, like, a thousand Earth-years ago! I'm burnt out. Done. Stick a fork in me." He belches, punctuating the point.

Pearly sits back on her stool, assessing. Across the bar, the Viking demi-god cracks a cue stick in half and hurls it at the wall, while the party of lost souls weeps over the harp's tender rendition of "Walk on the Wild Side." Everyone trying their best, doing what they've got to do to make it through the labyrinthine funhouse of existence. Pearly's aura crackles. She recognizes this as the kernel of an idea.

"What's your name?" she asks the White Robe.

"Mlkll'mkh'aalahem," he says, "but you can call me Malcolm."

Pearly drums her nails on the bar, considering. She signals to Diesel. "Pour another for my friend Malcolm." As she watches Malcolm's glass fill with ale, the kernel cooks and pops in the microwave of her mind. The idea is risky – lord is it ever. If it doesn't work out, she'd have to do more than reincarnate. That's for human mistakes. No, if this goes sideways, both her and Malcolm's souls could be wiped clean, scrapped for parts, recycled into the great cosmic womb. But if it works...

"You know what you need, Malcolm?"

"What's that?"

She leans in and grins. "A vacation."

"Ha! You're cute."

"Oh, I know. But I'm serious." She gestures in his direction. "Look at you. You're a train wreck waiting to happen – a danger to yourself *and* to the people you're guiding. A little R&R could go a long way."

His face pales. He shakes his head. "Even if that were remote-ly possible –"

"Let's say it was. Where would you go?"

He fiddles with an astral pearl on his ring finger. "Well...my soulmate's obsessed with the Hypogeal Dimension. We both are, really."

"Ooooh," says Pearly. "I heard the Cosmic Caves there are stuff of legend. You can even go spelunking with the abominable snow-bats."

"Yeah, that's the dream." He gets a wistful look in his eyes. "They say if you time it right, the fumes from the guano can make you go nova..."

"Listen, Mal—can I call you Mal?" She throws an arm around his shoulder. "What if there was a way for you to take some time off – treat your soulmate to a nice getaway – and still keep up with your cases? I'd be happy to take them off your hands. Temporarily of course. And if I do a good job, maybe you can put in a good word for me at the department. Help me cut through the red tape."

He frowns. "You mean like a con?"

"No, no, of course not! Nothing that sinister, Malcolm. Think of it more like a mutually beneficial arrangement. You need a break to save your sanity, and maybe your relationship." And frankly, I need a promotion to prove to my own soulmate that I'm better than a goddamn garbage-man."

He turns to her, those angelic eyes shining with compassion. "Is that what this is about? You know there's no judgment up here – no one is better or worse than anyone else —"

"Oh yeah? Try my job for a week and see if you still believe that."

Malcolm shifts back and forth on his stool, staring into his Nirvana Lite as if it contained all the answers to his woes. "I don't know," he sighs, "if the Higher-Ups find out—"

"With all their bureaucratic bullshit?" Pearly leans in, trying not to let the anxious excitement show. *This is it. You've almost got him. Go in for the kill.* "No one will ever know, as long as I keep up appearances."

"I mean, like..." He begins to nibble on his nails. "Do you even have any experience guiding humans?"

"Hmm." She rubs her finger along the rim of her glass. "Well, I ran a pyramid scheme once." Malcolm gives her a look. "I'm kidding, I'm kidding – of course I have experience. I'm actually waiting for the department to approve my application. Got caught up in that centuries-long vetting process you were talking about. But you could change all that."

This was not strictly what you'd call "a true statement." The department rejected Pearly's application twice before, precisely because of her "lack of experience." But how is she supposed to gain experience if they won't let her try? By gaming the system, that's how.

Malcolm glances at his scroll. "So you—you'd handle all three of my cases?" He thumbs down the screen. Photos, videos, and news updates pop up, along with what Pearly guesses are memories and dreams. Pearly recognizes some of the settings from her Chicago life.

"Sure," she says. "Easy-peasy."

"You say that now." He sets the scroll on the counter. "It's not that these are problematic cases, at least not any more than usual. But every individual responds to different methods, and sometimes they don't respond at all. Their lives can be a little..." – he wipes the sweat off his face, but he can't wipe off the centuries of fatigue – "complicated."

"What life isn't?"

Malcolm smiles. Laughs. Downs his beer. Apparently, that was the right answer. Pearly holds her breath, asks the cosmos for a break. She's not really the praying type, but it couldn't hurt, right? She watches the ball of light behind them. It's pushing one of the lost souls against the dartboard now. Bar fight? No, from the soul's flushed face and soft moans, it's clear another sort of exchange is in progress. Pearly wonders what Thunder's doing now. Probably curled up in a healing pod sobbing his guts out. She doesn't want to think about the alternative.

"If something goes wrong," Malcolm says. "If you need my help..."

"I'll message you." Pearly taps her forehead. "Interdimensional telepathy has improved by leaps and bounds since the

Higher-Ups launched those thought-form satellites." She has no idea if this is true, but she read something about it in the news.

"I'm sorry," he says, face hardening as stares into his glass. "It's just—it's too risky. I can't do it."

Pearly sets her shoulders. As much as she hates to admit it, she's desperate. And when she looks into Malcolm's eyes, she sees a lot of the same desperation. He might be a White Robe, but they're both about ready to crack.

"Look," she says. "You weren't off-base. I need this. But I think you need this too. If you keep pushing through the burnout for too long, it won't be good for anyone—not for you, not for the people you're guiding, not for the lives of the people they touch. I know it sounds crazy, but we could make a real difference here. All you have to do is give yourself the break you deserve."

Malcolm furrows his brow, weighing the pros and cons. He's probably picturing the cave-spelunking, or maybe the ecstatic face of his soulmate when he shows up with their travel itinerary. She winces, trying to bypass the stab of jealousy, the feelings of failure—

"Okay," he says finally. "You got yourself a deal."

Pearly's aura crackles. "Halle-fuckin-lujah!" She claps him on the back, knocking his halo to the counter. "Diesel, another round!" She's so jazzed she stands up and twerks, slapping her own gorgeous ass as Malcolm chuckles and patrons cheer. In the back of her mind, she imagines every worst case scenario. What if Malcolm's charges devolve under her watch? What if Malcolm has a crisis of conscience and reports her to the Higher-Ups? What if she really is only suited to Waste Management and her pride gets the both of them Recycled?

But she shoves her doubts aside. Maybe she is a mess, but she's always managed to scrape by. And if there's one thing she believes it's this: the universe should never bet against Pearly Gates.

Four

Pearly would give anything to wake up to the whine of Thunder's stupid blender. She'd give anything to taste his breakfast shakes again, to argue over his insistence on using only the fanciest ingredients from that astral market in Elysium. But there's an empty spot in the garage where Thunder's motorcycle used to be. She couldn't even bring herself to enter their bedroom last night. It still smells like him, like burning leaves with hints of tobacco and spiced vanilla. So she spent the night camped out on the living room sofa. She'd probably have insomnia, if souls needed sleep in the first place.

She throws herself into research to avoid throwing herself off the balcony. Malcolm left first thing, but not before providing Pearly with a manual and a mandate – "just keep their auras stable." He told her to make case notes to help him file his annual progress report, due each Earthly year on All Souls Day, aka November 1st.

Some of the rules in the manual are common sense:

- *Do not expose your supernatural abilities on Earth.*

- *Do not take clients to other dimensions.*

- *Do not provide financial advice.*

Some are woefully out-of-date:

- *Submit self-evaluations by messenger pegasus at the end of each universe.*

- *You may file a request for unemployment during periods of cosmic restructuring, such as continental drift, ice age, apocalyptic flooding, or giant asteroid.*

Some are almost incomprehensible, even to a cosmic being.

- *When faced with spiritual de-molecularization, channel the sixth ray of iridium light through the solar chakra. If problem persists, dance the Tri-Axial Watuzi and contact Operations immediately.*

Her eyes glaze after a while. She hopes Malcolm's own case notes will be more useful.

She pads into the kitchen in her chenille bathrobe and red-sequined house slippers, combining the aesthetics of Dorothy and the Dude, and summons a latte from the Cauldron. Most souls are capable of basic manifestation – turning thoughts into things – but it helps to have an object to focus on, a shadow on the cave wall. Thunder would've preferred one of those retro coffee makers, something sleek and mid-century, but Pearly has a fondness for reminders of her life as a "witch," even though that one ended with a lot of fire.

Armed with caffeine and case files, she sits down at the table. Pearly's always liked the kitchen with its cheerful yellow wallpaper featuring birds perched on flowering branches. When they're feeling frisky, the birds will detach from the wall and flutter around the room, singing paper songs. Today, their tunes sound like a dirge.

"I know," she sighs, as a sparrow lands on her shoulder with a whisper of paper against fabric. "I miss him too." The sparrow poops a crumpled wad of paper on the counter.

Pearly takes a breath, tries to center herself, spreads out the case files. There are three manila folders, each labeled with the name of one of the humans on Malcolm's roster: Hannah Cohen-Jones, Sam Garcia, Danielle Davis. A thrill runs up Pearly's spine. *This is real. Holy shit, this is real.* Her enthusiasm begins to morph into fear. *What if I ruin these people's lives?* Malcolm has had these three cases for a while now — souls are assigned a new guide for each incarnation on Earth, one best suited to the lessons they're working on in that lifetime. What made her think she'd be better suited than him? If they were struggling before, she could really fuck things up now. *Chillax, Miss Thing.* At the end of the day, all she has to do is fill out some paperwork and make sure they don't backslide. Then again — if she really wants that recommendation, she has to do better than maintain the status quo.

She opens one of the folders, labeled "Department of Human Relations." Stapled to the front are two photos. One is a wedding photo. Pearly recognizes the Palmer House, a fancy Chicago hotel. The young bride's gown has a vintage flapper vibe – Pearly approves – and she clutches a bouquet of oversized lilies. Holding her waist is a tall man with a short-cropped afro and a goofy grin.

The second shows Hannah ten years later, staring blankly as they lower a casket into the ground. Pearly touches the photo, and her heart fills with Hannah's grief. Overwhelm. Confusion. Hannah is a planner, and this wasn't the plan.

Pearly flips through Malcolm's case notes:

Name: Hannah Cohen-Jones
Age: 36
Aura: Yellow
Gender Identity: Female
Spiritual Orientation: Jewish *(emphasis on -ish)*
Childhood: Stable. Raised in Eenob, IL. Academic pressure from parents led to high achievement, competitive mindset.
Family: Mother (living), Father (living), younger sister* (living)
Janine—used to be closer, harder now that Janine has kids
Living Environment: Lake Forest, IL. *(Near Eenob. Fancy-schmancy!)*
Lives alone. *(With cat, Calypso.)*
Education: Masters Degree
Employment Status: Assistant professor, sociology, Lake Forest College
Significant Relationships: Theo Jones (husband, deceased)
Relevant Past Lives:
1) Mabel Harper, librarian, early 20th century Philadelphia
2) Ravi Kumar, social reformer and intellectual, 19th century British India
3) Urg, inventor of pancakes, ~30,000 BC (surprisingly tasty!)

Pearly's relieved – Hannah doesn't seem to be in dire straits. It looks like she just needs some help moving on. *You got this, girl.* She opens the second file. Again, there are two photos. One is a professional family portrait against a swirly gray background. Young Sam stands stiffly between his parents in a suit that matches his father's. No one is smiling.

The second photo tells a different story. Twenty-two year-old Sam stands proudly in front of an original abstract painting – his first "adult" purchase. There's a feeling of optimism, of finally getting to make his own choices in life. But there's something under the surface. Pearly touches the picture and finds herself in a too-cold doctor's office, crinkling on exam paper as she looks at a report. She remembers getting an MRI. Then a biopsy. Now the results. The oncologist points at a line highlighted on the chart: positive margin. There's a brief moment of hope. "Positive." That has to be a good thing, right?

"That means," the doctor says, "the cancer has spread beyond the immediate area."

Name: Sam Garcia
Age: 23
Aura: Orange-Yellow
Gender Identity: Male
Spiritual Orientation: Lapsed Catholic
Childhood: Stable; controlling parents
Family: Mother (living), Father (living)
(At arms' length for good reason)
Living Environment: Apartment (Eenob, IL).
(Moved to smaller town after diagnosis to escape big-city stresses. Still stressed.)
Education: Graduated early, UW-Eau Claire, degree in business*.
*(*Wanted to major in history & literature. Went to work for Dad.)*
Employment Status: Currently on disability.
Significant Relationships: Two year-long rela-

tionships, one in high school.
(No dating since diagnosis)
Relevant Past Lives:
1) Bella Morales, early 1900s muralist and activist,
Mexico City
2) Stuart Johnson, Union Army soldier, mid 1800s,
deceased age 16 at the Battle of Poison Spring
3) Kofi, griot and historian, Medieval West Africa

Pearly leans back, sips her coffee. She's died of cancer – several times. Sometimes it killed her fast, and sometimes it killed her slow, but it sucked every time. She stopped trying to understand the Higher-Ups' logic lifetimes ago. She knows there's a loving presence at the center of existence – that's the first thing they teach you in soul school. But it can be hard to reconcile with all the inhumanities that come with being human. From what she can remember, the only thing that really helped with dying was living. Maybe that's what Sam needs – to embrace the life he has left. She'll have to investigate.

The third folder is stained with rings of tea, and the notes inside are wrinkled. The first photo shows a young child with small bones and delicate features sitting on a kitchen counter, legs dangling as they lick cookie batter from an electric mixer. As Pearly touches the photo, she feels the bond between the child and the person taking the photo – Mom. Baking was their love language.

The second photo is actually a series of AI images from one of those gender swap apps – male to female, in a variety of styles from superhero to cowgirl to fairytale princess. Pearly senses the longing, the desire for this person's outsides to match her insides. And the fear.

Name: Danielle Davis
Age: 29
Aura: Green
Gender Identity: Female
Spiritual Orientation: Spiritual-but-not-religious
Childhood: Evangelical upbringing. Battled depression/anxiety/gender dysphoria. Showed interest in make-up, fashion, cooking.
Family: Mother (deceased), Father (living), Stepfather (living)
Living Environment: Stepfather's basement (Eenob, IL).
(Surprisingly, not the issue.)
Education: Three semesters community college.
Employment Status: Works part-time at local hardware store.
Significant Relationships: Childhood BF moved to Chicago. No significant romantic relationships.
Relevant Past Lives:
1) Lucian of Samosata, 1st century, Roman satirist
2) Marta Muller, 18th century, German pâtissier
3) Isaac Levi, 19th century, NYC tailor

Pearly closes the file. She feels less confident than she let on about taking these cases, especially after asking Malcolm what kind of guidance he tended to give.

"Oh, the usual," he waved her off, "dreams and synchronicities. Suggestions. Signs. Nothing that interferes with a human's free will."

Pearly scrunched her face. "Can you give me an example?"

"So, like, you can't make someone turn down a bad job offer that'll lead to overwork, irritability, and eventually divorce. But you can misplace their phone so it takes them an extra twenty minutes to leave work." Malcolm tapped his forehead. "By now rush hour's in full swing, and they're forced to take surface streets instead of the freeway," he traces their imaginary path along the counter of the bar, "and they drive by the pier at sunset where the happy couples ride the Ferris wheel, reminding them of their first date with their spouse, when they vowed never to let money stand in the way of a life well lived."

"Huh," said Pearly, as Malcolm polished off his drink. "That's clever."

"You'll get the hang of it."

"And dreams?"

"Tricky to produce," he admitted, "not for amateurs. We have a department for that, but anyway I doubt you'll need them. Also, please avoid direct intervention. We can't have everyone running around knowing the inner workings of the universe."

Pearly notes that all three cases are based or have roots in Eenob, IL. Could be common practice – if the Higher-Ups are forcing guides to juggle extra cases, maybe they tried to keep things local to make it easier. The only problem she'll have to face – besides the risk of getting Recycled – is her waste collection job. Mr. Mustard already has it out for her. Sanitation worker and guide are both full-time gigs, and she can't be in two places at once. The impossibility of her situation – the likelihood of getting caught – is starting to hit home.

"What the fuck are you doing?" she says aloud.

There's no reply. She watches one of the paper birds fly over with something in its beak. It lands on her shoulder, warbles, then drops a paper worm in her coffee. Pearly shakes her head.

If Thunder was here, the two of them would laugh about it. But Thunder isn't here.

***

"Did you check the oven?" Malcolm turns to his soulmate as they finally near the front of the line. "I might've left the oven on. Maybe we should go back." The transdimensional blimp that will take them to the Hypogeal dimension looms before them, taunting Malcolm for his indecision.

"You didn't leave the oven on, sweetie." Asprice rests a translucent hand on Malcolm's shoulder. Watching the lights swim beneath their skin like little fish always calms him down. "And even if you did, it wouldn't matter. If the house blows up, we can manifest a new one—"

"Form A-29!" he slaps his forehead. "Oh god, what about Form A-29? I think I remember filing it, but maybe I'm just remembering the memory of me telling myself to file it but really I'm just fooling myself..."

"Malcolm." Asprice puts a hand on their hip. "What is this really about? Do you not want to go?"

Malcolm hears the resignation in their voice. He stops inching forward up the ramp to take in his partner. Beautiful, patient Asprice, with their elongated head and zest for adventure, their willingness to relocate from Sirius to Earth when Malcolm got promoted from junior guide. They both love to travel – it was one of the things that bonded them – but Malcolm's schedule hasn't been so cooperative the past few millennia. "I do," he says, taking their hand. "I do. I absolutely want to go. I'm just worried about this Pearly person. I had a good feeling, sure, and her heart's in the right place. But I also had one too many, and her aura wasn't exactly the most stable...do you think I messed up?"

Asprice shrugs. "I've seen too much to believe in coincidences. You met. She presented you with a choice. You made it. I think you should let it play out — but if you're second-guessing yourself and it's going to make you crazy, we can go home."

Malcolm rubs his palms across his temples. He should've just booked them a spa day, something easier, less consequential. But the way Asprice glowed when he gave them the travel pamphlet—the whole room lit up.

"Tickets, please." A member of the ground crew in a 4-D jumpsuit holds out a hand.

Malcolm glances up at the blimp, with its Zeppelin-like shape surrounded by a glowing plasma field. It's a fancy way to travel, complete with luxury dining and accommodations and even on-board entertainment. It would be a shame to waste it all on—what? Some unfounded fear that this will all blow up in his face?

"Tickets, please."

Malcolm blanches. They'd reached the front of the line while he was agonizing. He takes a breath, steadies himself. His soulmate deserves better than his unchecked neuroticism. Dammit, he deserves better.

He hands over the tickets, turns to Asprice. "Let's see some fucking bats."

FIVE

Pearly trails Hannah at a reasonable distance in the most nondescript disguise she can manage – a dead ringer for Carmen San Diego in a teal trench coat and fedora. It feels a little weird for her astral body to imitate a denser physical form, like the skin is too tight. But no one could ever tell the difference just by looking at her. No human, anyway.

Hannah walks to work in "sensible sneakers," beige-and-Velcro monstrosities she must have purchased online. Pearly sees the shoes for what they are. They're a subconscious statement: don't look at me. She tries not to judge – as a drag queen, she did death drops in six-inch stilettos, but she knows her taste in footwear is not universal. Still, those things look like what a grandma would wear to Bingo.

Hannah moves like a carriage horse in blinders. Twice she misses friendly waves from fawning students. The tree-lined streets leading to campus are beginning to change from green to gold, but she never once looks up at the foliage, even when Pearly summons a breeze to blow leaves in her face. Hannah's route feels planned, her actions mechanical.

Eventually, she marches up the steps to Harris Hall. Pearly finds a seat in the back of the auditorium as Hannah walks onstage, head lifting and posture straightening. She makes eye contact and smiles, asking the students to quiet down. They listen. So does Pearly.

"In the past few decades," Hannah says, her aura blazing yellow in the midst of a lecture on gender and society, "the research has shifted. I don't need to tell you how important a role media plays in informing our cultural dialogue. In general, that dialogue has privileged the 'masculine' approach, which the media portrays as objective, rational, and unitary. On the other hand, we have the quote-unquote 'feminine' approach — supposedly subjective, irrational, and fragmented."

Hannah clicks a remote, displaying an internet meme with a quote emblazoned across the screen:

**For all men who say "A woman's place is in
the kitchen," remember –
that's where the knives are kept.**

"I pulled this from an opinion piece in the Tribune," says Hannah. "What do you think? Does an attitude like this liberate women or stereotype them?"

"I like it," says one student. "It's subversive."

"Maybe on the surface," says another. "It seems liberating, but an essential feature of the patriarchy is violence – 'I have to conquer you to make you believe in feminism' – and something truly liberating would have a more matriarchal approach to problem-solving. Wouldn't it?"

Pearly considers Hannah's case notes as the students continue their lively debate. This is a person who's been focused on doing everything right, meeting and exceeding the expectations set by society – now waylaid by the worst kind of plot twist. If she's unable to move on, she probably won't fulfill her life goals and will only end up getting the same lessons in her next incarnation. But purpose is personal, and it can change as a soul evolves. What does a life well-lived mean to Hannah? Was the plan to have kids? Or does she feel she's here to birth something else, like a new generation of feminists or maybe a book or two? Or maybe her soul needs to learn how to love and let go?

After the lecture, Hannah heads to the campus cafeteria for brunch. She declines an invite to eat with a colleague and instead sits alone with a sad sandwich reading an academic journal and scrolling through emails. She briefly checks Instagram, "likes" a photo of her sister's twin toddlers dressed up as matching scarecrows. Pearly tries her first nudge, sending an ad for the hot new dating app across Hannah's feed. But Hannah seems oblivious and just keeps scrolling. Pearly tries again with an ad for sexy-but-walkable boots, then an article that links good sex with longevity, then a press announcement for a play practically tailor-made for Hannah, one that she'd never attend alone. Nothing. Zero engagement. The woman really is wearing blinders.

Then Hannah's phone vibrates. Hallelujah, it's her sister to the rescue. Pearly holds her breath, aura quivering.

> **Janine:** so i invited my cute single neighbor to the twins birthday party
> **Hannah:** Ugh. Kill me now.

Not exactly the response Pearly was hoping for.

Janine: come on he's great!!
Hannah: You said that about the last guy. He thought "recidivism" referred to receding hairlines.
Janine: this guy has a graduate degree - and a cat!
Janine: aaaand he cooks!
Hannah: I cook.
Janine: yea if you count pancakes. come on sis, it's almost been three years. don't you think it's time?
Hannah: Why can't you just leave it alone?
Janine: uhh because your my sister and i love you and i want you to be happy?
Hannah: *you're
Hannah: And I am happy.
Janine: agree to disagree

Hannah huffs, puts away her phone. Damn. This isn't going to be as easy as Pearly thought. What are some other Malcolm-approved methods she could use? It's not like she has much Earth time. It's already September, and Malcolm's got to file that report on November 1st. Pearly needs to reach Hannah, and fast. She considers influencing the thoughts of a nearby driver to cause a minor accident that gets Hannah to realize how short life is and how she hasn't been making the most of it. But then she remembers that Hannah's husband died in an auto accident and that would probably just cause more trauma, and anyway that's probably not what Malcolm meant by indirect interference. If anything, it would only get Pearly Recycled.

A chill descends down her spine as this option becomes more and more real. She doesn't even really know what it entails — few souls do, unless they're about to face the music. Do they tranquilize you first, like when you put down a pet? Do they make you witness your consciousness breaking down, all those hard-earned memories dissolving like tears in the rain? Or do they just chuck you into the cosmic furnace without a second thought? She hopes she'll never be able to answer that question. And if she wants to keep it that way, she's going to have to come up with something more creative to break through Hannah's walls. Some other, safer way to bend the rules.

***

"Excuse me?" Pearly, clad in a cheetah-print jumpsuit and red chiffon headscarf, holds out a can of wet food. "You wouldn't know if this goat milk gravy is any good?" She shifts back and forth in her patent-leather heels on Kitty Kingdom's linoleum, giving Hannah her best suburban-cat-mom vibes. Is the big blonde beehive too much? Only time will tell.

"It is!" Hannah turns to her, eyes widening as she takes in Pearly's outfit. Pearly appears to Hannah as a flamboyant woman just-shy-of-forty — the age she died in her last life. It looks like Pearly's drag persona pulled a Pinocchio and became her own person. Hannah's brow furrows. Then the corners of her mouth turn up, exposing dimples. "My cat devours it," she says, "but she gets huffy if I give it to her too many days in a row. I recommend switching it out with the regular gravy and the aspic."

"That's so helpful, thank you." Pearly throws a few cans in her basket, then glances at the items in Hannah's cart – a climbing pole, a bubble bed, lumber, wire, shelving. "Looks like you're either building a bomb or a very small bunker."

Hannah laughs. "A catio, actually."

"A what-now?"

"It's like a screened-in porch for your cat. Calypso's always been indoor-outdoor, but when I woke up last week at 3 AM to a live mouse running across my face..."

"Ooooooh girl," Pearly shudders, crosses herself. "I'd be screaming my tits off."

"It was a shock," concedes Hannah, "but I surprised myself. Used a broom to shoo it out from under the bed and onto the balcony. That's when it came to me." She snaps her fingers. "Catio." Her face lights up, just like when she's lecturing.

"Smart," nods Pearly. "You're like the feline MacGyver."

"Ha! What's your kitty's name?"

Pearly looks around, sees a glittering toy. "Sparkle...thrust." She gestures to Hannah's cart. "That looks like a lot of work. You have someone to help you?"

"Oh, I...I..." Hannah looks down, bites her lip, and Pearly can feel the slideshow of emotions that start up. Pearly's own chest tightens, and her palms clench and release. "Theo would have thought I was nuts," Hannah says. "But then he'd geek out and get all into it. Probably end up turning the whole thing into a physics experiment." She shakes her head, looks up. "Theo was my husband. He passed."

"I'm so sorry." Pearly reaches out, gently clasping Hannah's hand. Hannah flinches, and Pearly fears she's gone too far. She can do that sometimes. But then Hannah softens, accepting the warm blanket of Pearly's kindness as she blinks back tears. This, Pearly realizes, is a woman who hasn't been touched in some time, not even in a friendly embrace.

"You know," says Hannah, "Theo was allergic to Calypso." She smiles. "Went in for allergy shots for years. It was one of the things he promised in his marriage proposal. He knew it would be a deal-breaker." She cocks her head, shrugs. "Theo was good like that."

Pearly spies a crack in the armor. She sets down her basket and puts her hands on her hips. "You know what you need? An ally. A co-conspirator, if you will. And I happen to be very good at conspiring, and also free this afternoon."

Hannah raises an eyebrow. "Really?"

"Yeah, really. So we building this thing or what?"

Hannah blinks. "You mean, like, now?"

"Yasss, girl, now!"

Hannah shifts her weight, considering. Pearly exhales, making herself wait. It wouldn't do her – or Hannah – any good to try to force things. It's like the manual says – "Above all, you must honor your clients' free will."

"I'd like to," says Hannah, "but…"

"You have a lecture to prepare."

Hannah quirks an eyebrow. "How'd you know that?"

"Oh, um…" Pearly cringes. "I'm a psychic. I see things."

Hannah doesn't seem convinced, so Pearly manifests a business card and pulls it out of her purse. "Pearly Gates: Psychic Readings, Life Coach, Lost Pet Locator." The picture shows Pearly in a turban with her hands covering her eyes, an open third eye staring out from her forehead.

"Wow. Have you found many lost pets?"

"Oh yeah, sure. Lots. Cats and dogs mostly. Couple of birds. Fish." She can see Hannah wondering if Pearly is delusional and not just kooky. She needs to try harder. "There was one, uh, tarantula. Escaped to the neighbor's house. Found it in the basement, in a kid's old shoebox diorama. Made itself right at home in the center of the volcano." She's rambling, but at least Hannah looks more amused than concerned.

"Tell you what," Pearly tells Hannah. "Go home, do your thing. You decide you want some help with the catio, give me a call." She hopes she doesn't sound desperate.

"Yeah? Thanks. Maybe I will." Hannah smiles, exposing those dimples.

Hot diggety! Score one for bending the rules. Pearly's really feeling herself today. She's sure Malcolm won't mind her going beyond the traditional subtle nudges— can't argue with results! In one clever move, she convinced Hannah to spend time with someone other than her cat. Well, probably. Hopefully. She'll have to wait and see if the call actually comes.

Six

Pearly pushes the wheelchair of a snoozing senior down the hall of All Saints Hospital, trying to look like she belongs here. It's not unreasonable – they've had drag queens come in before to cheer up patients. She's going for "vintage candy striper" with her red-and-white satin pinafore, old-fashioned nurse's cap, red fishnet stockings, and white patent thigh-high boots.

A few steps ahead, Sam's oncologist – Dr. Li, according to the nametag – hopefully has no idea he's being followed. Pearly could've made herself invisible, but that requires more concentration.

Her nose wrinkles as she breathes in disinfectant. She's been in a lot of hospitals over the years. It's not the worst place to die, not in comparison to some of her other deaths. Hospital definitely beats dying of the plague in a gutter.

She wheels her unsuspecting charge to rest against the wall as the doctor pauses outside an exam room to flip through a medical chart. He turns his pager to silent, sighs, runs a hand through his salt-and-pepper hair. Whatever's on that piece of paper – it isn't good news. Pearly can feel his fatigue. He's used to this, but it's never easy.

Dr. Li knocks and enters. Shit. Pearly's going to have to turn invisible if she wants to witness this; she doubts Sam would take kindly to a random candy striper eavesdropping on a private medical conversation. She glances around to make sure no one's looking, then – *Poof!* She doesn't need the sound effect, but it makes the transformation more satisfying.

She follows the doctor into the exam room, where Sam perches on an easy chair repurposed for medical use. Sam is a study in contrasts. Bright eyes, gaunt cheeks. Thick brows, shaved head. Clear mind, restless legs – bouncing against the chair in faded Packers sweatpants. One hand clutches the armrest, while the other fumbles with a vintage SpongeBob keychain. His aura glows orange-yellow – not so much because he's less evolved than Pearly's other charges but because he's a younger soul with less experience. Pearly doesn't have that excuse.

"Good morning, Sam," says Dr. Li. He heads to the stool, takes a seat. "How are you doing today?"

Sam stops bouncing, gives the oncologist a piercing gaze. "You're the one holding the chart. You tell me."

"It's not good news, Sam, I'll be honest." He spreads open the chart, revealing x-rays with several white-gray masses. "But there's always –"

"How long?"

Dr. Li blinks, then recovers. "What?"

"Come on, you know what. How long have I got?"

Pearly watches the doctor debate how to answer that question. "It's hard to say for sure. A few months." He pushes up his wire-framed glasses. "But that's just an average. There are patients who defy the odds. It does happen."

"Sure, but not to me."

"Once the cancer spreads to your lungs and lymph nodes..." He clears his throat. "There's only so much we can do."

Pearly gulps. This is a game-changer. Surely, Malcolm thought Sam's condition had been more stable. He wouldn't have gone on vacation if he suspected there was a chance Sam could pass on Pearly's watch. She squints at his aura, trying to detect any changes. Is there more orange at the edges?

Sam's eyes shift to the art print behind the doctor, a rendering of a local lighthouse. Several dozen steps lead up to a lantern room, casting a golden glow to welcome weary travelers. Pearly feels a wave of bitterness wash over Sam. Maybe it's the irony. Aren't lighthouses supposed to be a symbol of safety?

Doctor Li hands Sam a pamphlet. "Sam, you're not alone. We have grief counselors who can help you process all of this—"

Sam pushes the pamphlet away. "No thanks."

"Okay. Well. I'll leave this here in case you change your mind. In any case, it would be wise to get your affairs in order. Any friends and family who could help?"

Sam looks down, picks at a hangnail. "Not really." Pearly experiences a flash of memory – Sam arguing with his parents. They wanted to force him into some high-risk drug trial, controlling his treatment just like they controlled everything else in his life. Saying no to them was a big deal for Sam, but he doesn't have anyone to celebrate his independence with.

"I'm sorry, Sam," says Dr. Li. "I know this isn't what you wanted to hear. Contact me anytime with questions, okay? And let's stay on schedule with your infusions. In the meantime, try to get out, enjoy life." He doesn't say it, but Sam and Pearly both feel the implication. Enjoy life – while you can.

Sam waits for the door to close behind the doctor, then turns to Pearly. "Is this some kind of sick joke?"

Pearly gasps. "You, uh – you can see me?" This was not in the manual, but Pearly has heard rumors that people near death can see through the veil sometimes.

"I thought you guys wore black."

"Who?"

"You know..." Sam mimes the scythe coming down.

"Ah. Right. Only the ones from New York."

He fights off a grin. "I guess this means I don't have six months, huh?"

"Well, I'm not a reaper," Pearly shrugs. "And anyway, it doesn't really work like that."

"So you're, what, a guardian angel?"

"Yeah, you could say that. Point is, I'm here to help you."

Sam offers the most derisive laugh he can muster. "You're a little late."

"Why would you say that?"

Sam gestures to the x-ray. Pearly shrugs.

"You're not dead yet."

"Might as well be."

"Well, that's one way to look at it." Pearly feels the raw pain and anger flowing out of Sam. Anger can be destructive, of course, but it can also be useful. Clearly, Sam doesn't want comfort – not in the traditional sense. But maybe there's a way to present it as tough love, or even a challenge.

"Not the most interesting, though," she says. "I guess I expected more from you."

"So what, Clarence," Sam gets up in her face, "you want to show me how much worse off everyone would be if I'd never been born?" Apparently, he's seen *It's a Wonderful Life*. Decent movie. Kind of bland for Pearly's taste.

"Nah, not my style." Sam's anger doesn't scare her. She's dealt with worse before. Thieves. Mobsters. Zealots. Her boss. "And honestly, no offense, but I don't think the world would've been much different without you."

Sam cocks his head, taken aback by the honesty, but unoffended. Pearly was right. That's exactly what Sam wanted to hear. "So what, you just want to hang out with me until...?"

"I don't know, until you make peace? Fulfill your dreams?" Pearly adjusts her nurse's cap. The red-glitter cross glints in the light. "I hear people are pretty into that."

Sam scoffs, then his face falls. The weight of his anger is just too heavy. "Look, I – what did you say your name was?"

"Pearly. Pearly Gates."

"Uh-huh." Sam rolls his eyes. "Look. Pearly. I don't know if you're real or if the cancer has spread to my brain and this is some massive hallucination, but between the chemo, the radiation, the meds, and the bills, the last thing I need is some OnlyFans angel with a Mary Poppins complex forcing me to watch sunsets and smell the roses. So if you really want to help me, you can fuck off back to heaven, or wherever the hell you came from."

Sam gets up and storms out of the exam room. But he's obviously flustered. He left his keychain. SpongeBob grins at Pearly. She glares back at him.

"At least I ain't a fry cook, bitch." It was so easy with Hannah, she just assumed it would be the same with Sam. That was stupid. She has to remind herself some people are immune to her charms – or worse, some people are put off by her larger-than-life persona. Hard as that is to believe.

Sam re-enters the room, red-faced. "I, uh. Forgot my keys."

Pearly grins. "That was some Grade-A shade, slick. You got a way with words."

Sam makes a face. Pearly sees the snarky responses bouncing through his head, but none of them come out. "Thanks," he mumbles, as he exits the room again. That's progress. It's a tiny victory, but a victory nonetheless.

SEVEN

D anielle Davis cooks a fancy-ass grilled cheese.

This is Pearly's first field note as she invisibly watches Danielle placing four slices of sourdough on a sizzling pan, followed by layers of cheddar and camembert, sliced Honeycrisp apples, fresh thyme, and lemon zest. Between each step, Danielle puffs on her vape and blows it out the window, wearing a focused frown and layers of black-upon-black with over-the-ear headphones blasting Chappell Roan. The kitchen stands in stark contrast, all country quaint with its faded yellow wallpaper and rooster knick-knacks – they're everywhere, from the placemats to the cookie jar that cock-a-doodle-doos when you open it.

Pearly hears the hum of the garage door. An engine silences. Boots stomp. A bearded man in coveralls walks in from the mud room carrying a pair of work gloves and a bunch of mail. Blue-eyed and broad-shouldered, he holds himself with a sort of weary resignation. This has got to be Hank, Danielle's stepfather.

"Hey kiddo," he says, setting the mail on the counter. "You know, you don't have to cook *every* day." He heads to the sink.

"I know. I like to do it." She uses a spatula to flip the sandwiches and turns off the burner. "And I'm almost thirty, Hank. When are you gonna stop calling me kiddo?"

"When you get your own place." He turns on the faucet, starts to scrub. "Or when you stop asking to borrow money for reefer."

She rolls her eyes. "That was one time. And you can't say 'reefer' unless you want the Culture Assassins to bury you in a time capsule." She brings two steaming plates to the table, where side salads and iced tea await. Hank grabs a Bud Light from the fridge and plops down on the one of the checkered seat cushions. Danielle joins him, crossing her legs under the table. Pearly sits too, although of course they can't see her. For a few moments, the only noises are chewing sounds and the ticking of the wall clock.

Hank's brow furrows. He pulls a slice of Honeycrisp from the sandwich. "What's this?"

Danielle blinks at him. "They're apples, Hank."

He finishes chewing, swallows. "Huh."

"It's from a recipe in *The New York Times*."

"Gettin' back to your roots, I guess."

She smiles. Pearly glimpses a memory. Eight year-old Danielle proudly serves "Sandwich Surprise" to Mom and her new boyfriend, Hank: peanut butter and jelly sandwiches laced with Doritos and Hershey's syrup. "I'm still amazed you ate the whole thing."

"Yeah, well, I wanted to impress your mom." Hank's eyes get a little misty as he looks into the backyard, past the tall trees toward the lake. A covered pontoon boat painted with the name "Into the Sunset" sits at the end of a pier. It looks like it hasn't been used in a while.

Hank clears his throat. "How's the new gig?"

Pearly watches Danielle's jaw tense. She swallows, crumples her paper napkin under the table. "It's fine," she says. But Hank is waiting for more. "I mean, hey, I'm learning a lot about power tools. Thanks again for hooking me up."

He nods. "Eddie and I go way back. Used to play in the same softball league. We were the Maggots."

"The Maggots?" Danielle nearly chokes on her grilled cheese. "Why?"

Hank shrugs and picks another slice from his sandwich. "The Blue-Jays was taken."

She snorts. "Well, that's a name you don't forget. Were you guys any good?"

"Fair to middlin'." He takes a long sip of beer and sets the bottle down, picking at the label. "And, uh, how's...everything else?"

"Better." She tucks a strand of shoulder-length hair behind her ear. "The hormones are helping a lot."

He shifts in his seat, clearly uncomfortable. "Good," he mumbles. "That's good." Pearly senses that Danielle wants to say more, but she's afraid he won't be able to handle it. Instead, they both watch a chipmunk climb into the bird feeder and make off with a bunch of seed. "Excuse me," Hank says to Danielle, pushing back his chair. "Gotta teach those varmints a lesson." And he goes off to find the pellet gun, leaving Danielle alone with the roosters and Hank's uneaten apples.

***

When the dishes are done, Pearly follows Danielle into the basement. Danielle has done her best to make the space welcoming, playful and feminine, despite the lack of windows and the color beige spreading like a virus to the carpet, the walls, the sofa. She fights it with soft lighting. Floral accents. A carved oak vanity table lined with make-up and perfume. A framed photo of Tamara Rees, the legendary trans icon who went "from GI to girl" in the 1950s. A wall lined with old-fashioned ladies' hats – a bonnet, a pillbox, a fascinator, a fedora. It looks like the one place Danielle feels free to be herself.

After disappearing into the closet, Danielle emerges in a peach silk robe. She sits down at the vanity and takes a breath, as if steeling herself to see her own reflection. Pearly looks through Danielle's eyes, feels a combination of hope and de-spair. She sees a tall, lanky person with a square jaw, strong nose, and prominent cheekbones. Dyed red hair, cut in lay-ers, intentionally gender-neutral. Pale lips. Pierced ears. Neatly trimmed nails. She likes her legs. Her eyes. Her curves. The estrogen has led to softer skin, fuller hips, and less body hair, along with breast tenderness that she hopes will lead to actual growth sometime soon. But she still has masculine features that make it harder to pass, and then there's...down below.

For now, her genital dysphoria isn't her number one priority. She knows a lot of people have it worse. But it's still easier not to think about it. For the millionth time, she wishes she'd started transitioning earlier, when puberty blockers would've stopped some of the unwanted changes.

Pearly watches as Danielle starts with foundation – liquid then powder. After that comes contouring and bronzer, fol-lowed by blush. Then brow pencil, eyeshadow, and thick black mascara, which Pearly knows draws attention away from the stubble that's hard to fully erase even with the closest shave. But it's not until Danielle lines her lips and applies two coats of MAC's "Make Love to the Camera" shade that Pearly feels the mental cloud begin to lift. Dangling earrings and sparkly press-on nails complete the look.

After sitting for a moment, Danielle retrieves a shoebox from the under the bed and pulls out a pair of strappy red stilettos.

"Yas, girl," says Pearly, even though no one can hear her.

But Danielle doesn't put on the heels. She just looks at them – the same way she looked at Dorothy's ruby slippers in the display case at the Smithsonian when she was six. That was the first time Danielle *knew* she was a girl. Pearly travels back in time with Danielle, trying her damnedest to lobby her parents to let her dress as Dorothy for Halloween.

"But I don't want to be the Tin Man," she sobbed. "He's ugly and he has the worst song."

"Sweetie," said her mother, "you can't be Dorothy."

"No?" She wiped her tear-stained face. "Then what about Glinda the Good Witch? Or Jasmine? Or Ariel? Please, Mom, pleeeeeease?"

"Look, I'm..." Her mother wrung her hands. I'm willing to consider it."

Danielle's father was not. "My son is not a pansy," he declared. So, Danielle went trick-or-treating as the Tin Man, suffocating in a sweaty silver suit while all the cis girls lived her dream. So much for over the rainbow.

***

"I'm sorry," says Danielle, "I can't give you a refund without proof of purchase."

"Can't you just look it up?" Mr. Bloomington frowns through his jowls. "I bought the damn thing two weeks ago, Friday afternoon after physical therapy for my knee replacement." He waves his cane as evidence.

Danielle is not having a good day. She got yelled at by her nineteen year-old manager Kyle, then had a panic attack in the bathroom, which is why she's more frazzled than usual when old Mr. Bloomington comes in with a pizza oven he wants to return. Pearly guesses that Danielle's "Jake costume" doesn't help the situation, complete with its deadname nametag.

Mr. Bloomington has explained that his wife found a cheaper pizza oven online, but of course she can't find the friggin' receipt.

"Even if I can find a record," says Danielle, "the best I can offer is store credit."

"It's a five hundred-dollar oven! What am I gonna buy, two hundred hammers?"

Danielle wipes a bead of sweat off her forehead. "I understand it's an inconvenience, it's just that company policy—"

"Are you calling me a liar, Jake?" Mr. Bloomington crosses his arms in front of his chest. "Where's Eddie? I want to talk to Eddie."

Danielle's eyes dilate and she looks a little woozy, like she's fighting off a panic attack.

"I'm not calling you a liar, I just—"

"Do you know how long I've been a customer? Thirty-five years!" Mr. Bloomington gets in Danielle's face. "Have you even been alive that long?"

Kyle steps in, all acne and diplomacy. "Can I help you, sir?"

"I just want to make a return," he says, "but Jake here is telling me I can't do that." Every time Danielle hears her deadname, she cringes. Pearly cringes too. It's not technically their fault – no one here knows Danielle's true self. There's no way they'd let her work here if they did. "I've been a customer here since before you were born! This is bullcrap. Where's Eddie?"

Pearly has to hold herself back from swooping in and slapping some sense into that old man. She looks up at the light fixture, considers making it fall on his head. It begins to sway, just a little...but no, no, she can't do that.

"Good morning, Mr. Bloomington." Eddie-the-Owner emerges from the back of the store with a harried smile that says this is the last thing he needs. "Kyle, can you please take care of Mr. Bloomington's return?"

"Sure, Eddie. I was just about to do that." Kyle holds out his arm, and the old man takes it, praising Kyle's manners as they hobble toward the other register.

Eddie turns to Danielle. "Kyle told me no exceptions," she says, shifting from foot to foot. "He was very adamant about it."

"Look, son," he sighs, "it's not just about the return. You keep coming in late, or disappearing in the middle of your shift, and the staff is starting to complain."

Danielle bites her lip, looks down. "I'm sorry, Eddie, I can do this, I swear."

Eddie runs a hand through his hair, considering. "Alright," he says, "then get back on the floor and really show me you can do this."

Danielle's shoulders slump. "Okay, I just – I just need a little break." She raises her head, meets his gaze. "Five minutes to pull myself together."

Eddie grimaces, noting the growing line of customers waiting at the register. "Fine," he says. "Take your break. But don't bother coming back."

"Oh no," she says. "Please, no, don't do this—"

He shakes his head. "I'm sorry, Jake, I know I told Hank I'd help you out, but I've got a business to run."

"Yeah," she says, fighting back tears. "I understand." Pearly feels the rising well of grief and resentment. Danielle used to be so reliable. She's hard on herself, doesn't know if the regular panic attacks are because of the hormones or the trauma of working a job in the closet after finally coming out.

Danielle removes the "Jake" vest, sets it on the counter, and walks out the door. Pearly simmers with frustration. She's still tempted to intervene, but she feels the restraints of free will. She reminds herself it's not her job to magically fix her clients' problems – they're enrolled in Earth to learn something. To grow. Even if she was willing to bend the rules...as a guide, she has no influence on Eddie or Mr. Bloomington. And anyway, it's not like keeping this shitty job is in Danielle's best interest. It pains Pearly to feel useless. She's tired of feeling that way.

Unsure how to proceed, Pearly follows Danielle on foot past the town square to the local park. She finds Danielle shivering on a bench in front of a duck pond as she searches for jobs on her phone. Pearly takes herself off invisible mode and hovers a few feet away, tuning into her charge's inner world.

Danielle's worried about finding employment as a trans woman, about the hormones she depends on that require her to have health insurance. But after the shit-show at the hardware store, she doesn't want to hide anymore. She's tempted to dress hyper-feminine to avoid getting misgendered in job interviews, but she still has anxiety about passing, and she isn't ready to commit to the bra and silicone forms. Not yet. Maybe after a few months of electrolysis, which she can't afford but desperately wants. The two-hour sessions of needles getting jammed into her face sound like they'd hurt like hell, but she'd do it if it meant being seen for her true self. She'd also accept the boob job; that would make things obvious. She'd put bottom surgery on the list too, but who the fuck can take three months off work to heal? Assuming she could even get it covered...

At this point, Pearly's already bent the rules for Hannah—and really, they bent themselves for Sam. Would it really be so terrible to make it three for three? If they're going to Recycle her, one more offense won't make a difference.

Pearly strolls to the bench. She's going for autumn eleganza in a burgundy velvet coat with shiny satin lapels and brocade detailing. As she sits down next to Danielle, she adjusts the matching cloche hat perched atop her head – a statement piece adorned with a cascade of gold-threaded silk ribbon, a cluster of sparkling rhinestones, and an arrangement of hand-sewn silk flowers. It takes a moment for Danielle to notice Pearly, but when she does, her eyes widen.

"That hat!" she says. "It's spectacular. Is it Chanel?"

"Close," says Pearly. "Jean Patou."

"What year?"

"1929."

"Wow, those are rare. Where did you find it?"

Pearly runs her finger along the brim, considering how much truth to tell. "Oh, I, uh, inherited it. From my grandmother. Josephine. She was a real spitfire." It's actually a replica of a hat Pearly wore in a previous life. But the spitfire part is true enough. Pearly's always been a spitfire.

"That's so cool. The only thing I ever got from my grandma is a box of recipes."

"I don't know," says Pearly. "That sounds pretty cool to me. Do you make them?"

"Sometimes. More often before my mom passed. She was super into baking, and it was kind of our way to bond."

"That's very sweet." Pearly shifts her posture, holds out her hand. "I'm Pearly."

Danielle opens her mouth, then closes it, brow furrowing with indecision as a flock of migrating geese honks overhead. Pearly gives her a moment, contemplating the sky.

Some people think that if you fuck up your life you'll come back as a cockroach or whatever, but the Higher-Ups aren't that lame. Humans only reincarnate as humans. Still, if it were possible, Pearly wouldn't mind trying out life as a goose. They don't take any shit. Or maybe a redwood tree, or one of those sea otters who sleep holding hands.

"Danielle." Pearly feels the weight of Danielle giving that name, the hope. Danielle's still in her work clothes, minus the vest, and she's wondering how Pearly will read her. If she'll offer the conspiratorial wink, the condescending smile, or the unselfconscious stare. But Pearly just responds with a warm smile and shakes her hand.

She can feel Danielle grappling with uncertainty—how firm a shake to project "strong, independent, feminine?"—not to mention the exhaustion that comes with having to micro-manage every aspect of her gender presentation to avoid getting clocked.

"Pleasure to meet you, Danielle," says Pearly.

"You too." Danielle leans back into the bench, relaxing a bit as she takes in Pearly with less guarded curiosity. "Do you live around here?" Fair question. It's not like Pearly is the prototypical resident of the Corn Belt.

"Actually, I'm new in town." Pearly fishes out the same business card she gave to Hannah. "If you know anyone who might be interested in my services..."

Danielle reads from the card. "Psychic, life coach, lost pet locator. Huh. I could probably use the first two, but I'm kinda broke. Like, broke-broke. Like, just-lost-my-job broke."

"Been there, girl – I've had less dough than a Pizza Hut more times than I can count. But I'm in a better place now, and I believe in good karma. How can I help?"

Danielle shrugs. "I dunno. Maybe a reading sometime? Or hey, if you hear about any employment opportunities..."

"Of course," says Pearly. "I'll keep my eyes peeled." She watches Danielle pull her knees up to her chest and clutch them like a teddy bear. "Hey," she says. "It's gonna be okay."

Danielle nods, blinking back tears. "Yeah. I just – I don't know how I'm gonna tell Hank. My stepdad. He pulled strings with a friend to get me that job, and I don't want to mess things up for him.""I see," says Pearly, like she didn't already know this. "So you liked working there?"

"Well, no," says Danielle. "It was hell. Most days I'd rather rip off my fingernails."

Pearly laughs. "Sounds like the universe did you a favor." She closes her eyes and puts her hands on her temples, doing her best impression of a psychic. "I sense something much better coming soon. Something that allows you not just to survive, but to bloom. Stay open to possibility." She opens her eyes. "You willing to trust the universe?"

Danielle smiles. "Sure. I mean, it's better than the alternative, right?" She looks down at her phone. "I should go," she says, getting up from the bench. "Hank's gonna be home soon, and I want to talk to him before I lose my nerve."

"Sounds good." Pearly gestures to the business card. "Reach out anytime."

Danielle nods, picks up her things. "Thanks for being nice to me today. I really needed it."

Pearly can't be certain, but as Danielle walks away, it looks like her aura is a little bit bluer than the green it was when Danielle left the hardware store.

Score another hit for direct intervention.

Eight

Easy-peasy, just like Pearly told Malcolm. She's a natural at this guide stuff. Obviously, the Higher-Ups *did* have their heads up their asses when they rejected her application. As she strolls back through Eenob's town square – past the post office, the dollar store, and a bougie arts-and-crafts shop – she remembers the feedback she received with the rejection. It wasn't just lack of experience. They said she scored too high on "impulsivity" and "lack of respect for authority." Weren't high scores supposed to be a good thing? The situational judgment questions were the worst.

> *You are guiding a human who is stuck in a repetitive cycle of self-doubt and missed opportunities. They are afraid to take risks and avoid challenges, even though you sense they are capable of much more. You've encouraged them to take small steps, but they continue to retreat. How do you proceed?*

A) Create a turning point by subtly engineering a situation where they are forced to make a decision or face a challenge that can help them grow.

B) Focus on boosting their confidence by sending positive affirmations and synchronistic events to help them feel more empowered.

C) Help them see the bigger picture by sending visions or dreams that inspire them to look beyond their immediate fears and consider their broader purpose.

D) Impose a drastic event in their life, breaking the rules of free will to force them into action. While it may upset cosmic balance, it gets results quickly.

Pearly thought the answer was obvious.

The aroma of roasted coffee beans snaps her back to the present. She finds herself standing outside a cute bookstore-café. A banned book display in the window is wrapped in yellow caution tape, drawing attention to its subversive contents. Pearly's impressed – looks like the owner isn't just some yokel. The chalkboard sign on the sidewalk advertises fall specials like maple pumpkin scones and spiced hazelnut lattes. Pearly's mouth waters. While the spirit world offers all kinds of sights, sounds, and experiences unavailable on Earth, there's nothing like the physical world when it comes to taste. Pearly was actually one of the pioneers of what would come to be known as coffee. She was always telling Thunder she never got enough credit for being the first one to discover its effects, back when she was a goat-herder in the Ethiopian highlands. The love affair with the bean only strengthened throughout her incarnations. She decides to reward herself for her initial success with her charges with a congratulatory cappuccino.

As Pearly steps into the café, she's hit with a wave of nostalgia she can't quite place. There's nothing particularly familiar about the space. The décor is cozy chic, with mahogany floors, exposed brick walls and copper piping, walls hung with local artwork and historical memorabilia. "Would I Lie to You?" by the Eurythmics wafts through the speakers as Pearly winds through the mismatched vintage tables and chairs. It's late afternoon, and the only occupants are a handful of students on phones, a couple of chatty moms, a loner reading a book, and an old guy staring out the window.

A person in their mid-thirties stands behind the counter, preparing a drink. They're angular and lean, with a smattering of freckles across their cheekbones and dyed lavender hair falling over their eyes in uneven layers. Their black tank top shows off a sleeve of tattoos on both arms – Japanese cranes and plum blossoms – and their nose sports a septum piercing. They look up as Pearly approaches. Suddenly, Pearly feels a little woozy. The hairs on the back of her neck stand up. Weird.

"Howdy," says the barista. "What can I get started for you?"

As Pearly opens her mouth to order, a text bubble appears in the top-right corner of her vision.

WHERE THE HELL ARE YOU

Rather than allowing anyone and everyone to bombard each other's thoughts from across the sands of time and the manifold planes of existence, the Higher-Ups devised a mental inbox for telepathy. It's even possible to flag messages from certain souls as spam (where do you think Gmail got the idea?). Unfortunately, Pearly can't block her boss. For now, she just ignores the message.

"Hi there," she says. "I'm new in town. What do you recommend?"

"Welcome to Eenob," they say. "I'm glad you found your way to my little oasis. Charlie Tanaka, they/them."

"Pearly Gates," she says. "She/her." The weirdness is coalescing into a sense of déjà vu. Does she know this person?

Charlie cocks their head, brow furrowed. Like they too are grasping at something just beyond their reach. Then they smile, shake it off. "As for my recommendation," they say, "give me three descriptive words – don't think. First three that come to mind."

"Harvest," says Pearly. "Wizard. Glockenspiel."

Charlie laughs, a throaty chuckle that makes their eyes gleam. "Okay, okay, I know exactly what you need. Give me a sec."

As they turn to the espresso machine, another message pops into Pearly's peripheral vision, then another, then another.

HELLO?!??!?

GET YOUR ASS OVER HERE

EMERGENCY! WE'RE CIRCLIN' THE WAGON HERE,

PEARLY!

Not good. Pearly's going to have to deal with this – but not before she gets her coffee. Priorities. And anyway, she's curious what Charlie's going to come up with.

"Is this your place?" Pearly asks, watching Charlie select from an arsenal of spices and syrups.

"Yeah," they say. "I grew up here but lived in Chicago 'til recently. Found this place for sale and the price was too good to pass up. First time in my life I didn't play it safe."

"Congratulations," says Pearly. "That's no small feat."

"Thanks. I hope it pays off." They set a steaming mug on the counter. Pearly gets a whiff of exotic spices. "This here is a one of a kind Harvest Wizard Latte," says Charlie. "It's got a creamy spiced pumpkin base with a hint of maple syrup swirled with honey-lavender, a sprinkle of cardamom, nutmeg, and cinnamon, topped off with whipped cream laced with saffron-infused caramel. I predict that when you drink it, your brain will produce ecstatic glockenspiel chimes in your mind."

"Wow," says Pearly. "That's quite a concoction. I can't wait."

Charlie picks up the mug and hands it to Pearly. As their fingertips brush, a jolt runs up Pearly's arm and a flood of memories swirl through her mind. She realizes how she knows this person. She knows them from nights at sea on the Barbary Coast, their loyalty tested in every storm. She knows them from the German circus tent, where she watched them swallow swords, winning over the bawdy crowd – and from the cramped, back room of the Globe, where they snuck kisses between acts. She knows them from the rain-slicked street outside of Roscoe's Tavern, where the two of them walked hand-in-hand, her elaborate drag costume glistening under the streetlights as they both got drenched.

For the first time, Pearly is struck by the name of the café, inscribed above the counter:

THUNDERBOLT BOOKS & COFFEE

Pearly gasps, fumbles the latte and almost spills it. Charlie reaches out, steadies the cup. They watch the foam bubble up over the top.

"Are you okay?" Charlie looks Pearly over with concern.

"Oh, I'm fine!" says Pearly, much too loud. "Don't you worry about me! Just, um. Remembered something."

A final text from Mr. Mustard lands in her head like a lead balloon.

IF YOU'RE NOT IN MY OFFICE IN FIVE MINUTES
I'LL RECYCLE YOU MYSELF

NINE

What are the chances? Any fool knows that souls can choose to reincarnate at any point in history, and since Thunder's last life ended abruptly, it makes sense he'd have wanted to pick up more or less where he left off.

As Pearly steers Seraphina down the long, gravel drive of Waste Management HQ, she tries to piece it together. After their breakup, Thunder decided to reincarnate. He would have gone to the Screening Room, where he'd get a preview of several bodies chosen by the Higher-Ups. Those bodies – and the cultures, families, and conflicts associated with them – would present "ideal" scenarios for Thunder to evolve. He couldn't have known in choosing "Charlie" that Pearly would swindle her way into becoming Hannah's guide, and thus into his life. But the Higher-Ups – they're sneaky. They could have seen this coming. Hell, they could've even orchestrated it. To what end?

Pearly doesn't know. And right now, she has a more immediate problem – her boss. Mr. Mustard isn't a Higher-Up. The only thing he cares about is that she stays on schedule.

"I'm not all up in my panties," she says to Seraphina. "You know how he gets. I'll just tell him we had a Code Turquoise."

Seraphina revs her engine.

"No? Maybe you're right. What about a Handbag malfunction, or a TS-7?"

The dump truck shrugs her side mirrors. Pearly pulls into a spot in front of the poop-brown building. "I guess I'll wing it," she says. "Wish me luck."

Seraphina purrs, and Pearly marches up the steps in her hazmat uniform and hard-hat. As much as it pains her to leave her heels at home, there are times when it's best not to risk self-expression. There's no one in the lobby other than a gum-smacking hologram with big hair and pouty lips.

"You can go in, Ms. Gates." The hologram files her hard light nails. "He's expecting you."

"Thanks." Pearly wishes she'd come up with a few talking points. "What, uh...what kind of mood is he in?"

The hologram doesn't look up from her screen. "The usual."

Pearly smooths her hair and starts down the hallway. It smells like stale coffee and donuts, with a lingering aroma of lost hope. Framed photos line the walls under a banner reading "SANITATION IN ACTION," with a timeline of the Department's storied history.

She approaches a closed door with a nameplate – Bartholomew A. Mustard, Refuse Collection Supervisor – and is about to knock when she hears shouting coming from inside.

"...I don't care how you do it. But you pull your delusional head outta your barrel-boarded ass and deliver me that truck, or so help me, I'll tell Management you snuck moonshine into the reincarnation appreciation seminar—no, don't give me that horseshit! You told me you'd have it repaired by morning. You know, morning? The best time of day to go fuck yourself!"

Pearly hears a phone slam against its cradle. The receptionist was right. This is the usual. She steels herself, knocks.

"What?!"

She steps into an office decorated with gilded mirrors, wagon wheels, and cow skulls. It's like the Wild West had a midlife crisis, went on a bender, and threw up all over the room.

"Well, well, well." Mr. Mustard twists his well-oiled handlebar moustache. "If it ain't Pearly Gates herself. How convenient of you to make an appearance."

"Good morning, Mr. Mustard. Sorry to keep you waiting."

"Are you though?" His bolo tie has an amber-encased cockroach at its center, which glints in the light cascading through the window. "We got ourselves some hair in the butter, and as per usual, I'm the one who's got to pick it out."

"Yes, sir." Pearly takes a seat. "I'm sorry, sir."

"Do you know what happens when you're late for your shift?" Mr. Mustard looms over his desk, knocking over a mug that brags, "A little cup of GIDDY UP!"

"The drums get antsy, sir."

"And what do antsy drums do?"

Pearly sighs. "They leak, sir."

"That's right! And since you weren't there to deal with the leakage, your esteemed colleagues Hertz and Abathur had to chase down a renegade shame spiral into the alley behind Akashic Records. Broke a bunch of vinyls, caused a big foofaraw."

"Yes, sir. I can understand that. You see, the thing is –"

"Don't." He holds up a hand. "Just don't. If you think you can get one past me, you got the wrong pig by the tail."

"I don't think that, sir."

"I don't want flattery, Gates, and I don't want excuses. I want action!" He slaps the table, sending another few tchotchkes tumbling to the floor. "You think you got a shit job? Maybe so, but the only way out is through. You gotta show up every day, tougher'n nails and stronger'n steel. A few centuries of that, you could even make supervisor."

Pearly tries to hide her disgust. "You really think so, sir?"

"Maybe," he clucks. "But this is the last time I stick my neck out for your hooky-playin' ass. And if I hear anything – anything – that ain't on the up and up? I'm gonna come down on you so hard you're gonna wish you never popped outta the cosmic womb."

"Copy that, Mr. Mustard." Pearly stands, already devising a way out of her predicament. An idea is beginning to brew – she'll just have to call in a favor. "I won't let you down."

***

Bartholomew Ajax Mustard does not suffer fools. He can sniff out a fox in the henhouse faster than a bullet from his Black-Eyed Susan. And Pearly Gates is a fox – of that he is certain. The mechanism of her deceit may yet be unknown, but you can bet your fattest calf he's going to find out. After all, Mustard has a reputation to uphold. He didn't make supervisor by letting these lazy sons-a-bitches walk all over him. The very thought makes him so mad he could bite himself.

"Hertz!" he shouts this into the hallway. "Abathur! Get your be-hinds into my office, pronto!" He could use telepathy, or the intercom. But he doesn't trust that highfalutin tech. As he listens to their footsteps padding down the carpet, he pulls out a flask of bug juice and takes a long pull. The whiskey burns its way down, bringing him back to his senses.

A knock at the door. "You wanted to see us, sir?"

"Took your sweet time, didn't ya?" He seals the flask, places it on his desk. "Git in here."

Abathur enters first. Imagine an angel in board shorts with a Cubist face and long silver locks. One of the oldest beings in the afterlife, Abathur used to weigh the souls of the dead to determine their fates. But a decision was made to update the system, and Abathur was forced into retirement. His severance package included one "easy" life on Earth, when he took up surfing, and he's carried that affinity back into the afterlife.

"Morning, Mr. Mustard."

Hertz waddles in next, chewing a toothpick. Shifty-eyed, that one – short, balding, and rumpled in his gaudy bling and knock-off designer suit. There's still blood on the lapel from his most recent death via Canadian moose. He hasn't let go of that incident; it's a little too fresh. Hertz was a small-time crook with big dreams back in 1970s Toronto when he and some buddies pulled off a jewelry heist. Hertz betrayed his friends by hiding the loot, intending to recover it when the heat died down. He didn't anticipate the moose running into the road and foiling his plan.

These two are far from a dream team. But they're what Mr. Mustard's got to work with. He leans back in his chair. "You fellas up for a special assignment?"

"I am an instrument of cosmic justice, sir!" Abathur stands at attention. Silence. He elbows Hertz.

"Jeez man." Hertz rubs his ribcage, looks up at Mustard. "What do you mean by special? As in on top of, or instead of our regular duties?"

See? Lazy. Mustard clenches his fists, forcing himself to take a deep centering breath before he introduces Hertz to Black-Eyed Susan. "I mean I'm temporarily reassigning your shifts," he says. "I want you boys to keep an eye on Pearly Gates. Anyone can tell she's lyin' like a rug. But until I have evidence, it don't mean horseshit."

Hertz chews the same toothpick he's been chewing since he died. "So what, you want us to tail her?"

Mustard sighs. "Yes, Hertz. I want you to tail her. Follow her around. Take photos. Do whatever you need to do – as long as she doesn't see you. This is an undercover operation, y'hear?"

"I don't know," says Hertz. "What's in it for us?"

Mustard glares at him. "How 'bout I let you keep your job and not report you for improper relations with your vehicle?"

Hertz balks. "But I haven't –"

"Who do ya think Management's gonna believe?" Mustard morphs his head into a moose's, letting out an intimidating snort. Hertz shrinks back in his chair. Mustard laughs as he relaxes back into his usual form. "A Senior Supervisor, or some lowlife collection worker who can't even manifest a full head of hair?"

Hertz swallows. Mustard knows he's got the bull by the horns.

Abathur steps forward and salutes. "Sir, we are stoked for this bitchin' opportunity. We won't let you down."

TEN

Pearly Gates is a genius. That's what she's thinking as she flies into Sector 8. After parking Seraphina next to a sentient carousel horse, Pearly smooths the outfit she changed into after her shift – a rather conservative purple metallic toga and matching wig, with lace-up patent leather boots. She takes a breath and sashays into the three-story lobby of the Department of Design. Twirling fractals hang from the ceiling like a psychedelic chandelier. In the back, a three-headed receptionist in a couture business suit sits at a glowing, palette-shaped desk. Each head wears an earpiece. Pearly hands over her day pass – her aura only allows her temporary access to this sector – and addresses the middle head with the horns.

"I'm here to see Flaubert." She tries to say it with the same casual confidence she'd use to order a cocktail.

"Are they expecting you?" says the bespectacled head on the left.

"Tell them it's Pearly Gates." She glances at all three, unsure which to address. "I'm an old friend."

Horns looks skeptical. The three-eyed head on the right stares at Pearly, like it's trying to determine if she's full of shit.

Pearly tries not to flinch. After too long a moment, the receptionist gestures to a waiting area. "Have a seat," the heads say in unison. "We'll see if Flaubert is available."

"Thank you."

Pearly heads to the plush velvet sofa. It's shaped like a horseshoe, surrounding a coffee table laden with chic design magazines and a leather-bound binder. She picks up the binder, flips it open. The initial pages display the design of the spirit world, like a pop-up book of color and light. She looks at the honeycomb and wonders, as she often does, what happens when a soul evolves enough to enter Sector Zero. She likes to imagine there's a Big Bang, and a new universe is born with that soul as its Creator. At her current rate of evolution, Pearly figures that might happen to her in another 200 trillion years.

The contents of the binder start to download themselves into Pearly's mind – apparently, early versions of humans retained their past life memories, but this made it harder for them to live in the present. Someone bitten by a snake would fear snakes in every lifetime thereafter. Someone who drowned would never dare to touch the water. Someone betrayed would never trust again.

Pearly's reading up on the design contest for pets that led to cats, dogs, and something called a "schnitt" when Horns calls out to her.

"Ms. Gates? Flaubert will see you now."

***

Pearly takes the elevator to the fifth floor and follows a winding hallway to Flaubert's office. Floor-to-ceiling windows illuminate a vast warehouse filled with drafting tables, display cases, holographic models, and some kind of big, high-tech white box. She shakes her head – so Flaubert. The one thing missing is, well, Flaubert.

"Hello?"

No answer. Pearly walks up to one of the display cases, labeled "Transdimensional Tubeworm." At first she can't see anything amidst the colorful crystals lining the terrarium. Then the tubeworm – all six inches and sparkling rainbows – pops into existence, pulsing back and forth between this and some other reality.

"Absolutely sickening," Pearly marvels – and she's not easily impressed. "Why didn't this thing make the final cut to go to Earth?"

"Messed with space-time. We kept having to reset reality. Huge pain in the ass."

Pearly recognizes the voice. She turns to face Flaubert as they ooze from the ceiling, currently a squishy, many-limbed cephalopod. Some limbs are tentacles, while others are more human – some are crab claws, and some are eyestalks – at least one seems to be mechanical. Flaubert's always had a thing for the ocean, but they're looking more like a sea monster these days than the sailor Pearly remembers.

"Hey Bert," she grins. "You look like Nessie fucked the Terminator."

They grunt-whistle-click something that might be amusement. "And you look like the Statue of Liberty ditched the pedestal to turn tricks on Hollywood Boulevard."

Pearly chuckles. "Missed you, buddy. What's it been, three centuries?"

"Almost four, actually."

"Time sure does fly." She gestures around the warehouse. "Last I remember, your digs weren't this ritzy. Guess you're moving up in the world."

Flaubert does something with a tentacle that resembles a shrug. "Well, I helped design the internet. Higher-Ups got a kick out of that one. Latte?"

"Always."

One of the human arms reaches for a Rube Goldberg machine on the counter, while other limbs busy themselves with scissors, compasses, and paintbrushes. "So how've you been? Haven't gotten Recycled yet, I see."

"Please," she scoffs, watching a mouse eat a slice of cheese that releases a paperweight that pops a balloon that turns on a wand that steams some milk. "Like anyone could extinguish my big, beautiful light."

"I pity the soul who tries." Flaubert hands her a steaming mug. "Still working in Waste Management?"

"For now." She sips her drink, licking the foam off her lip. "But I'm up for a promotion. All that red tape, you know how it is. Takes forever."

"Right." Flaubert sketches something onto a drafting table, frowns, erases it. "How's Thunder?"

"Oh he's – he's great." Flaubert gives Pearly the oceanic equivalent to a raised eyebrow. She flushes, looks down at her boots. "He, um. He left me."

Flaubert sighs. "I'm sorry to hear that." One of his human hands extends to give her shoulder a squeeze.

"It's—it's fine. It's fine." She tries to keep the waver out of her voice. "I'm over it. Like so over it. Ready to sow my wild oats, hook-up with some lowlifes, maybe have an orgy. I hear the Olympians are into some kinky stuff."

Flaubert fixes their eyestalks on Pearly. She braces herself against a tenderness she can't bear. The two of them sit uncomfortably in silence, souls who've been through an incredible range of human trials and tribulations. It's impossible not to soften – at least a little – as the cycle of reincarnation progresses. And Pearly would know. Recently, she's been doing her damnedest to stay hard against the injustices of human life, but somehow, softness keeps creeping in.

"Why are you here, Pearly?"

She looks up, straightens her posture. "I need a favor."

Flaubert continues sketching on the drafting table. A hologram starts to take shape above the sketch – something oblong, vaguely human. "Nothing good ever starts with those words."

"Come on, Bert," she says, watching the hologram morph through artistic variations. "You still owe me for *The Bloody Shame*." That was the name of the ship they crewed together during the Golden Age of Piracy. In that life, Pearly was a big burly seaman, the quartermaster of the ship, and Flaubert was the captain. She'd saved them from starvation, shipwreck, and scurvy more times than they could count. Thunder was on that ship, too – a woman who stowed away and joined the crew disguised as "Mad Jack" McGraw. Pearly kept her secret, and they fell in love again—

"For godsakes, Pearly," Flaubert groans. "That was eight lives ago!"

"And have I ever asked you for anything in all that time?" She flutters her glittering lashes.

"Fine." Flaubert puts down the drafting pen, turns to her. "Lay it on me."

"So I'm in kind of a situation." Pearly braces herself for rejection. "I, uh, might need to be in two places at once. And maybe I could be..." – she runs a hand through her hair – "if you helped me build a body double. A Dumb Pearly, if you will."

"You mean a Dumber Pearly?" Flaubert jokes.

She rolls her eyes. "Sure, Bert. We could transfer, say, five percent of my consciousness into her. Just enough to do my job. What do you say?"

Flaubert's limbs stop working in the background, and they turn all their eyes on her. "What exactly are you up to?"

Should I tell them? Pearly could certainly use a confidant. But if she gets busted, Flaubert could go down too. Sure, it's been centuries – but they're pals. "It's really better if you don't know."

Flaubert sighs and turns their attention back to the drafting pen, back to work. Pearly holds her breath, watching as the hologram above the board morphs into her own image – then splits down the middle, reforming into two Pearlys. She hadn't realized just how much she needs this. Once she's got Mr. Mustard off her back, she can put all of herself into being a guide. She can make a real difference, her way, and earn that promotion.

Flaubert slithers to a control panel and presses a series of buttons. Then he waves a tentacle at the big white box at the center of the room. "Now get into the chamber before I change my mind."

Eleven

With her body double filling in at work, all Pearly can do is focus on her guide duties and pray for the best. She may be five percent dumber but she doesn't feel significantly impaired – unless you count her inability to remember all the lyrics to Salt-n-Pepa's "Push It" in the shower.

Hannah hasn't called, but Pearly didn't let that stop her from arranging a meetup. As Hannah was driving home through downtown Eenob, she just happened to hit a pothole – manifested by Pearly – that caused her to spill the coffee she was dying to suck down. And what was in front of her when she shouted "shit!" and slammed on the brakes? Why, Thunderbolt Books & Coffee – the very institution where Pearly happened to be waiting. For practical reasons, of course. Not at all because Pearly wanted to spy on Charlie, nothing like that. Okay, okay, it wasn't only that she wanted to spy on Charlie. Sadly, Charlie wasn't working the counter. Another barista took Pearly's order.

"Hannah!" Pearly waves to her charge from a table by the window.

Hannah's face lights up. "Pearly! I've been thinking about you." She clutches her to-go cup with care as she threads her way over. "Sorry, things have been nuts at work, plus family obligations, but I've been wanting to connect. Mind if I sit down?"

"Please." Pearly gestures to the cat whiskers face-painted on Hannah's cheek. "That's a good look for you."

Hannah blushes, touches her face. "Oh right. I've just come from my twin nieces' birthday party. Three hours of Musical Statues and Duck Duck Goose."

"I could get into that," says Pearly.

"Oh, for sure," says Hannah. "That wasn't the bad part."

"What was the bad part?"

Hannah groans. "The single dad my sister tried to set me up with."

"A single dud?"

"I don't know," she shrugs. "Janine's trying to get me back on the horse and she thinks she knows my type, but I think she's just projecting what she likes onto me."

Could this be an opening? Pearly will have to play this just right. "So," she says, "what do *you* like?"

Hannah's eyebrows raise. "You know," she says, staring out the window. "To be honest, I haven't really thought about it."

"Well," says Pearly, "there's one easy way to find out. I mean, if you're curious." She sips her latte and drums her nails on the table. She's going for 80s realness today with neon rainbows underneath painted black stars. "You could set up a dating profile." Hannah looks like she just got hit with a ping pong ball right between the eyes. "Now hang on, it doesn't mean you have to do anything with it. But it is an interesting way to find out more about yourself." Pearly leans in. "As a sociologist, I would think you'd appreciate that."

"Wow, you really are psychic," says Hannah. "I didn't even tell you I teach sociology."

Oops. Pearly will have to be more careful. But Hannah seems impressed, not suspicious.

"I guess I could try it," says Hannah. "As an experiment. For science. But I wouldn't even know where to start."

Pearly grins. "Leave that to me."

A few minutes, a couple of espressos, and one download later, Pearly pauses and looks up at Hannah. "Men? Women? Non-binary? Who are you interested in?"

Hannah leans over Pearly to stare into the depths of her phone. "Men?" she says, after a pause. But that was a long pause.

"You hesitated." Pearly gives her the side-eye.

"No, I didn't."

"Girl, you can't outfox the fox."

"I mean..." Hannah smooths her curly mane, suddenly self-conscious. "I date men. Or did. I've barely dated anyone other than Theo."

"Maybe it's time to branch out?"

Hannah shuffles her feet under the table, crossing and un-crossing her legs. Pearly can tell she feels a little uncomfortable — but even Hannah's not sure why. "I don't know. I'm not against it or anything, but aren't I too old to explore that stuff? I'm thirty-six. I'm supposed to be focused on, like, building a retirement plan."

"Pfft," says Pearly. "You're only too old when you're dead. Let me ask you this: have you ever found yourself checking out someone other than a dude?"

Hannah blushes, and Pearly peeks into the mental slideshow. There's that Janelle Monae video Hannah watched at least twenty times. There's that gender-fluid person she passed on the street a few months back. She caught herself staring while waiting at the stoplight, and told herself it was because they looked so interesting. But was that all there was to it? There's that dream she had that one time where Gollum was going down on her in the pit of Mount Doom and right after he breathed "my preciousssssss" under the covers he wasn't Gollum but Rachel Maddow, except she had blue hair and was wearing tap shoes?"I don't think so," she says, sounding strangled. Pearly wants to push a little further, but she senses it's not the right time. She scrolls through Hannah's camera roll, but it's slim pickings for dating profile pics. She's barely on socials – as a professor, she tries to maintain some level of privacy. There's a cute picture of her with Calypso, another with her sister at the Chicago lakefront, and one of her teaching a lecture. The others are too old, too out of focus, or feature her dead husband.

Pearly shakes her head. "Time for a photoshoot." She drags Hannah outside, exchanges the face paint for lipstick, and poses her in front of the café.

"Perfect," she says, before noting Hannah's stiff, slumped posture. "Now try not to look like you're grading a paper on the toilet."

Hannah frowns. "This is just how I look."

"No it's not!" She scrolls to the lecture photo. "You're so vibrant when you're up there in front of your whiteboard. Give me Hot for Teacher vibes."

Pearly captures a moment of Hannah's laughter, then shows her the phone.

"See?" she says. "You look fierce!" Hannah takes a look, can't help but smile. She does look fierce, in a professorial sort of way.

They go back inside, and Pearly sits down with a fashion magazine that somebody left behind on a nearby table while Hannah reviews the photos. Pearly flips through the pages with casual interest, curious to see how the trends have evolved since her last incarnation.

When Hannah's ready, they work on the prompts before getting to the juicy part—evaluating potential matches. Hannah has to get out her glasses so she can see the fine print.

They've been swiping for a few minutes when Hannah shivers and rubs her arms. "Is it just me, or is it cold in here?"

Pearly doesn't feel temperature the way a physical body would. She figures it's got to be a mental thing – change is stressful. "Let's stay on task," she says.

"This is so surreal," says Hannah, as they scroll through the options. She rejects the guys posing with fancy cars and fish, as well as anyone with bad spelling or bad politics. Actually, she rejects all of them. "It doesn't feel right. They're all just...not Theo."

"Isn't that kinda the point?"

Hannah takes off her glasses, rubs the bridge of her nose. "I guess?" Hannah places the phone on the table, screen down. "Look, I'm – I really appreciate you trying to help. I just don't think I'm ready for this."

Pearly slumps a little in her chair. "Of course. No pressure." She tries not to look disappointed. Patience has never been her strong suit. She wants so badly to succeed, and she's determined to make the most of every opportunity.

"Hey," says Hannah. "You wanna check out the bookshop?"

Baby steps, Pearly reminds herself through gritted teeth. "Sure."

They wander toward the back, where the café's cozy, modern ambience gives way to vintage chandeliers and the scent of old paper. The walls are painted a deep, rich green, creating a dramatic backdrop for the mahogany bookcases that line every inch of the space. Pearly's always been more of an adventurer than a bookworm, but the reading nooks with the plush armchairs and antique lamps create such an inviting atmosphere that even she's tempted to sit down and crack open a paperback.

"Wow, this place is something," Hannah marvels. She points to a display case housing a carefully preserved book. "First edition, *Little House on the Prairie*. God, I loved that story."

"Me too," says Pearly. "The scene with the Christmas presents always gets me. You know, where the girls get a peppermint stick, a tin cup, a heart-shaped cake, and—"

They say it together. "A whole penny for your very own!"

"Yes!" Hannah sighs. "Ugh, the beauty of simpler times."

Beauty, yes, thinks Pearly, but life's always complicated – at least, in her experience. Maybe she makes it complicated.

A person around Hannah's age stands behind the register reading Jesmyn Ward's *Let Us Descend*. As they look up, Pearly experiences a little jolt.

"Oh my god," says Hannah. "Charlie?"

What the what???

Charlie's mouth falls open, then turns upward in a grin. "Hannah fucking Cohen. You here for a book or a rematch?"

"Ha!" Hannah turns to Pearly. "Charlie was my nemesis in high school. We were neck and neck for valedictorian the entire four years."

Charlie sighs. "Cohen got me in the end, though."

"I did," says Hannah. "But you were the one they picked to go to that leadership thing at the Ronald McDonald House. I was so jealous."

"With good reason – free Big Macs all weekend." Charlie winks at Hannah, who blushes and fiddles with her hair. Pearly feels the spark from across the register. She puts a hand on the counter to steady herself.

Hannah stops fidgeting, clears her throat. "This is my friend, Pearly."

"Pearly Gates!" says Charlie. "We've met."

If you only knew. Pearly manages a weak smile. "That's right. I stopped in here the other day. What a find."

"I'm glad you think so," says Charlie. "Still trying to get the locals on board with gourmet coffee."

"They'll come around," says Hannah. "If there's one thing I know, it's that you're persistent."

Charlie grins at her. "That's true." There it is again, that spark. *What the actual fuck?* Isn't it bad enough that Pearly has to contend with her soulmate – okay fine, former soulmate – here in Eenob? Now she has to deal with this...complication. "Tell you what," says Charlie, gesturing toward the bookshelves. "Pick out anything you want – on the house. I know that big brain of yours needs to be fed on a regular basis."

"Really?" says Hannah, brightening. "Thanks!"

"Oh, and you too, Pearly," Charlie says, almost as an afterthought. Gut punch.

As Pearly and Hannah browse the shelves, Pearly can't shake the unease building inside her. She sidles up to her charge, all casual. "So," she says, "what's the deal with you two?"

"Who?" asks Hannah. Pearly gives her a look. "You mean, me and Charlie?" Hannah shrugs. "Classmates. Rivals. Friends, I guess, in a weird way." She brushes her hair behind her ear.

"So you're not, like, interested in them?"

"Interested?" Hannah's voice squeaks into a higher octave. "No, that would be...no. Definitely not. Nothing like that."

"Okay. Good."

"Good?"

"Yeah." Pearly rifles through a stack of staff picks. "You're just getting back into dating. You don't even know what you want. It would be a shame to ruin an old friendship for some lark or experiment. That's what the app is for."

"Right," says Hannah. "The app." She sounds about as excited as she would if Pearly had suggested a root canal without Novocain. "I don't know what book to get," she says. "It's been ages since I've read any fiction." Pearly senses she's trying to change the subject. Part of her knows she should press a little further, dig a little deeper, push it real good. Instead, she goes along with the subject change.

"Hard to go wrong with a romance novel." Pearly only feels a slight twinge of guilt. After all, there are billions of fish in the sea. Surely, someone other than Charlie is a good fit for Hannah. To think otherwise would be ridiculous. It's not like there's just one soul out there for everyone.

Everyone, that is, except for Pearly.

TWELVE

"**D**ude," says Abathur. "What's up with the flashcards?"

He and Hertz are parked outside a Tunnel in Sector 99, watching Pearly pick up a handful of barrels and load them onto her dump truck – a non-sentient model. Abathur isn't that close with Pearly, but he seems to remember that she's very attached to her sentient truck. What's its name? Sara? Spirulina? Anyway, it's weird for her to be using something different now. He should make a note of that for the case file.

Abathur's in the driver's seat, as usual, but Mr. Mustard arranged to swap out their own truck for a less conspicuous beige hover-sedan. Hertz, sprawled in the passenger seat, pauses on a card with a crudely drawn tree marked with an X under the roots. "Retrieval practice."

Abathur rolls his eyes, which disassemble and reassemble in a different shape and color. "Hertz, you gotta let it go. The Forgetting happens for a reason; no matter what you do now, the you in your next life isn't gonna find that treasure, because you're not gonna remember that it even exists. You really think you can outsmart the Higher-Ups?"

Hertz shrugs. "Hey man, you hear stories about people with past life recall all the time. That could be me! Or maybe I'll find my way to a regression hypnotherapist. All I know is what happened to me, it wasn't fuckin' fair. I mean a moose, seriously? I swear on the next go-round, I'm gonna dig up those damn jewels and do it right!"

Abathur pries a sour gummy wormhole from his snack pack, pops it in his mouth. It sizzles. "So what," he says, "you think the universe owes you a redo? A chance to relive your life as a petty thief?"

"Petty my ass. Those diamonds were worth at least a couple hundred Gs. And anyway, it wouldn't be the same old life once I cashed in. I'd buy an island – even a little one – maybe learn to play pickle-ball. "

Abathur rolls his eyes. "I don't think you've grasped the concept of karma."

"Oh come on. Karma's just a manipulation tactic invented by the Higher-Ups."

Abathur shakes his head. "I'm telling you, back in the old days—"

"Hey," Hertz cuts him off, eyes suddenly sharp. "What's she doing?"

Abathur follows Hertz's gaze to Pearly. She stoops to pick up an empty can. But she doesn't toss it in the recycle bin right away. She looks it over, sniffs it. And then she...takes a bite?

"Huh," says Hertz.

"Huh," says Abathur.

"That's weird, right?"

"Yeah, that's pretty weird, man. Snap a photo."

Hertz grabs the Polaroid from the backseat, points, and shoots. "Can we go home now?" The photo pops out with an electronic hiss. The rest of their equipment is more high-tech, but Hertz likes anything from the era that reminds him of his mission.

"It's not evidence of wrongdoing. Not yet." Abathur takes the photo from Hertz, inspects it as the image develops. "We need something more solid." In truth, he feels a little guilty about the whole assignment. He's always liked Pearly. Sure, she's a firecracker, and maybe a tad impulsive, but she's competent as hell. She's even been down to listen to his surf stories a couple of times over a pint at The Crooked Harp. Truth is, she reminds him of himself when he was a young soul, back when the universe was first being created. Not this one, the original one. Abathur was idealistic back then – ambitious, creative, fiery. He made a lot of mistakes. Souls don't get as much freedom to fail these days. But a job is a job, and Abathur's the kind of guy who gets the job done.

They watch Pearly lick her fingers as she polishes off the can. Apparently satisfied, she gets into her truck and takes off. They follow her back to the treatment facility, where she unloads the barrels without incident. Then she parks her truck and sashays into the plant.

"Let's go," says Abathur, donning shades and a sombrero. He hands Hertz a beanie with a fluffy knit pom-pom.

Hertz frowns. "Why do I get the baby's hat?"

"Why do you think? Come on, let's go."

They follow Pearly through the factory floor and into the breakroom. She's about to punch her timecard when a co-worker approaches her. It's Mooney, the little green Cyclops from Sector 23.

"Hey Pearly!"

She turns to him, grins. "Werk!" she says.

"How's life treating you?"

She flashes a smile. "Feelin' the fantasy!"

"Yeah? That's good." He lowers his voice. "Hey, I heard about you and Thunder. I'm sorry."

"Fuck them skinny bitches!" Mooney cocks his head. Not quite the reaction he'd expected, clearly. Not the reaction Abathur would have expected either. "Oh, was he – was he cheating?"

"Cooking and baking!" Pearly flutters her eyelashes.

"Is that...?" Mooney scratches his head, blinks his singular eye. "I'm sorry, I don't—I don't understand."

"I'm-a look sexy and make you eat it, bitch."

"Okaaay." Mooney begins to inch away. "Good talk. Enjoy the rest of your day."

"I liiiiive!"

Pearly slips her time card into the clock. *Ka-CHUNK!* Her face lights up like a kid eating ice cream for the first time. She does it again, apparently just to hear the sound. *Ka-CHUNK! Ka-CHUNK! Ka-CHUNK! Ka-CHUNK!*

Abathur and Hertz exchange glances. This is definitely Pearly – her energy signature confirms it. But still, something's off. Maybe the breakup's breaking her brain. But Abathur has a feeling that's not it. Mustard was right. She *is* up to something. And despite his reservations, he's damn sure going to find out what it is.

THIRTEEN

A day later and Pearly's still freaking the fuck out.

The Charlie-Hannah situation feels like a hornet's nest hanging on the edge of the door, but she can't get rid of the threat without poisoning her soul. So for now she just has to watch the hornets and try not to do anything stupid. At least her cover is intact — otherwise, she'd be getting carted off to Recycling right now. Of course, that means her responsibilities are still intact as well. She's got to guide her charges and nab that promotion.

It's time for her to check in on Sam. He clearly needs community – so why not bring him to Thunderbolt? She's pretty sure he'd love it there, and if it just so happens that Pearly can use that opportunity to continue to spy on – ahem, *observe* – Thunder in his new life, all the better. And anyway, Hannah said she wasn't interested in Charlie. Pearly could see through the lie, of course. But it eases her conscience enough to return to the café solo.

Anyway, Sam's got to get out of the house, even if Pearly has to pull a rabbit out of her ass to make it happen. And she could do that, if she really wanted to. As far as she can tell, he does little these days except play video games and dodge calls from the few friends and family he hasn't already alienated. It's not that he doesn't want to connect – it's just too painful. Why invest in people when you won't be around long enough to see a return?

Fortunately, Pearly has a plan. It took a little bippity-boppi-ty-boo to transform Seraphina from a pick-up to a pink Cadillac convertible, but hopefully it'll be worth it.

"You're checking yourself out, aren't you?" Pearly grins as Seraphina turns her side mirrors inward, assessing her sleek new lines. "Baby, you are killin' it. Gonna have to start calling you Hot Wheels."

Pearly feels pretty hot herself, driving down Main Street, hair billowing in the wind like some Old Hollywood starlet. Sam lives in an apartment a few minutes from downtown. He moved here from Chicago after his diagnosis, hoping to lead a less stressful life. But from what she's seeing, he's barely living at all. Well, that's about to change.

Pearly parks Seraphina and marches up to Sam's door with steel in her glitter-lined eyes.

Buzzzzz.

No answer, but she knows Sam's inside.

Buzzzzz. Buzzzzz. Buzzzzz.

Still nothing, so Pearly buzzes out the first verse in Run DMC's "It's Like That." *Buzzzzz- Buzzzzz- Buzzzzz- Buzzzzz... Buzzzzz Buzzzzz Buzzzzz- Buzzzzz Buzzzzz.... Buzzzzz-Buzzzzz Buzzzzz-Buzzzz Buzzzzz-Buzzzzz Buzzzzz-Buzzzzz Buzzzzz-Buzzzzz Buzzzzz Buzzzzz Buzzzzz...*

"Okay, Jesus, alright, just stop already!"

A bleary-eyed Sam throws open the door, standing barefoot in a Patti Smith t-shirt and sweatpants with a beanie covering his shaved head.

"Good evening!" Pearly holds out a steaming paper bag. "Hot barbeque wings, extra sauce? It's from Biiiiird's Neeeeest..."

Sam narrows his eyes at his favorite comfort food. "If I say no, will you go away?"

"Nope."

Sam sighs. Pearly hands over the bag, then squeezes past him to enter the apartment. A mishmash of cheap college furniture fills the cramped one bedroom, along with a few high-end items including the abstract art piece she saw in his case file. Sam must have made decent money post-graduation. But now that he's on disability, the only numbers he's crunching are hospital bills. A gaming console sits in the corner, and framed prints of cult-classic posters line the walls – *Night of the Living Dead*, *Flash Gordon*, H.P. Lovecraft's *The Call of Cthulhu.* These don't surprise Pearly as much as the stuffed-to-the-gills bookshelves.

"I thought you kids only read screens," she says. "You can tell a lot about a person by the books they keep." She runs her hand across a row of history tomes—works like Guns, Germs, and Steel, The Histories, The Immortal Life of Henrietta Lacks, and The Wright Brothers, along with A People's History of the United States. She pauses at a battered file folder labeled "Grade School Reports" and turns to Sam. "May I?"

He shrugs. "Go to town."

She carefully opens the folder to reveal an old report on the Great Chicago Fire, complete with hand-drawn illustrations and neatly written paragraphs. As her fingers touch the yellowed paper, she gets a flash of memory—Young Sam standing on his bed, holding the report, passionately reading about the fire to an audience of stuffed animals. His face is flushed with excitement, eyes shining.

She glances at him. "So you're a history buff."

He bites into a wing. "I'm a data analyst." He swallows, licks his fingers. "Or I was anyway."

Something pings on Pearly's radar of unexplored passions, but she doesn't think now is the time to push. "How're the wings?"

Sam gives a thumbs up and passes the bag to Pearly. She takes one and groans with satisfaction as smoky, sweet molasses with hints of fire and vinegar dances across her palate. "Now, that is slap your mama good."

"Right? Thank you." He wipes his mouth on a napkin, sinks into the futon. "So now what? We play Mario Kart and braid each other's hair until I kick the bucket? Will that convince the Top Brass you've earned your wings? Or do I need to, like, win a Nobel Prize to validate you?"

Pearly chuckles. "You just said you were a data analyst – do you have some Nobel-worthy talent you've been hiding?"

"Yeah, you got me. In my spare time, I split electrons and study nanocrystals."

"Cool," says Pearly. "I'll move you to the VIP section." Her eyes settle on a stack of dishes in the kitchen. "When was the last time you left this apartment?"

Sam shrugs. "What difference does it make?"

"It makes a difference to me. I don't want to see you squander the remainder of your one wild and precious life."

He rolls his eyes. "OK, Mary Oliver. I'll bite." He wipes his fingers on a napkin. "What do you want to do?"

"Me? I want to ride unicorns into the sunset. Make art in a white room dancing naked through paint. Build a treehouse, invite the whole neighborhood to bring some homemade instruments, and jam all night until the cops shut us down." She pauses, takes a breath. He's just staring at her. "Or we could just get coffee," she says. "Do you drink coffee? I know a place."

Sam glances back at the comfort of his self-imposed prison. "So," he sighs, "I guess we're not braiding hair and playing Mario Kart?"

"Don't worry," Pearly sashays to the window. "Our ride's way better." She pulls back the shades, revealing the Caddy gleaming a vivid shade of pink in the setting sun. "Say hello to Seraphina."

***

Thunderbolt is hopping, with a line of customers winding toward the back of the café. Pearly finds herself singing along to En Vogue, streaming through the Sonos speakers, as she and Sam place their orders with a jumpy barista.

This time, Charlie is managing the café floor. They see Pearly and wave. She wants very badly to run up and smack them into remembering she's their soulmate.

Former soulmate. Thunder cut the cord, Miss Thing. If you want to change that, you'd better get it together. Instead, she just waves back.

"It's cold in here." Sam shivers, tugging at the strings of his hoodie.

"Huh," says Pearly, "that's what Hannah said."

"Who?"

"Oh, she's um – a friend."

He raises an eyebrow. "You have friends. In Eenob."

"Yup." She'd rather not explain to Sam that he's only one of her three charges. He knows too much already and besides, he might feel slighted to learn he came as part of a package deal. "Why don't you go find a table?" she says, hoping to avoid further discussion. "I'll wait for our drinks."

"Okay," he says, and heads to the back of the café. It's a big space – ample room for a little stage if they wanted one – and she wonders if they use it for community gatherings. Then, out of nowhere, the lights begin to flicker. En Vogue turns to static and some old jazz tune fills the space. Charlie exchanges an anxious glance with the barista and heads to grab their phone.

"Are you sure you didn't touch anything?"

"I swear," says the barista, "it just did it all on its own!"

Charlie sighs. "I can't face the electrician again. He already thinks I'm nuts."

They fiddle with their app, but the music keeps switching back and forth between the two tracks as if it's some kind of rap battle, with loud static in between. Charlie shakes their head and sighs – looks like this isn't the first time this has happened.

"For Pearly," calls out the barista, "I have a maple pecan cold brew, a harvest wizard latte, an orange-pumpkin scone, a cinnamon-apple turnover, a banana walnut muffin, an almond croissant, a lemon gingersnap loaf, and a red velvet cupcake."

"Thank you!" Pearly loads the bounty onto a tray and brings it to the corner table where Sam sits, scrolling on his phone. When he sees how much she ordered, he rolls his eyes.

"What?" She hands him the cold brew. "Let me know what you want to try."

He inspects the offerings, pulls out a croissant, and takes a bite. "This has filling."

"Yeah."

He wrinkles his nose. "Travesty.""What are you, French?" She shakes her head. "Here, try this one instead." She passes him the scone. He takes a bite, chews with a look of deep consideration, and washes it down with his drink.

"What's the verdict?" she says.

"Kinda dry." He shrugs. "But you weren't kidding about the drinks – my coffee is fantastic."

"Good. So..." She settles back into her chair. "How've you been?" He looks about the same – still too pale, but she thinks maybe his eyes aren't as dull. His aura seems stable.

He dips a finger in the cupcake frosting. "You mean, like, have I magically regained my joie de vivre since you butted into my life and interrupted my stream of fatalistic thoughts with forced outings and sugary snacks?"

"If you want to put it like that."

He licks the frosting and recoils. "Too sweet." He sees Pearly waiting for more. "I don't know," he says. "I'm still tripping out on the diagnosis." He smears the rest of the frosting across a napkin. "But I guess it's nice to have someone who's invested in me – someone who isn't trying to guilt me into some experimental drug trial with horrible side effects."

"I'm sorry, Sam," she says. "That's not fair to you."

He nods, sighs. "My dad's kind of a bigshot in the construction business, and he's used to ordering people around, so..." He looks down, picks at the scone. "I figured I'd be in charge of my own life for once. Even if it's only for a few months."

"Yeah," she says, "I hear you." She leans back, reflects. "I spent a lot of my lives" – *you're not supposed to tell him about reincarnation!* – "I mean, uh, earlier parts of my life, being ordered around. But when do you get a chance to stand up for yourself, doesn't it feel good?"

He considers this for a few moments. "Yeah." He smiles. "It does."

A commotion up front draws their attention. Some frizzy-haired old guy in a coffee-stained sweater is yelling at the barista, who's holding up her hands like, "I didn't do it." Pearly watches Charlie rush over and attempt to make amends with an apology, an offer to pay for dry cleaning, and a gift certificate to the bookstore, but Frizzy isn't having it.

"This is an outrage," he spits, "and I'm going to report you on Yelp." As he turns around to stalk out of the store – with his gift certificate – Pearly recognizes the red, scrunched-up face. It's Mr. Bloomington of the Danielle-getting-canned disaster. Seems like he's a crummy customer everywhere. Pearly really should have dropped that light fixture on his head.

"Pearly..." Sam's voice is strangely calm, his gaze focused on something behind her.

"Yeah?" She's still watching the mean old man.

"I think you should turn around. Very slow."

Pearly's face freezes. Her stomach drops. It must be the cosmic fuzz here to Recycle her. Suddenly she has empathy for that negative energy leak with its litany of regrets. *Never got into Sector Zero,* she laments. *Never learned how to fold a fitted sheet. Never won back my soulmate...*

When she does turn around, though, she has to blink a few times to process what she's seeing. It's not some afterlife cop. It's a young Black woman, haloed by a luminescent glow. She's hovering near the barista, dressed like a 1920s showgirl with a feather boa draped around her shoulders. Her emerald satin corset, embroidered with gold, cinches her waist to Scarlett O'Hara proportions. Fishnet stockings and patent-leather heels complete the look. Her hair is styled in a bob, the ends curled just above her chin, framing a face that could stop time—a perfectly arched brow, full lips painted fire-engine red, and dark eyes lined with kohl, blazing with some mix of anger and amusement as she watches Mr. Bloomington storm off.

"Tell me that's not a ghost," says Sam.

"Oh, that's a ghost," says Pearly.

The young woman begins to glide around the café passing through tables and even customers as if they aren't there. Then she changes direction and heads toward Pearly and Sam. She stops at their table and scrutinizes them, like she recognizes something different about them. Pearly doesn't flinch as the young woman's eyes meet hers, and an unspoken recognition passes between them. But it's Sam who seems to interest the ghost more—she makes extended eye contact with him, searching his face for...what? He gulps, and a bead of sweat breaks out on his brow, but he doesn't look away. In fact, he seems mesmerized.

Then, just as suddenly as she approached, she turns and disappears through a wall, leaving them both to wonder what just happened.

"Well," says Pearly. "That was unexpected."

Sam turns to her, eyes wide. "That was wild. I mean, I don't...I've never seen a ghost before."

Pearly thinks before speaking, wanting to be sensitive to Sam's situation. "Sometimes when the veil is thinner between life and death," she says, "we see things we didn't use to see."

She expects him to argue, but instead he looks back at the wall, where the ghost disappeared. "Why was she staring at me?" he says.

Pearly shrugs. "Maybe you had food in your teeth." Seeing his face sag in disappointment, she adds, "or maybe she thought you were cute."

Sam blushes — but Charlie walks by before he can respond, looking more anxious than usual. Pearly straightens up. "Everything okay?"

Charlie sighs, glancing around the café. Pearly can tell they're considering how much to reveal to a customer. They may not know why they feel so comfortable with Pearly — only that it feels easy, natural. You can cut a soulmate cord, but you can't erase the history that comes with it.

"It's been a rough few days." They exhale, leaning against the table. "I've had all kinds of electrical problems, the radio is acting like it's possessed, and my barista swears that coffee spilled on Mr. Bloomington all on its own. Customers are starting to notice, and it's freaking them out. And to top it all off, Kylie just quit. Said she couldn't deal with the 'creepy vibes' anymore. This place is still a new business. Problems like this are just the kind of thing that drives off customers before they become regulars like you."

Pearly hesitates. She too wonders just how much to reveal to her former soulmate. She exchanges a glance with Sam, who raises an eyebrow as if to say, *isn't this right up your alley?*

She turns back to Charlie. "Have you considered that it might be a spiritual issue?"

"Spiritual?" Charlie raises an eyebrow.

"Yeah," says Pearly. "I'm a psychic, and I'm definitely picking up some strange energy. Maybe I can help. Me and my partner, that is. This is Sam. He's a...historical detective." She tacks on the "historical" part hoping that it might entice Sam to play along a little more. After all, he has all those history books in his apartment. Maybe this will be a good project for him.

Charlie looks back and forth between them. "You really think you could figure out what's been going on?"

"Totally," says Pearly.

"Okay." Charlie shrugs. "I've got nothing to lose at this point. If you can help, that'd be great. Just don't, you know, cross the streams in my cafe."

Sam chuckles as Charlie heads off to deal with more customers. "So," he smirks, "now we're ghostbusters?"

Pearly grins, leans back in her chair. "More like Holmes and Watson."

Sam scratches his head. "Holmes and Watson, huh? Guess that makes me Holmes."

Pearly gasps, pretending to be offended. "You? Please. Everyone knows I'm the legend. Besides, you're giving me trusty sidekick in that hoodie."

Sam crosses his arms. "Trusty sidekick? I don't think so. You just called me a detective."

"But I've got the flair," says Pearly. "The intuition, the genius."

Sam laughs, shaking his head. "Fine. We'll both be Holmes."

She bites into the cupcake, secretly pleased to have enrolled him in something – anything – that takes the focus off his diagnosis. "I can live with that."

FOURTEEN

Pearly fidgets on a meditation cushion. Her charges are all asleep, so she's back in the afterlife, trying to get Enlightened – or at least some semblance of peace after seeing Charlie stirred up so many feelings. But the house feels too quiet for her to concentrate. It reminds Pearly of everything that's missing. She closes her eyes and tries to visualize calming energy spreading through her astral form. Count to five. Hold. Release.

A loud bang interrupts her count. She opens her eyes and looks to the kitchen, where Dumb Pearly, her unofficial roommate, wrestles with her hazmat suit. The suit appears to be winning. Dumb Pearly spins in a circle, trying to zip up the damn thing, but one sleeve is still inside out, and she trips over her own feet as she fumbles with the zipper.

"Cheesecake!" she curses.

Pearly stops counting and opens her eyes. She glances at her body double with a mix of impatience and apprehension, then gets off the cushion and follows the noise into the kitchen. "Girl," she says, "you've got to get it together." She feels like she's giving a pep talk to herself – which she is, in a way. She helps

Dumb Pearly get the suit on properly, zipping and adjusting as needed.

"Get it together, girl," echoes Dumb Pearly. "Oh, snap!" From what Pearly has gleaned over the last few days, Dumb Pearly's vocabulary consists mostly of a mishmash of drag queen platitudes.

Riiiiing...Riiiiing...

Both Pearlys freeze. It takes the smart one a moment to realize what the sound is—a phone. It's out of place here since everyone in the afterlife uses telepathy. She suddenly remembers the business cards she gave Danielle and Hannah – the ones with her made-up phone number. The realization hits: someone is calling her on a phone, and it's actually working. It must be like a prayer; the way guides sense when their clients need help.

As she thinks about it, the phone materializes in her hand. Pearly takes a breath, forcing herself to get present.

"Good morning, Danielle."

"Pearly, hi...I guess I don't need to ask how you knew it was me."

"That's right, I am a psychic!" Pearly almost forgot. "How are things?"

"Okay, I guess. Not having much luck in the job search." Danielle pauses. Pearly can feel her struggling to put words to something. "The thing is, maybe you already picked up on this, but um...I'm trans." The silence hangs heavy as they sit with the vulnerability of this share.

"Thank you for trusting me," says Pearly.

"Yeah," Danielle swallows. "I don't know why, you barely know me. I just felt like...I don't know." Pearly has always had that way with people. Besides, she assumes she pings on the queer radar, even if Danielle can't pinpoint why — maybe she senses a certain fluidity that makes Danielle willing to confide in a relative stranger. "Anyway, I decided I didn't want to work in the closet anymore. It's too stressful, and everything triggers me, and I always feel like I'm on the verge of a panic attack. But being broke is stressful, too, and it's not like the job offers are rolling in. So I thought...I don't know...maybe you could give me a reading or something? Over the phone? Something to help point me in the right direction."

"How about a lead?" says Pearly. "I was in a new café the other day. "Thunderbolt Books & Coffee – ever been there? I hear they're short a barista."

"Oh, um, maybe..." Pearly can hear the insecurities bouncing through Danielle's mind — *how do I present myself? Will they accept me as Danielle?*

"The owner's non-binary," Pearly says, answering Danielle's unspoken question. "And the whole place seems super queer-friendly. If you want, I can introduce you."

She feels Danielle perk up, even from the afterlife. "Okay, yeah! I'd love that." She sighs. "I just wish I felt more confident. People talk about transition like there's this finish line—like one day I'll just wake up and be complete. But I don't think that's how it works. I'm afraid I'll keep changing but never arrive. Like I'll always be in this awkward in-between space, wanting more, never satisfied with where I am, or who I am."

Pearly shakes her head. "I don't think it's about crossing some finish line. I think it's about becoming more of who you already are. And that never ends. We're always evolving – right up until we die." And it doesn't stop there. To Pearly's annoyance, even in the afterlife, the Higher-Ups are into self-development.

Danielle stays quiet for a bit, and Pearly wonders if she said too much. Then her charge continues. "I guess you're right, but

I swear my brain is my own worst enemy. What if I always feel like an imposter?"

"Oh honey," says Pearly, "I still feel that way sometimes. I don't know if that stuff ever totally goes away."

She glances at Dumb Pearly, her own imposter, wriggling on the floor like a turtle on its back. And isn't she herself an imposter, trying to do Malcolm's job? There've been plenty of times she's felt like an imposter with Thunder – like maybe she didn't deserve him. Like someday, he'd find someone better. "But I promise, you are enough. You don't have to prove shit to anyone, least of all society. I think it's about trying to cultivate more acceptance, which hopefully leads to peace. And that peace doesn't come from a final transformation—it comes from loving yourself at every stage of the journey." Pearly is not unimpressed by her own advice. Now all she has to do is take it.

"Yeah," says Danielle. "Something to work on. Thanks, Pearly. And thanks for the lead. I'll take you up on that."

Pearly hangs up the phone, feeling accomplished. She turns back to Dumb Pearly and pulls her off the floor. Even after all that struggle, her double's helmet is still on backward. Pearly sighs and adjusts it for her.

"Try not to fuck everything up for me, okay?"

Dumb Pearly gives two thumbs up. "Werk!"

As her body double marches out the door, Pearly wonders if she's getting in over her head. But it's too late to worry about that now.

***

Pearly marches into Thunderbolt the next morning, determined to Make Things Happen. But something's off. Even though

she's only been here a few times, she senses a weird energy. The volume of customers is starting to overwhelm the
staff—more specifically, overwhelming Charlie, who's trying to
be a one-person band behind the counter, managing the line of
customers, making drinks, and working the register all at once.
They're doing pretty well, all things considered, but Pearly can
see the strain.

She finds an empty table near the window and slides into it,
keeping an eye on Charlie as they fiddle with the café's sound
system. Charlie keeps looking around nervously as if expecting
something to go wrong. But there's no sign of the ghost today.
Maybe because Sam isn't here? She seemed particularly attract-
ed to him. Even still, Pearly's on her toes. She knows negative
energy from her sanitation job, and she can feel it starting to
swirl and coalesce here.

Pearly is sipping her coffee, casually scanning the room when
she spots someone new—a young woman, casually dressed,
holding a coffee cup in one hand and a folded resume in the other. The way she sits on the edge of her chair and the occasional
glance she shoots toward the counter suggests that she's here
for the same reason Danielle will be soon: an interview. Which
sucks, because Pearly's pretty sure Charlie can only afford to
hire one person.

Oblivious to Pearly's attention, the competition bites into
her cinnamon roll. Pearly glances at Charlie, who's still juggling
orders and attending to customers. Then she looks back at
the young woman. A thought creeps into her mind—she could
intervene, just a little, to give Danielle a better shot.

*It's just a nudge. A minor inconvenience for a worthy cause.
Nothing Malcolm wouldn't do... right?*

She focuses all her energy on the candidate's pastry, manifesting a tiny clump of mold – not enough to kill her or anything, but

enough to cause discomfort, and fast. The woman takes another bite, and after a moment, she makes a face and squirms in her seat. She looks at her phone – checking the time – then pushes out of her chair and hoofs it to the bathroom, leaving all her stuff behind. Pearly watches her go with some combination of guilt and glee.

Danielle arrives a few minutes later, entering the café with the same determined look Pearly had earlier. She's going for casual eleganza in a powder blue blouse, skinny jeans, black ballet flats, and light make-up. As the door jingles behind her, Pearly hears the toilet flush. Then a groan. Yeah – that one isn't going anywhere for a while.

"Danielle!" Pearly calls out, waving her over. She gets up and pulls Danielle into a hug. "You look great."

Danielle laughs nervously and tugs at an earring. "I just tried on, like, twelve different outfits. Eventually, my closet staged a revolt."

"You're gonna own this," says Pearly. "Just be yourself." She guides her charge over to the counter. "Hey, Charlie, I want you to meet Danielle. I know you're looking for a barista, and I think you two would hit it off."

Charlie smiles and holds out their hand. "Pleasure to meet you, Danielle." They wave toward the line of customers. "I'm sure you can see, we definitely need the help. Sit tight for a bit while I take care of this."

When the rush settles down, Charlie takes Danielle to a back corner of the café for an interview. Pearly uses her heightened senses to listen in. Danielle struggles a little over the usual dry opening questions, but she perks up as she talks about her passion for baking. Then it gets personal.

"You know," says Charlie, "when I first moved back from Chicago, I wasn't sure how people would deal with the new me.

I'd already come out as a lesbian, and now I was coming out as non-binary. It's a small town, and sometimes that leads to small-mindedness."

Danielle fidgets with her collar. "Did it?"

"Surprisingly, no. I mean, sure, there are always a few assholes, but most folks here have been more open and accepting than I expected. Times are changing, I guess. But that didn't stop me from creating all these expectations in my head—like I had to prove something to them, or to myself."

"Yeah," says Danielle. "I know that one." She stops fidgeting and tucks an errant strand of hair behind her ears. "I keep thinking I should have started sooner – like, before puberty."

"I get that," says Charlie. "But sometimes it takes a lot of questioning and pushing away those questions before you're ready to accept, much less move forward with transition. It's all a part of 'queer time,' you know?"

"Yeah, exactly."

"You know what, Danielle?" says Charlie. "Thunderbolt would be lucky to have you. If you're ready to start watching latte art tutorials, I've love to bring you on board."

Danielle clasps her hands in victory. "Really?" she squeals. "Yes, absolutely!"

Charlie glances around and leans in. "I should probably mention," they say, voice lowered, "some folks say this place has a bit of a...supernatural element."

"Supernatural," says Danielle, doubtful. "You mean like a ghost?"

Charlie shrugs. "You'll have to ask Pearly. She said she's looking into it."

"That's fine," Danielle grins. "It's not the dead who scare me. It's the living."

Charlie laughs, and they shake on it. Pearly does a little booty dance in her seat. But just as she's about to join them, a mental text bubble pops up in the corner of her vision.

Sector 23 – Hostile Energy Leak detected.
Immediate containment required.

Pearly groans. There's no way Dumb Pearly will be able to handle something like that on her own. She knew it was only a matter of time before her body double got in over her head. She sits straighter and steels herself for the message from Mr. Mustard:

PEARLY, ARE YOU ON THIS???

Fifteen

As Pearly steps into the waste processing center in Sector 23, the stench of negative energy assaults her senses. The center looks like a subway station, only not as grimy, with translucent walls made of light. The Tunnel looms overhead. It's a passageway from death to the afterlife, and it's designed to strip away the burdens of the living as they transition. Usually, each sector's Tunnel glows with a steady, soothing luminescence. But today, the light of Tunnel 23 is anything but steady or soothing.

Pearly hurries through the station, searching for her dumber half as souls move through the Tunnel. Many are still in shock, having only just died. But their forms seem dimmer and heavier than they should be. Pearly moves further into the station, feeling the cold, damp air pressing in. All around her, she can hear machinery groaning under the strain. The air is oppressive – toxic – and Pearly's grateful for her spare hazmat suit.

She spots Dumb Pearly standing in the center of the chaos. The problem is clear: Pearly's counterpart must have decided her hazmat helmet looked better as a hat, and the way it sits on her head – unattached to her suit – is allowing negative energy to seep in. Dumb Pearly appears to be completely unaware of the danger. She's obsessively mopping up a glowing blob of negativity on the floor – without realizing that she's pulling more toxic energy into herself than into the bucket.

Pearly rushes forward, cornering her double. "What the hell are you doing?" At least the Tunnel has a high enough vibration to keep the leaky blob locked in place.

Dumb Pearly looks up, eyes glazed. "Werk....werk..."

"You can't clean a toxic leak with a mop!" Pearly snaps, but Dumb Pearly just continues, her movements growing frantic and erratic. "Filthy, filthy, filthy..." she mutters through clenched teeth as more negativity seeps in.

As she continues to clean, her body begins to jerk and spasm, until eventually she starts to merge with her cleaning tools. Her hand becomes a mop, wiping furiously at a spot on the floor. Then it's a sponge, soaking up the toxic liquid only to wring it back out. Her arm reforms as a bucket, spilling out its contents onto a bottle of household cleaner that replaces her foot before snapping back to form.

The malfunctioning Tunnel overhead flickers again, and Pearly knows she doesn't have much time. She can't use the Handbag to suck up this negative energy—it would trap Dumb Pearly too. Well...that certainly *is* an option—maybe her double has served her purpose? But Pearly feels bad. Her counterpart has experienced too much to be thrown away like that. And anyway, Dumb Pearly isn't a robot – she is literally Pearly. Pearly can't just Handbag herself. She needs something to counter the negative energy, something that will snap Dumb Pearly out of this trance and separate her from the negative energy. Something like...

"Are you ready to lip-sync...," Pearly raises her voice dramatically, "...for your afterlife?"

For a moment, the manic fog lifts, replaced by a spark of recognition—something deep within Dumb Pearly remembers the thrill of performance.

"You want to be legendary?" Pearly challenges her. "You and me, right now. Show me what you've got!"

Dumb Pearly straightens, a gleam of defiance in her eye. "It's on, bitch."

Pearly manifests a boombox. She stands at one end of the room, her aura shimmering with determination. Across from her, Dumb Pearly clutches the mop, her movements rigid and compulsive, the negative energy clinging to her like climbing ivy. Souls in various stages of purification float nearby, momentarily distracted by the spectacle.

Pearly applies a final swipe of glitter lipstick—a bold, iridescent purple that catches the light—then locks eyes with her double. She tosses the lipstick aside, cracks her neck, and nods to the soul floating next to the boombox.

"Hit it."

The soul presses play, and "I Wanna Dance with Somebody" fills the station. Pearly opens her arms, Whitney-style, and lip-syncs the opening with that iconic Pearly charm.

Dumb Pearly begins to shuffle her feet to the chorus. She clutches the mop and tries to copy Pearly's moves. But she's not exactly graceful, and the negativity clinging to her makes her moves even more stilted and awkward.

"Come on, girl, bring it!" Pearly turns to her counterpart and belts out the bridge, asking if Dumb Pearly wants to dance. She extends a hand.

Dumb Pearly *does* want to dance. Her movements are loosening up as the music begins to break through her trance.

Then, something shifts. Dumb Pearly lifts the mop to her mouth as it morphs into a makeshift microphone. She lip-syncs along with Pearly, her awkwardness giving way to a surprising playfulness.

Pearly belts out the first line in the chorus, giving it her all.

Dumb Pearly sings the second line. They keep taking turns, sharing the mop as a mic. Each time they switch, their moves become more joyful, their energy more infectious. The negative energy clinging to Dumb Pearly begins to lose its grip, weakened by the sickening performance.

The souls in the room watch enamored as both Pearlys strut and shimmy across the floor, their every move reflecting each other.

As the song peaks, they both do a death drop, their bodies hitting the floor at exactly the same time. The souls go wild as the impact reverberates through the room. The negative energy clinging to Dumb Pearly shudders and separates, spiraling in the air, disoriented and vulnerable.

Pearly sees her moment – she pulls out the Handbag and snaps it open, capturing the rogue energy before it can latch onto anyone else. The audience of souls bursts into applause.

Pearly and Dumb Pearly rise to their feet as the last notes of the song fade into silence. They hold hands and bow to the crowd.

Pearly gives her a wink. "That's how you take out the trash, girl." She's surprised and relieved by the success, but as the applause fades, a knot of worry tightens in her chest—that was a close call, and she's not sure she'll be able to save the day if there's a next time.

***

Hertz and Abathur are parked outside the treatment facility, the hover-sedan idling quietly. Both received the same alert: *Sector 23 – Hostile Energy Leak detected. Immediate containment required.* Mr. Mustard sent Pearly to handle the situation—and then sent them to handle the aftermath.

"Shouldn't take her long to clean up," Hertz mutters, keeping an eye on the facility's entrance while fiddling with his energy signature scanner.

Abathur pops a Flaming Cheeto into his mouth. "You're awfully optimistic today." He gets comfy, leaning his chair back in the driver's seat. "Hoping the containment chutes clog up again so we get overtime?"

"Ha. Mustard would sooner hand out free donuts." Hertz rolls his eyes, tapping his toothpick against the dashboard. "Speaking of which, the break room's looking pretty empty lately. Any idea why?"

Abathur smirks, offering the bag of Cheetos as a peace offering. "At least I'm not hoarding the good coffee like some people I know." He eyes Hertz's gaudy suit. "Dude, that knock-off's seen better days. Aren't you tired of wearing that old thing?"

"This?" Hertz plucks at the bloodstained lapel, grinning. "This is my lucky suit. Wore it for every big job, and it never steered me wrong."

"Yeah," Abathur mutters, "until you steered yourself into that moose..."

"Hey, shut up! At least I'm not dressed like a beach bum. Those board shorts don't exactly scream consummate professional."

Abathur chuckles and crunches another chip. "I stopped caring about appearances a long time ago."

The scanner beeps before Hertz can retaliate, drawing their attention.

"One day you'll learn, Hertz," Abathur says. "It's the work that matters." He leans in, his focus sharpening as he wipes his fingers on his shorts. "Two energy signatures?" he says, squinting at the screen. "And they're reading exactly the same..."

Hertz frowns, tapping the scanner. "That doesn't make sense. Mustard sent her in alone. Maybe this thing is on the fritz."

"Maybe. Or it could be a residual effect from the leak." But even as Abathur says it, he doesn't fully believe it. Before they can decide what to do about it, though, the scanner's readings begin to fluctuate and fade.

"Looks like the leak's getting weaker," says Hertz. "But we're still getting two identical signatures. We should go check it out."

The rational part of Abathur agrees. He knows there's more to this than meets the eye. Back in that older, darker age, when he once sat in Judgment of all the trembling souls who came before him, he learned the taste of deceit, of hidden machinations, of defiance against the will of the Higher-Ups. But the emotional part – the part that's still rooting for Pearly – is holding him back. "Let's not push our luck," he says. "If we go in there now, we'll have shown our cards." He knows he's stalling, giving the kid a chance she might not deserve.

"So what," says Hertz, "you just want to let it go?"

"No." Abathur leans forward with an ancient gleam in his eye. "Ever shall the morning light reveal the sins of the guilty, wherever they may hide, and blessed shall be the hunter who drives them out."

Hertz blinks. "The fuck is that supposed to mean?"

Abathur chuckles. He crumples the empty chip bag and stuffs it into his pocket. "It means we need more intel. Let's head to The Crooked Harp. If she's up to something, someone there might know. Not even Pearly can keep a secret forever."

Sixteen

Pearly's getting the stink eye from Hannah's sister. It's understandable – Pearly is a stranger intruding on the rare kid-free sister-time these two get nowadays. Even worse, Janine decided Thunderbolt was the perfect place to meet. Pearly was hoping she could keep Hannah away for a little longer — but no such luck.

"So..." Janine raises an eyebrow at Pearly as she settles in with her coffee and scone. "Why are you here again?"

Hannah glares at her sister. "Pearly's new in town," she says. "I thought it might be nice for her to get to know some locals." This is not a complete lie, but it's not the truth either. The more accurate answer would be that Hannah wanted moral support. Maybe it doesn't seem like a big deal just to put yourself out there, but for Hannah it is. Especially given the pressure Janine's been putting on the subject. Hannah knows her little sister is just trying to be supportive, but her support can come off as...intense.

"Fine, fine," Janine relents. "Really, it is nice to meet you, Pearly. I'm just a little grumpy after spending all night at Urgent

Care. Silas thought it would be hilarious to shove a miniature brontosaurus up his nose."

"I totally understand," says Pearly. "I hope it was retrieved without incident."

"It was," says Janine. "Ten hours and nine hundred bucks later." She turns to Hannah. "So, how are things?"

"Well..." Hannah rearranges the sugar packets in the tray, alternating pink and blue, pink and blue. "You'll be pleased to know that I've decided to start dating."

Pearly takes a sip of her latte and watches the Cohen sisters across the table. Hannah's trying for casual and composed, though Pearly can't help but notice she's a bit more dressed up than usual. Nothing too obvious, just a nicer top and an extra coat of mascara.

Janine claps her hands. "Finally!" She grins. Janine looks pretty put-together, if you don't count the crayon markings on her purse and the applesauce in her hair. For an overworked mother of toddlers, she's ahead of the curve. "I've been trying to tell her this for ages." She turns to Pearly, levels a finger at her. "Did you do this? Is that why you're here?"

Pearly shrugs. "I don't know. I might've tipped the scale."

"Well, I'm ecstatic to hear that. So who's the lucky guy?" She winks. "Or guys?"

"Uggghh, Janiiiine, stooooop." Hannah buries her head in her hands. "No one's getting lucky yet. All I did was put myself online, which is weird enough for me."

"You gone on any dates yet, or you just window shopping?"

Hannah sits up, pauses. "I did have a video date the other day."

"Yeah? How'd it go?"

Hannah shakes her head. "It started out alright. Then he decided to give me a tour of his apartment. He's got, like, a whole room devoted to props from film and TV sets."

Janine gives an encouraging smile. "Hey, that could be cool!"

"Oh yeah—that absolutely could be cool," says Hannah. "I mean, if it was stuff like Indiana Jones' whip or a typewriter from *His Girl Friday*. But these were kind of...bizarre."

Janine quirks an eyebrow. "Bizarre how?"

"Bizarre as in, he had a life-sized 'Chairry' – you know, the talking chair from *Pee-Wee's Playhouse?* It was all downhill from there."

Pearly chuckles. "That sounds like a – what do you kids say nowadays – swipe left?"

"Hundred percent," says Hannah.

"Hey," says Janine, "at least you found out before you went to the movies together."

Hannah shakes her head. "See, this is why I didn't want to put myself out there."

Janine shrugs, take a bite of her scone. She grimaces. "These are terrible." She forces herself to swallow, wipes her hands on a napkin. "Look, we all know it's a numbers game."

"That's what I said!" Pearly chimes in.

"God," says Janine, "I went through so many guys before I found Bill. I guess I got lucky that the weirdest thing he does is sing to his tomato plants."

"I don't think it's luck," says Pearly. "I think it's fate. But it's hard for fate to find you unless you tell it you're available. Don't give up!"

A small crash in the background makes them glance to the front of the café, where Charlie's picking up a community bulletin board that fell onto a table.

"We're good!" they say, when nothing's broken. This gets lukewarm applause from the crowd. Pearly can't help but notice Hannah's gaze lingers on Charlie.

Hannah pushes back her chair. "My caffeine buzz is reaching dangerously low levels. I'm going back for seconds. Anyone want anything?"

"Nope," says Janine.

"I'm good," adds Pearly.

Hannah adjusts her hair and sidles up to the counter, where Charlie is bent down rearranging the display case. Pearly and Janine watch Charlie break into a grin as soon as they see Hannah. "Back for more?"

"Couldn't resist," Hannah grins back. "Surprise me with your most exotic latte."

When Charlie hands over the steaming mug, Pearly watches their fingertips graze the top of Hannah's hand. Just like they did with Pearly's.

"If you ever want to brush up your Quiz Bowl skills," Charlie teases, "you know where to find me."

"You're on." Hannah's still smiling as she heads back to the table. Pearly tries to unclench her jaw. There's an ease to their banter, not unlike the kind Pearly has with Thunder. *Had* with Thunder.

"Speaking of fate," says Janine. "There's something going on between those two."

Pearly takes a sip of her drink. "Why would you say that?"

"Come on, isn't it obvious? Look at them. Even back in high school, Charlie had that effect."

"Yeah," says Pearly, "I heard they were rivals."

Janine rolls her eyes. "Rivals, uh-huh, sure. Oh, you should've seen them. They were always finding new things to compete at. But as much as Hannah complained, I think she secretly loved it. They both did."

A pit forms in Pearly's stomach. This feels like soulmate territory. Theo was Hannah's soulmate—but Theo is dead. There's no reason a person can't have more than one soulmate in their life. It's not even always romantic. But Pearly and Thunder – they always just had each other. Did he make another agreement after their breakup? The possibility is a knife in the gut.

Hannah rejoins them at the table, setting down a fresh latte. "So," she says to Janine, "did you ever hear back from that pre-school?"

Janine ignores the question. "What's the deal with you and Charlie?"

"What? What—what do you mean?"

"It always kinda seemed like you guys had a thing."

Hannah laughs – a little too loud. "Oh, come on. Like I told Pearly, Charlie and I were classmates. You know, nemeses. Competitors. There was never any...I mean, I wouldn't say...anyway, that's all it was."

Janine shrugs. "If you say so."

The pit in Pearly's stomach expands. Is it possible that Hannah and Charlie are meant to be together in this lifetime? Could she really guide Hannah to be with Thunder—her Thunder? She glances at Charlie, who's looking at Hannah – or was, until Pearly caught them. Charlie averts their gaze, but it doesn't make Pearly feel any more at ease. She smells a love triangle brewing, and she doesn't know if there's a cure for that. Better to take preventive measures.

"Well, I believe you, Hannah," lies Pearly. "Now, let's get back on the horse— by which I mean the app, of course. Somewhere in that avalanche of 'likes' is someone worthy of an in-person date."

"Ugh." But Hannah pulls out her phone. "You know," she says, as she begins scrolling through candidates, "I keep picturing Theo sitting on my shoulder, like some angel or something, telling me this is all wrong. Is that crazy?"

"Look…" Pearly reaches across the table, takes Hannah's hand. "I know life hasn't worked out the way you thought it would. But that doesn't give you an excuse to stop living it."

Hannah blinks back tears. "You're right." She takes a breath, squares her shoulders. "But shouldn't I be, like, trusting my intuition or something? No one on the app has felt like a 'fuck yes,' or even much of a 'fuck maybe' to be honest."

Pearly waves away Hannah's doubts. She takes Hannah's phone, begins scrolling. "Everyone's going to feel like that at first." *Everyone except Thunder.* "You need to go on some dates, give people a chance. Hey! What about this guy?" She holds out the screen. "Nice smile, no kids. He's a composer – ooh, for the Joffrey Ballet! Janine, what do you think?"

"Yeah, totally," says Janine. "He even sent you a rose, whatever that means."

"It means you should at least meet him for coffee," says Pearly. "Come on, what do you think?"

"Okay, okay," Hannah sighs. "Just swipe right before I change my mind."

Pearly thought steering Hannah away from her own soulmate would lift the weight off her chest. But if anything, it's only heavier. Okay, sure, she just advised her own charge not to trust her intuition. And maaaaaaybe Pearly's being a tiny bit manipulative. But the Charlie thing could blow up in Hannah's face, and a breakup with someone important from her past would be a lot more devastating than a breakup with some random person from the internet. Right?

As Hannah and Janine continue talking, Pearly glances at a mirror hanging on the wall. She's probably just imagining it, but she swears she sees flecks of yellow in her green aura. It didn't occur to her to worry about her own metrics. If Malcolm returns to find that Pearly herself has devolved, he won't be chomping at the bit to give her that recommendation.

But as Pearly watches Charlie charming customers, she can't bring herself to change course. It's like one of those "train in danger!" cartoons she used to watch as a kid in Chicago. Some evil villain sabotaged the track, and now they're headed for disaster. Will the hero show up in time to save the passengers? And the real question of the hour – can the hero be the same person who sabotaged the track?

Seventeen

Hannah went out with the composer twice. The first time was pleasant enough. They had coffee, talked about music and education and the crazy state of the world. He drove her back to her car and they exchanged a chaste peck on the cheek. The second time was a disaster. He invited her to his place under the guise of "cuddling" and "sharing energy," which apparently meant asking if he could masturbate while they kissed.

"Maybe that's just par for the course these days," she told Pearly the next day. "But it creeped me out. I mean, I didn't even like him much to begin with. So...that was the end of that."

Now that made Pearly wince. Hannah deserved respect, romance, connection – and it was Pearly's job to help her find it. She needed to get her head out of her ass and rethink her priorities. Pearly never claimed to be a saint, but what kind of guide – what kind of soul? – would make her charge suffer just to push back her own pain? Thunder said he left because she was becoming "spiritually stagnant." She couldn't accept that accusation — until now, when the evidence was slapping her in the face.

"Well," Pearly said to Hannah. "Don't give up. Remember what Janine said – it's a numbers game."

"Ugh." Hannah cradled her head in her hands. "I don't know if I have it in me."

"Sure you do." Pearly tried to sound upbeat, but even she could hear how hollow it sounded.

Hannah sighed. "Maybe I'm just meant to be a perpetual widow." She said it in that half-joking-but-actually-kind-of-serious way that made Pearly realize the amount of damage already done. The only option now was to throw caution to the wind – to try to cancel out one stupid thing with another.

***

Astral Alley is a popular gathering place for the dead. Bowling has always seemed a bit pedestrian to Pearly; she scoffed when Thunder invited her to join his afterlife league. But as she looks up at the flashing marquee, she scolds herself for not being more open-minded. This does look kind of fun. Kitschy. Pearly likes a bit of kitsch. Maybe if she'd been more open to new experiences, it would've been enough to convince Thunder to stick around.

Today, though, Pearly's not here to socialize or to make up for missed opportunities. She's here on a mission: to convince Hannah's late husband Theo – an avid bowler – to appear to Hannah in a "healing" dream. Seems easy enough, except for one complication: Theo doesn't know she's not-exactly-officially taken on Malcolm's job, and she'd really like to keep that information on the down low. So, she's walking into this bowling alley disguised as Malcolm. Surely, Theo will listen to Hannah's guide. The only tricky part is mimicking Malcolm's aura. She's green and he's indigo. But with a little black market energy dye, she can fake it...for maybe an hour.

Pearly squares her shoulders, adjusts the clichéd angelic robe, and steps inside. The space is vast yet cocoon-like, with low ceilings amplifying the dim glow of black lights. The air is alive with the rumble of balls rolling down lanes and the occasional crash of pins scattering. From the arcade, games beep and coins jingle, while laughter from the bar mingles with an 80s rock station. Pearly looks up sharply when a bright light flashes above her head. On the ceiling, a holographic comet streaks across the simulated night sky, its fiery tail a cascade of vivid colors.

Okay, well, no time to sightsee. She scans the lanes looking for Theo. After a moment, she spots him in lane six. He's standing with a group of four other souls in matching red polo shirts declaring them "The Lab Rats." Pearly starts in that direction, but pauses when an emo teenager behind the rental counter clears his throat. When she turns toward him, he taps the sign:

BOWLING SHOES REQUIRED

"Oh," says Pearly, "I'm just here to talk to someone."

The teenager rolls his eyes. "I didn't make the rules."

Don't make a scene. "Okay, okay. I'll take shoes."

"Size?"

How big are Malcom's feet? "Uh...twelve?"

The teen disappears into the back room as Pearly looks out at the alley. There are a few fantastical flourishes, but the game itself is the same as on Earth. Sometimes human "inventions" are things that got their start in the spirit world, but bowling is about as Earthly as it gets. Pearly imagines that's why it's so popular – it can be a long time between incarnations, and some souls don't incarnate at all anymore. This gives them a taste of warm-and-fuzzy, without having to deal with all the inconveniences of material reality.

"Malcolm, y'old son-of-a-gun!"

Pearly whips around to see a fellow White Robe in a "Pin-Heads" t-shirt. The stranger beams at Pearly as if she's a long lost cousin. He looks kind of like a genie, with blue skin and a top-knot.

"Heyyy....you!" She searches for a reasonable explanation as to why "Malcolm" might not recognize this guy, but she comes up short. Bullshitting it is, then.

"Are you back to school the amateurs? Or just to remind Magog why you're still in the top five?" He gestures to an illuminated scoreboard near the entrance to the lanes. At the top, in bold, shimmering letters, it reads "All-Time High Scorers." Sure enough, there's Malcolm at number five, with Magog trailing just a few points behind him. She groans inwardly. Of course Malcolm's an expert bowler.

"Nah," she says. "I'm here on business." She tries to make her face look as "Malcolm" as possible, but she's pretty sure her attempt to duplicate his overworked expression just makes her look constipated.

The White Robe leans back, assesses Pearly. "You feelin' okay, buddy? Your vibration seems a little...off."

If Pearly had a physical body, it would be sweating right about now. "Yeah, well, you know how it is,"—she tugs at the collar of her robe—"getting back to the grind after a vacation."

"Boy, do I ever. Hey, have you ever tried the Golden Glow spa? It's—"

"I'm so sorry, man," Pearly cuts him off. "I'm running late for my meeting, but it was so nice running into you."

She gives him a fist bump and scurries off toward lane six in shoes that she realizes too late are at least two sizes too big.

A few souls give her give her the nod as she passes. Stepping past the rack, where an assortment of gleaming balls shine under the black lights, she finds Theo in the scorekeeper's seat at a console equipped with a holographic display. His fingers glide over the floating keyboard, deftly inputting scores and updating the digital leaderboard.

"Theo?"

As he turns to Pearly, his eyes widen. "Malcolm, hey! What are you doing here?" His brow furrows. "Did something happen to Hannah?"

"No, no, nothing happened," Pearly assures him. "But I am here to talk about her."

"Yeah, sure. We just finished a game. How about I punch you in and we can go a round? You don't mind, do you, guys?"

"Hell, no," says one, pumping his fist. "It'd be an honor."

Another practically bows. "You're a legend, man. I'm here to learn."

Fuck me on a piece of toast. "Uh, well..." says Pearly, "I'm a little out of practice."

"Ha! Good one." Theo turns to the scoreboard. "Best of three?"

Pearly gulps. She doesn't see a way out of this. It's not like she can fake a heart attack, what with already being dead. "Alright."

Theo steps up to the lane, cradling a glowing green ball. Everything looks normal to Pearly – that is, everything except for the astral pins, which jostle one another in their pyramid formation, whistling and shouting from the end of the lane.

"Hit me with your best shot!" "Bombs away!" "Let her rip!" they call.

Theo executes a confident frame, knocking down nine pins on the first roll. His teammates cheer.

"Don't celebrate too soon!" yells the last pin standing. "I am the Highlander, there can only be one!"

"And now, there can be none!" Theo shouts back at it, and sure enough, his second roll knocks it out and clinches the spare.

"So," says Theo, stepping off the lane like that was nothing and gesturing for Pearly to take his place. "What's going on with Hannah?"

Pearly picks up a ball, feeling the pressure. Maybe this wasn't the best idea, but it's too late to back down now. "Well," she says, as she approaches the line. "She's stuck. And I think she's using your death as an excuse not to move on."

She mimics Theo's style, rolling the ball with a flourish. It ambles down the lane before veering to the right and knocking down a mere four pins. "Guess I'm a little rusty." She shrugs as the pins boo behind her.

Pearly shakes it off and bowls again. This time she only hits one. A ripple of disgruntled murmurs make their way across the room. Pearly winces—she didn't realize she'd drawn an audience.

"Sorry about that!" she calls out to the crowd. She turns back to Theo, looking for any sign he's seeing through her disguise. Fortunately, he seems preoccupied.

"How long has it been for her?" he asks. It's a fair question. Time isn't really a thing in the spirit world.

"Three years." Pearly hesitates. Now that she's bringing it up, she realizes this is a big ask. If someone had approached her with this request, she might have punched them. But not everyone is Pearly, and anyway she's doing this for Hannah. "I think she's getting lonely."

Theo looks down at his hands, at the place where his wedding ring used to be, then meets Pearly's gaze. "Yeah," he says. "Actually, I've been meaning to talk to you about that. Maybe it's about time she started dating again."

"Wait, what?" Pearly picks up her jaw. "You're into it?" She thought this would take more convincing. Who wants to see their beloved with some other person?

"Of course." Theo spins the ball in his hands. "I mean, yes, she's my soulmate, and it's hard not to be with her. But love is – it's bigger than us. Hannah and I can't be everything to one another all the time. We both have lessons to learn, and sometimes other people are the best teachers. I want her to have the fullest possible experience in this life." He looks up at Pearly, face glowing from the light of the ball. "I'm pretty sure there were some ways I held her back in that life, and now she has the opportunity to find out who she is, apart from us. I trust that it'll only make us stronger when we come back together. And if for some reason we don't – well, I trust that too. The Higher-Ups – they know what they're doing. Right?"

That's what Thunder said too. But the very thought of it gives Pearly heart palpitations. Still, if it gets Theo to agree with her proposition...

Theo bowls again. This time he crushes it in one roll.

"Steeeee-rike!" The pins get up and perform a choreographed dance. Pearly's pretty sure she sees some moves from Janet Jackson.

Her turn. She picks up a ball, trying to project confidence. "I know Hannah. And I think what she needs right now is a healing dream – one where she hears from you directly. It would mean so much to me if you could be part of that."

"Of course." He smiles warmly. "If you think it's the right thing to do, I'm all in."

Invigorated by the victory, Pearly rolls her ball with precision. It knocks down eight pins, leaving one at each end.

"Ooooooh, split happens!" shout the pins.

Pearly forces a grin. "I guess even the best have their off days." She bowls again, aiming for the pin on the right. Looking good...looking good....fuck.

The remaining pin moons Pearly. "Never a good time to clean the gutters!" The crowd laughs. Pearly flushes as Malcolm's ranking inches below Magog's. Not good.

Theo shakes his head. "You must be really worried about Hannah."

"Totally." Her hands are shaking – as much from her emotional discomfort as the concentration required for her ruse – and she's starting to feel her hold on the disguise slip away. Her aura crackles, fighting the dye. She knows if she bowls again, it's over. "I think I should tap out," she says. "Hard to focus with so much on my mind."

Theo places a hand on her shoulder. "Listen, I appreciate you going the extra mile for Hannah. I know you've got a lot on your plate, but you're a good guide, Malcolm. She's lucky to have you."

Pearly nods, feeling a mix of relief and resolve. "Thanks, Theo. That means a lot."

As she turns to leave, she can't shake the weight of deception. She glances back at Theo, hoping her intentions shine through the façade. Helping Hannah is worth it, she assures herself, even if she has to bend a few of the rules. Besides, who's ever going to know?

***

Pearly paces in the background of an afterlife soundstage, just outside the dream bubble. Hannah has entered R.E.M. sleep, and the director is about to cue the dream Pearly commissioned – as Malcolm.

"3...2...1...Action!"

Pearly holds her breath as Theo steps out of the unfinished shed and into Hannah's garden. It's been painstakingly recreated, with the autumn colors enhanced to make the setting even more vivid. He's dressed in what used to be his favorite clothes, his well-worn Levis and his favorite "mad scientist" sweater, patterned with beakers and exploding brains. Hannah opens the sliding glass door and stares out, confused.

"Theo," she says. "What are you doing here?" It's a dream, so she's not exactly surprised to see him. But she knows something is off. She just can't quite place it.

"I missed you," he says. "And I think we're overdue for a talk." He turns to look at Hannah, swallows a lump in his throat – this is the first time he's been with his wife since he died. Pearly's afraid he's going to freeze, but he shakes it off. "Want to join me out here?"

"Sure." Hannah enters the yard in a fluffy robe and a pink beehive wig. Pearly smiles, realizing her influence has infiltrated Hannah's subconscious. For a moment, Hannah and Theo sit on a bench and stare out at the garden.

"Sorry I never finished building the toolshed," he says. "I see you decided not to either."

"I couldn't," she says. "Well I guess I could've. I didn't want to. It was comforting, living with your messes. Like you were still around. If I finished those projects..." She looks down, rustles some leaves with her foot. "If I finished, we'd be finished."

He cradles her face. "Hannibal." His pet name for her. "It's time. You've got to let me go."

"I can't." She slips out of his grasp. "I know, I know, everyone's telling me I'm supposed to get on with things, but I can't imagine life without you. Every milestone, from the time we turned eighteen — we celebrated them together. Birthdays, anniversaries, promotions, publications. And the hard stuff too – the fights with my dissertation adviser, those stocks that tanked, the abortion – we survived them together. I just – I don't know who I am without you." She starts to cry, wipes the tears with her sleeve. "I don't think I want to find out."

They sit there in silence for a moment, watching leaves blow in the wind. Then Theo takes Hannah's hand and gently lifts her head so he can look into her eyes. "I died, Hannah," he says. "Three years ago. But you're living like it was yesterday. Like you're permanently on pause. And that's not what you came here to do. There's a whole world beyond campus, and unexplored parts of you that deserve to be brought into the light." He searches her face for a recognition of this truth, but she's unreadable beyond the tears. "You could keep playing it safe, and maybe you'd even convince yourself you were happy – but I know you." He walks over to a rosebush that was never there before, plucks one and hands it over. That rosebush wasn't from set design, or even Pearly. That one's all Theo. "You're a lover, Hannah. And the only way to be a lover is to open your heart to love."

She reaches out to take the rose, then hesitates. "I'm scared, Theo."

"I know. But you're brave, too. And you don't let life stop you when it doesn't go your way. Remember the story you told me about the little girl who was so mad she didn't get the part of the Cheshire Cat in the school musical?" A grin breaks through Hannah's tears. "She refused to be a flower in the chorus with the girls, so she petitioned the principal to let her be a playing card with the boys. Ace of Hearts. That's still you, Hannibal."

She finally takes the rose. "Damn, Theo, when did you get so wise?"

"Don't give me too much credit. I still watch you shower from the afterlife."

They both chuckle at that, and so does Pearly. Theo pulls Hannah in and wraps her in a warm embrace. Pearly actually feels the shift in Hannah's consciousness, the opening to something new.

"And cut!" yells the director.

The dream dissolves, and Hannah disappears. Pearly, still in the Malcolm suit, walks up to Theo and shakes his hand.

"Thank you," she says. "That was beautiful."

"Thank *you*, Malcolm. I wasn't sure what to expect, but I feel lighter now, and I know Hannah's in good hands."

"I hope so. She deserves it. That rose bush was a nice touch, by the way. Maybe you should consider training in dreams."

Theo quirks an eyebrow. "You really think I could?"

"Sure."

"It's a fun idea," he says, "but I think I'm going to reincarnate. My last guide was in Italy during the Renaissance and said she could hook me up. I might get to meet da Vinci!" That's the thing about reincarnation – you can choose any point in time to be born. The Renaissance makes sense given Theo's scientific nature, but...

"What about Hannah?" she says.

"We'll find each other again, in some form or another." He smiles at Pearly. "True soulmates always do."

"Yeah," she says. "Absolutely." She believes it, too. So why is her throat so dry?

A production assistant comes by with champagne. Theo takes a glass and turns to Pearly. "You staying for the wrap party?"

"Nah," she says. "I've got to get back." It's not like Pearly to skip a party, but something Theo just said is weighing on her – true soulmates come back to one another. She wonders if that will happen with her and Thunder. Because if not – and she can barely stand to think the thought – it means the two of them were never true soulmates in the first place.

Eighteen

As Pearly and Sam browse the bookshop at Thunderbolt, she has to smile at the spring in his step. He's in his element surrounded by old books, but as they continue to look around, Pearly has a feeling they're not alone. There's something in the air, swishing between the shelves and rustling along the stacks. Then, a book slides out from a shelf just behind Sam, teetering on the edge before falling to the floor with a THUD. They both jump.

"Did you see that?" he whispers.

Pearly nods, all casual. "I did."

Sam picks up the book – a hardcopy of *The Great Gatsby*. "You think it's...her?"

Pearly eyes the book. "Could be."

She turns around, half-expecting to catch a glimpse of the ghost in her periphery. Nope. All she sees is Charlie waving at them from the café.

"Come on," says Pearly. "Let's grab some lattes before she chucks the whole shelf."

After ordering drinks, they find an unoccupied corner to settle down. She hates to admit it, but Pearly's glad Hannah isn't here today. She needs more time to adjust to the new normal. But she's not the only one with a cloud above her head. Something has shifted in Sam. She sees it in the tension in his shoulders, the way he slumps in his chair as he stares into his cold brew, a million miles away.

"Hey." Pearly pulls him back to the moment. "What's up?"

He hesitates, looking out the window as if the trees might have the answers. "I've been thinking about where I'm at and what's next. Not just with my chemo infusions and all that. I mean the big-picture stuff. I know I'm running out of time, and I've started wondering, like, have I done enough? Have I ever done anything that's mattered at all?"

Pearly senses this is a rhetorical question and waits for him to continue.

"You ever read *Fahrenheit 451*?" he asks. "There's this line in it about leaving something behind when you die. Bradbury says it doesn't matter what you do, as long you make your mark in some way. So your soul has a place to go when, you know...'" He pauses, pushing away his coffee. "What have I left behind? A bunch of spreadsheets no one even wanted to look at? That's not how I want to be remembered."

Pearly feels an ache in her chest. She's tempted to spill everything she knows — about the afterlife, about reincarnation, everything. But she doesn't think that's such a great idea. It's not just about Pearly's fear of getting Recycled. Sam needs to learn to live with impermanence, to accept his impending death without the reassurance of knowing he'll come back. So she settles on something simpler.

"It's never too late, Sam."

"Sure, whatever." He tugs at his beanie. "It's your job to say that."

Pearly senses a ripple in the air around them—probably the ghost, eavesdropping on their conversation. She considers saying something but decides it's better to let her come to them. She's no expert on ghosts, but if they're anything like cats, they play hard to get.

"You're in flux," she says to Sam. "Okay, yeah, maybe that's scary, but it doesn't mean you're powerless. You can still shape your own story and do something meaningful with the time you have left."

Sam meets her gaze. "You really think so?"

"Of course. And I'm going to help you figure out what that is. Now that I'm here, you can't get rid of me, okay?"

Sam nods, and Pearly can tell he feels a little bit lighter. Sam starts perusing the walls while they drink their coffees. He stops on a framed program hanging on the wall above them.

"What is it?" Pearly asks, watching him get up and approach the frame.

Sam gets up closer, studying the details with a historian's eye. "Pearly," he says. "You need to see this."

Pearly joins him, her eyes narrowing as she studies the program. It's old and yellowed, depicting a young woman wearing a stunning burlesque costume. The title reads, *Ruby LaRue in Mystique of the Midnight Lotus*, dated July 15th, 1928.

"That woman looks like the ghost," he says. "Doesn't she?"

"Sure seems like it," says Pearly. She tries to take a sip of her latte when a wind rises out of nowhere and whips around them. Pearly's hair flies in her face, and their coffee cups ripple.

"Boy," a man at the other table clucks to himself. "Sure is drafty today."

"Hey," his friend shrugs. "It's the windy city."

A crackle of energy appears in front of them, in the outline of a person — and then the young woman materializes, filling in the outline with her presence. She reaches out and touches the program, but her hand passes right through it.

"That's you," Sam whispers. "Isn't it?"

"Hot damn!" she says. "You nearly scared the life out of me."

Pearly and Sam exchange an awkward glance. "Jeez Louise, I'm only joking." The ghost crosses her arms. "Maybe humor's changed in the last century? Sorry, I – I'm just surprised you can see me. It's only happened a couple of times, and those people skedaddled and never came back."

"Their loss," says Sam. He blushes right after it comes out of his mouth. "You're, uh, Ruby, right?"

The ghost gives him a penetrating stare. He gulps. "Yes," she says. "Ruby Mae Davis. My stage name was Ruby LaRue."

Pearly glances around the café, but no one seems to be paying much attention to the two people talking to no one. There's a glance or two, sure, but Pearly figures they see her tarot cards and crystals and assume it's some psychic thing.

The ghost nods to the program. "That—that was supposed to be my big debut. As a headliner, I mean."

"Supposed to?" says Pearly.

"Yeah, supposed to." As Ruby floats away from the program, the radio turns to static. The lights flicker on and off, and a cold draft sweeps through the room. "As in it never happened."

"Why not?" says Sam.

"Why do you think?" snaps Ruby. "Because I died, you moron!"

The wind swirls again, crackling with emotion. As Ruby's anger sweeps through the café, the pastry case cracks and collapses in on itself. The crash sends nearby patrons jumping to their feet.

"Ruby!" says Sam. "I'm sorry. I didn't mean to pry." He makes eye contact with the ghost. "I just – well, I just wanted to get to know you. I think you're...kind of amazing." Pearly can almost feel his heart racing.

Ruby holds his gaze. For a moment, nothing changes. Then the wind dies down, and the charge leaves the air. Everyone looks around, unsure of what just happened. A few people start to file out.

"Sorry about that, folks!" Charlie calls out, trying to hide their worry. "I think it's a barometric pressure thing?"

But there's a lingering unease in the café. This incident isn't just going to be forgotten. People talk – especially in small towns. But for now, Pearly has to think about Sam. She can almost see him putting the puzzle pieces together.

He steps closer to Ruby. "You were listening, weren't you? When I was talking about...not leaving anything behind?"

Ruby nods. "I heard you. And I understand. This," she gestures to her spectral form, "isn't how I want to be remembered, either."

"That's probably why you can't move on," Pearly says. "Something's keeping you here. Something unresolved."

Ruby reaches for the program again, then recoils as she seems to remember it's out of her grasp. "And what if...what if I don't like what I find?"

"I can see why you'd be afraid," Sam says. "But you won't have to do it alone." He glances at Pearly, then back at the ghost. "We want to help you, Ruby."

She searches their faces. "Thank you," she says. "I—I haven't had anyone to talk to. In such a long time."

Pearly feels for Ruby. She doesn't know how ghost-time works, but a hundred years of solitude can't be good for the soul. She can see it in Ruby's aura – a heaviness holding her down. Shouldn't ghosts have guides too? Pearly knows the

White Robes are short-staffed, but Ruby's situation is a travesty. She makes the decision — she's just picked up a bonus client.

Nineteen

For the first time since Malcolm and Asprice went on vacation, the two aren't together. His soulmate wanted to shop for edible crystals at the local market, while Malcolm was pulled toward a café nestled at the base of an underground river. He's sitting cross-legged at a stone table in the cozy cavern, lit by bioluminescent fungi clinging to stalactite chandeliers. Being away from work has had something of a calming effect on Malcolm – but now that he has a few minutes alone, he reverts to his usual state of worrywart. He hasn't checked in on Pearly – after all, what could he do from another dimension? But she hasn't checked in either, and he's beginning to catastrophize. What if she got overwhelmed and bailed? What if the Higher-Ups figured out *he'd* gotten overwhelmed and bailed? What if—

"Refill?"

He looks up to find a five foot glow worm standing over him with a kettle of moss-infused tea. It's nearly impossible to get coffee in the Hypogeal Dimension, and it wouldn't be polite to just manifest a cappuccino in someone else's establishment. Besides, Malcolm likes to observe the local customs when traveling.

"Er, yes," he says. "Thank you."

He waits for the tea to cool, then takes a sip. *Ahhhhhhhhhh.* The moss brightens his mood and stabilizes his aura, enough for him to decide it's appropriate to contact Pearly. He sets down the mug, closes his eyes, and makes mental contact.

How's it going, Pearly?
Holding up okay?

As soon as the message goes out, three dots appear in the corner of his vision. Hopefully those new thought-form satellites are working. Malcolm waits, watching a cavehound saunter in with a yappy human on a leash. Finally, a message pops up:

I'm good!
A few bumps here and there
But nothing I can't manage.
How's the Hypogeal Dimension?

Malcolm exhales. Thank god, she hasn't bailed! With new-found enthusiasm, he messages her back:

Amazing! I'll send pics.
But get this—
We're in the Cosmic Caves, right?
And my soulmate gets nervous—
They whistle when they're on edge.
Apparently that summons the bats.
Suddenly, we're surrounded by
a swarm of abominable snow-bats!
They're usually pretty chill
but when they're disturbed,
whoo boy...
So we're ducking and dodging,
thinking we're gonna get eaten alive.
Our guide had to use a cosmic flare—
He was so annoyed

we almost got booted off the tour.
LOLOLOL!

He chuckles. It wasn't so funny at the time, but it sure makes for a good story. The dots reappear, then...

Earning your adventure badge, huh?
Everything's fine here.
Just the usual morning chaos.
The cases are under control.
And no one's the wiser.
So when are you coming back?

He considers, then...

Not too much longer.
Still gotta see
the Upside Down Pyramid
And the 5-D Rock Circus—
Don't let your guard down.
I'll be back before you know it.
Gotta make sure that report's spotless.
How are the case notes coming?

This time, the dots pulse much longer. Malcolm is expecting a long-winded reply – but when it finally comes through, it simply says:

Great.
Totally on top of it.

Worrywart Malcolm might wonder whether she's telling him the truth. But Vacation Malcolm decides not to bother. He'd rather spend that energy meeting Asprice at the market, sampling those edible crystals...

***

Pearly has in fact made zero notes to date. But honestly, there's only so much multitasking a soul can handle. Look what happened to Malcolm when he tried juggling three cases. Total burnout. And he didn't even have a reincarnated soulmate to contend with! All she can do at the moment is focus on what's in front of her. And though Pearly is not the "rest on your laurels" type of soul, she has to admit, things are going pretty well. As she watches Danielle and Charlie working together to accommodate the morning rush, she reflects that it's much easier to guide her charges now that they're all regularly coming to Thunderbolt. They're even getting to know one another. Meanwhile, Pearly's begun to carve out her own niche at the café as the quirky-but-surprisingly-wise resident psychic who people sometimes come to for life advice. It's actually kind of nice.

Pearly's reverie lifts as she senses something going on with Danielle. Her charge is doing her best to keep up with the Saturday morning rush, but her anxiety is growing. Instinct tells Pearly to step in, but she hesitates. Maybe this is one of those moments when Danielle has to find her own way to prove to herself that she can handle it. When is a guide supposed to step in, and when are they supposed to step back? Malcolm would know. Pearly has to guess. For now, she stays seated.

Her gaze shifts to Charlie. They're all business, but there's something in the way they look at Hannah, at a corner table sipping espresso and grading papers. It's a subtle thing – a softening – and it's clear to Pearly what it means. Thunder used to look at her that way.

The thought makes Pearly a little nauseous, but right now she's got to focus on Danielle, whose anxiety is turning to panic. It's time to step in.

Pearly rises from her seat, approaching the counter as Danielle opens a box from their bakery supplier. A customer has just asked for their pre-ordered gourmet pastry tray for a large group. Danielle's face falls as she sees the disaster inside the box. The croissants are burnt beyond recognition. Panic flashes in Danielle's eyes, the stress of the morning rush tipping into something more dangerous.

Pearly leans in, all casual. "Hey, Danielle, everything alright?"

Danielle looks up, alarmed. "These croissants are supposed to be for that big order. Now they're a mess, and I've got nothing decent to serve. I don't want to bother Charlie, they look..." She glances at Charlie, who's animatedly telling some story to Hannah. "Busy." She wrings her hands, anxiety spiraling. "What am I supposed to do? If I can't handle this, I'm gonna get fired again and I'll never find another job and Hank will kick me out and I'll have to live in a cardboard box as yet another trans tragedy in the news—"

"Hey, whoa, hang on," says Pearly, resting a hand on Danielle's shoulder. "I totally get that this is scary, but do you really think Hank would kick you out?"

Danielle looks up, sheepish. "Well, no."

Pearly nods. "And I'm sure there's a solution. You're creative. Maybe there's a way to turn these lemons into lemonade."

Danielle stares at the charred croissants. "I don't know. What if I just make them worse?"

"Hard to be worse than that. And anyway, I trust you. Let me know if you need any help."

Danielle takes a breath, then sets her mouth in a firm line. "Okay," she says. "I'll give it a shot."

As Danielle gets all Dr. Frankenstein on the croissants, it occurs to Pearly that a little mood music wouldn't hurt. She remembers seeing Danielle rocking out to Chappell Roan while cooking earlier in the week, and with a subtle nudge of her manifesting powers, she shifts the song on the café's playlist to "Hot to Go." The upbeat anthem fills the room, and Danielle immediately perks up. "Hey!" she says, turning to Pearly. "What if we rebrand them as crispy caramelized croissants?"

"Perfect!" says Pearly. As the catchy beat of "Hot to Go" spreads through the café, she can't resist busting out some dance moves. Without missing a beat, she starts spelling out the letters with her arms—H-O-T-T-O-G-O—just like Chappell does on stage.

Danielle grins and jumps in. The two of them start dancing through the prep, turning what could have been a disaster into a fun musical interlude. Charlie laughs and starts recording a short video on their phone.

The energy in the room is so contagious that even a few customers get up and join them in the dance. Charlie pockets their phone and heads to Hannah. "Come on," they say, holding out a hand.

Hannah hesitates for a moment—she's been a Serious Professor for so long—but the song, the energy, and Charlie's invitation are too hard to resist. She takes Charlie's hand, and they join Pearly and Danielle in spelling out the letters with their arms, adding some extra hip-shaking and freestyle flow.

"You've got some moves!" Charlie says.

Hannah smiles, a little breathless. "I was in a musical theater troupe back in the day. Guess it's like riding a bike."

Pearly watches from afar. She has to remind herself that she's committed to helping Hannah move on. She just never imagined it would be with someone she herself loved. Loves. But she pushes those feelings aside. There is so much joy and beauty in this moment, and Pearly wants to savor it.

When the song ends, the mood in the café is buoyant. Danielle returns to the croissants with renewed confidence. She and Pearly slice the black parts off the mutant pastries, cut the remainder into triangles, and add gourmet spreads from the stock room including Nutella, honey butter, and berry compote. Even Charlie and Hannah pitch in. The customer is surprised but pleased with the changes and even gives them an extra tip. Mission: success.

As the morning rush dwindles, Pearly returns to her usual spot. The good vibes linger, but Pearly is distracted. The laughter, the dancing, the collective energy of the space begins to stir something up – something she'd rather keep buried. She watches Charlie and Hannah giggle at the video of the dance party on Charlie's phone. Hannah teases Charlie about their dorky dance moves and Charlie eggs her on by doing The Sprinkler, holding one hand behind their head while the other arm "sprays" like a sprinkler. Hannah cracks up. Pearly swallows a lump in her throat. That was Thunder's signature move...

***

Chicago, 1995

It's a Friday night, and Pearly is in full drag, decked out in a Bob Mackie-inspired gown that glitters under the lights. Club Steel is the go-to spot in Boystown. The drinks are strong, the DJs are good, and the dance floor is always packed.

Pearly moves through the mass of sweat and cologne, feeling the bass thump-thump-thumping through her bones and into her heart. She's just finished a performance—a classic lip sync to Donna Summer's "Love to Love You, Baby" that had the crowd going wild. Her makeup is beat, her lace-front wig is perfectly coiffed, and she feels fucking glorious. She did her job, raked in a boatload of tips, and now it's time to let loose and have fun.

That's when she sees him—Thunder. In this life, he's Matthew, a skinny little white boy, all corn-fed and bright-eyed, trying to look like he belongs in a city with his black leather cap, sleeveless vest, and a stupid studded collar. He's leaning against the bar drinking a highball and watching her come toward him. The strobe lights only partly show his face, but Pearly can tell he's impressed. There's a lot of pretty people at the club, but he only has eyes for her.

They move toward each other like magnets as the DJ drops Robin S.'s "Show Me Love." Face to face, body to body, they find a rhythm that seems so easy, so natural, it's like they've been doing it for lifetimes. Matthew isn't exactly an amazing dancer, but his enthusiasm is so infectious that Pearly is swept off her stilettos. The electricity between them is undeniable, and every time they touch, Pearly feels a tingle in her chest – and not only in her chest. They dance and laugh, bump and grind, lost in the rhythm and in each other. This goes on for hours, but to Pearly, it feels like no time has passed at all. When the house lights come up and they're finally kicked out, Pearly knows she isn't going home alone. Ever again.

***

The memory is so vivid that it feels like yesterday. Pearly shuffles through the milestones of their relationship: the firsts, the lasts, the good times, and the bad. Losing Thunder felt like losing her anchor, and she's been drifting ever since.

Pearly takes a breath, exhaling grief. Enough – she can't get all tangled up in seaweed, choked by her attachment to the past.

Her charges need her, and this life—like all her lives—demands her full attention. Charlie may have thrown a wrench in her plan, but Pearly is nothing if not adaptable. She can work with this. She has to.

TWENTY

Pearly and Seraphina – rocking her pink Cadillac form – cruise the tree-lined streets of Lake Forest on the way to Hannah's house. Unlike the more modest homes in Eenob, this neighborhood oozes old money. While Pearly admires the well-kept Georgians and Tudors, it's all a little hoity-toity for her taste. Inside the Caddy, it's a different vibe. The radio blasts "Venus" by Bananarama, and Pearly sings along with the band.

She's used to lip-syncing, but her actual singing voice is better than she remembers. Seraphina seems to agree, revving her engine in time to the rhythm. That, or she's trying to drown out Pearly.

As they hit a stop sign, Pearly thumps the steering wheel. "Come on, girl, show me that bounce!" Seraphina responds with a playful low-rider hop that makes Pearly burst out laughing.

Pearly stops speeding as they approach Hannah's grey and white turn-of-the-century Victorian. She pulls into the driveway, shifts into park, and pats the dashboard. "You still got it, baby. Now go on and flirt with the neighbors while I talk to Hannah." Seraphina's side mirrors shift to check out the Mercedes Benz next door.

Pearly steps out of the car and rings the bell, still humming the song to herself. Hannah greets her at the door with a smile.

"Come in, come in." Hannah dumps a box of chicken wire in the foyer and ushers Pearly inside, blushing as Pearly takes in the upscale furnishings. "Theo's dad made some good investments," she explains. "No way we could've afforded this place on assistant professor salaries."

"Good for him," says Pearly, who's never been known for her business acumen. "Could've used his advice when I went all in on etoys.com. Total disaster."

"Well anyway," says Hannah, "I really appreciate you helping me with this catio." She gestures to the chicken wire. "All this stuff has just been sitting around."

"No problem." It's also a perfect opportunity to hear about Hannah's and Charlie's recent "outing" – Hannah's term – to the farmers market.

"And speaking of the devil," says Hannah. "Calypso!" But no cat comes running. She looks around, shrugs. "She'll come around eventually. Would you like a drink? Water, lemonade, coffee? My lattes aren't anywhere near as fancy as Charlie's, but if you're into caffeine…"

"Oh, girl,"—Pearly pumps her hands in the air—"I started the fan club."

"Coming right up." Hannah picks up some papers and straightens a wobbly stack of books. "It's a little messy, but you're welcome to look around."

Hannah heads to the kitchen, and Pearly opens the door to the yard featured in Hannah's dream. Sunlight beams through the branches of sturdy maples and oaks, illuminating a tire swing and a rusty set of garden tools. Amidst the shrubbery, a long-haired marmalade cat splays out on a patch of concrete. It hears Pearly approaching, lazily opens one eye — then springs to its feet as it takes her in.

God's teeth! Pearly, you old coxcomb. What brings you to my estate?

"Scurvy!" Pearly grins, tickled to see the soul of an old friend. They knew each other back when Pearly was a costume designer for the Globe Theater, and Scurvy was the tomcat who lived behind it. Cats are possessed of many unique gifts, including short-range telepathy, if you're on a high enough frequency to hear them. They're also burdened with a special relationship to time — not only can they remember their past lives, they can shift between them. So when your cat stares off into space, then suddenly yowls and bolts, who knows? It could be some terrible creature chasing them in another life.

"Believe it or not," Pearly says, "I'm on a job."

Yea verily, I believe it. Who are you hornswaggling this time?

"I'm not!" Pearly crosses her arms. "This one's totally on the up and up." She stands tall, straightening her posture. "I'm actually training to become a guide."

Oh, forsooth? Calypso's tail flicks in amusement. *And I'm Cleopatra's lost familiar.*

"Fine, be a skeptic, but it's true."

Hannah approaches with two steaming mugs. "Ah, I see you've met Her Royal Highness."

And I see you've met my most loyal maidservant.

"Oh yeah," says Pearly, bending down to stroke Calypso's fuzzy orange head. "She reminds me of a kitty I used to know."

"That's sweet." Hannah hands Pearly a mug and points through glass doors to a spacious yard covered by a blanket of leaves. "That's where we'll be starting construction. Want to see what you're in for? I found a YouTube video with step-by-step instructions."

"Lay it on me."

Hannah presses play on her phone. An illustrated slideshow begins, with a narrator speaking over a wordless funk track. "The first step in building a catio," he says, "is to measure your space and make a plan. Will your enclosure be large or small? One story or two? Will it feature perches? Steps? A climbing pole? Make sure you have enough material for the fencing..."

Why, you finical jackanape! Calypso leaps up, stares daggers at Pearly. *You intend to build a prison around me, turn my mansion into a gilded cage! Well, beshrew thee! This treachery. Shall. Not. Stand!*

"Sorry, bud," Pearly whispers. "You brought home too many mice."

But that is my calling, my sacred duty! I am a mouser! I have always been a mouser! You of all people should know that, you traitorous son-of-a-biscuit-eater!

Calypso hisses, sticks her butt in Pearly's face, and saunters away.

"Sorry about that," says Hannah. "She can be a little temperamental."

Pearly shrugs. "I can relate." She picks up a measuring tape. "Let's do this."

It goes well enough at first. Following the instructions in the video, they measure, mark, and cut with a rusty saw. Or rather, Hannah does those things while Pearly plays the video and cheerleads. She's got a valid excuse: her nails don't fit into Theo's gardening gloves.

"Get your angles right!" warns the narrator.

"Yeah, girl, watch those angles," jokes Pearly. "Unless Her Royal Highness prefers an Escher catio."

"She really might," laughs Hannah.

"So now you gotta pre-drill and, uh, countersink your joins?"

"What are joins?"

"I don't know. Neither does Google, apparently. Maybe it's a typo. I see stuff about 'butt joints' in other articles." Pearly scrolls through Hannah's phone. "I think it just means you're supposed to make a U-shape with three pieces of wood."

As they continue to work, Pearly glances at her charge. "So," she says, acting casual, "how was the date?"

Hannah flinches at the word. She shakes her head, picks up a drill and some screws. "I don't know. I wasn't really sure what to expect. The market was cool. Crowded, but not overbearing or anything. There was live music, and the cider doughnuts were to die for, and I can't believe how many stalls there were with handmade crafts. Some lady was selling mushroom sock puppets. They had googly eyes."

"Uh-huh." Pearly doesn't care about sock puppets. She cares about this date with her soulmate of the past thousand years. She wants to know every gesture, every flirtation, every sordid detail — but she also doesn't want to know.

Hannah drills a screw – almost straight – and sighs. Pearly can tell she's choosing her words carefully. "Charlie was great. They asked a lot of questions – I mean, it's been eighteen years since we really knew each other. But there weren't any of those long, awkward silences I've had on other dates. We wandered around for a while, just talking. I was having a good time, but it was also kinda weird? Like I'd swapped places with someone in a rom-com and was watching from the outside."

"Ha," says Pearly. "First dates can be a little surreal."

"Yeah..." Hannah rests a hand on the catio frame. Pearly can see in her expression that this date was special, not like the one with Mr. Cuddly Composer. "We stopped by this plant stall at one point—I told Charlie I'm notorious for murdering anything green, and they said we'd find a plant that wouldn't make me a criminal."

Pearly forces a smile. That sure sounds like Thunder—always the nurturer. "Did you?"

"I did! A spider plant. Actually, Charlie picked it out." Hannah gestures to an open window, where the elegant plant sits on the sill. "They said it's nearly impossible to kill and apparently it even purifies the air. But I'm still worried. What if I water it to death? I thought about bringing it to Thunderbolt; it might stand a better chance there. Honestly, after Theo, I'm afraid to commit to anything – even a plant."

"You know," says Pearly, "it helps to give it a name."

"A name?"

"Yeah. It's harder to kill something when it's personal."

Hannah nods. "Sure. That makes sense. I'm not the most creative with names."

Pearly walks over to the window and picks up the plant, holding it up to the sun. "What do you think it looks like? Snuggles? Seymour? Supercalifragilisticexpialidocious?"

Hannah laughs. "Hmm. I don't know, maybe Shelob?"

"Shelob it is. See, now you're invested."

Hannah clears her throat, and Pearly senses it coming – the reason Hannah really invited her over. "So, uh, when we were leaving," says Hannah, "Charlie walked me to the car. We ended up...you know...making out. And I just – ugh, I mean, I liked, it, but I had no idea what I was doing. I didn't even know where to put my hands, so I just kind of left them hanging like a ragdoll. I felt like I was back in seventh grade."

Calypso's voice sounds in Pearly's mind from across the yard. *God's fish, she's a doddypoll. Perhaps the runt of her litter?*

Pearly would laugh if she wasn't struggling to contain her jealousy. "I'm pretty sure that's normal, Hannah. First kisses—or second, or third—can be a big ole' jumble of nerves. Especially when you care – and I think you do."

Hannah bites her lip. "Yeah, I guess." She bangs the hammer with extra zeal.

Pearly gives her a look. "What's wrong?"

"Nothing...okay, maybe not nothing. I just – well, I asked Google about queer sex and I thought I'd get a few pro-tips, like curl your fingers to hit the G-spot or keep your nails short or whatever. And I mean, yeah, there was some of that – but I looked up queer sex scenes in novels and there were all these lines like," she lowers her voice, blushing, "'she shoved her fist up my... c-word'...and 'I will ride you like a nightmare,' and what's up with the daddy stuff and what is frog fucking and is scissoring really a thing? I mean, I guess it's a lesbian thing, but I don't even know if I'm a lesbian, I'm – I don't know what I am. And maybe that's not even a term Charlie's comfortable with anymore now that they're non-binary—"

"Whoa." Pearly holds up a hand. For a moment, she wrestles with her inner demons. The temptation is there to steer Hannah away, to scare her off from dating Charlie by suggesting her sex life is about to turn into some dark web horror show.

But when Pearly looks at Hannah, really looks at her—she sees an innocence, a vulnerability that she can't just ignore. She sighs. This is what being a guide is all about. She can't put her own self-interest above her charges. Well, she could – but that's not the kind of soul she wants to be. And anyway, they'd 100% Recycle her if she did.

"Okay," she says, "first of all, take a deep breath. It's okay not to know everything. And come on, you gotta know the internet is maybe not the most trustworthy source for advice."

Hannah blushes. "I know, I know, it just made me feel so...u nprepared. Like I'm supposed to know how to do all this stuff, and I don't even know what half of it means. With Theo it was easy – I'm on top, he's on top, we're done."

"Look," says Pearly, "I don't think Charlie's expecting you to be some connoisseur of kink. What's important is communication and connection. The rest is gravy. Who knows? Maybe you'll find some new things that you turn on. But ultimately, it's about what feels right for both of you." She raises an eyebrow. "And for the record, 'I'm on top, he's on top, we're done?' Sounds like it might get stale after a while."

Hannah's brow furrows. Pearly senses some combination of guilt and relief. "Yeah." Hannah exhales and looks at Pearly. "So, I don't need to buy a strap-on for my second date?"

Pearly laughs, shaking her head. "No, girl. Just keep showing up, being you. The rest will work itself out. And if you have questions, Charlie is probably a better resource than ChatGPT."

Hannah nods. She sets her tools down by the catio, which lurches in response. "Yeah. Thanks, Pearly. I guess I just needed to hear that I'm not, like, some imposter in my own life."

"Not at all," says Pearly. Danielle had similar concerns. And so did she. And so did Thunder, believe it or not — even if he was Employee of the Year, he still worried he wasn't doing enough. "I think we all feel like frauds at one point or another. It's just a part of being human. But you, honey, are one of the most authentic people I know." She comes up to Hannah and gives her a hug. The two smile at one another, then step back to assess their progress. "Not bad, huh?"

As if on cue, Calypso bounds across the yard and leaps onto the roof of the catio. Pearly holds her breath as the structure shudders from the impact, waving oh-so-slowly to the right, then the left, before toppling to the ground, leaving a smug feline shaking herself off amidst the wreckage.

Your petty schemes are no match for me, ye furless knaves.

Pearly cracks up, followed by Hannah. It's one of those big, belly laughs that only comes after a hard conversation.

At the door, Hannah gives Pearly another big squeeze. "I really appreciate you coming over on such short notice. You're a life-saver, Pearly."

"Anytime. Sorry the catio didn't work out."

Hannah shrugs. "Probably for the best."

"Yeah, Calypso seems like a real free spirit, if you ask me. And I am a psychic." She wiggles her fingers. "He prefers the open air and the open sea."

Pearly steps out into a twilight sky filled with deep blues and purples – her favorite eye shadow palette. As she heads down the driveway, she wonders what grade she'd get as a guide. The conversation went well—better than she could have hoped. She managed to advise Hannah without letting her own shit get in the way, but she feels like she has permanent heartburn as a result of all the pain she's forcing down.

Young souls assume life gets easier as you evolve, and in some ways it does. But your choices only grow more complicated, in life and in the afterlife. The Higher-Ups want you to be challenged.

Pearly leans against Seraphina and gazes up at the sky. She's always loved the stars, no matter when or where or who she was. But tonight, they offer little comfort. She used to wish upon the stars — but how can she do that when the only thing she'd wish for is the one thing she can't have?

TWENTY-ONE

There's a Minotaur outside The Crooked Harp – and he's knitting. He looks fierce, with impossibly strong arms and shoulders, curved pointy horns, and a glistening snout. Maybe that's why it's surprising to see the beast work the needles with a precision and delicacy generally associated with proper young ladies. As Hertz and Abathur approach, he looks up with a set of gentle brown eyes that Abathur finds quite soothing.

"Gentlemen," the beast rumbles, checking their energy signatures on a scanner. He hands them each a tiny crocheted scarf. "On the house. I'm practicing."

Hertz scoffs and Abathur gives him a nudge. "Be polite." Abathur smiles and accepts the gift. "Thank you," he says. "I haven't seen craftsmanship like this since the cosmos itself began to stitch together." He wraps the scarf around his wrist. Hertz rolls his eyes and does the same.

"You know," says Abathur, as they open the flaking green and gold door. "You might attract more flies with honey."

"You know," says Hertz, annoyed, "you don't have to lecture me on how to extract information. It's kind of my thing."

Abathur sighs and follows Hertz inside. The place isn't as packed as he expected, but then he and Hertz have only been here a handful of times. Abathur prefers Tubular, where all the dead surfers hang out, but tonight they're on a mission.

They head to the bar, where the bartender, Diesel, is busy wiping down the counter. His hair is tied back in a ponytail, and he's wearing a cross on a pendant, which might or might not be ironic if you believe the Jesus rumors.

"What'll it be?" he says, placing two coasters on the bar.

Abathur nods to Hertz. "A couple of Flaming Swords for me and my friend here."

Diesel raises an eyebrow, but he clearly knows better than to comment. "You got it."

"Hey man," says Abathur, sliding onto a barstool. "Since when have you guys needed a bouncer?"

Diesel sighs, glancing toward the Minotaur at the entrance. "Ah, we got a busload of Doppelgangers on leave from the Mirror Dimension a few days back. It's become more important to double-check IDs these days." He reaches for a couple of glasses. He lines them up on the bar top, then unlocks a cabinet and selects a bottle of a shimmering liquid with a faint red glow. He pours the liquid into the glasses.

Next, he adds drops from a vial filled with a glowing blue substance and strikes a match, holding it just above the surface of the glasses. The liquid ignites, and flames dance above the drinks. Hertz leans in – but Diesel isn't done. He picks up a blade and slices the air above each drink, causing the flames to rise higher, forming the shape of a sword above each glass. Pleased with himself, he sets the shots on the counter.

"Two flaming swords," says Diesel. "Some people sip them, but it goes down easier if you shoot it."

Hertz thumps his fist on the counter, almost knocking over the glasses. "Enough with the chit-chat," he says. "We've been trying to catch up with Pearly Gates. Seen her lately?"

Diesel narrows his eyes at Hertz's blood-stained suit. "We get a lot of customers," he says. He turns back to the bar, begins putting bottles back on shelves.

Abathur gives Hertz a glare—way too soon, man. "Don't mind my friend," he says to Diesel. "We're concerned about her. Pearly's been acting strange at work. We just want to offer her support, keep her out of trouble. Waste Management – it can get to you sometimes. Happens to the best of us."

Hertz and Abathur exchange a glance before downing the shots in unison. The moment the fiery liquid hits Hertz's tongue, his eyes bulge. His face begins to flush, and it looks like all the blood in his body has rushed to his head. The color spreads and his skin begins to glow, radiating hotter and hotter until, with a sudden whoosh, he bursts into flames.

Meanwhile, Abathur is unfazed. He swallows the shot with a contented sigh. As the flames consume Hertz, Abathur simply lets out a deep, rumbling burp that releases a small puff of smoke from his mouth.

Hertz, now fully ablaze, frantically pats himself down, while Abathur watches with amusement. "Ah," he says, "that always hits the spot. Little weak for my taste, though."

Diesel seems unimpressed. Hertz, meanwhile, is still sputtering and coughing.

"But like I said,"—Abathur pops a handful of peanuts into his mouth, crunching them with an almost casual indifference—"we really need to know what's going on with Pearly...before someone gets hurt."

Diesel's hand pauses mid-polish on a glass, his discomfort becoming palpable. "Look, guys," he says, 'I don't really have anything to tell you. Bartenders hear a lot, but we don't always listen, you know?"

Abathur isn't buying it. His senses, honed over eons judging souls, are exquisitely tuned. Diesel knows more than he's letting on.

"Look, we're like therapists," says Diesel. "Gotta respect customer confidentiality. It's an unspoken code."

Abathur leans forward, his presence suddenly more menacing. As Diesel stares into Abathur's eyes, the flickering flames reflected there seem to grow darker, more intense. Abathur offers Diesel a glimpse of something terrifying—visions of ancient hells that have long since been sealed, places where fire and brimstone consumed the damned without mercy. Not to mention Abathur's true form, a monstrous, eldritch entity of unfathomable power, exacting judgment on souls lost to time. Cataclysms of Biblical proportions flash before Diesel's eyes—cities turned to salt, worlds obliterated in divine wrath, universes collapsing into nothingness.

Hertz shifts uncomfortably beside him, his usual bravado completely gone.

Diesel's hands tremble, and the glass he's holding slips and falls to the ground. "All right, all right," he stammers. "I've seen Pearly here. Twice, actually. Once, she was with some White Robe. Looked friendly. Then later, she came in alone, but something was off. She was...different, not her usual self. She even ate the glass after finishing her pint, like it was nothing."

Now that's familiar. Abathur glances at Hertz, who seems to be thinking the same thing.

"You're not, uh, going to do anything, are you?" asks Diesel. "To Pearly."

Abathur leans back, his intense aura receding as quickly as it came. He offers Diesel a nonchalant shrug. "Dude, all I can promise is that justice will be served." He slides off the bar stool, motioning to Hertz that they're done.

Diesel nods stiffly, not wanting to press any further. "Have a good day, gentlemen. And, please," he mutters as politely as he can, "don't come back."

Abathur gives him a friendly smile, completely unbothered. "Thanks for the drink," he says casually before turning and walking out with Hertz.

Hertz remains silent as they get into the car.

"See?" says Abathur. "Told you to let me do the talking. More flies with honey than with vinegar, my friend."

Hertz shakes his head. "You got a funny definition of honey."

Abathur gives him a little glare.

Hertz winces. "So anyway, what do you think is going on?"

Abathur frowns, his mouth shifting and reshaping as he considers his next steps. "I'm not sure," he says, then sighs with resignation. "Maybe it's time we paid Pearly a visit."

***

Pearly's dump truck is parked at an unfathomable angle, as if she'd executed a twelve-point turn to fit between the driveway, the flowerbed, and the mailbox.

"You think she's on a bender?" says Hertz, as he and Abathur approach the front door.

"I wouldn't put it past her." Abathur peers into the house. The shades are drawn, and the light filtering through is too weak to make out much. "But something tells me it's not so simple."

Hertz raises his fist to knock, but Abathur catches it before it hits the door. "You gonna let me talk this time?"

Hertz sticks out his tongue. "Fine. But I'm taking photos." Hertz snaps a Polaroid of Abathur to prove his point.

Abathur snatches the photo as it spits out of the camera, stuffs it in the oversized pocket of his cargo shorts, before his face can develop — his true face, too terrible for Hertz to behold.

"Hey man," he says. "You gotta warn me next time."

"Ooh-la-la, look at Mr. Vain." Hertz snickers. "So much for that whole 'hang loose' thing."

Abathur knocks on the door. Crashing and banging erupts from the other side, followed by something that sounds like a police whistle. Then the door opens and Pearly's standing in front of them, wearing an inside-out bathrobe and a spaghetti strainer as a shower cap.

"Hey hunties!" she says, setting down a casserole dish filled with marbles. "What's the tea?"

"Hi Pearly," says Abathur. "Hope we didn't catch you at a bad time. You remember my associate, Hertz?"

Pearly eyes Hertz's cheap suit. "Bar queen," she gasps. "Busted!"

"Uh...yeah..." Abathur rubs his chin. *Damn,* he thinks, *this Pearly is one tough nut to crack.* He doesn't want to reveal their assignment, but he would like to get more information. "You mind if we come in for a minute?" he says. "We were in the neighborhood, and we thought it might be nice to have a little chat. Colleague-to-colleagues."

Pearly's brow furrows. If she was thinking any harder, steam would be coming out her ears. "Chicken cutlets," she announces, then opens the door wide enough for them to enter.

Abathur steps inside, followed by Hertz. Pearly removes a giant handcuffed teddy bear from the living room sofa and disappears into the kitchen.

"Nice place you got here!" says Hertz. He begins snapping photos: the teddy bear, a trio of half-eaten bananas stuck to a hover-board, a brochure for something called "The Phantasmaguffin Experience," the mantel with several photos facing backwards – presumably of Pearly with her ex. He moves to the coffee table, where a holographic tablet displays a blank screen except for the words "Case Notes."

"Hey," whispers Hertz. "Check this out."

Abathur shuffles over. "Why would she be making case notes? We don't have cases. Unless you count our case on Pearly."

Hertz slaps the table, like he's had some brilliant idea. "Maybe she's secretly following us following her?"

Abathur rolls his eyes. "What would be the point?" His face shifts and reforms as he considers. "Maybe it has something to with the soulmate. They did just break their contract—"

Pearly flounces into the living room and hands them each a mug topped with white foam. Abathur accepts his and takes a sip. "Is this....shaving cream?"

Pearly grins. "Read that bitch."

Abathur sighs. His standard interrogation tactics don't feel appropriate for the situation. He decides to be honest – to a point. "Pearly," he clears his throat. "I realize we don't know each other well, but I care about you, kid. If there's anything going on – anything at all – that you feel like you need to get off your chest, you can tell me. I, we – me and Hertz – we're here for you."

Pearly considers this. She takes a sip from her own mug and emerges with a shaving cream beard. "She owns everything."

"Who does?" says Abathur, leaning in.

She blinks at them, like it's obvious. "Pearly."

Abathur exchanges a glance with Hertz. "Are you Pearly?" he asks.

"Yaaaaaaas, girl! Dumb Pearly in the house!" She makes a popping sound with her mouth.

"Uh-huh. Well..." Abathur flashes back to what Diesel said about doppelgangers. Suddenly, it all clicks. It wasn't quite the same thing—Abathur knows you can always tell a doppelganger by the eyes — but the dots are connected. He sets his mug on the coffee table. "We'll let you get back to...whatever it was you were doing. But my offer still stands. Reach out anytime."

Hertz stands up. "So we done here or what?"

Abathur follows suit. "For now." He gives Pearly a nod. "You take care of yourself."

Pearly blows air kisses as her visitors head to the door, then dances back toward the kitchen, humming the wrong chorus to some pop song.

As they walk back to the sedan, Hertz shakes his head. "Well that was a waste of time. I tell you, that Pearly is a real loon."

"No, dude." Abathur hops in and turns to his colleague. "I think we got two Pearlys on our hands."

TWENTY-TWO

"What's your take, Holmes?" says Pearly.

She and Sam are back at Thunderbolt, ready to dive deeper into their investigation as they study the poster advertising Mystique of the Midnight Lotus. The photo of Ruby stares back at them, all magnetism and mischief — but the real Ruby is nowhere to be seen.

Sam shakes his head. "It's a tough nut to crack, Holmes, but I suspect the answers are close." He turns and looks around, taking in the café full of soccer moms, students, and a handful of retirees. "Kinda weird she's not here," he says. "She seemed pretty interested in solving her own mystery."

Pearly shrugs. "Maybe she got scared. But I have a feeling she'll be back."

As they consider their next step, Charlie sees them and heads over from the counter. "You two look like you're up to something," they say. "What's going on?"

"Actually," says Pearly, "we're working on the case of your haunted café. We think it might have to do with the speakeasy that used to operate here."

Charlie raises an eyebrow. "The speakeasy? I don't really know much about it. I think it burned down in the twenties or thirties. There's a bunch of old records and stuff down in the basement. You're welcome to go through them if you think it would help."

"Hell yes!" says Sam. "Maybe we'll find the Holy Grail, or the Ark of the Covenant."

Pearly smiles. It's nice to see Sam excited about something. "Thanks, Charlie," she says. "If you're sure you don't mind."

"Knock yourself out. Honestly, the rumors are starting to scare away customers." Charlie makes a face. "Someone even mentioned it in a Yelp review." They pull out a key from their pocket. "Anyway, take this," they say. "There's a storage area under the breakroom. It's kind of a mess down there, but I know there are some boxes and trunks from the old days."

"Amazing." Pearly takes the key. As her fingers touch Charlie's, she experiences a little jolt and she has to steady herself. "We'll be careful with everything."

***

The basement air is musty, and the space is dark. Pearly turns on a light, illuminating bulk supplies, old furniture and appliances, seasonal decorations, overstocked books – and in the very back, as Charlie promised, a stack of trunks and boxes.

"Those look promising," says Sam.

Pearly joins him, sorting through papers and other mementos. Most of it isn't that interesting – illegible receipts, outdated menus – until they find a large trunk labeled "Moonshine." Pearly pulls out some vintage barware that would probably fetch a good price on eBay.

"Look," says Sam. He holds out a sepia-toned photo in a brass frame. It features a working class Black family squinting against the sun in front of a modest brick home. Laundry lines flutter behind them, and factory smoke poofs in the background. Dad looks like a laborer, with scuffed boots and one of those flat caps Pearly remembers the railroad workers used to wear. Mom stands next to him in a cotton dress and apron – even from that far away, she looks tired. Sandwiched between five boys is the youngest child, a girl with braids in her hair. She holds a paper fan in one hand, flicking it at her siblings like she's shooing a fly.

"My brothers razzed me something awful for that fan."

Ruby materializes beside Sam, making him jump. "Holy hell, Ruby," he says. "I guess I won't have to worry about the cancer if you give me a heart attack first."

"Now we're even," she says, bending down to study the photo. "I kept that photo in my dressing room," she says. "I don't really know why. It's not as if those were the best of times."

Pearly looks at Sam like, *this could be a clue*. "What do you mean?" she says.

Ruby straightens up. "Well," she says, "growing up poor on the South Side wasn't exactly a riot. My father broke his back to put food on the table, but he could be...well...he could be real rough around the edges." She swallows. "He didn't have much use for girls—thought I should be cleaning the house or going to church instead of sneaking out to jazz clubs. And my mama..."—she runs her finger along the outline of the woman in the photo—"she tried, but the white family she worked for took up most of her time. So I spent a lot of time on my own, daydreaming. Planning my escape."

"And dancing?" Sam says. "When'd you start dancing?"

Ruby laughs. "Right after the doctor cut the cord. We didn't have money for lessons, so I had to teach myself. I'd watch the street performers and try copying their moves with other girls in the neighborhood. When I had money, which was hardly ever, I'd go to shows, and when my brothers weren't around, I'd practice in front of the mirror. Eventually I got good enough to get noticed. The other girls – they just danced for fun. But not me. I was on a mission."

"Sounds like a lot of self-imposed pressure," says Sam. "I can relate—maybe not to the dancing part, as anyone who saw me doing the robot at my junior prom can attest. But I used to work for my dad. And I always felt like I had to prove myself to him – to everyone who thought I didn't earn my place in the company. I acted like I wasn't bothered by it, but inside, I was suffocating."

"So what happened?" Ruby asked.

"Cancer," he says, watching her face soften. "Suddenly, it was like, all those hours I wasted trying to meet his expectations – they didn't mean shit. I started asking myself what I'd really accomplished, and the answer was pretty bleak. It felt like I'd spent my whole life climbing a ladder, only to realize it was leaning against the wrong wall."

"Yes!" Ruby floats a little closer. "That's a great way of putting it. Every night when I stepped on that stage, I had to prove I deserved to be there. It was even harder as a Black woman dancing for a white crowd, like some spectacle for them to gawk at. But the hardest part was coming back to an empty dressing room. There were flowers and gifts, sure – but none of it really meant anything."

He nods. "No one to share it with."

"Right." She sighs. "I always told myself that the next performance would be the one that would go down in history. And then, well — tuberculosis went down in history instead. Talk about a spotlight stealer."

"I'm sorry," says Sam. "It's hard, isn't it? Feeling your body fail you — knowing you're slowly dying — and not being able to do jack shit about it?"

She nods. "In some ways, knowing it's coming only makes it worse. Almost wish I didn't."

Sam reaches out for her arm — but of course, he can't touch her. His face reddens, like he's embarrassed by his desire, but he shakes it off. "You might not have it all sorted out yet, but the answer is here." He waves a hand around the space. "Somewhere. We'll figure it out."

"You really think so?" She's already beginning to fade. Pearly guesses she's had enough excitement for one day.

Sam nods. "I really do."

And they watch her disappear through a wall, giving a little wave before her hand dematerializes.

"So," Sam turns to Pearly. "Now what?"

Pearly considers. She feels pretty confident that she understands Hannah's needs, Danielle's, Sam's – but ghosts? Not her forte. "I'm not sure," she says. "Ruby's obviously holding onto something, but I can't tell exactly what."

"Too bad you're not really a psychic," he smirks.

"Ain't that the truth."

"It's okay," he says. "Holmes and Holmes are on the case. We'll get there."

As they leave the basement behind them, Pearly feels the thrill running up Sam's spine. A haunted café, a dancing ghost, and a team of unlikely detectives—it's the perfect twist for the universe to throw his way. Who would guess that a ghost would bring Sam back to life?

TWENTY-THREE

"I had another date," says Hannah, looking up from her laptop. "With Charlie."

Pearly inhales, counts to three. Charlie's not working today, so Thunderbolt is open for gossip. She sets down *The Eenob Times* and looks across the table. There's a sparkle in Hannah's eyes that wasn't there before, and even her aura looks brighter. Pearly's stomach churns. *Do your job. Don't be an asshole.* "That's great," she says, swallowing her jealousy. "How'd it go?"

"Honestly, it was magical." She shakes her head, like she's still trying to believe it actually happened. "When Charlie heard I grew up in Illinois and had never experienced a corn maze, they were horrified. So we drove to some big farm and did all the things – the maze, a haunted castle, a hay ride, and for some reason, pig races? Anyway, it was super fun, and this time I took your advice and didn't get all in my head during the car make-out at the end. It was"—she blushes a little—"it was pretty hot. And of course, now it's all I can think about."

"Wow." Pearly doesn't know if she has it in her to form anything more encouraging than this. Fortunately, her phone buzzes, saving her from further reply.

Sam: Just got results from the scan.

Pearly's jaw tightens. She'd asked him to keep her updated and she's glad he's reaching out, but this doesn't sound promising. She tries to keep her mind neutral as she types a response.

Pearly: And?
Sam: Not looking so good.

Pearly feels a rush of panic. She knows she's supposed to be calm and supportive, but she's not any more ready for Sam to die than Sam is himself. He's just starting to wake up to life again, dammit. It's too much, too soon. She knows better than to ask for fairness. There's an old saying in the afterlife: "What we consider to be fair from our limited perspective is a mere thread in the great and ever-evolving cosmic tapestry of existence." But if she could bargain for a little more time...

Pearly: Come to Thunderbolt?
Sam: Don't really feel like talking about it.

"What is it?" says Hannah.

"Sam." Pearly sighs, setting the phone on the table. "He could use some cheering up. A distraction."

"Okay," says Hannah. "What's he into?"

Pearly considers. "History? Nerdy sci-fi stuff?"

"Hmmm..."

"*Invasion of the Body Snatchers.*" Danielle approaches as she finishes wiping down a nearby table. "Sorry, couldn't help overhearing. It's playing at the local drive-in." She taps an advertisement in the paper. It's the version from 1978 with Donald Sutherland and Leonard Nimoy. Pearly perks up. Wasn't that one of the posters on Sam's wall?

"Danielle, that's brilliant." Pearly grabs her phone.

> **Pearly:** I'm picking you up at 6. Dress for warmth. Confirm with "okay whatever."

He responds with an eye-roll emoji. Pearly smiles. He's in. She assesses her other two charges. It would be great if she could foster more connection between them. And if it makes her job easier, all the better. "Y'all have plans tonight?"

***

The Eenob Outdoor Theatre sits on the outskirts of town at the intersection of farmland and nowhere. Pearly steers Seraphina onto the lot. The carload of passengers displays varying levels of excitement: Sam sits stone-faced in the front, while Hannah and Danielle chit-chat in the back. As Pearly pulls up to the ticket stand, a sign for Golden Age Cinemas advertises:

Set your radio to 88.9 FM, and tune in to the Golden Age!

($14/carload)

"Tuning in!" says Pearly, as she flips on the radio. She finds a spot in the U-shaped lot surrounding the massive screen. A few people give Seraphina, still in her favorite pink Cadillac form, appreciative glances.

"She's a beaut!" says the dad parked next door. "That chrome detailing, those fins – pure magic."

"She sure is." Pearly pats Seraphina, who purrs until Pearly cuts the engine. She turns to her charges. "Popcorn?"

"Extra-large," says Danielle.

"Extra butter!" says Hannah.

Sam just shrugs.

Pearly feels the tug-o-war in his mind. Part of him wants to join the fun and part of him just wants to stew in his misery. "Come on, sunshine." She wraps an arm around his shoulder. "We already drove out here. You might as well get into it."

Pearly leaves Hannah and Danielle to set up the lawn chairs and folding table while she and Sam make their way through the lot. It's a warm night for early October. Families are staked out around their cars, playing board games and tossing around footballs. The concession stand is concrete and halfway underground, like some kind of nuclear bunker. Posters like the ones in Sam's apartment line the walls – *Forbidden Planet, Bride of Frankenstein, The Blob* – and an old Cinex movie projector sits next to a classic juke box. Pearly forces Sam to take a photo with his head in the cardboard cut-out of an enormous bowl of popcorn before gesturing to the snack options.

"Anything you want," she says, flashing some bills. "I'm buying."

"How do you even have money?" he asks.

"I manifest it." She rubs her fingers together, and dollars appear between them. Sam raises an eyebrow. "What? It barely contributes to inflation."

Sam orders a small popcorn and a Diet Coke. Pearly orders 3 extra-large popcorns, a Slushie, a slice of pizza, a tray of nachos, Twizzlers, Raisinets, and a beer.

"Go big or go home," the cashier chuckles.

"Always." Pearly winks.

They make their way back to the car and settle into the lawn chairs. Pearly hands out the goodies, and they chew in awkward silence. Hannah, Sam, and Danielle have met at the café, but this is the first time they've hung out. It probably wouldn't have happened without Pearly. They all come from different social circles. Sam's even from a different generation, the youngest of the gang. Pearly watches him watching the cute couple on their right. They're about his age, snuggled together on a sleeping bag in the back of a pickup, sipping hot cider from Styrofoam cups, steam rising into the crisp autumn air.

"When does the movie start?" asks Hannah.

"Not until it's fully dark," says Pearly. "We have some time. I wish I'd thought to bring a game or something."

"I know!" Danielle swallows a mouthful of popcorn. "How about a tarot reading? I've been so curious ever since you said you worked with cards."

Tarot, Pearly wracks her brain, *that's, like, swords and wands and dishes, right?* Pearly's only past experience with divination was as a seer in ancient Egypt. It was a good gig — plenty of perks, not to mention the respect — until she "misread the signs" and advised a swift and immediate attack against the Hittites. Unfortunately, they were better prepared than anticipated. You can really only fuck up that kind of thing once. It wasn't her first public execution, and it wouldn't be her last.

"I mean, if y'all are into it," she says, hoping the skeptics in the group will shoot it down.

"Yeah, sure," says Hannah. "Show us what you do."

They look at Sam. He snickers, the only one of them who knows she's not really a psychic. "Go for it."

If there's one thing Pearly's good at, it's bullshitting – or rather, shaping facts to suit her needs. Whether it's cards or tea leaves or entrails, divination's always been less about telling the future and more about creating it. Right?

"Okay," she says, reaching into her handbag and emerging with a newly manifested deck. "I'll pull one card for each of you. Danielle, you want to start?"

"Sure!"

Pearly spreads the cards across the table, claps her hands together. "First, I need you to close your eyes. Go on, close 'em." Danielle obliges. "Now, focus on an intention. What is it you want to know?"

"Uh...next steps?"

"Great." Pearly hovers her hands over the deck. "Just feeeeeeeelin' the energy..." Then she cracks her knuckles, draws a card, and flips it over. It features a young person with a joyful expression about to walk off a cliff, either unaware of the danger or totally unbothered by it. "Ah," she says. "The Fool. My favorite." In truth, it's one of the only cards she actually recognizes. But she's damn sure going to milk it.

Danielle frowns. "I thought that one meant you're being naïve or reckless."

"I never saw it that way," says Pearly. "The Fool doesn't buy the shit society is selling. They're a radical, a risk-taker, ready to take a leap into the unknown and carve out the life *they* want to live. It's a place of possibility. And if that's not magic? Girl, I don't know what is." Pearly sees Danielle's aura brighten, like someone just threw her a life preserver. Pearly brightens too, inspired by her own pep talk. She's good at this. She's going to get that promotion, carve out her own afterlife. She's the Fool, just like Danielle, a risk-taker, a truth-teller.

"Okay," says Danielle, "I'll buy that interpretation. But living your truth is hard. How do I know I won't just fall off the cliff?"

"You don't." Pearly shrugs. "No risk, no reward. Now obviously no one's suggesting you do anything unsafe – but if you have enough support, I'd advocate for the leap of faith. Be the you that makes you feel the most alive." She looks up, assessing her charge. "Is there anything you've been wanting to do but afraid to try?"

Danielle leans back in her chair. Pearly can tell she's debating how much to reveal, and in what category. "I mean," she says, "sometimes I think about doing more with baking."

"You're a baker?" says Hannah. "That's so cool. I tried to get on that sourdough trend during pandemic and failed miserably."

"What do you bake?" asks Sam.

"I'm kind of all over the place," Danielle shrugs. "But I like to cook with seasonal ingredients, so right now it's mostly fall-inspired pastries. I just made a batch of apple cardamom turnovers that my stepfather said were amazing. But this is a guy who's content with a 'Hungry Man' frozen dinner if I don't cook, so I'm not sure his opinion counts."

"You should bring some into Thunderbolt," says Pearly. "We will happily provide feedback."

Danielle shakes her head. "I don't want to step on Charlie's toes. I'm so grateful to have a job – I wouldn't want to fuck that up by side-hustling my pastries."

"I don't think they'd mind," says Pearly. "Why don't you ask them?"

"Maybe. I'll think about it." Danielle turns to the others, eager to change the subject. "Now, who's next?"

Hannah looks at Sam. "Go ahead," he says.

"Okay." Hannah puts down her popcorn and sits up. "Next steps works for me, too. Not so much for career, but, uh..." She blushes. "Relationship stuff."

"You got it," says Pearly. She pulls a card for Hannah — a figure sneaking away from a campsite, holding five swords and leaving two behind. The figure is looking back over their shoulder with an expression of caution, or maybe even guilt.

"Ooooooh," whispers Danielle. "Seven of Swords."

"What?" says Hannah. "Is that bad?"

"Oh, um, I'm not the expert." Danielle tucks a strand of hair behind her ear. "Sometimes they say it's about betrayal, but Pearly would know better."

Betrayal. Is that the universe trying to warn Pearly? She's determined to do right by Hannah – to table her personal feelings with the Charlie situation – but she's never taken on this kind of dilemma. Pearly's ethics hold up, as long as you don't look too closely. And she's never had to look – not like this. But there's poor Hannah squirming in her lawn chair, probably wondering if she's just made a huge mistake.

"The card *can* signify betrayal," says Pearly. "But that's not what I'm getting for you. I see it more as...thinking out-side-the-box."

"Oh yeah?" Hannah perks up. "How so?"

Pearly takes a breath, hoping she can spin this. "It's like you're betraying your old belief systems and forging a new way forward – one you've never considered before. Just because you did relationships a certain way in the past doesn't mean that's how you have to do them now. You're allowed to break the mold."

Hannah's brow furrows as she thinks about this. Then she smiles. "I like it. Thanks, Pearly."

Yaaas, girl, nailed it. "Anytime." Pearly glances at Sam. "What about you, Holmes?"

"Holmes?" says Hannah.

"That's right. Sam and I are co-detectives, working on the case at Thunderbolt. Did you know the café is haunted?"

"Seriously?" Hannah looks skeptical.

"It's true," says Danielle. "I can't see the ghost, but I can feel her presence sometimes. I don't think she's mean or anything, maybe just...I don't know, fragile."

"I know, it sounds wild," says Sam, "but they're right. There really is a ghost – Ruby LaRue. She's connected to the café in ways that go deeper than just a few spooky incidents. We're trying to get to the bottom of it, unearth the real history."

"Huh." Hannah adjusts her glasses. "Well, I guess I'm broadening my horizons. Normally I just hang out with stuffy professors. This is much more interesting."

If you only knew, thinks Pearly. "So," she says to Sam. "Any particular intention?"

"Not really. Let's just see what comes up." He knows she's full of shit. But is she? So far, her readings have been pretty on point.

"You got it." Pearly runs her hand over the deck, hoping for something good — so far, she's two for two. She flips a card, revealing a stately figure holding a golden staff. He's seated on a raised platform, draped in a thick red cloth and lots of bling.

"Ah," she says, with a triumphant air. "The Elephant.""Um," asks Danielle, "do you mean the Hierophant?"

Whoops.

"Yeaaahhh," says Pearly. "Too, uh, patriarchal. I call him the Elephant." Sam covers his face to hide his laughter.

"I like it," says Danielle. "You put your own spin on it. Like the non-gendered decks."

"Exactly. Anyway," she looks up at Sam, his face still red. "This card embodies wisdom. For you, I'm feeling the wisdom of...acceptance."

His smile fades. Pearly senses he's considering a snarky reply, but it never comes. "Yeah," he says finally. "That would be wise. But, like, how do you cultivate it? You can't force acceptance."

Good question. Pearly doesn't have an answer. She's not so great at accepting things she doesn't like. If she was, she wouldn't be here. But Sam can't do anything to change his diagnosis. He can only change his attitude. So how does he get there?

"I don't know if this helps," says Danielle. "But when I was struggling to accept my gender, I had this moment where I realized how much energy I was spending just fighting reality. It was, like, eighty percent of my total output. And, I don't know, something just clicked. I realized that embracing my transness was actually easier than constantly pushing it away. Plus now I had all this energy I could put into other things. That's actually when I started baking again."

Pearly is floored. She didn't expect Danielle to reveal something so vulnerable, especially to people she doesn't know very well. But the look on Sam's face tells all of them it was worth it.

"Thank you for sharing that," he says, blinking back what might be tears. "It does help."

Well, wouldn't you know? Pearly wasn't sure if bringing her charges together was a good idea, but this officially confirms it. As the screen lights up and a hush comes over the crowd, she looks at each of them in turn. Hannah. Danielle. Sam. Individually, they have their struggles, but together there's a strength that makes each of them shine brighter. Pearly's relied on Thunder – her one and only – for so long that she's forgotten the value of community. Maybe there's a lesson in this for the Higher-Ups. She could show them a better way of guiding, one that embraces direct intervention and client intermingling. She'll blow the cobwebs off their archaic system, infuse new life into the afterlife!

An annoying little voice in the back of Pearly's mind says she might not be getting the point about acceptance. But she doesn't feel like she's fighting reality. She feels like she's kicking its ass. And that is perfectly acceptable.

Twenty-Four

Thunder.

No, not *that* Thunder. The kind that comes with lightning. Pearly feels it rumbling as the storm closes in on Eenob. It's been raining since dawn. As she lounges at the cafe window with her cinnamon roll latte, fat drops pound the glass. It's a rhythm that she usually finds soothing, but for some reason...not today.

Instinct tells Pearly to seek Danielle. She's behind the counter, grinding espresso beans and steaming almond milk as she laughs with a customer about some stupid plot twist in a show they're both watching. Pearly smiles. She's over the moon to see how much progress Danielle has made since starting at Thunderbolt. Still...something feels off.

Maybe it's Ruby? The ghost has started "helping" around the café. She said she felt bad for scaring away customers, so she restocks books and buses tables when no one's looking. Today, she's helping Danielle with the morning rush. When she searches for a particular flavor of syrup, it seems to appear in front of her. As she reaches for a spoon, it almost slides into her hand on its own. Danielle smiles at her unseen ally, bolstered by the loving support. It warms Pearly's heart to watch. *All is well*, she tells herself. *All is well.*

The storm kicks up a notch. Rain comes in driving sheets as the storm rattles the windows. Pearly squirms in her seat, unable to shake her vague sense of dread. Just as she's convinced herself it's her own head trip, the door swings open, and a very wet woman steps inside. She stops in the doorway and wrestles with her dysfunctional umbrella, trying to get the damn thing to close. Pearly guesses she's in her late fifties, with iron-gray hair and a navy blue raincoat that matches her loafers.

Her face tightens as she finally snaps the umbrella shut – spattering drops onto the floor and nearby customers, including Pearly. She sets it aside with a huff and heads to the counter. As she makes her way to the front of the line, her eyes fix on Danielle with a pointed intensity. Danielle's customer-service-smile falters as she meets the woman's eyes.

"Good morning," she says, "What can I get started for you today?"

The woman gives her the once-over – noting everything from Danielle's makeup to her ruffled top and bangle bracelets.

"It's been a long time," she says. "I almost didn't recognize you."

"Hello, Margaret," Danielle says with a sigh.

Ruby and Pearly watch from the sidelines, their own anxiety rising along with Danielle's.

"You've changed so much since we saw you at church," says Margaret. "How long ago was that again? Anyhow, we've all been praying for you, Jacob."

Pearly can tell that hearing her deadname hits Danielle hard. But she raises her chin and looks Margaret in the eye. "I go by Danielle now."

"I see." Margaret shakes her head. "It's not too late, you know. If you get tired of this...phase. I'm sure your father would be relieved to have you back."

Danielle looks down. It's just too much. Should Pearly step in? As she debates how to handle this, the storm rages harder, slamming against the windows and pelting the sidewalk with drops approaching hail.

Pearly senses the shift in Ruby – a storm is brewing in her too. The temperature drops and the lights in the café begin to flicker. As the ghost approaches Margaret, the air around her seems to thicken. Pearly holds her breath. If Danielle hits a breaking point, Ruby might too.

Margaret throws Danielle a pious look of thinly veiled pity. "You don't have to live this way, Jacob," she says. "God is waiting for you."

Danielle's eyes well up, and Ruby's anger flares. The lights flicker, then go out completely. Customers must think it's the storm, but Pearly knows better. Just as she pushes up out of her chair, Charlie approaches the counter. It's clear they've heard enough of the exchange to know what's going on.

Charlie steps between Danielle and Margaret. "Is there something I can help you with?"

Margaret shifts her focus to Charlie. "I was just reminding Jacob—"

"Her name is Danielle," says Charlie. "And in this café, we respect who people are, not who others want them to be."

Margaret grimaces, but Charlie doesn't back down. "If you want to order something, fine. But if you're here to cut someone down, I'll have to ask you to leave."

Yaaaaaaaass, thinks Pearly. *That's my Thunder.*

Standoff. Margaret glares at Charlie. Then she smooths her coat and gives Danielle one last condescending look. "You might think you're helping him," she says to Charlie, "but you're just encouraging confusion."

Charlie stares her down. "No, I'm encouraging you to leave, and never come back."

Margaret seethes, but she's not stupid enough to respond. Instead, she turns and marches out into the storm, slamming the door shut behind her.

Pearly exhales, but she knows this isn't over – Ruby's only getting more upset. Pearly feels the negative energy building...

CRACK!

A pipe bursts overhead before anyone can react, a surge of water spewing from the ceiling. Shocked customers grab their belongings and scramble out of the way as the water spreads across the room and into the bookshop. Pearly's gut wrenches — the books on the lower shelves are already getting soaked...

The door to the breakroom opens and Charlie emerges with an armful of supplies. "The storage room's flooding!" they shout. "We gotta move everything out!"

Pearly wants to help, but when she looks back at Danielle, she sees her breath coming in shallow gasps.

"Danielle." She comes up behind the counter and takes her charge's hands. "Let's breathe together." Pearly glances at Ruby. The ghost is assessing the damage she caused with wide, panicked eyes. "You too, Ruby. Come over here."

Danielle manages to nod. Ruby floats over. They both echo Pearly's slow, deep breaths.

"One...two...three..." says Pearly. "Hold. Exhale."

After a couple of rounds, Pearly feels both of them stabilizing. Charlie's still across the room dealing with agitated customers and wonky equipment, so Pearly knows it's up to her and Danielle to help out.

"Now," she says to Danielle. "The water – we need to shut it off. Can you do that while I help Charlie?"

"Yeah," Danielle says. "I know where the valve is."

She heads to the pipes, while Pearly turns her attention to Ruby.

"This is all my fault," the ghost laments, wringing her hands. "Sometimes, I just – I get so agitated. I didn't mean for any of this to happen."

"I know, Ruby. We've got to work on stabilizing your energy. But your intention was good – you were upset about an injustice and wanted to protect Danielle – and that's the most important thing."

Ruby nods, but she doesn't look convinced. "What's wrong with me?" she whispers. "Why can't I just move on like everybody else?"

"We're trying to figure that out. When Sam and I said we wanted to help you, we meant it. I know it's tough to be patient, but I need you to try. Can you do that for me?"

Ruby straightens her posture, and for a moment Pearly sees the confident performer she'd been onstage. "Yes. I can do that."

"Good," says Pearly. "I believe in you."

Danielle reenters. She gives a thumbs up, indicating the pipes have been shut off, and the remaining customers cheer. Pearly takes the reins. She runs up and grabs Danielle into a mama bear hug.

"I'm proud of you, girl," she says. "That was a lot, and you did great."

"Thanks, Pearly." She leans back against the counter, recovering from the adrenaline rush. "But I feel about as soggy as these pastries." She indicates a ruined batch in the display case.

"No real loss," says Charlie, emerging from the bookshop with a stack of water-stained mysteries. "Everyone knows they suck anyway." Pearly catches Danielle's eye as Charlie continues. "But I do want to save as many books as I can. Pearly, would you help me clear the bottom shelves? And Danielle, we need to dry the floor before it molds. I'll join you in a bit but I need to spend a few minutes offering free drinks to the few customers who haven't left." They sigh. "The PR on this could be a disaster, on top of all the damaged stock and repairs."

"Yes, of course," says Danielle.

"You got it," says Pearly.

Charlie pulls their gaze from all the empty chairs and turns to Pearly. "I guess you weren't pulling my leg about that ghost..." Their brow furrows, as if trying to figure out how to add this problem to their "to-do" list.

"No," says Pearly. "But you leave that one to me." Technically, helping Charlie helps her charges. Danielle's employment is tied to the café, and they all have an investment in it, emotional or otherwise. But it's not just that.

Charlie looks up at Pearly with the first hint of vulnerability she's seen – soft eyes beneath the 'tough guy' exterior. It reminds her so much of Thunder that her breath catches in her throat. "Thanks, Pearly," Charlie says, stepping close enough for her to feel their breath on her face. "I really feel like I can count on you."

Pearly swallows, nods. She really hopes to prove them right.

TWENTY-FIVE

"It's not usually this quiet in here, is it?" says Hannah, glancing around the café.

Pearly shakes her head, trying to ignore the pit in her stomach. "No, not usually."

She looks over at Charlie, pacing back and forth behind the counter, negotiating with a vendor on the phone. It doesn't seem to be going well.

"I understand the delivery was delayed," Charlie says, "but we can't afford another shipment of stale beans...yes of course, we've gotten complaints...no...no, I don't want a discount – I want fresh beans...yeah, I get it. I get it...we'll be in touch." They end the call, shoving the phone into their pocket with a sigh.

Pearly shakes her head. "That can't be good. Thunderbolt's got enough problems." Charlie told Hannah this morning that the café needs a miracle to stay afloat, between all the new repairs and the drop in business. And of course, Hannah told Pearly, in a game of telephone.

"Yeah..." Hannah stares into her latte. "On the bright side, Charlie finally believes you that the café's haunted."

"Don't worry, Ruby's a nice ghost." Pearly smiles. "Not one of those head-spinning, barfy types."

"You mean like *The Exorcist?*" Hannah raises an eyebrow. "That wasn't a ghost, that was a demonic possession. And anyway, doesn't seem like such a nice ghost to me." She gestures all around them. "She wrecked this place."

Pearly winces. She and Sam know Ruby. They've talked to her about her story and have sympathized with her struggles. But she has to remember that everyone else has only seen the destruction.

"I know, honey." Pearly nods to the program featuring Ruby's likeness. "But you have to understand she didn't want to do this. She just got out of control." She leans in. "That's why Sam and I are trying to help her find closure. Maybe then she won't take it out on the café."

As if on cue, the door chimes as Sam enters, a bit lost in his own world. Pearly waves him over.

"Sam! Come join us."

He hesitates briefly, then makes his way over to the table.

"We were just talking about our case," says Pearly, as he sinks into a chair. "I don't see Ruby today. I'm sure she still feels bad about what happened."

Hannah grunts, and Sam raises an eyebrow. "What?" he says. "It's not her fault."

"Then whose fault is it?" says Hannah.

"No one's." He takes off his beanie, setting it on his lap. "How would you feel trapped as a ghost in some café while everyone you knew moved on? Ruby deserves compassion, not judgment."

"I guess," says Hannah. "You might feel differently if it was your name on the lease."

"Yeah, maybe." But Sam doesn't look convinced.

The door to the breakroom swings open, and all three of them turn to look. Danielle comes over carrying a box, which she sets on the table. "I made these," she says, glancing at Pearly. "I'm going to see if Charlie's interested in selling them, but I figured I'd take you up on your offer to test them first." She opens the box. "I have a cinnamon-spiced pear danish, maple-pecan sticky buns, and pumpkin spice scones with maple glaze...Want one?"

"Hell yes, girl!" Pearly immediately grabs a sticky bun.

"Wow, these look amazing," says Hannah. She pauses over the Danish but picks a scone. "And they smell even better. You made them all yourself?"

Danielle yawns. "Yeah. I've been getting up at three in the morning."

Charlie walks over, drawn by the spicy, nutty scents. "What's this?" they ask.

Danielle steps back to let them take a look. "Remember how I mentioned I like to bake? Well...I made these. I thought you might...uh..." She trails off, suddenly nervous.

"She thought you might fare better with these than the garbage you've been peddling," says Pearly.

Charlie leans in to inspect the pastries. They pick up a sticky bun, examining it with a critical eye. Then they take a bite.

"Holy shit," Charlie says, only it sounds like "holla shift" with their mouth full. "These are ridiculous, Danielle. If you're up for daily batches, I'm more than happy to put them on the menu."

Danielle hops back and forth like she just won the lottery. "Really?"

"Absolutely," says Charlie. They gesture to the empty tables. "Maybe it'll help bring back some business."

As the group devours the pastries and settles into a contented sugar high, Pearly clears her throat. "All right," she says, "I think it's time we had a little meeting. I've got an idea that just might turn things around for the café—and it involves all of you."

Heads turn. Eyebrows raise. Pearly's got them where she wants them.

"So I've been thinking," she begins, "Thunderbolt has quite a history. Some of you know it used to be a speakeasy – the Moonshine Lounge – featuring Ruby, the café's resident ghost."

Charlie flinches at the name. Pearly can't help thinking Thunder would understand – he's such a caring soul. That's why they gave him that award. But she gets how from Charlie's perspective, Ruby is some out-of-control pest infesting her business.

"Due to...recent events," Pearly continues, "the café needs our help. And I thought there might be a way to make use of its history. What if we hosted a 'Save the Café' fundraising event with a 1920s theme, turning the place into the Moonshine Lounge for a night?"

Pearly looks around the table for reactions. Sam, Danielle, and Hannah all seem interested, but Charlie is frowning.

"I don't know, Pearly," they say. "I mean, it sounds great on paper, but that's a huge undertaking. I'm already stretched thin, and now you want us to put together some big event with, like, period costumes, decorations, and I don't even know what else? It sounds expensive – and a pain in the ass to organize."

Pearly feels a flash of irritation as her grand vision collides with Charlie's practicality – just like it used to do with Thunder. If she's being honest with herself, this is bigger than the café. This is her opportunity to prove herself before her report is due. But she catches herself, forces a smile. "I'd be happy to take the lead and MC the event," she says. "You'd be surprised what a little creativity and community spirit can accomplish." She looks at Sam. "You could help with the historical aspects—"

"I'd love to!" Sam's face lights up.

"And you," Pearly turns to Danielle, "could do the catering."

"Ohmygod, yes!" she says. "We could do classic hors d'oeuvres—maybe mini beef Wellingtons, or Oysters Rockefeller, or deviled eggs with a twist. I could make an old-school coconut layer cake or maybe even a Baked Alaska..." She stops herself, giggles. "Sorry, I'm getting a little ahead of myself. I've barely made more than a batch of pastries."

"You can do it," says Pearly. "We'll help you."

"Oh, and Pearly," says Sam, "what about all that vintage stuff we found in the basement? Some of it's got to be valuable. Perfect for an auction."

"Now we're talkin'," Pearly grins.

"What if we did it the weekend of Halloween?" says Hannah. "It would give people a reason to go all out on costumes."

"Hell yes!" Pearly slams her hand on the table. They'll be cutting it close to Malcolm's November 1st deadline, but it's all coming together. Everyone starts chattering at the table, excited by the prospect — everyone but Charlie.

"Hey, simmer down everyone," they cut in. "I'm not trying to be difficult. It's just – things have been rough. We only opened six months ago and we're barely hanging on. This idea – it's risky. If this flops, it could be the last straw."

They slump back into their chair, and Hannah takes their hand. Pearly feels a twinge of jealousy. It's unsettling how much Charlie's gestures and mannerisms mirror Thunder's – from the way they rub the back of their neck when they're feeling overwhelmed to the way they pinch their lip when they're considering something serious.

"I'll help too," says Hannah. "Honestly, if it's a chance to keep you in business, why wouldn't we give it a shot?"

"Exactly!" Pearly grins, feeling the group's energy shift as the idea takes hold. "Charlie, I can help you with logistics—figuring out where the stage will go, coordinating with vendors, all the headache-inducing stuff." Details have never been her strong suit, but she's sure she can handle it.

"Well..." Charlie says, a hint of relief creeping into their voice. "That would make things easier."

"I can do some marketing," says Sam. "You have an Insta, right?"

Charlie nods.

"Oh!" says Danielle. "We can also put up flyers at the Halloween Festival. That always gets a lot of traffic."

"Definitely," Hannah agrees. She turns to Pearly to explain. "The festival's kind of a big deal around here—it's what the town's known for. Especially the pumpkin pie baking contest." She turns to Danielle. "I hope you enter. You'd slay it."

"I admit, I've thought about it," she smiles.

"Yes! Great!" Pearly turns to Charlie with a hopeful smile. "So...?"

Charlie crosses their arms, tapping their fingers. After a moment, they sigh and look directly at Pearly. "If this goes south, I'm blaming you."

Pearly shrugs, unfazed. "I get that a lot."

Charlie studies her, all tight-lipped and furrowed brow, but then a smile breaks through. "Okay, okay, you sold me. Let's do this."

"Yaaaaaaaasssss!" Pearly pushes her chair back and instigates a celebratory duck walk down the aisle. The others laugh and cheer her on. She's so caught up in the moment that she almost doesn't notice Charlie lean across the table and kiss Hannah. Almost.

TWENTY-SIX

Pearly's not what would you would call a "numbers person." She's a Big Ideas kind of girl – the kind who makes magic, not spreadsheets. Just like Thunder, Charlie is all about the details. "I don't know, Pearly," they say, running a hand through their lavender hair. Their mouth keeps doing frowny things as they scroll through projected expenses on their laptop. "We can fund this thing – barely. But if we don't raise enough money…"

Pearly leans back in her chair. "Come on, Charlie," she says, forcing a smile, "where's your sense of adventure? We've got the community, we've got the creativity, and once we start rolling, there's no stopping us. Sky's the limit! No, bigger – shoot for the stars!"

But even as the words leave her, Pearly can feel the weight of her own doubts. This isn't just about saving the café. It's something deeper—something in the way her heart skips a beat whenever Charlie's around, the way every little gesture echoes something from a life she's trying to leave behind. She tells herself she's doing this for her charges – and for Charlie – but she'd be lying if she said it didn't occur to her that putting on this event would be an opportunity to spend more time with her soulmate. *Former soulmate.*

"Besides," she adds with a wink, "if it all goes to hell, we can always blame it on the ghost. Ruby's already spooked half the town away—maybe she can scare 'em back in."

Charlie rolls their eyes. "I'm serious, Pearly. If this flops…"

"It won't," she says, more confident than she feels. "Trust me."

"Alright, what's next?" Pearly finishes the last of her third straight latte and looks up with a semi-maniacal buzz. "Costumes? Decorations? Supplies?"

"Yeah…" Charlie closes their laptop with a grimace. "We'll need to get a lot of stuff in bulk—plastic drink cups, napkins, trays, string lights… the works. Costco should have most of that—"

"Costco?" Pearly's eyes light up "I've heard of this legendary land…"

Charlie raises an eyebrow. "You've never been to Costco?"

"Nope," she says, "but I've always wanted to. I bet it's filled with magic and mayhem."

"Well, don't get too excited," says Charlie. "It's pretty much just a warehouse with oversized everything."

Pearly waggles her fingers. "Magic is what you make of it. Lead the way, Captain Practical."

***

As they pull into the football-field-sized parking lot, Pearly's jaw drops. The massive building looms ahead, its gleaming exterior promising endless aisles of goods inside. Rows of cars stretch out in every direction, asphalt farther than the eye can see.

"Whoa," she says, watching wild-eyed people come out with carts piled high with jumbo packs of paper towels and industrial-sized jars of peanut butter.

Charlie grabs a cart. "Oh, you ain't seen nothin' yet."

The automatic doors slide open, revealing the cavernous interior. Pearly cranes her neck to stare at towering shelves crammed with everything from patio furniture to mega-jars of multi-vitamins. "Holy shit."

"Stick with me. We've got a lot to pick up."

But as they begin to browse the aisles, Pearly's all over the place. "Oh my god, look at the size of that thing!" She points to a giant sack of kettle corn. "It's big enough to drown in."

Charlie grins and shakes their head. "We're here for drink cups and string lights, remember?"

"Right, right," Pearly says, but she's already on her way to a display of gourmet cheeses. She grabs a sample of truffle cheddar and swallows it one gulp. "Oh god, you've got to try this," she says, grabbing another piece and practically stuffing it into Charlie's face.

"Okay, yeah, it's great," they say, gently pushing Pearly away. "But we really don't need gourmet cheese for the event."

Pearly's face flushes. She realizes it may have been a bit overly intimate to put her fingers in the mouth of someone, who, from Charlie's perspective, she barely knows. It's a struggle for Pearly. She feels her bond with Thunder so strongly in the presence of Charlie. But Charlie isn't struggling with anything. It's just Pearly – and if she wants what's best for them, she'll keep it that way. "Who said anything about need?" Pearly forces a grin, popping another piece into her mouth. "We're creating an *experience*, Charlie."

"Yeah, well, *experiences* can be expensive – and we're on a budget, remember?"

"Right." Pearly considers manifesting an unlimited charge card, but that would probably get her in a lot more trouble than a few concessions at the drive-in. "Hey, look at this!" she calls out, holding up a massive inflatable flamingo. "Centerpiece? It's only twenty bucks."

Charlie throws her a look. "Pearly, we're trying to channel 1920s elegance, not a cheesy Hollywood pool party."

"Details, psssh," Pearly says, but she reluctantly puts the flamingo back.

Charlie takes a breath. It looks like they're counting to five. "Are you even taking this seriously?"

"Yes!" says Pearly. "I am living for this."

As they continue through the store, Pearly insists on trying every free sample, dragging Charlie along to taste-test things they clearly don't need, like frozen mini quiches and pizza bites. She's delighted to get to try out a new experience like this, especially with Charlie, and she notices them shifting from annoyance to amusement at her childlike enthusiasm. They stop briefly at the electric fireplaces, and Charlie looks at them with longing. "Wouldn't one of those be great in the reading nook?" they say. Then they shake their head, dragging Pearly away muttering mantras like "stay on target" under their breath.

Eventually, they find the aisle with the string lights, and Pearly examines each option. "These!" she declares, grabbing several boxes. "They'll add just the right amount of sparkle. Elegant with a touch of mischief, like fairies."

"Okay," says Charlie. "I've got to admit, you have a good eye. Now, let's get those trays and cups."

As they turn into the aisle with the heavy-duty tools, Pearly glances at a display of rivet guns. Something about them stops her in her tracks. Before she knows it, she's no longer at the warehouse...

***

Detroit, 1943

The factory floor buzzes with the clanging of metal and the hum of machinery, air thick with hot metal and engine oil. Rows of women in bandanas move with purpose, their faces set with determination as they assemble B-24 bomber parts destined for the front lines. Gladys – Pearly in this lifetime – rivets panels with swift precision. Her once-blue overalls are a patchwork of oil stains and wear. Her face drips with sweat, and her hands are smudged with oil.

Across the floor, young Marjorie struggles with a heavy metal sheet, her slender frame buckling under the weight. Just as Gladys moves to help, a sneering voice cuts through the din.

"Come on, doll face," shouts the foreman, "put some muscle into it. We're not baking banana loaves here. If you can't hack it, there's the door."

Marjorie's face flushes with embarrassment, her eyes welling up. Before she can respond, Gladys is at her side, eyes blazing. "Hey chucklehead, lay off her."

The foreman's face twists in annoyance. "Take a powder, Gladys. This ain't your fight."

Gladys's face hardens. She tells him off in her head: *"Listen, bub, we're on the same team, so why don't you clam up your bone box before we stage a walk-out and leave you alone with your willy swinging in the wind?"*

But she knows she can't say any of that, not if she wants to keep her job. Not to mention Marjorie—it would only hurt her in the long run. Instead, Gladys swallows her pride and goes back to work.

"Don't let him get to you," she whispers to Marjorie as she passes. "He's all hooey and hot air."

She's still steaming on the streetcar back home. But the closer she gets, the more her mind fills with worries about Vic, her Thunder in this life. His letters from overseas have gotten scarce lately. Each newsless day only adds to her growing dread.

The city is alive with the hustle of wartime activity. Gladys approaches her modest apartment building, a sturdy structure of faded brick with ivy creeping up its sides. As she climbs the steps, she notices the door is slightly ajar.

Gladys's breath stops. An intruder? She pulls her pocket pistol from her purse and stalks down the hallway, eyes adjusting to the warm glow of the lamps within. And there—sitting in the armchair in the living room...who's that?

She trains her gun on him before she realizes. It's Vic. Vic!

Her heart expands, then sinks into her stomach. But he doesn't notice her, or even the pistol pointed at his chest. He's staring blankly at...what, the wall? His uniform is neat but worn. The olive jacket, decorated with medals and insignia, is carefully buttoned up. But his left pant leg is empty, the end knotted at the waist. A prosthetic wooden leg leans against the chair.

"Gladys." He lifts from his reverie enough to notice her, and breaks into a small smile. "Now, that's what I call a welcome wagon."

She drops the pistol and rushes to him, wrapping her arms around his neck, sobbing with a mix of relief and joy. "Jesus, Vic. I thought I'd never see you again."

"I promised I'd come back to you." Vic holds her close, his grip strong despite his exhaustion. "And look, most of me did."

She snuggles into him, then meets his gaze. "What happened to you?"

He flinches, rubbing his forehead as if to wipe clean the memory. "We were advancing," he says. "Got caught in a barrage. And when I came to, well..." He swallows hard. "They got me out fast, but the damage was done. I'm not – I'm half a man, Gladys. I'd understand if..."

Gladys cups his face in her hands, her thumbs brushing away the tears on his cheeks.

Does he really think she'd leave him? Because of some stupid inconvenience? "You'll always be my man," she promises. She leans in, kisses him long and slow and sweet. Then she pulls back, takes a breath. "I was so scared," she admits. "Every day, I worried. I even went to goddamn church and prayed."

"I guess it worked." He smiles.

As Gladys grapples with this, her gaze lingers on his leg. "Did they give you anything for the pain?"

"Pumped me full of morphine," he says. "It did the trick, but it made everything hazy. Those first few days in the field hospital are a blur. The nurses said I kept trying to write you, but it was all gobbledegook."

She hugs him again, tighter this time, as her whole body shakes. "I just – I can't believe this is real."

"It's real," he says, nuzzling into her neck. "I'm here now. And I'm not leaving. Ever again."

***

"Hey," says Charlie. "You okay?"

The vision fades, leaving Pearly back in the brightly lit aisle of Costco. Charlie's standing next to her with a furrowed brow. "What?" Pearly blinks, disoriented.

"You – well, you kinda went away for a minute there." Charlie laughs nervously. "You okay?"

"Oh yeah," says Pearly. "I'm fine. I swear. It's, uh, a psychic thing." She makes a swirly gesture leading out from the center of her forehead. "Happens sometimes. Nothing to worry about."

"Okay," says Charlie. "If you're sure..."

"I'm sure! Now show me those cups."

***

After hauling their Costco finds into Thunderbolt, Pearly and Charlie settle down at a corner table, ready to brainstorm how to transform the café into the Moonshine Lounge. Charlie opens their laptop, ready to get serious.

"Okay," says Charlie. "We got everything on our list. But I don't know if any of this screams speakeasy."

Hannah walks up to the table, shaking off the early autumn chill. She leans in to give Charlie a quick hug, their shoulders brushing as she settles into the chair next to them. Pearly feels the spark as if it happened to her. Sometimes, guide-empathy is confusing.

"What if we make the entrance part of the experience?" Hannah suggests. "Like, turn it into a secret passage? We could have guests enter through the bookshop and create a swinging door that leads into the café. That screams speakeasy to me."

"I love it!" grins Pearly. "We could have a sign at the front of the bookshop—something subtle, like 'Closed for Inventory'—and only those who know the password get in. Then, when they give the password, we lead them to the secret entrance."

"Right." Hannah looks around the café. "And once they step through, they're transported back to the 1920s. We could even decorate the bookshop with some period props—maybe a few vintage books or a typewriter, or whatever you guys find down in the basement that you don't sell at the auction."

"I don't know," says Charlie. "That sounds like a pretty big undertaking."

"It doesn't have to be," says Hannah. "There's already a door between the bookshop and the café. Couldn't you just, like, attach some shelves to make it look like a bookcase?"

Charlie considers. "That actually could work. Good thinking, Cohen!"

Hannah blushes.

"And," says Pearly, "we could have a bouncer at the door—someone who's sort of nice but also menacing. Maybe even dress them up like an old gangster? Fedora, pinstripe suit, the whole deal. They could ask for a password—something like 'bananas foster' or 'jazz hands'—just to throw people off. And if a guest doesn't get it right, they have to do the Charleston before the bouncer lets them in."

Charlie shakes their head. "I'm not sure we want to scare off the few customers we have left, Pearly."

"Oh come on," says Pearly. "Everybody loves a little role play." She tries to mask her frustration with a cheerful tone. Why does Charlie have to be such a sourpuss?

"Oh hey!" says Hannah. "What if we used the bookshop, too? We could have a display on flapper culture and the way it challenged traditional gender roles. That would add historical context, and maybe you'd sell some extra books!"

"Okay, sure," says Charlie, getting into it. "That would be easy to set up. We could even include a section on the influence of jazz music, and some local history from that era."

"This is all great," says Pearly. "We're only missing one thing – but it's a big thing. The performances."

They both stare at her. "What performances?" says Charlie.

Pearly clucks. "You can't have an event like this without performances. It's like an open mic night or a reading, only bigger and with more flair."

Charlie sighs. "You're right. A gala needs performances."

"That's fun," says Hannah, "but who would we get to perform?"

"Well, you for one, Miss Professor. I could see you doing a short lecture on flappers—maybe even in costume."

Hannah laughs. "Oh God, you want me to give a lecture? At a fundraiser?"

"Okay, point taken." Pearly throws her a mischievous grin. "Don't you sing? I'm pretty sure I remember you saying you were in a musical theater troupe. You could give us a jazz standard – maybe even dressed as a flapper."

Charlie leans in, a teasing glint in their eye. "I, for one, would love to see that."

"Okay, okay." Hannah blushes. "I'll think about it."

Pearly grins, happy to see her idea coming to life. Underneath it, though, she's still bothered by Charlie's prickliness toward her. It doesn't totally seem in character – but then again, she doesn't really know Charlie. Is it possible there's some unconscious bleed-through from Thunder causing these reactions? It's not like Thunder has no grounds to be annoyed with her after all the shit she's pulled. Maybe it's good that this energy is finding its way up and out. It could clear the air between them...possibly even pave the way for a reunion in the afterlife. She can take whatever Charlie wants to serve up – she's been read far worse. Not just by her fellow queens. The shadiest shade always seems to come from herself.

TWENTY-SEVEN

It's getting dark as Holmes and Holmes return to café after an unfruitful trip to the Eenob Historical Society. While Pearly found it cute to see Sam geek out on the town's history and the rise and fall of the Moonshine Lounge, they didn't learn anything to help them with Ruby's inability to move on. Tired and somewhat discouraged, they step through the door to find Danielle closing up. Charlie is busy tallying up receipts, but they tell Pearly and Sam they're welcome to stay. As soon as they sit down at a table, Ruby materializes beside them.

"Did you find anything?" she says. "Tell me – no don't tell me – no tell me."

"Not really," says Pearly. "We know there's something un-resolved from your life, something that's keeping you here. It obviously has to do with the old speakeasy, but it might not be directly related to your career."

"Well what then?" Ruby kicks at the wall, but her foot just goes right through it. "I don't know what's wrong with me. I mean, I'm already dead, so I know I'm not afraid of death."

"I'm sorry, sweetie," says Pearly. "I know you're frustrated." So is Pearly. She wishes she could do for Ruby what she did for

Hannah with the dream, recreating her charge's former life to spark new insights and healing.

That's when she gets the idea. It's one of *those* ideas – as in, unlikely to be found in the guidebook, unless it's filed under "don't." But it feels like it could really help. And isn't that what she's supposed to be doing – helping? "What if I could bring you back there?" she says. "I mean, to Moonshine as it existed in your day. It might offer some new insights..."

Ruby stops in her tracks. She looks between Sam and Pearly. "You can do that?"

Pearly shrugs. "I guess we're about to find out."

She closes her eyes, hoping all that damn meditating finally has a use. She concentrates on the ambient energy of the café and feels it humming beneath her fingertips, ready to be shaped. "Stay open, Sam," she says. "I want you to see this, too."

Sam nods, watching in awe as Pearly begins to weave her magic. The air around them grows warmer, the lights more golden – and little by little, the café begins to change. Velvet drapes materialize along the walls. The cheap wooden tables dress themselves with white tablecloths and flickering candles. The counter melts into a polished mahogany bar as the room fills with upbeat jazz, and the smell of coffee fades into cigar smoke.

Sam turns in a circle, taking it all in. "Damn, Pearly," he says. "You're like a living holodeck."

"Well not living exactly – but yeah, it helps to set the right mood."

Ruby is also affected by Pearly's little stunt. Physically, she doesn't look any different, but somehow she's more vibrant. More real. With the way she looks around her old haunt, she also seems more sad, more aware of what she lost.

"Ruby," says Sam. "You're so...so..." He trails off, speechless for once.

She wipes a spectral tear and puts on a brave smile. "Welcome to the Moonshine Lounge."

Pearly glances at Sam, who's practically got emoji-hearts for eyes. "Why don't you show Holmes here around?" she suggests.

Ruby, more confident in the familiar surroundings, floats toward the young detective. "Come on." She curls her finger in that 'come hither' gesture. "Let me show you where the magic used to happen."

Sam turns a shade of red that matches the velvet drapes, but he tries to play it cool. "Lead the way, Miss LaRue."

Pearly lingers a few steps behind, watching with interest as Ruby takes the lead. The ghost gestures toward a corner of the room, now transformed into the main stage area. "This is where I performed," says Ruby. "We had all kinds of dancers, but I specialized in burlesque. It's an art, you know, to bring the tease, the timing. The feathers, the sequins, the way the lights catch my costume—it's all part of the seduction."

Sam nods repeatedly. "Right, right. And, um, where did the big shots sit?" he asks.

Ruby sweeps her hand out like a game show hostess, pointing out a row of tables near the stage. "Right here, close enough to feel the heat of the stage lights." Her eyes go distant for a moment, and Pearly sees the bitterness and nostalgia battling it out. "The big spenders, the ones who thought they owned the world—they'd lean back, puffing on cigars, watching every move I made." She shifts back to the present and leans in closer to Sam, her lips almost touching his ear. "But the truth is, they were putty in my hands."

Sam chokes a little, and Pearly can't help laughing to herself. "Y-yeah," he says, "I bet they were."

Ruby winks and continues the tour, pointing out other easter eggs —the spot where the piano player sat, the door to her dressing room, the hidden alcove where she'd sneak a moment of peace or a shot of bourbon between acts. Sam hangs on her every word.

"You know..." Ruby pauses near the stage, tapping her heel on the floor, "I wasn't always the headliner. I had to prove I was more than just a pretty face. It took years."

Sam shakes his head. "You're a force of nature, Ruby. I don't know how you kept going all that time."

"Up there, under the lights, I could be anything—anyone. It was the one place where I was truly free, where I felt...invincible."

Pearly's feeling a vibe between the two of them, and she decides to double down. "Hey Ruby," she says, "why don't you show Holmes here a bit of that magic? Give him a taste of what it was like."

Ruby seems quite happy to oblige. She directs Sam to one of the "big spenders" tables and heads offstage. As a sultry new song begins, she makes a dramatic entrance – one leg through the curtains, followed by the rest of her. As a ghost who's stuck in the outfit she died in, she can't do burlesque reveals in the traditional fashion, so instead she plays with visibility, fading parts of her costume to suggest a slow reveal. She shimmies, rolls her hips, drags the feather boa across the stage. At one point, she comes right up to Sam, teasing a fingertip up the length of his shirt. He can't feel it, of course, but you wouldn't know that from the look on his face. When she hits the "big reveal" finale, she glows brightly, flips her hair, and gives Sam a playful wink.

As Pearly watches this exchange, seeing how both Sam and Ruby light up with shared energy, she decides to change the music from a jazz tune to a waltz. This one's more about connection than performance. Ruby pauses, sensing the change, and meets Sam's eyes again. He stands, and without a word, they fall into step together. Sam tries to lead, but he doesn't know the waltz – or any other dance from the looks of it – so he lets Ruby guide them. It's intimate...one might even say romantic. They can't touch each other, but they romp and twirl around the stage like kids. There's a mismatch between Ruby the professional and Sam the total amateur, but neither of them cares. They're actually having fun.

As the song ends, they shuffle-glide to a stop. Ruby's laughter becomes a giggle, then fades to silence. "Thank you," she whispers.

"No, thank you," says Sam. "That was incredible." His brow furrows. "Did it help? I mean, did it bring up anything new?"

"I can't say it unlocked anything," she says. Then she flashes a huge smile. "But I assure you it helped."

As the café closes for the evening, Pearly leaves with a sense of accomplishment, but there's a nagging unease she can't quite shake off. The amount of energy she used for that stunt, the way she brought Sam into Ruby's past—it wasn't exactly conventional guide behavior. For a moment, she wonders if she might have crossed a line. Well...another line. She dismisses the thought, telling herself it's all for the greater good, but the doubt lingers, like a shadow at the edge of her mind.

***

Hertz and Abathur sit in their usual booth at The Great Beyond Burger. The checkered floors gleam under the lights, and a jukebox plays an endless loop of rock 'n' roll classics. The smell of greasy fries and sizzling burgers fills the air, mingling with the slightly metallic scent of old machinery.

Hertz stabs at his plate of pancakes with a fork. "You ever wonder why they make breakfast an all-day thing?" he asks, voice muffled by a mouthful of syrup. "And why just breakfast – why not all-day dinner?"

Abathur, lounging across from him, sips on a milkshake that occasionally changes flavors on its own. "Because, man, breakfast is the only meal everyone can agree on."

As Hertz chews his pancakes, the scanner goes haywire. At first he ignores it, but the beeping just gets more insistent. Abathur raises an eyebrow as Hertz pulls out the device.

"This can't be right," Hertz mutters, tapping the scanner. "The readings are off the charts. Pearly...she's using a ton of energy."

Abathur, midway through a fry, leans in to get a look at the scanner. "Dude," he says. "That signature's not coming from here."

Hertz scrunches his nose at his partner. "Where's it coming from?"

Abathur drops the fry as the realization hits. "Earth."

TWENTY-EIGHT

I t's so early, even the rooster knick-knacks are sleeping. But Danielle is up, slicing butter into cubes with laser focus. She's been up since 4 a.m., determined to get her baking done before her shift starts at the café. In her oversized hoodie and leggings, hair pulled back into a bun, she moves around the kitchen with practiced efficiency. Pearly sits at a stool by the counter watching Danielle work. She has embraced the role of "baker" – or maybe "baker's bitch" – with a hot pink chef's hat and matching apron emblazoned with the slogan "Serving Looks & Pastries."

Today's project is pumpkin pie with a twist—a salted caramel version Pearly's sure will be a hit at the Halloween Festival. Danielle's croissants for the café are almost ready to leave the oven, and Pearly hopes she gets to taste test.

"Okay, Pearly," says Danielle, "can you grab the roasted pumpkin from the fridge? It's in the big white bowl."

Pearly hops off the stool. Even if she's never been at home in the kitchen, she's more than willing to help. "You know," she says as she hands the container to Danielle, "my partner..." Pearly trails off, the lightness in her voice faltering for a split-second. "Well, my ex-partner—he was always the one handling the kitchen stuff. I was more of the 'order takeout and mix a mean cocktail' type."

Danielle looks up. "Really? You don't seem the type to let anyone else take charge."

Pearly shrugs, a hint of nostalgia in her smile. "You'd be surprised." She pops a roasted pumpkin cube into her mouth. "He was good with logistics," she says, swallowing. "Planning trips, coordinating schedules, making sure we had regular date nights. And in the bedroom – oh girl, I just surrendered. He was my..." her voice trails off. "My rock." Suddenly, she feels exposed. She's not used to talking about her personal life. Is it against the rules to open up to someone you're guiding?

"That sounds nice," says Danielle. "I've never had a partner like that. Someone I can count on."

Pearly hears the longing in her charge's voice. "Are you dating?"

"Not exactly. I've got a lot to work on by myself right now." Danielle starts mashing the pumpkin cubes, but there's a hint of a smile on her face. "I have started talking to someone online. Travis. A trans guy in Chicago. I'm finding I prefer T4T." She smiles at Pearly's confusion. "Trans for trans."

"Ahhh," says Pearly. "Does that feel safer?"

"Yeah. And it's nice to talk to someone who really gets what I'm going through."

"Absolutely." Pearly grins. "I can't wait to hear more. That is, if you're comfortable sharing. No pressure."

"Thanks." Danielle finishes mashing the cubes into a creamy mixture. "I think I'd like to keep it to myself for now. But I'm glad you're here to help. Even if you're not the baking type, you make a pretty glamorous assistant."

Pearly strikes a defiant pose. "I'll have you know, I can whisk with the best of them!" This is a lie, and they both know it. Pearly has never whisked a thing in her lives. Well...not that she can remember.

Danielle adds sugar, cinnamon, ginger, and cloves to the bowl of mashed pumpkin, followed by a dash of nutmeg. Pearly watches with fascination. She's starting to understand why people are so into those baking shows.

"You've got a real knack for this," she says. "That pie is going to snatch their wigs at the festival."

"I hope so. It would be nice to feel like I know what I'm doing for a change."

As Danielle pours in heavy cream and cracks a couple of eggs into the mixture, she glances over at Pearly. "You think I really have a shot?"

Pearly smacks the table. "Absolutely. You've got the skills, and that caramel pumpkin combo is pure genius. Mouths are watering from here to Jupiter."

"That sounds promising." She pours the filling into the handmade crust, spreading it evenly with a spatula. "I'm just glad we haven't burned anything yet."

Pearly laughs. "Small victories, girl. Small victories."

Danielle takes the croissants out of the oven. The rich buttery scent is so enticing that Pearly can't help reaching for one. Danielle moves the tray just out of Pearly's reach. "Sorry," she says. "If you want one, you can buy one at Thunderbolt." She slides the pie onto the oven rack and closes the door, ignoring Pearly's grumbles.

They hear footsteps on the stairs. It's Hank, still groggy in his flannel shirt and sweatpants, guided by the scent of coffee and croissants.

He rubs his eyes as he takes in the scene. "Well, would you look at that," he says. "Up before the sun and already at it. I remember when your mother practically had to set off fireworks in your bed to get you up for school." He too reaches for a croissant.

Danielle slaps his hand away. "Don't eat those! I'm selling them at the café."

Hank steps closer, eyes landing on Pearly. He tilts his head, clearly trying to process the glittery anomaly standing in his kitchen. "Hello," he finally says. "I'm Hank."

Pearly flashes a warm smile and extends her hand. "Pearly Gates, at your service. Well, technically at Danielle's service. She's the master chef—I'm just here for taste-testing and moral support."

Hank chuckles, shaking her hand with a firm grip. "Well, you picked the right kitchen to be in if you like good food. Danielle here's got a real gift, just like her mother. I swear, their chocolate chip cookies taste exactly the same."

Danielle looks up at her stepfather, eyes misting a bit. "Thanks, Hank. It means a lot to hear you say that."

Hank just grunts and pours himself a cup of coffee from the pot.

"So," says Pearly. "Danielle tells me you're a plumber. You must have some wild stories from the job."

Hank grins, leaning against the counter. "Oh, I've seen some things. A few weeks ago, I got called to a middle school where the toilet had been backed up for lord knows how long. The kids kept using it like some kind of science experiment, and by the time I got there, it was like something out of *The Blob*. Had to burn my clothes after that one."

Pearly chuckles. "Oh, man, can I relate! I once had to—" she catches herself, realizing she's about to share something from her afterlife gig, "—um, deal with a disaster like that. In one of my odd jobs." She clears her throat, addresses Danielle's raised eyebrow. "I've done a lot of weird shit in my day."

Danielle nods, seeming to accept this.

Hank glances at the clock and drains the rest of his coffee. "Well, I'd better get going. Don't want to be late for work." He nods to Danielle. "You're doing great, kiddo. And in case it matters for future baking experiments – I sure do love custard...just puttin' it out there..."

Danielle smiles. "I'll put that on my list."

With a final nod, Hank heads out the door, leaving Danielle and Pearly alone in the kitchen once more.

"So, now what?" says Pearly. "We just sit around and wait?"

"Yeah, pretty much." Danielle wipes her hands on a dish towel. "The pie needs time to bake."

"Cool," says Pearly. "Wanna show me your hat collection?"

Danielle's eyes light up. "Sure."

Pearly follows Danielle into the basement, doing her best to feign surprise. Pearly's already seen this space—and the hats—during her invisible observation. But Danielle doesn't know that. The soft lighting, floral accents, and cluttered vanity all look more or less the same, yet there's a noticeable lightness in the air compared to what Pearly felt before.

They move toward the wall where Danielle's hat collection is displayed, from the cloche to the bonnet to the pillbox and the fascinators. Pearly's eyes finally land on a particularly dramatic wide-brimmed hat, decorated with peacock feathers and a bold satin ribbon.

"Yaaaaaaassss!" she marvels. "This is stunning." She turns to Danielle. "They all are. You've got an eye for elegance."

Danielle's cheeks flush. "Thanks. I've added a few new pieces. Each one has its own story."

Pearly steps closer, her fingers brushing the brim of the hat. "I can tell. You'd give Jean Patou a run for his money."

Danielle laughs. "That's high praise coming from someone with your taste. You should try one on."

Pearly picks up the peacock-feathered creation, playfully placing it atop her head. "How do I look?"

"Like you're ready to make your entrance at a grand Edwardian Ball."

Pearly grins. She did do that, a few lives ago.

As Danielle watches Pearly model the hat, her face falls. Pearly can feel Danielle wishing she could be more like Pearly – never second-guessing her self-expression. The sight of Pearly's confidence seems to stir something in her. She crouches down, pulling out a shoebox from beneath the bed.

Pearly raises an eyebrow. "What've you got there?"

Danielle hesitates, her fingers brushing over the lid of the shoebox. "These," she says, lifting the lid to reveal a pair of strappy red stilettos — the same ones she'd looked at longingly so many times before. "I bought these a while ago. I've just...never worn them."

"Why not?" says Pearly. "They're fabulous." She's aware of the painful memory attached to these shoes – her father's rejection – but maybe this is the moment for Danielle to open up and actually talk about it.

Danielle shrugs. "It's stupid, really. I had a thing for *The Wizard of Oz* as a kid. And the ruby slippers in particular. I thought they were, like, the pinnacle of footwear – and I wanted a pair so badly."

"Oooh, girl, I get it. Magic and high fashion and they even repel wicked witches! Who wouldn't want to wear those?"

"Exactly!" Danielle sits on the bed, picks at a thread in the comforter. "I guess there's still a part of me that's afraid to step out, or maybe to step into myself. These shoes," she gestures to the stilettos, "they represent everything I want to be, but...I don't know, I'm still scared. So they just sit in the box."

"Well, sweetheart," says Pearly, looking around. "This is a pretty low stakes situation. Maybe you could try them on. Just for a minute."

Danielle laughs nervously, glancing at the shoes. "Yeah? You want a private fashion show?"

Pearly grins. "Does a bear shit in the woods?"

Danielle cocks her head, confused.

Pearly laughs. "Hell yes, I want a private fashion show!"

"Okay, okay." With trembling hands, Danielle slips off her ballet flats and carefully steps into the red stilettos. She looks a little awkward at first, but as she straightens up, something visibly shifts inside her. Pearly watches as Danielle takes a tentative step, then another.

"That's good – now let's get you strutting like you own the place! First things first—posture." Pearly straightens her back, lifting her chin high and pulling her shoulders back with exaggerated elegance. "Chest out, shoulders back, chin up. The world is your runway and you, girl, are the headliner."

Danielle copies Pearly. "Like this?"

"Perfect! Now, start to move. Not too fast, not too slow. It's like a dance—let the heels guide you, heel to toe, heel to toe. Feel the floor beneath you, and let it carry you forward."

Danielle tries again, this time with more confidence, but her arms hang awkwardly at her sides.

"Ah, those hands!" Pearly grins, takes Danielle's hands, shakes them out. "Be free! No clenching!"

Danielle nods. Her nerves ease as she lets her arms relax, taking another step, more fluid this time.

"Good! Amazing! And most importantly—" Pearly taps the brim of the peacock hat. "Eyes forward! Don't look down. The runway is ahead of you, and so is your future. You've got places to be and everyone else is just background scenery."

Danielle takes a deep breath, channeling Pearly's wisdom. She strides across the basement carpet with a bit more flair, her gaze fixed ahead. When she reaches the other side, she twirls around, her Dorothy-red heels clicking confidently on the floor.

Pearly cheers. "Own it, girl! You're a natural!" She sticks her butt out and twerks. "There's no place like home! Mmmm, yeah. There's no place like home!"

Danielle bursts out laughing. "That...actually felt kind of amazing."

***

Back in the kitchen, the scent of pie is even more tempting than before. Pearly has to sit on her hands not to take it out and scarf it down.

"Is it done yet?" She crouches down to peek through the oven window.

"No," says Danielle. "You gotta be patient, let it rise on its own."

Pearly is not known for her patience. She plays with the cock-a-doodle-doo cookie jar until Danielle has to take it away from her.

"You know," Pearly says, sitting down at the table, "it's great that you're catering the 'Save the Café' event. You're so talented and this is a great chance for your baking to shine. But I was thinking...what if you did a performance, too? It could be a powerful way to express yourself. Healing, even." She grins. "You could wear those ruby slippers of yours."

"A performance?" Danielle's hands still over the dough she's rolling out. "What, like, singing or dancing?"

Pearly shrugs. "Whatever feels right for you. I used to design costumes for the drag community, and I have some history as a performer myself, so I could help you out."

Danielle bites her lip. "Sounds exciting, but I don't know if I'm ready for that."

Not the answer Pearly was hoping for. If she wants to prove herself before her looming deadline, she's going to have to push her charges out of their comfort zone. But it will have to be done with care. Too much too soon could dissolve the trust that's emerging between them. "Of course," she says. "No pressure. Just something to think about."

"Yeah," Danielle says. "I will."

And that's good enough for Pearly. Even the longest journey starts with a single step—or in this case, a strut in red stilettos.

TWENTY-NINE

"Who's ready to build some shit?"

Pearly swaggers into Thunderbolt in "construction chic." This includes violet sequined overalls, a rhinestone tool belt complete with a very shiny hammer, and oversized safety goggles lined with bling. The Timberland knockoffs add just the right touch of realness – even if they are gold.

Hannah and Charlie just stare.

"This is going to be legendary," says Pearly. She's ready to get hot and sweaty testing out Hannah's "secret passage" idea. Well, maybe not sweaty. But she will get hot.

Charlie's already standing by the door between the bookstore and the café with a (not-shiny) tape measure. It's early and the café hasn't opened for business, so now's the time to get crackin'. Pearly notices a bit of fatigue in Charlie's eyes – they're working overtime managing the café and the gala. Right now, they're trying to figure out the logistics. Their lavender hair falls in their eyes as they spread the tape measure across the door, and Pearly can't help noticing how adorable they look.

"Gotta make sure everything's aligned," says Charlie, holding a pencil in their teeth. "We're gonna build shelves onto the door and fill them with books to create a swinging bookcase effect."

"Roger that," says Pearly. "Thank god one of us knows which end of a hammer to use."

"Thank my dad," says Charlie. "I was always helping him build stuff – treehouse, bird house, dog house..."

"Ooh, you should help Hannah finally finish that catio."

"Yeah," says Hannah. "That'd be great." She glances at the door. "Are we sure this is going to be stable with the added weight?"

Pearly waves her off. "It'll be more secure than a pair of boobs in an iron corset."

"I hope so," says Charlie, but they seem more relaxed than at their planning session.

As they work, Pearly and Charlie discover a shared love of iconic Chicago diners. "Lou Mitchell's," says Pearly. "Hands down the best. How can you top an institution that hands out free Milk Duds and donut holes?"

"That is a classic," Charlie admits. "But the shakes at the Chicago Diner are pretty epic. Plus, all day breakfast..."

"Valid argument," says Pearly. "Or, oooh, what about the Pick Me Up Café? That was always my go-to late night spot."

"Me too! You know they moved to Uptown a few years ago?"

"Oh really? Did they keep the purple ceiling?"

"Of course! Wouldn't be the Pick Me Up without it."

Pearly steps back, evaluating their progress. "This is gonna be epic," she says. "I can see it now – guests throwing dollar bills everywhere. Maybe even hundos!"

Charlie giggles, and they share a look with Pearly that sends tingles down to her toes. She can't help remembering the last time she and Thunder were intimate – his astral body meshed so perfectly with hers, it was hard to tell where one of them ended and the other began. This same look seems to send a pang through Hannah – which in turn sends a pang through Pearly. She notices her charge standing off to the side, smiling in kind of a distant way.

Pearly turns to Hannah. "What do you think, Hannah? Have we thought of everything?"

Hannah steps closer. "Yeah, I think so." Pearly detects a strain in her voice. "Let's just make sure to test it before anyone walks through this thing."

"Of course, darling," says Pearly. "Safety first—glamour second."

They get to work. Charlie takes the lead, assembling the shelves. Pearly offers pep talks, tool-assists, and the occasional dance break.

Hannah steps back to look at their work-in-progress. "I just thought of something," she says. "What if the secret entrance could be triggered by pulling an actual book?"

"Goosebumps!" says Pearly. "You're giving me vintage Nancy Drew!"

Charlie pinches their lip – one of Thunder's classic "I'm thinking" gestures. "It could work," they say. "We'd need to rig up some kind of mechanism. A latch behind the shelf, attached to one of the books."

"Yeah!" says Pearly. "And the book should be something from that era."

"Like *The Great Gatsby*?" says Charlie.

"Yeah, but less obvious." Pearly flashes a smile. "Make 'em work for it!"

"What about *This Side of Paradise*?" says Hannah. "It's still Fitzgerald, but less well-known."

"That could work," says Pearly. "But what about—"

"People. Please." Charlie's tone is stern, but it looks like they're trying not to laugh. "We can't 'make 'em work for it' if we want to raise money."

"Sorry," Hannah blushes. "Got a little carried away."

Charlie gives Hannah a kiss on the cheek. "Don't worry about it," they say. "You're cute when you get carried away."

Turns out building a secret passage is easier said than done. After a series of smaller mishaps, Pearly tugs just a little too hard on one of the books — the door swings open, and a pile tumbles off the shelves. Pearly loses her balance and falls right on top of Charlie, their faces inches apart. It would be so easy to kiss them. Pearly's stomach drops. *Shit. Pretty sure love triangles aren't in the manual. At least, not when the guide is part of the triangle.*

Pearly scrambles to her feet. "Sorry!" she says too loudly, adjusting her tool belt with a nervous laugh. "Category is...awkward!"

Charlie pushes themselves up from the floor. "All good," they say. But they look shaken. Pearly wishes she could read Charlie's thoughts in this moment. Are they shaken because they're uncomfortable with Pearly? Or because they felt the connection too? Or maybe they're just shaken from the fall? But Pearly's powers only extend to her charges.

She tries to act casual, but her heart is still racing. "Well, at least we know the bookcase isn't the problem. It's me!"

They get back to work. Pearly can't help noticing how Hannah reaches out to help Charlie with the secret book. Hannah's fingers brush over Charlie's with deliberate slowness, the contact lingering in a sexy, intimate way. It turns Pearly's stomach into a pretzel, even though it's totally to be expected – after all, they're dating. Still, as Pearly watches Charlie respond by running a fingernail lightly down Hannah's arm – and Hannah lean into the touch with a sigh of pleasure – Pearly feels the pretzel twist even further. She wonders if Charlie feels as guilty as she does. But how could they? Only Pearly knows their shared history.

What's wrong with me? Pearly's supposed to be Hannah's guide, her mentor. This isn't about Pearly. But the jealousy buzzes around her like one of those tiny mosquitoes you can't see but know is going to get you. She's well aware that, as a guide, she should be focusing on the bigger picture, on the success of the event and the well-being of her charges, but her gut – and her heart – refuse to get on board. She rolls her head a few times and shakes out her hands, but she can't shake the ick.

"Well," she says, "looks like someone's getting 'nailed' today!" No one's laughing. The moment the words are out, she wants them back. "That was, uh, a construction joke."

"Yeah," Charlie clears their throat. "I got it." They step back, probably trying to distance themselves from the situation. "Why don't we take a moment to admire our handiwork?"

They all take a good, hard look at their progress. Pearly thinks it's pretty damn impressive, actually.

"This is coming together so well," says Charlie. "You know," they turn to Hannah, "none of this would've happened without your ideas—the secret bookcase, the hidden trigger. You're kinda brilliant, you know."

"Gosh," Hannah beams. "I wish my end-of-course evaluations were that glowing."

Pearly looks down, shifts her weight. Shouldn't she, as Hannah's guide, be the one to recognize insecurity and offer reassurance? That's Thunder, always outshining her just by doing what comes naturally.

"Alright," Charlie claps their hands together. "Let's see how this thing works. How about someone walks through it pretending to be a gangster or something? You know, for flavor."

Hannah raises an eyebrow. "Obviously, that someone should be you, Pearly."

Pearly doesn't need to be told twice. She straightens her overalls, raises her goggles, and adopts an exaggerated swagger. Strutting through the bookshop, she puffs out her chest and impersonates Lucky Luciano – another friend from a former life.

"Say, toots," she growls, "what's a dame gotta do to get a drink around here?"

Charlie and Hannah burst into laughter as Pearly hams it up. The whole scene is stupid, but, like, stupid good. Enough to ease the awkwardness, at least a little bit. Enough to make Pearly forget how complicated her job is. How easy it would be to put her own heart first. How thinly she's riding the line.

THIRTY

Hertz and Abathur materialize on Venice Beach, spewing out a tidal wave of energy as their feet hit the sand. They blink in the sunlight, adjusting to the density of a physical world.

"Jesus H. Christ." Hertz shields his eyes. "Feels like I just got a full-body wedgie."

Abathur just manifests some shades and takes a deep breath of ocean air. "You'll get used to it."

Nearby, a group of tourists peeks out from under an umbrella, wondering if maybe they smoked a little too much Purple Kush.

The two colleagues shuffle from the sand to the boardwalk, where the scent of pizza, pot, and kettle corn mingles with the algae-and-sewage breeze wafting in from the ocean. Sunburned tourists in matching T-shirts shout over reggae music blasting from beachfront cafés, while Speedo-clad dudes with boom-boxes strut along the path.

"Why here?" asks Hertz, shaking sand out of his beat-up platforms as they dodge a stoned chick on a skateboard weaving through the crowd.

Abathur can't help feeling nostalgic as they pass a street performer pantomiming in silver body paint. "I used to surf here," he says, "before it turned into a tourist trap. All we know is that Pearly's on Earth, so I figured we might as well start somewhere familiar."

Hertz pulls out his scanner, already grumbling as they weave through the crowded boardwalk. He fiddles with the settings, and the device begins to beep. "Okay," he says, "looks like we've got something. It's faint, but it's there. Somewhere in the Midwest—Illinois, maybe."

They pass vendors hawking flashy souvenirs – "your name on a grain of rice," pewter R2-D2s, crystals, hemp bracelets, prints of Jesus smoking dope.

"Midwest, huh?" says Abathur. "Well, we can't just teleport there. Our energy's too dense down here, and you don't have 'in-and-out' privileges. We'll have to get there the old-fashioned way."

Hertz grunts. "I hate road trips.Abathur rolls his eyes. "You hate everything." His expression brightens. "Hey, if we've got to drive, that means we can take Route 66! The Mother Road! It'll be fun."

"Fun? We're here to catch Pearly, not take a vacation." Hertz gives him a sideways glance. "You sure you're not making this harder than it needs to be? I know you got a soft spot for Gates."

"Why, I would never! How dare you besmirch my good name! The very idea..." That is, in fact, exactly what Abathur's doing. But he'd never admit it to his colleague. "Anyway, Route 66 is iconic! And it's a straight shot to Illinois. We can track her down and enjoy the ride."

Hertz sighs, still focused on the scanner. "Fine, whatever. But no unnecessary stops, okay?"

Abathur tears his gaze away from the water. "Let's find some wheels," he says — promising nothing.

Leaving the chaos of the boardwalk behind, Hertz and Abathur make their way to the nearest rental kiosk. The bright, sterile space is a stark contrast to the beach, and Hertz immediately gravitates toward a flashy Mustang GT.

Hertz whistles. "Now this is a car."

But Abathur is drawn to an old VW bus. Sure, it's faded and more than a little rusty, but the thing has spirit. "Look at this beauty," he says, running a hand along the exterior and flaking off some paint. "Perfect for a road trip."

"That hunk-a-junk?" says Hertz. "It's one pothole away from wherever cars go to die."

"It's got character," says Abathur, admiring the flower vase built into the dashboard. It's empty, but he manifests a white daisy to brighten up the place. "And besides, no one's gonna give us a second glance in this. We'll blend right in."

"Whatever man," Hertz grumbles. "If it breaks down, you're pushing."

Soon enough, they're on the road. The old bus chugs along with a slight rattle as they pull onto Route 66. The sun is high, and so is Abathur's mood. He turns on the radio and finds a station playing "L.A. Woman" by The Doors.

"Now this is music," he says, turning up the volume.

"Seriously?" Hertz snorts. "I can't deal with this hippie crap. Let's see what else is on." As he reaches for the radio dial, Abathur's face darkens, a force of nature unleashed. A flash of rage passes through his eyes. The air around him charges as shadows gather in every corner of the bus—

"Fine," Hertz says. "Keep your damn channel."

The air calms as Abathur smooths back into his usual surfer vibes, all mojo rising.

***

A few hours later, Hertz notices a billboard for "The World's Largest Thermometer." Only five miles ahead! "Are people really into this crap?"

"I like it," says Abathur. "It's quirky."

"I guess when you got nothing better to do..."

Abathur sighs. "That's the thing, Hertz. There's never anything 'better' to do." He taps the wheel as they take the exit towards the Thermometer. "I've seen civilizations rise and fall, entire worlds go up in smoke. It's all the same in the end. The monuments, the so-called great achievements—everything fades. Doesn't mean it's not worth something."

Hertz raises an eyebrow. "So what, you're happy just cleaning up cosmic garbage? You think our shitty jobs are just as good as anything else?"

"Exactly! Now you're gettin' it."

With a primal scream, Hertz grabs the daisy from the vase and flings it out the window. "I've had it to here with you!" he says. "You are by far the most infuriating soul I have ever had the displeasure to work with! You're worse than the shit we have to clean up! Always spewing garbage about bright sides and silver linings. Do you know what that's called? Toxic positivity, bub." He pulls at his face. "Okay, yeah, I know I fucked up in my lives, but what did I do to deserve getting stuck here with you? I wasn't a mass murderer, just a thief! All I've ever wanted was to get enough respect for someone to love me...is that too much to ask?"

Abathur rubs Hertz's shoulder. "That's right, buddy. Let it out. Maybe after you purge all that negativity you'll see the glass as half full."

"You're a nutcase," Hertz grumbles. "You know that?"

Abathur laughs, the sound deep and rolling. "Been called worse. Usually by someone who thought they had it all figured out."

***

The Thermometer fades into the distance as they head farther east. Hertz only gets more and more impatient, but Abathur wants to make the most of this little jaunt – who knows when they'll get another chance to visit Earth, after all? He insists they stop at every kitschy roadside attraction they encounter.

"Hey, check that out!" he says, pointing to a sign reading "The Blue Whale of Catoosa." He takes the exit. "We gotta stop."

Hertz groans. "No. I'm not doing this again!" He gestures at the Polaroids all over the seat—Giganticus Headicus, the Cadillac Ranch, Totem Pole Park. "Isn't this enough for you?" But he knows it's no use. He follows Abathur out of the bus and across the parking lot. The whale is even more absurd up close—its enormous, grinning mouth is wide enough to fit a small boat, and a faded, chipped paint job that gives it a strangely endearing, yet also sort of creepy, vibe.

Abathur pulls out his camera and snaps photos from every angle. "Pretty groovy, dude."

Hertz grits his teeth. "Yeah, you got that right," he says. "I got to say, you totally changed my mind on all these roadside attractions. It's all about the scenic route, am I right? Hey, you know what would really be groovy? I hear there's a pinball museum over in Asbury Park, we oughta check it out..."

Abathur narrows his eyes. "Asbury Park?" he says. "As in, New Jersey?"

Hertz pretends to think. "Huh, I guess it is New Jersey."

"Give it up, man." Abathur snaps another picture of the whale. "That loot is staying buried. Just like you." Abathur hands Hertz the camera. "Now take my photo." He climbs onto the whale's back, posing like he's riding a wave.

***

Two thousand miles and several stops later, they cross into Illinois. The landscape has shifted from open desert to endless cornfields. The old bus rattles along the road, and even Hertz has gotten used to the sound by now.

Suddenly, the scanner starts beeping. Hertz pulls it out, frowning as he studies the display.

"What is it?" says Abathur.

Hertz adjusts the scanner's settings, trying to get a clearer read. "Pearly's energy signature," he says, "it's getting stronger."

Abathur leans over to look. "Good," he says. "We're almost there."

The sun dips below the horizon, plunging the road ahead into twilight. As they near the small town of Eenob, the bus begins to sputter and jerk. Whatever is happening with the transmission doesn't sound good.

"Oh, come on!" Hertz pounds the window.

Abathur glances at three flashing warning lights. "Welp. Looks like the old girl's finally giving out."

Hertz rests his head against the dashboard. "Man, I told you we shoulda gone with the Mustang."

Before Abathur can respond, the VW bus gives one final, pitiful groan and rolls to a stop on a deserted stretch of road.

"Perfect," Hertz groans. "Fucking perfect."

"Well, we're not far from this Eenob place." Abathur shrugs. "We can just hoof it the rest of the way."

Hertz lifts up his head to glare at his tormentor. "You've got to be kidding me."

"How else are we *going* to get there? You're not suggesting we abandon our duties, are you? Why, then you'll never get reincarnated."

The scanner beeps again. Abathur glances at the screen over Hertz's shoulder. "The readings are getting stronger, aren't they? We're close."

Hertz massages his temples. "Yeah," he says. "We'd better get moving. We can't let Pearly get away—not after all this."

"Chill, man." Abathur gives him a pat on the back. "We'll find her."

Leaving behind the bus, Hertz and Abathur set off down the darkening road, kicking up dust as the scanner's persistent beeping guides them toward Eenob. Toward Pearly.

THIRTY-ONE

"**G**uys, check this out!"

Sam blows the dust off a top hat and replaces his beanie with a flourish and a sneeze. They're back in the Thunderbolt basement, searching for clues in a pile of old costumes and props. He poses for Pearly and Ruby, twiddling an imaginary moustache in the style of the Monopoly Man.

"Well, don't you look dapper!" Ruby marvels, as Pearly pillages a pile of feathered boas in the trunk.

"Lookin' good, Sam," she says with a glance over her shoulder. "All you need is a wand and some fake flowers, and you've got a magic act."

Sam grins, but Pearly notices a hint of fatigue in his eyes that wasn't there the last time they met. Before she can comment, Ruby floats closer to examine the hat.

"That's from the Moonshine era," she says. "It belonged to Vincent. He did comedy sketches—a real charmer. That hat saw more standing ovations than I can count."

"It would be great if we could incorporate it into the event," Pearly says. "Sam, you're not secretly a comedian, are you?"

"If I was, you wouldn't know. It's a secret, remember?" He might be joking, but there's no gleam in his eyes. His shoulders sag a bit. Maybe he's just in a mood. Not like it doesn't happen to Pearly. She doesn't want to think about the alternative – that Sam's health is taking a nosedive.

She pulls out an old beaded vest and holds it up. "I think this might fit you. Why don't you try it on?"

Sam hesitates, but when he sees Ruby beaming at him like he's the cutest puppy in the pet store, he can't resist. He slips the vest over his T-shirt. It's a little loose, but it doesn't look half bad.

"Sharp as a tack," says Ruby. She winks at Sam, making him blush.

Pearly rummages through the trunk for any other fun finds. Her fingers hit something cold and metallic at the bottom. She digs a little deeper and comes out with an old skeleton key. It's heavy and tarnished, with a fleur-de-lis carved into the handle.

"What's this?" Pearly holds the key up to the light.

Ruby floats closer. "Ahh," she says. "That was a key to the speakeasy. It unlocked the doors to a hidden room in the back."

"Oh yeah?" says Pearly. "What went down in there?"Ruby grins. "All kinds of things. Private shows, high-stakes gambling, secret meetings between all the fat cats of the city."

"Amazing." Pearly turns the key over in her hand. "I doubt this is worth selling, but maybe Charlie would want it. It's part of the café's history, after all."

Thunder would've geeked out over something like this—he loved hidden pieces of history, the thrill of discovery. But Charlie...the thing is, she doesn't really know Charlie. Not the way she knows Thunder. She wants to, but she knows that could be dangerous.

Shaking it off, she plunges her hand back into the trunk and emerges with an elaborate burlesque costume. The deep red sequins sparkle under the lights.

"Eleganza!" Pearly lifts the costume out of the trunk and inspects the detailed beadwork and lace. "This is stunning."

"That was one of my favorites," says Ruby. She reaches her hand out, only for it to pass right through the corset. "I wish I could wear it again. Oh, but Pearly! Maybe you can."

Pearly laughs, draping the costume across her body. "I wish, honey, but this was made for someone with half as much ass. Someone like Hannah—or maybe Danielle."

"That costume was a gift from my mentor, Sadie DuBois," Ruby reminisces, but she doesn't seem too nostalgic about it. Her face tightens into something resembling a scowl. "She was a burlesque queen back in the day—tough as nails. She ran the underground jazz club where I got my start." Ruby pauses, tracing the hemline of the costume. "I say 'gift,' but it really wasn't. With Sadie, everything was a transaction. I think she saw me more as an investment than a person."

"How so?" asks Sam.

"Sadie saw potential in me," says Ruby. "She helped me refine my stage persona – she's the one who made me Ruby LaRue. I learned a lot from her—how to control a crowd, how to sell a moment. But it was all business. She never even gave me the occasional 'good job, kid.' Just silence or critique."

Pearly's starting to see the shape of Ruby's regrets more clearly now. She spent her whole life seeking validation from people who couldn't – or wouldn't – give it to her. Pearly knows that quest all too well.

"You were always performing, weren't you?" says Pearly. "Not just for the crowds, but for her."

Ruby floats in between Pearly and Sam, seeking a buffer from the pain. "Yes," she says. "I wanted...I wanted so badly for her to approve of me. I thought if I was good enough, if I could be what she wanted, she'd finally care. But that was never part of the deal. Sadie didn't do love—she did success."

A heavy silence settles over the room. Pearly can see that her last life was all about validation through performance. She thought she'd moved beyond the need for other people's approval—by the end of that life, she was performing for herself and the people she loved. And even if that wasn't *always* the case, there were benefits that rippled outward, like the permission she gave to others to express their truest selves. But now here she was again, seeking validation. After all, isn't that what she's been doing in her stint as guide? Proving to Malcolm and the Higher-Ups and Thunder that she's worthy of love? She's trying so hard to make progress, to move forward in her afterlife — but is this just regression?

"You know," says Sam, "maybe that's why you're still here, Ruby. You were always looking for someone to see you. Not just the dancer under the stage lights, but the real you." Pearly swallows a lump in her throat. It feels like Sam's speaking to her, too.

Ruby curls inward as her grief drops the temperature of the room. Pearly braces herself in case the shelves start to topple over. But they don't. When Ruby shows her face again, she just looks sad and exhausted. Raw. Ghostly tears run down her face as she absorbs the truth she's been running from.

"I just wanted to be remembered," she says. "I wanted to matter."

"You do matter, Ruby," says Sam. "And people did remember you. We found your name, your story—it's still here. It deserves to be told." Sam glances at Pearly, the idea forming as he speaks.

"And I'm going to tell your story—at our fundraising event. We'll honor you the way you deserve, Ruby."

Ruby floats closer to Sam. "You...you'd do that for me?"

He nods, and even though he can't hold her hand, he brings his fingertips up to hers so they're almost touching. Her emotions settle, and so does the room.

Pearly lets the beauty and tenderness of the moment wash over her. In every life, it's been human connection that's saved her, that's made her feel whole. But it's easy to forget. We chase money and fame and variety and control. Right now, she's missing the most important human connection she's ever made. Still, she has to remind herself, she's making real connections with real people here in Eenob. They're helping her too, enriching her life, making her grow. And it feels healthier than just relying on Thunder for all of her needs. There's something healing about helping other people heal.

THIRTY-TWO

Pearly sashays into Thunderbolt, ready for her daily fix of sugar and caffeine. As she steps inside, Danielle waves her over, apparently reading her thoughts. "Pearly! You've got to try this."

With a nod to the other regulars, Pearly makes her way to the counter. Danielle starts slicing a piece of pie from a tin. "After a lot of experimentation," she says, "and a couple of massive failures involving lavender and chili pepper, I think I've finally perfected my entry for the Halloween Festival." She places the pie in front of Pearly. Its golden crust is still warm from the oven. "Pumpkin pie with a twist – chai-spiced streusel and roasted hazelnut caramel."

"Ooooh," says Pearly. "The wait is finally over." She shovels a large bite into her mouth. The pie is so creamy, with the pumpkin and the chai and that caramel teaming up to do crazy things to her taste buds – and then that graham-cracker crunch. "Girl, they should serve these in heaven, because they are divine," she says, as the homemade whipped cream slides down her throat. "You're going to have those judges jizzing in their pants."

Danielle giggles. "Thanks, Pearly. I hope so. There's supposed to be some big-deal food critics and bloggers there. You know that guy Bennnett Hawthorne? He's got, like, two million followers. So I really want to impress him."

"Oh, you will," Pearly says, scooping up the last crumbs of crust. "I can see the write-up now."

Sam joins them at the counter, ordering a cold brew as usual. "Hey Sam," says Danielle. "Heard you had a doctor's appointment this morning. How'd it go?"

"Oh, um, everything's fine," he says. Pearly can tell it's a lie even without hearing his thoughts. She tries making eye contact but he won't look at her. "So..." he clears his throat. "What's everyone dressing up as for the festival? I'm told it's kind of a big deal in these here parts."

"I won't be dressing up," says Danielle. "Unless it's as Julia Child. I've got to work my pie booth and impress the judges."

"Fair enough," says Sam. "I haven't worn a costume since seventh grade, but I don't think Creeper from Minecraft is the way to go. Honestly, I just don't want to look stupid."

"Good luck," Danielle teases. "What's your plan for that?"

Sam glances at Ruby, who gives him a nod. "I've, uh, been encouraged to wear that old vest and top hat I found in the trunk downstairs – an ode to vaudeville. According to a certain someone, it makes me look 'dapper.'"

"It's true," Pearly nods, all serious. "I heard her say it."

Hannah sidles up to them, plopping a stack of textbooks on the counter. "I'm going as a flapper," she says, standing on her tip-toes to give Charlie a kiss. "It's good practice for 'Save the Café' and I don't want to double up on costumes."

Charlie peeks out from behind the espresso machine. "Sensible *and* sexy. Can't wait to see it."

"Thanks, babe," Hannah grins. "What about you?"

Charlie taps the porta-filter against the knock box and wipes down the steam wand. "I'm thinking of going medieval? Not sure what though – maybe a knight or a bard or something, I don't know."

"A bard, huh?" Hannah appraises Charlie with a gleam in her eyes. "Does that mean you'll be regaling us with a song?"

Charlie winces. "OK, not a bard then."

Hannah turns her attention to Pearly. "What do you think you're going as?"

"I'm not sure yet," she lies. In fact, she knows exactly who she's going to be. And she wants it to be a surprise. "By the way," she adds, "I think it's time we gave our fundraising event a memorable name. 'Save the Café' is a bit vanilla, don't you think? I was thinking of something more glamorous, like 'Gin Joints and Jazz Hands' or 'Moonshine Revival Gala?'"

"Moonshine Revival Gala," says Hannah. "I love that!"

"Me too," says Charlie. "I'll get it on the flyers."

As the afternoon goes on, the café gradually empties, and Danielle finishes her shift. Pearly hangs around, getting high on caffeine as she waits for the right moment to introduce her next brilliant idea. When Danielle is finally free, Pearly packs it up and heads to the counter.

"Danielle," she says, "wanna come with me downstairs? There's something I want to show you."

***

They head down into the basement, where Pearly turns on a lamp. In the corner, Ruby's burlesque costume hangs on a dress form near a pair of matching red feather fans. It occurs to Pearly that the costume is the same vibrant, sparkly red as Danielle's secret stilettos.

Danielle's jaw drops. "You found this in a trunk?"

"It was one of Ruby's," Pearly says, stepping closer to the dress. "I wanted to show it to you because—well, I've been thinking about everything we've talked about. How you're working to love your body, how you want your outsides to match your insides. What if you gave it a shot at the gala with a performance? A little razzle-dazzle routine could bring the house down." She glances at Ruby as the ghost floats into the room. "And it could be a beautiful way to honor our resident star."

"I'd be so touched," says Ruby.

"I mean, it's gorgeous," says Danielle. "But burlesque? That's...a lot."

"Yeah," says Pearly. "It could be more drag than burlesque – no stripping required. Whatever you feel comfortable with."

Danielle looks at the glittering costume. Pearly senses her excitement, and also her apprehension.

"Do you want to try it on?" Pearly asks gently. "See how it feels? No commitment."

Danielle brightens. "Okay," she says. "Sure."

"Let's get you some privacy." Pearly hangs a curtain from some hooks, creating a makeshift dressing area. "And voila!"

Danielle offers a grateful smile. "Thank you," she says, slipping behind the curtain.

Pearly and Ruby take seats on empty crates, listening to the soft swish of fabric. Pearly can sense the weight of the moment, and she knows how vulnerable Danielle must feel.

A nervous laugh emanates from behind the curtain. "This is...I don't know what this is."

Danielle steps out from behind the curtain with flushed cheeks and question marks for eyes. But there's something so perfect, so right, in seeing the little girl forced to be the Tin Man finally getting to wear the pretty dress. Tears spring up in Pearly's eyes.

"Beautiful," says Ruby. "Truly," says Pearly. "More dazzling than a field of poppies."

As Danielle adjusts the corset, she hesitates, gaze lingering on her chest in the mirror. Pearly tunes in, sensing the confusing combination of feelings moving through her charge. On the one hand, Danielle has never worn anything this brazenly feminine – or sexy. She feels a little like a goddess from one of Pearly's cards. On the other hand, the costume shows her all her dysphoria, the laundry list of things she wants to change.

"This would look better with implants," she sighs. "I've been saving up now that I have a job, but that's a ways down the road."

"No problem!" says Pearly. "Trust me, you can make magic with breast forms and a little strategic positioning."

"Okaaaay," says Danielle, turning to look at the side view. "As long as they're, not, like, super-sized. I know you're used to the drag world, but femininity isn't just a performance for me. It's an identity I want to live in full-time."

"I hear you," says Pearly. After all, though it was a persona in her previous life, she's currently identifying and appearing to her charges as a bio queen – a woman. "Thank you for being clear."

"And what about...." Danielle looks down, blushes.

Pearly smiles. "Have you tucked before? It can help create a smoother silhouette."

"I want to, but..." Danielle bites her nail. "The tape freaks me out."

Pearly waves a hand. "It's not that bad, I promise. But we can worry about that later. Why don't you see how it feels to move?"

Danielle nods, takes a few steps, and gives an awkward twirl. "I don't know what to do," she says. "I'm probably gonna need some coaching."

Pearly gets up, stands next to Ruby. "Girl, we've got you covered."

They start with the basics. Ruby shows Pearly how to move in the costume, and Pearly shows Danielle. "Ruby says this isn't a runway strut, it's a dance." Pearly rolls her shoulders back. "Your body's telling a story...with sequins."

Ruby demonstrates a graceful glide across the floor, which Pearly mimics for her charge's benefit. "It's not about the steps," says Ruby, and Pearly repeats. "It's about the feeling you evoke. The audience is here to be enchanted, not to judge every move."

Danielle's brow furrows. "So how do I enchant them?"

"Practice," Ruby shrugs. "The more you do it, the more natural it feels."

"Anyway," says Pearly, "what really matters is how you carry yourself. When you believe in what you're doing, the audience will too."

They move on to the gloves. Pearly translates for Ruby as they show Danielle how to peel them off, slowly, seductively, one finger at a time. "You want them to ache for what's underneath," she says. "But don't give it to them 'til they're begging for it."

Danielle tries to copy Pearly, but she stops and rolls her eyes. "I feel ridiculous!"

"Embrace it, girl!" says Pearly. "It's all confidence and attitude. There's nothing sexier than a woman who's having fun and isn't afraid to show it."

"Yeah," says Danielle, but she sounds a little discouraged. "Maybe we can move on for now? I'll practice and we can try again next time."

Pearly gives her shoulder an encouraging squeeze. "Okay, honey."

They move on to the fans. As it turns out, gliding across the stage while trying to wave and twirl four-foot plumes of feathers is seriously hard. She fumbles one of the fans and nearly careens into the mirror. Ruby and Pearly can't help but laugh.

"How do you do this without falling over?" says Danielle, shaking her head.

"You'll get it," says Pearly. "But you know what? That stumble? You can even make that work. It's all about how you recover."

As they continue practicing, Danielle gets more into it and starts to find her rhythm. Pearly offers confidence tips, while Ruby gets more technical.

"Your face is your secret weapon," says Ruby. She demonstrates an over-the-top wink, and Pearly copies it for Danielle. "Flirt with the audience, give them a wink, a smirk—then they're yours to play with."

To bring it all together, they cue up a traditional burlesque song. Danielle starts her walk, trying to embody the character Ruby and Pearly have guided her to become. But she has trouble connecting with the music, and Pearly can see her getting frustrated. Eventually, she stops, puts down the fans.

"I don't know," she says. "It just doesn't feel right."

Pearly considers. "Maybe we need something a bit more current – modern, but still sexy and playful. Something like..." She thinks for a moment, then her eyes light up. "Madonna!"

Danielle perks up. "That sounds fun."

Pearly finds the track. Madonna's "Fever" fills the basement, and Danielle starts to get into the groove. She picks up the fans, this time moving with more grace and swagger. As she reaches the center of their makeshift stage, she removes one glove with a flick of her wrist and flashes a seductive smile.

Ruby claps her hands in delight, and she glows a little brighter. "Perfect!"

"Girl," says Pearly, "you're gonna have them eating out of the palm of your hand."

Danielle beams. "I can't believe I'm actually doing this."

Pearly wraps an arm around Danielle's waist. "Believe it, honey. You're gorgeous, inside and out. Eenob is in for one delectable treat."

As Danielle admires herself in the mirror, pride swells in Pearly's chest. She sees herself in Danielle—those early days of drag, the thrill of success, of liberation. It felt so goddamn good to express her truest self. Danielle is still new, and Pearly wants to be tender. But she can see Danielle's potential to blossom — and can't help but think of how it might impress Malcolm and the Higher-Ups. Sometimes you have to take risks. And let no one say that Pearly's not a risk-taker.

THIRTY-THREE

P early always got a kick out of Halloween, or harvest festivals in general. Samhain, Día de los Muertos, Pomona, Gai Jatra — whatever humans call it, the veil between seen and unseen feels a little thinner this time of year. Though the costume part hits a little different when you're a soul, and you can be whatever you want at any time.

Anyway, Halloween is a major deal in Eenob, and the annual festival is the star on the tree. Or the stem on the pumpkin. It takes place in the third week of October – a week before the fundraising gala and Pearly's looming deadline with Malcolm and the Higher-Ups. Pearly heads to the town square clutching a stack of event flyers. She passes booths draped in orange and black, trees decorated with hanging ghosts and crashed witches. The sidewalk is lined with glowing jack o' lanterns, and the air smells like a mix of spiced cider, caramel apples, and roasted nuts. She feels pretty snazzy in her costume — a glam version of a medieval noblewoman with her flowing empire-waisted dress, fur-trimmed surcoat, bejeweled crownlet, gold brooches, and embroidered gloves.

She looks around for her charges. There's Sam in his vest and top hat, holding court by the cider stand. He's totally in his element, telling a group of Boomers about the history of the Moonshine Lounge – and using the conversation to drum up interest in the upcoming fundraising gala at the café.

"Before Hollywood took over," says Sam, "it was vaudeville that had the real stars. Those performers could do everything, and man, did they do it with style. The Moonshine Lounge was a perfect example—a place where the spirit of that era thrived right here in our little town." He glances at Ruby, hovering at his side, invisible to everyone but him and Pearly. "One of the performers, Miss Ruby LaRue, was a real sensation. I wish you could've seen her."

One of them laughs. "What kid, like you have? Even I was just a twinkle in grandma's eye back then."

Sam glances at Ruby, then looks back to them. "Spend enough time at the cafe, and you might feel like you know her too. Some even say her spirit still lingers there..."

Pearly sees her moment and approaches with her most charming smile. "Speaking of the Moonshine Lounge," she says, fanning out the flyers. "We're actually bringing it back for one night only. We're hosting a 1920s-themed gala next weekend at Thunderbolt Books & Coffee to raise funds for the café. There'll be live performances – music, dance, maybe even a bit of vaudeville magic. Plus, you can get liquored up on vintage cocktails and bid on some super cool stuff at our auction. It's going to be epic, darlings, and we'd love to see you there."

After making sure no one leaves empty-handed, Pearly looks around for Hannah. There she is, weaving through the crowd in a beaded fringe dress, long pearls, and feathered headband.

"Fuckin-A, girl!" Pearly barrels in for a hug. "Belle of the ball. I want to drink champagne and do the Charleston just looking at you. If your students could see you now, they'd all be crushing out!"

Hannah giggles. "I have to say, this is more fun than my usual suits and sneakers."

"For sure," says Pearly. "How's the prep going?"

"A bit more work than I expected, but I think it's coming together. It's been a while since I've hit any notes other than lecture notes."

Pearly grins. "I'm sure you'll find the perfect balance. I can't wait to see it."

"Thanks, Pearly." She smiles, looks around. "Oh, and Charlie's just closing up. They'll join us soon."

"Great." Pearly takes a breath, tries to keep her face neutral. "So how are things going between you two? Seems like you've been spending a lot of time together lately."

"We have." Hannah blushes, fiddling with her pearls. "It's been a while now since I've spent a night alone. We've mostly been at Charlie's place – it's still a little weird to be at my house with all the memories of Theo. I don't think Calypso is too happy about it, but she seems to like Charlie, which is surprising as she barely likes anyone."

"That's great, Hannah. I'm really happy for you." Pearly hears herself saying the words, but they feel like swords in her gut.

"The only thing is..." Hannah bites her lip.

"Yes?"

"Well, it's just – I mean, it's all happening so fast. Don't get me wrong, I really like Charlie, but..."

"Ahh," says Pearly. "You're worried about U-hauling."

"Kinda?"

Pearly smiles. The tightness in her chest lifts a bit. Part of her feels relieved that Hannah has some doubts. Maybe Hannah and Charlie aren't destined to be together after all. "Trust your gut,"

she says. "And give it some time. I'm sure things will work out."
One way or another.

"Yeah," says Hannah, adjusting her headband. "You're right."

Pearly takes Hannah to meet up with Sam and Ruby. The
ghost blends right in, and Pearly wishes more people could see
her. Ruby's usually bound to the café, but at this time of the year,
her movement extends to the town square. The group links arms
and goes exploring — of course Pearly wants to try everything.
She insists they all eat the biggest caramel apple they can find
and cracks up as Sam takes a huge bite, caramel sticking to the
mustache he grew just for this occasion. Hannah snaps a picture
on her phone, and Ruby poses with them — though they all
know she won't appear in the photo.

As they wander over to the games, Sam spots the classic
strength test – hit the lever, ring the bell.

"Step right up! Step right up!" A booth attendant calls out to
Sam. "Hey, how 'bout you in the top hat?"

Sam picks up the mallet, flexes his puny muscles, and takes a
hefty swing. The mallet hits the lever, but the marker only climbs
halfway up the scale, falling way short of the bell.

"Ooh, too bad! Better luck next time, kid!"

Sam's face falls. Pearly knows what he's thinking — *there
won't be a next time.* He may have been teasing with the mus-
cle-flex, but even he didn't seem to realize how much the chemo
has sapped his strength.

Hannah puts an arm around him. "That wasn't bad," she lies.

"Why not give it one more try?" says Pearly. "Just for shits and
giggles."

Sam hesitates, looking up at the bell, then picks up the mallet.
As he prepares to swing, Pearly focuses on the mallet, channeling a bit of her magic to bolster his strength. This time, when

Sam brings it down, the marker shoots up, ringing the bell –
CLANG!

The booth attendant hands Sam a plush black cat with a tiny
witch's hat. "Well, shit," he says.

"That's right," says Pearly. "Who's the stud now?"

He grins, turning the cat over in his hands. "For you," he says,
offering Pearly the prize.

"Aw, thank you, Sam," she says, accepting the cat. "I have a
special fondness for witches and felines."

Hannah practically drags them to the Ferris wheel next.
"We have to ride this!" She grabs Pearly's hand and pulls
her toward the line. They pile into a gondola, with Sam—and
Ruby—squeezing in beside them. As the wheel begins to turn,
they rise high above the festival, giving them a birds-eye view
of downtown Eenob. The lights below twinkle like stars against
the deepening twilight, and for a moment, Pearly allows herself
to get lost in the magic of it all. Sometimes, life on Earth isn't so
bad.

As the ride ends, Pearly spots Danielle at the pie-baking
contest booth, making last-minute adjustments to her entry.

Pearly approaches, passing by other contestants who are fidgeting with their pies or making final tweaks. She resists an urge
to tamper – Danielle can win this on her own. "How are you
feeling, honey?" she asks.

Danielle looks up, wiping her hands on her apron. "Ready as
I'll ever be," she says. "I know it's a kickass pie. I just hope the
judges agree."

Pearly puts a hand on Danielle's shoulder. "That pie is fit for
the gods. Whatever happens, you're a winner in my book."

Ruby materializes beside them. "And if the judges don't agree,
I'll scare the shit out of them."

Pearly relays the comment to Danielle, who laughs. "You guys are the best."

As the pie-baking contest gets underway, festival-goers gather around the booths. The judges begin making their rounds — a mix of local critics and chefs, including Bennet Hawthorne, a prominent food blogger from Chicago. Pearly stands off to the side, eyes locked on Danielle as the judges approach her booth.

Maybe Pearly's a little biased, but she's sampled a few of the other pies and Danielle's is a hundred times better. As the judges take their first bites, Pearly holds her breath, crossing her fingers and toes and even her aura.

The judges confer in a whispered huddle, making notes and occasionally glancing back at the contestants. Are they looking at Danielle more than the others? Is that a good look or a bad look? After what seems like eons, Bennet Hawthorne himself steps forward to announce the winners. Pearly's heart pounds.

"...And in first place," he declares, "Danielle Davis for her pumpkin pie with chai-spiced streusel and roasted hazelnut caramel!"

The crowd erupts into applause, and Pearly lets out a whoop of joy. "That's my girl!" she shouts, beaming with pride. Danielle accepts the ribbon with trembling hands.

"Congratulations, Danielle," says Bennet. "It's rare to see such a thoughtful blend of flavors and textures. The streusel added a warm, aromatic complexity that took the filling to a whole new level. Simply divine."

"Oh, thank you!" Danielle dances on her tip-toes. "I can't believe this is really happening."

Pearly doesn't want to eavesdrop, but she can't help but catch a snippet or two of their discussion — words like "profile" and "interview."

"Look at her go." Ruby shakes her head, looking pleased as punch. "Unstoppable."

"That's right – you saw it here first," Pearly boasts. "Celebrity chef in the making."

Pearly notices Charlie entering the town square and peels away from the group to say hello. Apparently Charlie vetoed both knight and bard. But they are wearing a burgundy vest, a billowy white shirt, and leather pants tucked into knee-high boots — so they're still going for medieval chic. A fake saber hangs at their side, strapped to a wide, leather belt.

"Hey Pearly," Charlie says as they approach. "Looks like the Middle Ages called to you, too."

"That's right. They wanted a makeover." Pearly bats her eyelashes, and nods to Charlie's costume. "So, uh, what are you supposed to be?"

"I don't know," Charlie shrugs. "I guess I was going for sword-swallower? Is that a medieval thing?"

Pearly's throat constricts. Could it be a nod to the life they shared all those years ago? Thunder was a sword-swallower back then. It feels too specific to be a coincidence. Besides, a lot of things we like are callbacks to past lives – pirates or cowboys or Impressionist painters. Pearly wonders if they could still swallow the real deal. They're only about eight hundred years out of practice.

"And who are you exactly?" asks Charlie. "The Queen of Eenob?"

"Sure, darling. You may bow and kiss my hand." She gives a regal smile, but inside, she's struggling. The pull to tell the truth to Charlie is intense — to reveal their shared history, the connection that spans lifetimes. But she knows the consequences could be disastrous. Not just for her mission as a guide. For Thunder's sake, and her own.

Pearly feels the tug of the past. This time, she doesn't resist. She closes her eyes, and the sounds of the festival become those of a circus in 13th century Bohemia...

***

Prague, 1224

Thunder—Kaspar, in this lifetime—is dressed in flowing burgundy breeches, standing in the center of a makeshift stage, sword gripped firmly in his hand. The audience gathers in the tent getting drunk as the circus prepares for its next act. And Pearly—Milena, in this lifetime—is among them. She's a noblewoman dressed as a commoner, after sneaking out of the manor during afternoon prayers. Kaspar catches her eye, grins. She can tell he senses the truth — she's just slumming it in disguise.

"Ladies and gentlemen," says Kaspar, "and who knows, there could even be a real lady in the crowd!" He gets a laugh, gives a wink to Milena. She flushes, feeling a little hot under the collar. "Gather 'round and behold — with no trickery, no sorcery, I shall now command this blade to travel where no blade ought to go!" Another peal of laughter ripples through the crowd, which Kaspar cuts short with a finger to his lips. "Oh, I pray thee dear audience — hold your breath and silence your murmurs! Just one slip could spell my doom..."

Kaspar lifts the sword to his lips and Milena gasps, watching him tilt his head back and lower the blade inch by inch into his mouth, the metal sliding smoothly down his throat. After years of practice, he's mastered the instinct to resist. Milena's heart pounds —not from fear, but from the thrill. Her life has been dedicated to child-bearing, household management, religious devotion. There has been no place for adventure...or desire. Watching him makes her long for both.

The crowd oohs and aahs as the sword disappears down Kaspar's gullet. He holds the pose, relishing the attention — before pulling it out and raising it high above his head. "It is said the gods smile upon the fools and the fearless," he boasts, to thunderous applause. "Today I may be both." He bows, waving to the crowd, but his eyes are only for Milena.

Kaspar works the crowd, making jokes and collecting coins. The last of the onlookers drift away, but Milena lingers, heart pounding in the shadows. When he finally reaches her, he pauses. His eyes meet hers, and someone is seeing her for the first time. Not her name or her dowry or even her beauty, but her soul. She reaches into her borrowed tunic for a leather pouch. The weight of it feels conspicuous, out of place.

"Quite the show." She pulls out a silver coin and places it in his outstretched palm.

"Milady," he curtseys, slipping the coin into his pocket. "If only we were all so blessed to carry a purse so generous."

"Ah, but you're the blessèd one," she says, "to roam where you please and live as you like."

He tilts his head, a smile forming at the corners of his mouth. "You think so?" He closes his hand around hers. Even through her gloves, a rush of fire runs through her. His body is so close, so warm. She should turn away, she should leave – but she doesn't. For a moment, neither one of them moves. Her face flushes. Her teeth chatter. The breeze blows leaves all around them, urging her lips to part like some magical spell. Closer. Closer. Closer...

***

Pearly blinks back the memory, but its pull is strong. The laughter and light of the festival swirl around her, but the past lingers at the edges of her thoughts. That's when she notices — she and Charlie are face-to-face now, breathing cool air in the centimeters between them. Pearly's aura crackles, and she feels the negative space where their soulmate cord once bound them together. Reality warps. Lines blur. Charlie becomes Kaspar. Pearly becomes Milena. It's too powerful to resist. Milena cups Kaspar's face and pulls it in for a kiss that melts through time. Soft lips. Open mouth. The taste of joy and caramel apples. Kaspar's rigid posture relaxes as they surrender to the moment, Kaspar's hands around her waist, Milena's fingers running down his back—

And then it's over, and Pearly is herself again, and Charlie's looking at her with a mix of confusion, guilt, and overwhelm. Oh God, what did she do? "I'm sorry," Pearly breathes. "I'm so sorry."

Charlie stumbles back, their face drained of color. "I don't..." They struggle for words. "I didn't—"

"I did," says Pearly, struggling to hold back tears. "It was me."

Charlie swallows, searching Pearly's face as the energy continues to pulse between them. Then they turn around and disappear into the crowd.

Shit. Shit-shit-shit. Should she go after Charlie or leave them be? What would she even say beyond admitting she's the worst, most selfish soul who ever lived?

But just as she decides to sit down before her legs give out, Pearly sees two familiar figures entering the square. Her jaw drops. Hertz and Abathur—what the hell are her coworkers doing here? A realization settles in, a knot forming in all of her chakras as she watches them scan the area. This isn't some bizarre coincidence. Mr. Mustard must've sent them. If Hertz and Abathur are here on her boss's orders, that means her secret work on Earth is no longer secret. They're looking for her, or worse—they're here to cart her off to get Recycled.

She spots Sam and Ruby on a bench and hurries over. Sam notices the frozen look on her face. "Pearly," he says. "What's going on?"

"They're not supposed to be here," she mumbles to herself.

"What do you mean? Who's not supposed to be here?"

Oops. Shouldn't have revealed that. "Listen, Sam," she says, "do you trust me?"

"Of course."

"Then I need your help. You and Ruby."

"Okay..." The ghost floats up to them and nods – she's in.

"I need to disappear for a bit," says Pearly. "Can you find a way to distract those guys?" She gestures to Hertz and Abathur.

"Copy that, Holmes. We're on it."

Pearly crouches behind a stack of hay bales and peeks through the gaps. She can almost feel the shift in the air as Ruby does her thing, crackling with energy in a way that messes with all nearby electronics. Pearly watches Hertz frown, tapping at his scanner in frustration as it starts to beep erratically. She can't hear their conversation from her hiding spot, but she sees Hertz gesturing at the thing and making some excuse or another.

"Keep it up, Ruby," Pearly whispers. "You're a superstar." Ruby cracks a smile, then closes her eyes tight in concentration. A few seconds later, everyone's cell phone goes off simultaneously, but the ringtones are all static. It's just enough of a distraction to pull Hertz and Abathur away from their search.

Seeing her chance, Pearly weaves through the crowd, ducking behind a row of market stalls. Just as Abathur turns to look, Sam kicks over a display of pumpkins, allowing Pearly to slip away. As Sam and Ruby book it from the scene, attracting Hertz and

Abathur's attention, Pearly finds an empty storage tent at the edge of the festival grounds. She dashes inside, waiting until she's certain her pursuers are gone. Pearly sinks to the ground and puts her head between her knees. That was a close call – too close. They may not have found her today, but she knows they will...and soon. Can she finish the job and hand it back to Malcolm before they turn her in? Every day now is a liability. She's not sure how much longer her luck will hold out.

"Pearly!" Ruby's voice cuts through Pearly's musings. "Come quickly. It's Sam."

Oh no. Not this. Not now. Please God, not now.

She follows Ruby to a circle of festival-goers surrounding Sam. He's lying on the ground, eyes closed. His face is pale – too pale. And his breathing...there's something wrong with his breathing. Pearly kneels beside him. She checks his pulse with trembling hands, vaguely aware that Ruby has vanished.

Her mind spins. She can't move. She can't breathe. Maybe she's too late. Maybe Sam will die while she sits here frozen into inaction. She can't let that happen. Not again.

Suddenly she's back on Belmont Street, feeling Thunder's blood seeping through her fingers. Sirens blare in the distance, too far away to matter.

No, no, no! Sam is finally coming out of his shell – finally living, dammit. How can it all be taken away from him now? She should do something. Anything.

"Sam?" says Charlie. "Pearly?"

Charlie reappears with a couple of paramedics in tow, and Ruby floating behind. "Our—our friend just collapsed," they say, trying to keep it together. "He has cancer, and he just collapsed."

Sam's eyes flutter open. "M'okay," he mumbles. "M'okay." Clearly, he's not okay.

"You don't have to talk," says Charlie. "Just keep breathing."

One of the paramedics checks Sam's vitals, putting an oxygen mask on his face, while another gathers further details from Charlie. Pearly hovers at the edge of the scene, stuck in her own mental sludge. The paramedics lift Sam onto a gurney and wheel him to the ambulance parked on the street. Charlie glances back at Pearly, like "are you gonna come?" But Pearly can't move, can't speak. It's like she's on a different plane of existence, and all she can do is watch the scene play out – like she's become the ghost. Charlie climbs in behind Sam, and the doors close with a heavy thud.

As the ambulance pulls away, its flashing lights reflect in Pearly's eyes and its sirens gradually fade into the distance. She watches until it's no longer in sight, feeling more helpless than she ever thought possible.

THIRTY-FOUR

Pearly should be at Thunderbolt. There's gala prep to be done, and she's needed. But she only got as far as the parking lot. Her legs seemed to have a will of their own, carrying her away from the café and into the park where she first met Danielle. She watches the ducks foraging for food, building up their reserves for the long journey south. Maybe she should join them. She'd probably be more welcome in some South Carolina swamp, where the biggest thing she could screw up was quacking at the wrong time.

She hasn't spoken to Charlie about the kiss, but they have exchanged texts about Sam. Pearly sent flowers to the hospital, along with a coffee mug that has Cthulhu sitting on the bottom. Seraphina even drove her to the hospital and tried her best to get Pearly to go in, tilting her side mirrors and opening the driver's side door, but Pearly couldn't walk in there either. The trauma of Thunder's death keeps hijacking her mind, and she's terrified she'll fail Sam the way she failed Thunder in their Chicago life. So instead she's slumped on a bench like some abandoned marionette, unable to pull her own strings.

"May I?"

Pearly looks up to see Abathur blocking the sun. He's disguised his face to look more human, but he's still wearing his standard Hawaiian shirt and board shorts. If he really wanted to blend in, he'd put on a coat – it's freezing out here – but Pearly doesn't feel the need to offer tips. Anyway, she's not all that surprised to see him.

"Just get it over with and Recycle me already," she sighs.

"May I?" He gestures toward the bench. She nods, and Abathur takes a seat beside her. They sit in silence for a few moments, watching the ducks.

"So," she says, "where's your partner?"

"In the car." He pulls a bag of Slim Jim Fire Fries from his pocket, takes one, and offers her the bag. She shakes her head. For once, she's not hungry.

"I guess you met Dumb Pearly."

"We did." Abathur chuckles. "She's quite a character. Got your spunk, if not your brains."

Pearly's stomach churns as she imagines the paddy wagon coming for her body double. "Look, whatever you need to do to me is fine, but leave her out of it, okay? She's innocent, and she doesn't deserve to be punished for my mistakes."

"You know, Pearly," Abathur crunches on a couple of Fire Fries, "we don't believe in punishment – well, not anymore. Back in the old days, well. That was a different story." He wipes his hands on his board shorts. "These days, we try our best to rehabilitate souls, instead of just chucking them back into the cosmic womb for a redo. I mean hey, it happens. But it's rare. And listen —the fact that you're pleading with me to save your dumber half, and not yourself? That tells me your soul just might be worth preserving." He sighs, puts down the bag. "Still, you got a lot to answer for. What the hell were you thinking, kid?"

Pearly squirms in her seat. "I don't know, I just – I felt like I needed to prove myself. To show everyone that they're wrong about me. That I'm more than just some fuck-up." She sucks in her cheeks, marveling at the irony of it all as the ducks swim in circles. She used to think it was because they were stupid — until Thunder told her it was all a strategy, stirring up food from the bottom of the pond. "Can I ask you something?" she says. "Why did they assign you to Waste Management? You were such a big shot back in your day."

"It wasn't an assignment." Abathur digs his hands into the bag, searching for the last fiery crumbs. "I volunteered."

Pearly gapes at him. "Are you shitting me?"

"I shit you not."

"But...why?"

He sucks on his fingers, balling up the empty bag. "Walk with me."

Pearly gets up from the bench. If she knew she'd have to do nature today, she wouldn't have worn the thigh-high platforms. At least the red vinyl is a perfect complement to the red and golden leaves on the path.

"I was a lot like you when I was younger," says Abathur. "Eager. A real boundary-pusher. Obsessed with getting ahead. I was convinced I could work my way into Sector Zero and impress the Big Boss with my spiritual portfolio. I went after the jobs other souls were afraid to take on – the ones with the hardest choices and the gnarliest moral dilemmas. That's what led to my career weighing the souls of the dead to determine their fate in the afterlife. It was epic, and I was good at it. Then the system got revamped, and I was out on my ass with a severance package, including one reincarnation pass for an 'easy life' on Earth." He shakes his head and sighs. "As if any life is truly easy. Anyway, that's when I took up surfing. I was never really any good, but I didn't care – I was stoked just to be in the water. The first time I caught a wave, I experienced what the Buddhists call 'satori.' It was a perfect moment, a profound connection with the wave, no longer separate, but one with it. After that, it didn't matter where I went or what I did. That thing I'd been chasing – that need for validation – it was an inside job."

"Wow," says Pearly. "That's so...bumper sticker."

"You'll get it someday. All souls do, eventually." He moves to the side to let a couple in matching jogging outfits run past them. "In the meantime, I've got our pal Mustard on my ass and I can only hold him off so long. You broke a lot of rules, Pearly. We have to bring you in."

She stops, takes his arm. "Listen, I get it, I really do. But if you could just wait a few more days – until after the fundraising gala – it would mean the world to me. After that, you can do whatever you need to do. But my charges are counting on me, and without this gala, the café will go under and the sweet community we've worked so hard to build will disappear." She looks up at him, oozing vulnerability. "Please, Abathur – I'm begging you. If not for my sake, for theirs. Just give me a little more time."

He looks back toward the parking lot, where Hertz is waiting. "I'll see what I can do," he says. "But I'm warning you, kid – this is your last chance. Don't fuck it up."

***

The good news: Sam's out of the hospital, and he's planning to give Ruby's tribute at the gala. The medium news: Charlie still hasn't said anything to Pearly about their impromptu kiss. The bad news: Pearly feels so guilty about her crappy guidance of

Sam and Hannah that she's continued to find excuses to stay away from them – and Thunderbolt.

While her charges were sleeping, she dreamed up a complex new choreo routine for Danielle, filled with manic energy from the Abathur encounter. If she could give a confidence boost to at least one of her charges, maybe she could start to make up for her failures with the other two.

The next morning, she finds Danielle practicing in front of the mirror in her costume and heels. "How are you feeling, honey?" Pearly sashays in with a can-do attitude and gives her a big squeeze.

"Good...I'm good." Danielle glances in the mirror. "Well, actually, I'm a little nervous. I feel like I just memorized the choreo, and now you want to add more? And a lip sync on top? I'm worried I might mess it up." *And justify people's stereotypes of trans women.* That's what Pearly hears Danielle not saying.

"Let me ask you something," says Pearly. "That food blogger was so impressed with your pie that he scored you an interview with a pastry chef in Copenhagen. That's an incredible opportunity! But you said you're not sure if you're up for it, right?"

"Right..."

"Well I think this performance could be just the thing to help you strut into that interview like you own the kitchen."

"Yeah," she says, biting a nail. "Maybe?"

"Maybe? Maybe? I want them to hear your 'hell yes' all the way in Europe."

"Alright, alright," Danielle concedes. "Hell yes!"

"Great." Pearly pulls out a print-out with the lyrics to "Fever" from her handbag and gives it to Danielle. "First priority – memorize this. Every time you practice the routine, I want you to sing along until it becomes second nature."

"Okay..."

"And it's not just about getting the words out. Exaggerated facial expressions can really help you connect with the audience and make the performance feel more emotionally charged."

Danielle wrinkles her nose. "I mean, I've seen that in drag shows, but I'm afraid I'll just look ridiculous."

"You won't, I promise. Let's try it together." She cues up the track and presses play. They practice singing with "en-hanced e-nun-ci-a-tion." Danielle mirrors Pearly, who's totally in her element as a performer. "Yes," Pearly encourages. "More. Big-ger."

When Pearly's satisfied that Danielle has it down enough to keep practicing on her own, she asks her charge to pull up the video to "Fever" on her laptop. They watch Madonna, dressed in a black sequined bra top and hot shorts, expertly move and groove with two sexy backup dancers while playing to the crowd with seductive winks and smiles.

"God," Danielle chews on a chunk of hair. "She's so good."

"A legend," agrees Pearly. "And you will be too when we add in some of her choreo."

"Uhh...I don't know. That looks pretty hard."

"How do you know until you try?" Pearly leads Danielle to one end of the room and positions her in a statuesque opening pose. As the song progresses, she demonstrates fluid, wave-like arm movements, shimmy kicks, and hip rolls, extending her arms and arching her back to convey seduction and heat. Danielle tries to keep up, but even after she gets the steps, she looks a little fidgety. Pearly figures it's just pre-show jitters. She knew lots of queens who'd barf backstage then go on to own the spotlight.

"It's okay to be nervous," she says. "But don't let it stop you. From the top?"

Danielle nods. They start the routine again. Pearly pushes a little harder, adding some additional floor work. Her voice cuts through the music as she directs —maybe even micro-manages – everything Danielle is doing.

"No, honey, on the beat, not after it...Chin up, smile...Lock your elbows...Stop slouching...Pivot, darling, pivot!"

As Danielle struggles to keep with the pace, she stumbles on a tricky move. Pearly shakes her head. "Come on, Danielle! Don't get into your head."

"I know, I know – I'm trying."

Pearly urges her to repeat the sequence – "Again! Again! I want to see you turn it!" – but each time, Danielle gets further and further behind until finally she lowers her arms in defeat.

"I'm tired, Pearly," she says, sinking onto the bed. She does look tired, and Pearly feels a little guilty. Is she pushing too hard?

Pearly walks to the foot of the bed and kneels down so she's eye to eye with Danielle. "I know you are," she says. "But we only have two more days. If you want to stop, we can stop...but a superstar would try it one more time. Just channel Ruby!"

Danielle looks at Pearly, considering. "Okay," she says finally. "One more time."

Pearly settles onto the vanity stool to watch, but she can't relax. An inner voice warns her that she might be going off the rails—that obsessing over Danielle's performance isn't the best way to manage her own anxiety. But it feels too late to change course. The gala is almost here, and with it Pearly's deadline. *Tick-tock, tick-tock.* The countdown's getting louder in her mind. She just hopes it's not counting down her last days as a soul.

THIRTY-FIVE

Tomorrow night is the night. The apex. The peak. The culmination of everything Pearly's been working toward as a guide. But no pressure or anything.

Pearly shoves aside her anxious inner narrator and slips in through the hidden bookcase to assess the scene. The café has become the Moonshine Lounge once more. String lights line the ceiling, and the tables are draped in black and gold linens, topped with pearl-and-feather centerpieces. There's a stage in the corner lined with burgundy curtains – rented, since they didn't have them at Costco – and a cute little vintage mic stand. It's a bit chaotic, as she'd expected, with Charlie at the center of the cyclone giving last-minute instructions to the staff. Even Charlie looks stressed, and they rarely get ruffled. Is it just the show? Or did Charlie tell Hannah about the kiss?

Across the room, Hannah is helping with decorations. As she fiddles with the centerpieces she silently mouths words – it looks like she's mentally rehearsing her number. But Pearly can tell it's more than pre-show jitters. Part of Pearly hoped they could brush it under the rug until after the gala. But she sees now that she has to do the hard thing – or there might not be a gala. Her hands shake as she approaches her charge. Hannah looks up with ice in her eyes. *She knows.*

"Hannah, can we talk for a minute?" says Pearly. "Outside?"

Hannah doesn't say anything, but she drops the centerpiece materials and marches out the front door. Pearly follows, gut twisting with each step she takes. Hannah shivers in the crisp autumn air, crossing her arms in front of her chest. She locks eyes with Pearly. "What the hell were you thinking?"

Pearly cringes. "I wasn't," she says. "And I know that's no excuse. I just got caught up in the moment and acted impulsively. It's been awkward and confusing, and I obviously haven't handled it very well." She swallows, clenching her fists. "I never meant for anything to happen, but I want you to know it wasn't Charlie's fault. I kissed them. It was my mistake."

Hannah glances through the window, where Charlie is fiddling with the stage curtains. "Look," she says, "I don't care what excuses you come up with. There's obviously something going on between you two. And that something is making Charlie pull away." Hannah takes a breath, searches Pearly's face. "I need you to be honest with me. Do you want to be with Charlie?"

"No! I mean...it's complicated. But listen, I would never—"

Hannah cuts her off. "You're the one who told me – repeatedly – to put myself out there after Theo died. You encouraged me to take a chance, to let someone in. And I did—I let Charlie in." Tears prickle at the corners of her eyes. "But now, you're the one taking them away from me. And when they say they want to be with me, I don't even know if I can trust them. How am I supposed to feel about that, Pearly? Because I have to be honest, it's feeling pretty shitty right now."

Pearly feels a wave of guilt wash over her. She did encourage Hannah to date, even helped her make that damn profile. She'd been so proud of Hannah for taking that step, for finding the courage to move forward.

"I'm so sorry," she says. "That was never my intention. I wanted you to find happiness again. I didn't think..."

"Didn't think what?" says Hannah. "Didn't think that your feelings might get in the way? Or did you just not care?"

"Hannah, I care about you. I care about both of you."

"Are you sure about that? Because it sure feels like you're more focused on being there for Charlie than on being here for me. If you're letting your personal feelings cloud your judgment, then it's not just me you're failing—it's our friendship."

Pearly flinches. "Hannah, I promise, I'm going to fix this. Just give me a little more time, okay?"

Hannah shakes her head. "The gala is tomorrow, and it's not fair to Charlie—to any of us—to have this hanging over our heads. You'd better figure something out, and fast." With that, Hannah turns and stomps back inside, bell jingling as she slams the door.

Pearly's pretty sure there's nothing in the guidebook to help her through this one. That's probably why the application process is so rigorous – they weed out souls who do selfish shit like this. But what else can she do at this point except keep plowing ahead?

Pearly centers herself as best she can and returns to the café. On the stage, Danielle is rehearsing her routine. Pearly weaves between tables and sits down in the front row next to a hovering Ruby. Danielle is trying her best, but it's not going well. She's wearing a fitted jacket over her costume – another recent addition, to give a nod to the striptease part of burlesque. But as she attempts to slide it off her shoulders, the fabric catches on her corset. Danielle grits her teeth and stops the music.

"Damn it!" One of the buttons pops off as she tugs at the jacket with a little too much force. "Ugh! This isn't working. I can't do this."

Pearly's about to respond when a text bubble appears in the right-hand corner of her vision. It's from Malcolm.

I'm baaaaaaack!
How's the homestead?
Catch up @ Crooked Harp?

He's going to have to wait.

Pearly shifts her focus back to Danielle. "You've got to play with it. Not shuck it like you're coming home after a hard day and can't wait to get the damn thing off."

Danielle sighs. "I'm trying, Pearly, but the jacket keeps getting stuck, and I can't seem to do it in time to the music."

Pearly steps onto the stage and takes the jacket. "It's not just a strip," she says, demonstrating, "it's a tease. Slow down, let them savor the reveal. Try it again, and don't rush."

Danielle takes a breath, resets the music, and tries again. But her body is rigid, her breathing is shallow. When the jacket catches on the corset again, she yanks it off and throws it on the floor. Ruby glares at Pearly. OK, maybe she should tone it down.

"Danielle," Pearly softens her tone. "I know it's hard, but you've come so far. This is just one more hurdle. I wouldn't ask you to do this if I didn't think you could do it. It's normal to be a mess before a show, but when you hit that spotlight, I promise it'll all fall into place."

Danielle shakes her head. "It's not just about the routine. It's everything. The performance, the interview—it's too much. I feel like I'm gonna crack."

"You won't, honey, I've got you—"

"Dammit, you're not listening to me!" Danielle throws her hands up. "I'm telling you, I can't fucking do this! It's too much pressure. I'm done. I can't—"

Without warning, the string lights overhead flicker and pop, sending tiny shards of glass to the floor. A handful of centerpiece vases shatter.

"Shit," Pearly says, snapping out of her tunnel vision. Ruby pulls back, guilt pulsing in static around her edges.

Danielle takes off the stilettos and steps down from the stage. "Sorry, Ruby." She shakes her head, then turns toward Pearly. "I quit. You can get someone else to be your punching bag."

"Danielle, wait—"

But Danielle doesn't wait. She heads for the exit, leaving Pearly standing there amidst the shards of shattered glass.

Pearly???

***

The café has returned to nearly normal. A few centerpieces have been replaced, and the glass has been vacuumed. The once-bright string lights hang dimly overhead, like a smile with missing teeth. Pearly stands near the stage trying to regroup, but she's having trouble focusing after the recent blow-outs.

The door opens and Pearly looks up, bracing herself for the next disaster. When she sees Sam standing in the doorway with his laptop bag, her heart sinks further. Doesn't take a psychic to predict this isn't going to go well. But she has to try.

"Sam," she says, reaching out for a hug. "I'm so glad you're okay." But he backs away.

"I don't think that's how I'd put it," he says. It's true – his shoulders are hunched, his face is especially gaunt, and his eyes are framed by dark circles. And then there's his aura – normally orange-yellow, it's now a deeper orange with alarming flecks of red. "I'm here because I promised to show up for Ruby. And unlike some people, keeping my word is important to me."

Ouch.

"Sam, please," she pleads. "I know I said I'd be there for you. I was thinking about you all the time—"

"Gosh, Pearly, thanks. Thoughts and prayers are so helpful. Honestly, this whole spiritual manifesto you've been selling is a load of crap. Anyway, it doesn't matter. Charlie and the gang actually showed up for me."

Pearly shifts her weight, searching for anything to salvage the situation. "I tried to come to the hospital – I really did. It's not that I didn't care. I just – I froze. I let my own shit get in the way. I'm sorry, Sam. I never meant to hurt you."

"But you did," says Sam. "You did hurt me, Pearly. I never wanted a guide in the first place. You forced your way into my life, and I let you do it because I was lonely and you were so damn insistent. Well, here I am, officially insisting that you please leave me the fuck alone. You've done enough damage, and I don't want my last days to be filled with fake cheer from a fake guide who keeps telling me to be brave when she couldn't even muster up the courage to be with me the one time I really needed support." He collects himself, shuddering with raw emotion. Pearly can feel him trying to keep it together. "Now if you'll excuse me, I have a tribute to write, and I no longer want to do it here." He turns and leaves.

Three strikes. You're out, Pearly.

She stands there, staring at the door. She wants to rewind and start the whole damn day again. How could she have been so stupid? She's lost Danielle's trust, driven a wedge between

Hannah and Charlie, and now, she's alienated Sam too. *Dammit, dammit, dammit!*

She sinks into a chair. A zillion excuses pop into her head. *Three cases is too many. The guidebook is too vague. Mercury is in retrograde.* But no matter how hard she tries, she can't escape the fact that she's failed—not just as a guide, but as a friend.

THIRTY-SIX

Failure. Fuck-up. Fraud.

Pearly's slumped on the sofa in her bathrobe and red-sequined house slippers, staring at her holographic tablet. She's on her third latte, but even her old friend caffeine isn't helping her write case reports for Malcolm and the Higher-Ups. It should be easy. Just talk about their progress. But that's the problem. All her charges are struggling right now—and it's Pearly's fault. She squirms on the cushion as she tries to think of something—anything—positive to report about her work with Sam, Danielle, and Hannah.

But she can't. What's she going to say? That she abandoned Sam? That she made Danielle spin out and bail on the event? That she undermined Hannah's trust so badly she actually, almost, sort of tried to steal Hannah's love? She wasn't even supposed to intervene directly, but she did – and she only made things worse. Like, much worse. Ludicrously worse. She did all the things a guide is not supposed to do. Misread situations. Pushed too hard. Prioritized her own feelings.

Pearly forces herself off the sofa and into the kitchen, where she summons her fourth latte from the Cauldron. She wonders why it's so quiet, then realizes the wallpaper birds have gone missing. Maybe they're ashamed of her too.

What the hell is she gonna do? Malcolm's back, and she can't ignore him forever. She has to face the music – even if it's a funeral dirge. She just wishes she had more time. The fundraising event is about to happen, Hertz and Abathur are hot on her tail, and Malcolm could report her to the Higher-Ups to save his own skin if he realizes just how terribly things are going. Okay, sure, they made an under-the-table deal, and it isn't like he'd want to expose his own involvement. But that doesn't mean he won't be nervous—especially if he knows how many rules she's bent. The case reports could've been her saving grace, a way to reassure him that she has everything under control. But she doesn't. Not even a little.

She looks at the case files on her tablet. It makes her sick to think of these souls in her hands – souls she convinced Malcolm to trust her with while he was away. She pages through Sam's file for something, anything, that might redeem her. There isn't much to work with.

- **First Meeting**: *Showed up at his oncologist appointment. Sam saw through invisibility cloak. Thought I was the Grim Reaper. Set him straight – sort of. Should I have told him about Malcolm?*

- **Ruby**: *Sam's falling for a ghost. Is this a distraction from making peace with death or something deeper to encourage?*

- **Health Scare**: *Collapsed during the Halloween Festival while saving my ass. Scared the shit out of me. Health seems to be rapidly declining. Might be in a worse place* *spiritually than when we first met.*

None of it seems like it would help.

She opens the report template again and starts typing some generic shit about companionship and comfort. Nothing sounds right. Nothing feels honest. And she doubts she can bullshit Malcolm – not about this. He might even think she's been avoiding him. And, well, he'd be right.

Pearly drains the rest of her latte and leans back against the sofa. The truth is sinking in: she's in way, way over her head. Maybe she isn't cut out to be a guide after all. Maybe she should've stayed in Waste Management and minded her own business. Now she's sure to get Recycled. And maybe she deserves it. At least that way, she wouldn't leave any more messes for other people to clean up.

The hum of an engine interrupts her pity party. Pearly blinks, turning her head toward the garage.

Seraphina.

Pearly hesitates. She shouldn't let herself get distracted. But Seraphina keeps honking, insistent. With a sigh, Pearly pushes the tablet aside and gets her ass off the sofa. She trusts her emotional support vehicle more than she trusts herself. Anyway, a ride might help her find some clarity. Who knows? Maybe even a miracle.

As she enters the garage, Seraphina's headlights turn on. Pearly slides into the driver's seat as Seraphina closes her own door and adjusts her mirrors. Pearly's happy to relinquish control. The truck knows where to go. The truck always knows where to go.

"Okay, baby," she says. "I trust you."

Seraphina rev-rev-revs out of the garage and onto Lightbody Lane. Pulling away from the house, Pearly casts one last glance back at the living room window. At all the unanswered questions she's left behind. Then she turns around and embraces the open road.

As they drive through the neighborhood, the sprawling campus of Elysium University comes into view, with its ethereal, multidimensional architecture and lush green quad. This is Pearly's old alma mater, the place where souls study between incarnations before graduating to full-time jobs in the afterlife — the place where Pearly first imagined becoming a guide, where she and Thunder first found each other. Pearly catches glimpses of young souls, eager and curious, just as they'd been all those lifetimes ago.

Pearly wishes she could return to those simpler times. Times when everything seemed possible – when the worst thing that could happen was flunking an exam. Not ruining everyone's life, including your own.

Seraphina guides Pearly farther into the sector. They pass the farmers market, where souls are busy bartering for all sorts of cosmic goods. Pearly can almost hear Thunder's voice, cheerfully debating the merits of compost made from starlight vs. astral manure. This was their Saturday morning ritual, and it was always Pearly's favorite part of the week. Seeing it now is bittersweet. She doesn't know if she could shop there without Thunder.

Seraphina senses the shift in Pearly's mood and carries her away from the market, toward the Astral Highway Overlook. They pull up to the secluded spot where Pearly and Thunder used to park, gazing out—and making out—over the swirling energy of the highway below. This was where they dreamed together, mapping out future lives and adventures. Pearly had so many dreams back then. What happened? She used to be all about self-actualization. Thunder was right. She did get complacent.

Seraphina rounds a bend, and the Cosmic Rebirth Center comes into view. Pearly winces as they pass the building's towering, crystalline structure, where souls go to begin their new lives. It's a place of renewal, of fresh starts—everything Thunder embraced and Pearly has resisted. The sight of it fills her with a profound sense of loss. Not just for Thunder, but for the part of herself that used to believe in the future they would build together.

Seraphina slows as they approach the Nursery. Thunder's workplace. Seraphina must be trying to take her back to her soulmate, not realizing he's incarnated.

Seraphina opens her driver's side door. Pearly hesitates, so the truck tilts until Pearly gets dumped out onto the street.

"He's not there, baby."

Seraphina flashes her headlights, urging Pearly to go inside anyway.

"All right, all right, fine."

The Nursery's large, ornate doors glide open silently as she approaches, revealing a hospital-like space bathed in iridescent light. It's peaceful inside. On the walls are glowing murals depicting the journey of a soul from creation in the Great Cosmic Womb to incarnation on Earth. Each panel is a masterpiece, capturing the essence of existence in swirling colors and light. Pearly pauses to take in the beauty. She doesn't know why the universe exists, why consciousness divided itself up into trillions of souls. But in this moment, it's impossible not to feel like there's some meaning in it all.

As she walks down the gleaming corridor, Pearly passes several rooms where nurses tend to young and injured souls. Eventually, she arrives at the main nursery, where rows of incubators cradle the newborn souls. Above each one, tiny mobiles made of stardust, suns, planets, and glowing crystals gently spin, tinkling a sound like wind chimes. The baby souls are like little blobs of light, hovering in that delicate space between energy and form.

Pearly hesitates at the entrance. This is Thunder's domain. And after everything that's happened, does she even deserve to be here, in this sacred space?

"Can I help you?"

One of the nurses must've noticed Pearly standing around like a fish out of water, or a drag queen at a gun show. It's Sen-Sen, Thunder's coworker. The one who Thunder took under his wing when Sen-Sen was in dark place.

"Oh—must've gotten turned around. Sorry, I was just leaving—"

"Wait," he says. "It's Pearly, right? From Thunder's party?"

She was hoping he wouldn't recognize her. Sen-Sen wasn't especially nice to Pearly back then, but he seems to recognize something in her now.

"Wait," he says. "Don't go. Why don't you come with me?" He offers a hand. At first, she's not sure if she wants to take it — but what does she have to lose? Pearly finds herself holding her breath as he guides her into the Nursery, as if she might break the fragile souls with her too-muchness.

"Ah," Sen-Sen says. "Here we go."

He stops at one of the incubators and carefully lifts out a newborn soul, placing it in Pearly's arms – just like Thunder did for Sen-Sen so long ago. Pearly's heart races. She's visited Thunder a couple of times, but she's never held a newborn soul, and the sudden responsibility sends a wave of anxiety through her. The tiny being pulses in her arms. It's warm and luminous, like a piece of living stardust. The pulse syncs up with the beat of her own vibration. *Thump-thump. Thump-thump. Thump-thump.*

There's something about the soul's innocence that pulls out of Pearly a pure, unconditional love – one devoid of any judgment or expectation. Tears prick at the corners of her eyes as the truth settles in. The soul in her hands doesn't need to prove anything to anyone. It doesn't need to validate its existence with achievements. It's worthy of love just – well, just for existing. Just because. And that means Pearly is too.

"Enchanting, aren't they?" Sen-Sen's eyes gleam as he stares down at the soul.

"Yeah," Pearly marvels. "They really are."

She hands the newborn back to Sen-Sen, her heart a little lighter, her mind a little clearer. She steps out of the Nursery feeling renewed. Her spirit is back.

Seraphina's door swings open as Pearly approaches. She slides into the driver's seat and puts her hands on the wheel.

"All right, girl," she says, "take us home."

Seraphina hums, then pulls out of the parking lot. The ride home is calm, but Pearly's already thinking about her next steps. She knows she can't avoid it any longer. She needs to fess up, to confront the mess she's made. She steadies her mind, composes a message to Malcolm:

Meet @the Crooked Harp?

The response is almost instant.

See you there!

THIRTY-SEVEN

Pearly fidgets on her stool at The Crooked Harp. The glass of Shangria-La she ordered from Diesel sits in front of her, untouched. She's still in her bathrobe — she just didn't have it in her to put on makeup, do her hair, or even paint her nails. The self-playing harp mimics her mood with its somber version of "Toxic" by Britney Spears.

Pearly swills her drink, thinking about what she's going to say as she waits for Malcolm to arrive. She feels strangely exposed in her bathrobe, and part of her wants to run home and change.

Too late. The door opens and Malcolm enters. He looks refreshed – but still high-strung, as usual. He spots Pearly at the bar and makes his way over.

"Pearly!" he says, standing there awkwardly before reaching into his pocket. "I got this for you." It's an abominable snow bat on a keychain. Pearly smiles, accepting the gift.

"Thanks, Malcolm." She places the keychain on the bar next to her drink, then glances up at him, trying to gauge his mood.

Malcolm settles onto the stool beside her, signaling Diesel for his usual Nirvana Lite. "You know," he says, "you were right about how much I needed that break. Those caves were something else. And the bats—seeing them glow in the dark right in front of you, especially after that close call—unreal. I still can't believe we didn't get kicked off the tour."

Pearly nods absently. "Sounds like a great time."

Diesel sets Malcolm's pint on the bar-top. "Here you go, Malcolm." He starts to move away, then turns back. "Oh, Pearly, by the way," he says, "some guys were asking about you recently—one with a bloodstained suit, the other looking like he just walked off a beach. Seemed real interested in finding you."

Malcolm raises an eyebrow, looking to Pearly for an explanation.

"Oh, them." She forces a laugh. "Thanks Diesel, nothing to worry about." She tries to mask the alarm surging through her. She'd hoped she wouldn't have to tell Malcolm she's being followed. But Malcolm catches the unease in Pearly's eyes. He sets his drink down, his casual air fading.

"What do I need to know?" he asks. "Are we screwed, Pearly?"

"Things are...well..." Pearly takes a deep breath—and a big fruity gulp of wine. "Things haven't exactly gone as planned."

"Oh God." Malcolm buries his face in his hands. "Oh God..."

Pearly swallows, feeling the knot in her chest tighten. "I thought I could handle it. I was gonna prove to you I was this A+ guide – and show the Higher-Ups they made a mistake when they assigned me to waste management. But the thing is...it's been a little harder than I expected. And more complicated." She sighs. "Much more complicated."

She keeps going, confessing the challenges her charges are facing, along with her part in it. The only thing she doesn't tell him is that Charlie is Thunder reincarnated, and that she kissed them. What if Malcolm sees her attachment as a liability? He might think she's too compromised to be objective with Hannah. And could she blame him? But she can't have him questioning her decisions. Not now, when everything is hanging by a thread – if that. So she swallows that tidbit and continues on. "Every time I've tried to help," she says, "I've fucked it up. I know I'm no angel, but I'm not a great guardian either."

But when Malcolm finally looks up at Pearly, it's not with the disgust she imagined, but something else...compassion? "You know, Pearly," he says, "change – real, lasting change – isn't easy or linear. And it doesn't happen instantaneously. I don't know what kind of results you were expecting in such a short amount of time, but it actually sounds like you've been a good guide." He takes a long pull of his pint. "Sure, you made some mistakes, but if I'm hearing you right, you managed to help Hannah clear her stagnation and find new love. You got Sam out of his house and into community, giving him a sense of purpose for the first time since his diagnosis. And the last time I checked in on Danielle, she was suffocating in that dead-end job that kept her in the closet. Look at her now, shining in a new career while finding acceptance and belonging at Thunderbolt. These are all meaningful spiritual advancements. You're too hard on yourself."

"Really?" It comes out hoarse, choked with emotion. It's true – she is hard on herself.

He rests a hand on top of hers. "Really."

She swallows, blinking back tears. "Thanks, Malcolm." She's tempted to leave it at that, but he deserves to know about Hertz and Abathur. "There is one other thing. The guys who were asking about me—the ones Diesel was talking about? They're closing in, Malcolm. They work in Waste Management, and they know I haven't been showing up for my shifts. So my boss sent them to investigate. I've managed to stall them until the gala, but they'll be coming for me." She doesn't say "us," even though she has to admit it's a possibility.

"What?" says Malcolm. "Why didn't you tell me about this?"

"I know, I know," she says. "But you were busy with the snow bats, and I thought I could handle it on my own. Anyway, they've been digging around, trying to figure out what I'm up to." She sighs. "I guess they realized I had a body double."

Malcolm white knuckles the handle of his glass. "A what?"

"Never mind. It doesn't matter."

Malcolm doesn't respond, just thousand-yard-stares into his beer. Pearly feels guilty, but she knows she needs to turn this around. She adopts the same tactic she used on Abathur. "Malcolm, please," she says. "Just give me one more chance. This 'Save the Café' event—if I can pull it off, it could really change things for Hannah, Sam and Danielle. I've worked too hard to let them down now...and besides, I'm hosting the event, so if I don't show up, they're fucked."

Malcolm hesitates. He has every reason not to trust her. Would she trust him if it was the other way around? She'd like to think so, but she's more impulsive than he is. "Alright," he says. "But this is it, Pearly. If you screw this up, I won't be able to protect you from the Higher-Ups. Or your co-workers."

Pearly nods. "I won't screw it up," she says. "I promise."

Malcolm drains his pint, stands. "I hope that's true – for both our sakes."

His words echo in her mind as he exits the bar, leaving her to figure out how on Earth she's going to get herself out of this one...

***

Think, Pearly, think.

Pearly's back at the kitchen table, the surface almost buried under a sea of case files, hastily scribbled notes, and half-empty coffee cups. She begins to type ideas into her tablet—each one more desperate and convoluted than the last.

Like, what if she temporarily swapped her charges' souls into each other's bodies? If they experienced each other's struggles firsthand, they could have huge breakthroughs in empathy and understanding. But what if she got Recycled anyway, and they never got swapped back? Or what if they liked their new bodies too much to switch back?

Maybe she could create a time loop in the café? Force her charges to relive the same day over and over until they achieve personal breakthroughs? The more she thinks about it, the more she realizes trapping them in a never-ending loop might actually drive them insane. Plus, there would be the small issue of breaking the loop once they've learned their lessons...and of course, the damage to the space-time continuum...

You're being ridiculous, Miss Thing.

As the minutes tick by, her frustration grows and no solutions magically appear. Pearly tosses aside the tablet in frustration. She's running out of options. And time. And hope.

Suddenly, the door flings open, and Dumb Pearly sashays through in her hazmat suit.

"Jeez, Dumb Pearly! You scared the glitter out of me!" Pearly clutches her chest.

Unfazed, Dumb Pearly marches over to the desk, glancing at the mess of papers and notes. "What in the name of tacky, girl?"

Pearly watches as Dumb Pearly picks up one of her discarded print-outs, squinting at it like it's written in a foreign language. "People are mad at me," says Pearly. "I fucked up, and I'm trying to fix things. But nothing's working, and it's driving me nuts!"

Dumb Pearly nods, gives the corner of the page a thoughtful nibble.

Pearly slumps back on the sofa. "I know, I know. But what else am I supposed to do? Malcolm's breathing down my neck, Hertz and Abathur are watching, and probably the Higher-Ups too. If I don't figure this out, I'm toast."

Dumb Pearly rolls her eyes, tossing the notes onto the ground. "You gotta sissy that walk."

Pearly glares at her double, frustration bubbling up. "And how exactly do I do that?"

Dumb Pearly fixes her gaze on the original, and for a moment Pearly swears she sees the deepest, wisest part of herself reflected back.

"Tell the truth!"

Pearly freezes. The simplicity hits her like a ton of bricks, and it's exactly what she needed to hear. Her counterpart isn't much different from a newborn soul – she has that same innocence, that same unclouded view of life. The truth? It's daring. It's brave. It's so dumb, it's genius.

THIRTY-EIGHT

P early catches her reflection in Thunderbolt's front window. She looks less frazzled than the last time she was
here, but no less determined. Taped to the window is one of the
event flyers with a handwritten message across the top: "Moonshine Revival Gala – Tonight!" Pearly remembers handing out
those flyers just last week. Back when everything was under
control, or at least under the illusion of control.

She takes a deep breath and pushes open the door. The café
is closed for the day – the staff needs to prep for the gala. It
looks like it's going well, with everyone engaged in last minute
tasks. No one even looks up when Pearly enters.

Danielle's at the back counter unloading trays of hors d'oeuvres from insulated carriers. Hannah's up front repairing the
damage from Ruby's outburst, putting feathers and pearls back
into centerpieces. A broom and dustpan sit beside her, filled
with shards of glass from the popped bulbs. Sam's at a table
in the back, typing away, probably revising his tribute speech
for Ruby. The ghost of honor isn't present. Maybe she's still
embarrassed about what happened yesterday.

As Pearly steps further into the café, she spots Charlie grabbing their coat from the hook by the door. "Running a quick errand," they say. "Back soon." It's hard to tell from their expression if Hannah told them anything about yesterday's conversation, so Pearly just nods. It's actually perfect timing. Pearly needs to talk her charges – alone.

She clears her throat to get their attention. "Hannah, Danielle, Sam. Would you mind if we, uh, all sat down for a minute. There's something I have to say – to all of you."

No one's jumping up, but Pearly didn't expect that. Sam is the first to move, smacking his laptop closed. Danielle and Hannah exchange a glance before following suit, taking seats beside Sam and Pearly around a table.

Now that the moment has arrived, Pearly feels a knot form in her stomach. She's better at roasts than serious speeches.

"First," she says, "I want to thank you. You've all worked so hard to make this night happen. But before we step on that stage, there's something I need to tell you." She sighs. "Something I should have told you a long time ago."

Her charges all look at one another, and Pearly feels like a silent decision is being made.

"We're listening," says Hannah.

"Okay. Thank you." Pearly takes a deep breath. "So...I haven't been completely honest with you. About who I am, and why I'm here. The thing is, I'm not really a psychic. I'm actually something, well...more."

Sam looks surprised, while Danielle and Hannah just look confused.

Pearly ignores her pounding heart and presses on. "I'm a spirit guide," she says. "My job is to help souls—people—you, specifically—navigate the challenges in their lives."

"A spirit guide?" says Danielle. "You mean like a guardian angel?" She doesn't look totally weirded out. Pearly guesses it's not such a far stretch for someone who's already into psychics and tarot cards.

"Not exactly," says Pearly. "I don't grant wishes or perform miracles. That's more the fairy godmother department. My role is to guide you through hard times, to help you find your way. But I guess I haven't done a great job of that. I know I've let you down."

Danielle frowns. "Why didn't you tell us this before? Why pretend to be a psychic?"

Pearly sighs. "I didn't tell you because I'm not supposed to. There's a guidebook, and revealing our true identities is, like, one of the most important things they tell you *not* to do. But I couldn't just sit back and give you subtle nudges. Actually, I tried,"—she looks at Hannah—"but it didn't work. So I decided to do things my way." She takes her hands out of her lap and lays them flat on the table – showing her cards. "The other thing is, I kind of made a deal with this guy Malcolm—he's your real guide. I convinced him to let me sub for him while he went on vacation. I thought I could prove myself. But I got caught up in trying to fix things my way, and I lost sight of what really mattered."

Hannah scoffs, crosses her arms. "A spirit guide? Really? I don't know, Pearly. This is pretty hard to buy."

Sam clears his throat. "She's...actually telling the truth."

Hannah turns to Sam, eyes narrowing. "And how would you know?"

"Because she can do things," he says. "Things that no ordinary person could do. I've seen her when she was invisible. No one else in the room, not even my oncologist, could see her. I could—but only 'cause I'm on the brink of death." He shrugs. "Oh, and she teleported me into the 1920s, or at least some kind of simulation. It was wild. Anyway, she's not perfect, but she's not lying either."

Pearly's grateful for Sam's support, but Hannah still looks dubious. Pearly's going to have to do some bippity-boppity-boo to prove herself. She looks at the table, focusing on a spoon until it begins to shimmer. It twists and turns like it's possessed, then grows points and transforms into a fork.

Danielle gasps. "Wicked."

Hannah blinks at the fork, closes her jaw. "Okay," she concedes, "so you're a spirit guide. But that doesn't mean you're a good one."

"You're right," says Pearly. "I've been a shit guide, and I'm so, so sorry. But I'm here to ask for a second chance. Look, I don't know if it matters to you, but there's a reason I needed to redeem myself. A reason I got assigned a crappy job in the afterlife. I made a mistake."

This is new information even for Sam. "What kind of mistake?" he asks.

Pearly's jaw tenses. She hasn't processed this with anyone – not even Thunder. He wanted to, but it was just too painful. "In my last life," she says, "I was a drag queen. My birth name was Isaiah, but everybody called me by my drag name, Pearly Gates..."

***

Chicago, 2009

Club Berlin is packed, with an eclectic crowd mingling under the pulsating lights and flashing strobes. In the corner, a DJ spins a mix of 80s new wave, house, and pop. The sound system is state-of-the-art for the time, filling the space with a thump-thump-thump that vibrates through the bodies packed onto the dance floor. The crowd is a sea of vibrant colors and textures—sequined dresses, leather jackets, neon wigs, fishnet stockings—anything goes.

Pearly's backstage, applying the finishing touches to her makeup. She's giving Space Queen in a floor-length purple sequined gown with huge angular shoulders, and an enormous metallic wig. She grins at herself in the mirror and waits for her cue.

The crowd erupts as Chaka Khan's voice fills the room. The track builds, and Pearly gives it everything she's got. She is so every woman. The words, the moves, the emotion – she is more Chaka Khan than Chaka Khan.

Pearly casts a spell. The crowd is mesmerized by her, their cheers growing louder with each chorus.

In the audience, Thunder – Andrew, in this life – stands near the front, eyes glued to Pearly. He's wearing a red velvet blazer over a black mesh shirt, offering just a glimpse of the tattoos on his chest—most of them tributes to his love for Pearly. They make eye contact, and for a moment, the rest of the world fades away.

The song hits a crescendo, and Pearly brings the house down. She basks in the crowd's adoration – ooh, she feels so utterly alive!

After the performance, she makes her way backstage, still riding the high of the show. Andrew wraps her in a hug and lifts her off the ground.

"You," he says, "are a wonder. Every time you perform, you just get better and better."

Pearly grins, smudging her mascara as she brushes his neck. "You might be a little biased."

"Yeah." He leans in to kiss her. "But that doesn't make it any less true."

Pearly takes off her heels, wincing as she rubs her sore feet, and Andrew kneels down to massage them. They spend a few moments winding down in the dressing room, talking about their future—plans for the next big show, maybe even taking her act on the road.

The cold November air hits them as they leave the club, whipping through the streets and carrying the threat of impending snow. The ground is slick with a layer of almost-frost – the kind that's easy to slip on, even easier in heels. They walk hand in hand, still buzzing – until they turn a corner.

A group of sketchy-looking guys in dark hoodies hangs around an alley. They smirk as they spot Pearly, still in drag. One of them leans forward, a skinny guy with a scruffy beard. "What's this?" He stubs out a cigarette. "A little late-night show?"

Pearly lowers her gaze. "Just ignore them," she whispers.

But the men refuse to be ignored. "Where do you think you're going?" says Skinny, blocking their path. "We're just trying to have some fun. Isn't that what you 'ladies' like to do—have fun?"

Andrew's jaw tightens, but he stays calm. "Hey man, we're just passing through."

One of the men sneers, coming up close to Pearly. "What's the rush? Didn't your mama teach you about sharing?"

Andrew moves in front of Pearly, shielding her. "Look, we don't want any trouble. Just let us pass, okay?"

For a moment, it seems like they might actually back off. But then one of them lunges forward and it all becomes a blur. Pearly senses Andrew moving in front of her — then a scuffle — then a sickening thud. Pearly's heart stops as she sees Andrew stagger, his hand clutching his side.

"Andrew!" Pearly catches him as he sinks onto the sidewalk. She holds his head in her lap. His face is so pale — scary pale — and when she looks down, she sees the dark stain spreading across his shirt.

"No, no, no," Pearly pleads, as the blood seeps through her fingers. "Stay with me." The men scatter, but Pearly barely pays attention. Andrew's breaths come in ragged gasps. His grip on her hand is weakening.

Someone in a nearby building leans out a window as she fumbles for her phone. "I'm calling 911!" She hears the distant wail of sirens, but Pearly knows they won't get here in time. They could never get here in time. Tears blur her vision as she clutches Andrew's body, feeling his life slipping away.

"I'm here," she whispers. "I'm here. Please, don't leave me..."

Andrew tries to speak, but no words come. His hand clenches around hers. And then he's gone.

***

Pearly forces herself back to the present. She swallows hard. It still hurts. Even after all these years—all these lives. It still hurts.

"I couldn't live with the guilt," she says. "After Andrew died, nothing was the same. I kept telling myself that if I'd just been stronger, braver...if I'd done something to protect him, maybe...maybe he'd still be here."

She pauses, eyes glassy as the memories threaten to pull her under again. "I tried to keep going," she says. "To keep perform-ing. But every time I stepped on that stage, I saw his face. The pain, the loneliness, it haunted me. I thought I could handle it, that I could push through, but I was spiraling. The pills—they were just supposed to help me sleep, to take the edge off, you know? But one night, after too much tossing and turning, and a few too many drinks, I took more than I should have. Maybe deep down, I didn't care if I woke up."

She lets out a shaky breath. "And I did wake up—only it wasn't in Chicago. As soon as I crossed over, it all came flooding back. I remembered everything—who I really was, who I had been, and all the lives I've lived. I got assigned to Waste Management after that. I thought it was a punishment, and I swore I'd get out of it. And, well, that's how I ended up here, with you. I wanted a chance to prove that I could help others in a way I couldn't help myself."

Pearly exhales, waiting to see how her confession lands. A bit of the weight has been lifted. Even if they still hate her, she came clean.

Danielle is the first to speak. "That must have been so painful," she says. "Losing someone like that, and then...everything that came after. I can't even imagine."

Pearly nods.

Hannah meets Pearly's gaze. "I'm sorry that happened to you," she says. "I can see why you'd want to help us. But you have to understand, it's hard for us – for me anyway – to trust you after everything that's gone down." That makes sense. Hannah's the one Pearly hurt the most.

"About that," Pearly winces. "There's one other thing I should tell you. Charlie — was Andrew. Was my soulmate, for a long time. But they're not anymore. And I have to accept that."

Pearly glances at Hannah, who looks stunned. Not surprising – that was quite the admission. "I don't expect everything just to go back to normal," Pearly says. "But I still want to earn your trust back, and I still want to help you – if you'll give me a chance."

"We've come this far," says Danielle. "I'm willing to give her that chance."

"Me too," says Sam.

Hannah picks up the spoon-turned-fork, running it between her fingers as she considers Pearly's proposal. Eventually, she sighs. "Alright," she says. "Let's do it." She glances at the wall clock. "The truth is, we need you. You're our MC. It'll all fall apart without you—and Charlie will suffer the consequences. So for now,"—she places her hand on the table—"we're a team."

One by one, the others place their hands on top of Hannah's. Pearly hesitates for just a moment before putting her hand on the pile. The gesture fills her with a gratitude she hadn't expected – for the grace of her charges. And for the chance to make something beautiful out of the wreckage.

THIRTY-NINE

Pearly may be out of Waste Management, but she's still got some messes to clean up. Starting with Danielle. She finds her in the breakroom arranging one-bite beef Wellingtons on a platter. On the counter is a silver dome with something coconutty inside, and Pearly knows there's more in the mini-fridge. Danielle glances up when Pearly enters, then returns to the hors d'ouevres. She looks a bit on edge, like she's not sure how to feel about Pearly. Pearly understands—she's not sure how to feel about herself, either.

"Those Wellingtons look amazing," says Pearly, approaching the counter. "But I have to admit, I was sad to see they don't come with galoshes."

"That would actually be kinda cute."

"Right?" Pearly moves closer, picking up a sprig of parsley to garnish the platter. "Look," she says. "I know yesterday was – well, it was a lot. And I want you to know that I'm really sorry. Not just for hiding the truth from you, but for how I pushed you into doing something you weren't comfortable with. I wasn't listening, and I overstepped."

"Yeah," says Danielle. "You did." She wipes a hand on her apron, looks up at Pearly. "I just feel like I'm being asked to be someone I'm not."

"You're right," says Pearly. "I made some assumptions, and I projected my own experiences onto you." She finishes with the parsley and presses her hands on the counter. "In my last life, when I was struggling to come to terms with who I was – drag saved me. It was like...for the first time, everything I'd ever felt ashamed of – who I was, how I loved, the way I expressed myself – became my superpower. And damn, was I good at it." She shakes her head. "I never had a drag daughter, and I guess I got a little over-excited. I saw all this potential in you and just wanted to see you blossom. But I think I turned into one of those crazy stage moms."

Danielle nods. "You know, despite what the media would tell you, not every trans woman wants to be a drag queen."

"I know, I know." Pearly cringes. "I'm sorry. That was stupid of me. Your journey is your own. You do you, girl."

"Thank you for saying that." Danielle sighs. "The thing is, I'm just not even sure what 'me' is. That's what's scaring me about the performance, as much as your ridiculous routine."

"Tell you what," says Pearly. "What if we simplified things? Cut the complex choreo – just do what feels good."

Danielle's shoulders relax. "Yeah? You don't think Ruby would mind?"

"Hell, no! I think Ruby's over the moon just to be honored. No one expects you to be some master of burlesque – or drag. You don't have to be perfect. You just have to be you."

Danielle hesitates, shifting the Wellingtons around the platter, trying to arrange her way to decision. "Okay," she says. "I'm in. But if I'm really doing me, don't be shocked if I swap the evening gloves for oven mitts."

Pearly laughs out loud. "That would be epic. Gotta make sure someone's getting video."

As they finish arranging the food, Pearly glances at Danielle. "So...have you thought any more about the apprenticeship interview?"

Danielle heads to the sink to wash her hands. "I have, but... honestly, it still scares me. It's such a big step. I mean, I've never even been to Europe."

Pearly sets down the parsley, turning to face her. "I think you'll love it – you'll finally have a place to wear all those hats! And, hey, it's okay to be scared. This is a big step. Maybe just take one at a time, starting with tonight."

Danielle smiles, a little more confident this time. "Okay, Pearly. One step at a time."

***

Next up, Hannah. She's at the front of the café, working to replace the shattered bulbs of the string lights. As much as Pearly would like to intrude on Hannah's thoughts to help her figure out how to handle this, it doesn't feel respectful after everything that happened. So she does the hard thing and opens her mouth without knowing if she's about to put her foot in it.

"Hannah," says Pearly. "We should talk."

Hannah doesn't look up. She unscrews a cracked bulb and sets it on the table next to the others. "Ever since you dropped the bombshell," she says. "I've been thinking about you and Charlie. Obsessing, if I'm honest. And now, after what you told us..." She finally meets Pearly's gaze. "Look. Maybe you should tell Charlie the truth—"

"Hannah, no—"

"Just hear me out. If they knew who you really were, it would clear up the confusion and help them understand why they've been pulling away from me."

Pearly shakes her head. "Trust me. It's better if Charlie doesn't know." She takes a deep breath, exhales. "As hard as it is to swallow, I'm learning that sometimes loving someone means letting them go."

"But isn't it kind of important?" says Hannah. "If Charlie knew that you've been soulmates in so many lifetimes..." She retreats inward, wraps her arms around herself. "Maybe they'd decide, you know, that they're better off with you."

Pearly's heart aches, for herself and for Hannah. *How many asshole guides does it take to screw in a lightbulb?* Then she thinks about the newborn soul in the Nursery, and it strengthens her resolve. "Real love isn't about clinging to what was," she says, "or forcing someone to relive a past they're not meant to remember. It's about letting them find their own way, even if that takes them away from you."

"But what about me?" Hannah says. "I don't want to be anyone's second choice. If Charlie still has feelings for you, if they're meant to be with you, then I'm just some backup option."

Pearly sets down the bulb she's been holding and turns to face Hannah. "Hannah, you're not a backup option. I've seen the way Charlie looks at you. There's something real between you two, something that deserves to be explored."

She pauses. There's still one thing she hasn't told Hannah. The most painful thing. The most embarrassing thing. But she deserves to know. "After our last life together," Pearly says, "it wasn't just death that separated us. Thunder – Charlie – left me. They moved on because I couldn't. I was clinging to what we had. So Thunder cut the cord."

Pearly swallows hard. "Letting go isn't easy, but I have to do it. For Charlie's sake, for yours – and for my own. I can't make the same mistake twice. I need to step aside and let them find their own path. And I'm pretty damn sure that path leads to you."

Hannah looks up at Pearly, choking back tears. "You really think so?"

"I do."

Hannah nods. They continue replacing the bulbs, but Pearly senses that telling Hannah isn't enough. Hannah needs to feel that Charlie is genuinely choosing her, with her whole heart – and that needs to come from Charlie.

As she mulls it over, an idea begins to take shape, a way to bring Hannah and Charlie together without upending everything all over again. It'll require a delicate touch, which isn't exactly Pearly's specialty — but if she can pull this off, she's pretty sure even Thunder would be impressed.

Forty

Pearly steps outside, trying to give herself a break from the guilt parade. But no such luck – there's Charlie, unloading bags of ice from their truck. And worst of all, they look so sexy doing it. Charlie glances over, then gets back to it. But their hands are shaking. *Come on, Pearly, get your shit together.* It's too easy to linger on "what ifs" and "could've beens."

"Hey, Charlie," she says. Charlie puts down the bag and looks back. "I, uh. I wanted to apologize. For what happened. For the, uh...well, the kiss. I was way out of line."

Charlie wipes their hands on their pants. "What the fuck did happen? I'm still trying to wrap my head around it."

Pearly takes a deep breath. "I can't speak for you, but I've been feeling – I don't know, a vibe between us. I thought I could just ignore it, but as you saw the other day, that didn't work out too well. The thing is..." She tries to choose her words carefully, deciding how much truth is too much. "You remind me a lot of someone from my past. And I don't think I've a done a good job separating my feelings for that person from my feelings for you. I got all twisted up, and I crossed a boundary I swore I'd uphold. It wasn't fair to Hannah, and it's not fair to you."

"Honestly, it was super confusing." A chunk of hair falls over Charlie's eyes, and Pearly has to restrain herself from not brushing it back. "I mean, I really want to be with Hannah. We're good together."

"Yes!" says Pearly. "You are. Everyone can see it."

"But..." Charlie rubs their face, as if they're trying to remember a dream. "When you kissed me, I felt something too. I didn't think it was...well, I didn't know what it was. It was like – I don't know, like we have this deep connection. I care about you, Pearly, in ways that I don't totally understand."

"I care about you too," Pearly says, fighting the constriction in her throat. "But maybe we don't have to understand it all. Hannah is your present and your future, and she's what you need. Not...whatever this is between us."

Charlie nods. Their face softens. "I do really like Hannah," they admit. "But I don't know that I've done a great job of showing it lately."

Yaaaaas, queen! Just the opening Pearly was hoping for. "I think you're right. Hannah deserves to know she's the most important person in your life. And tonight could be the perfect opportunity to show her. I'm talking about a romantic gesture – something swoon-worthy, you know? It doesn't have to be anything big. Just something that shows her she matters to you, something that connects you."

Charlie leans against a bag of ice, thinking. "Something that connects us..."

Pearly grins, a little sparkle in her eyes. "You've got this. You and Hannah share something special. I'm sure the perfect gesture will find its way to you."

Charlie's face brightens a bit. "Yeah, yeah, I may have an idea." Pearly can't help but feel a tiny surge of satisfaction. Maybe she's finally perfected the art of the "gentle nudge."

***

Pearly finds Sam behind a feather-and-pearl centerpiece at a table in the back of the café. His laptop is open in front of him, the screen reflecting the furrow in his brow as he types, then pauses, his fingers hovering uncertainly over the keys. She takes a deep breath, marches over, and sits down next to him. When he finally looks up, his eyes meet hers, but there's a distance there—a guardedness she's seeing a little too often for her comfort. His arms are crossed, his posture defensive, as if bracing himself for another blow.

Pearly hesitates, then decides she might as well just go for it. "Holmes," she says. "This is my last stop on the official apology tour. Saving the best for last."

He doesn't respond, but he does look up. God, he looks tired.

Pearly forces herself to meet his gaze. After her win with Charlie, she thought this might be easier. "I'm starting to feel like one of those canceled celebrities," she says. "Only without the fame, which really adds to the sting."

Sam's lips twitch, but he fights back a smile. "That's too bad," he says. "I would've liked to see some tragic meme."

Pearly smiles. She rests her hands on the table, considering her approach. The chair creaks under her as she shifts her weight. "I know you feel betrayed, Sam. And I understand. I underestimated my capacity as a guide, and I failed you when you needed me most. It was stupid and irresponsible. I should've told you about Malcolm from the start. I guess I just thought – I mean, you were already on the fence about having a guide. I figured if I told you I was just a temp, you'd have told me to fuck all the way off." She smiles. "Which you kind of did anyway."

"Not that you listened," he mumbles.

"You're right," she says. "I didn't listen. Maybe Malcolm would've listened." She leans in. "Actually, Malcolm wouldn't have interfered at all. He doesn't believe in direct intervention. But can I ask you something? Do you think you'd have been better off that way? Because I'm pretty sure if I hadn't dragged your ass out of the house you'd still be alone in your apartment playing Mario Kart instead of earning your chops as a detective and making new friends and maybe even falling in love with a ghost."

He leans back. "I can see your point."

"Okay," she says, relaxing slightly. "Good."

"But I wish you'd trusted me enough to tell me the truth."

"You're right," she sighs. "I should've trusted you. I was just scared."

He closes the laptop and nods. "Yeah, I'm scared too. I'm dying." He picks up a napkin and crumples it in his palm. "Why do you think Ruby's still here?" Pearly blinks, jarred by the change of subject. "We brought her back to the Moonshine Lounge, got to see her doing her thing. We even made new, happy memories there. Shouldn't that have, like, unshackled her? That's how it works in TV shows."

The question had occurred to Pearly too, but she hadn't had time to dwell on it. "I don't know," she admits. "I guess that isn't what she needed. Maybe tonight – your tribute – will be the key."

"Maybe," he says. "I'm just…" His voice cracks, and he quickly looks away, blinking back tears. "I'm running out of time, Pearly. To do something that makes a difference. To leave something behind."

His admission hangs heavy in the air. Pearly wants to offer comfort, but she knows words alone won't be enough. Instead, she sits in silence, wishing she did have the power to perform miracles.

"Sam." She reaches across the table, takes his hand. "I can't pretend to know what it's like to be in your shoes, to be facing what you're facing. But I do know that you've already made a difference. Just by being here, by caring, by becoming part of this community. That might not seem like a lot to you, but I'm coming to realize that the things I thought were important are superficial at best. It's not about what you do. It's about who you are, and how you love." She squeezes his hand. "I think you're a great man, Sam Garcia – and I'm not even your real guide, so I don't have to bullshit you."

This time he does laugh, even as he's wiping his tears. "Okay, okay, whatever." He reaches for his laptop. "Now will you scram already, Holmes? I gotta finish this tribute."

Pearly smiles, pushes back her chair. "You got it, Holmes."

Forty-One

Pearly Gates does not get stage fright. Then again, she's never performed with her ass – check that, her soul – on the line. As she peeks out from behind the curtain, she's pleased to see the space is packed. Guests decked out as flappers, gangsters, old-school aristocrats – even a Charlie Chaplin! – sit at tables surrounding the stage, sipping champagne and eating Danielle's hors d'ouevres. The servers keep going back for refills on deviled eggs and coconut layer cake — apparently, they're both smash hits.

Pearly notices Ruby, the guest of honor, drifting through the room, blending in perfectly in her burlesque costume. She floats over to Sam and hover-sits beside him. He smiles, as always comforted by her presence. But he looks almost as pale as the ghost. It worries Pearly.

She takes a breath to steady herself. This is it, Miss Thing. Tonight isn't just about putting on a show or even saving the café. It is all that, but it's also about proving to herself and her charges that she deserves another chance. She wishes Thunder could be here. Well, technically, he already is. He just doesn't know it.

Pearly glances at Charlie, standing near the back in a tailored suit with a velvet burgundy jacket and art deco tie. They fidget with the edge of the jacket. When they see Pearly, they smile, like they're trying to reassure both Pearly and themselves that the night will be a success. Pearly smiles back. She hopes she looks more confident than she feels.

A rustle from the side of the stage catches Pearly's attention. Danielle and Hannah are waiting in the wings in their period costumes. They both look nervous – especially Danielle, who keeps adjusting her corset. Pearly tries to catch her eye, but Danielle is off in her own world.

A tap on Pearly's shoulder—she spins around to find Malcolm standing in front of her in a midnight blue tuxedo and matching bow tie. Pearly's heart races. "Malcolm?" she whisper-shouts. "What are you doing here?!"

"Well," he says, "you told me it all came down to tonight. And my report's due tomorrow. I wanted to see for myself how you're handling things." He glances around the room. "Quite the little shindig."

"Yeah, well, you know me. Can't resist a good party."

"I know...just remember, Pearly, this is about making good on your promises as a guide."

Before Pearly can respond, she notices movement at the entrance. Her stomach drops as she spots Hertz and Abathur slipping into the room. They're dressed like 1920s coppers in trench coats and fedoras. Hertz is even slapping a billy club against his palm. They may have taken up the theme, but Pearly knows this is no casual visit.

"Oh shit," she says. Didn't Abathur tell her she had until after the gala? Maybe he couldn't hold back the Higher-Ups any longer. But why are they just standing there? Are they going to make a big, splashy arrest in the middle of the show? Or are they actually interested in what she's done as a guide?

Malcolm follows her gaze, tensing up as soon as he sees who she's looking at. "That's them, isn't it? The guys who've been following you?" He pulls at the collar of his robe.

Pearly nods. "Just act natural, Malcolm. Go sit down. We can't afford to draw any attention."

Malcolm heads to the front row. As the lights dim, Pearly takes one last glance at Hertz and Abathur. They don't seem to be moving toward her.

Pearly smooths her silver sequined gown, making sure the long glittering train isn't twisted on the floor. She's paired the dress with a massive crystal-and-pearl headpiece that sits on a wig of long sculpted waves. She takes a breath and straightens her shoulders.

Showtime.

She parts the curtain and steps onto the stage. The room hushes, all eyes on her. Pearly swallows. Then a smile spreads across her face. "Hello, gorgeous people," she says. "Welcome to the Moonshine Revival Gala!"

Applause erupts, and Pearly lets it wash over her. She's in her element now, anxiety melting away as she takes command of the room. "I have to say," she says, "you all clean up so well, I hardly recognized you! But that's what tonight is all about, isn't it? A chance to step back in time to a world where the champagne flowed freely, the music never stopped, and everyone knew how to have a damn good time."

Laughter ripples through the audience. This is what Pearly lives for—the connection, the thrill of holding a crowd in the palm of her hand. She glances back at Hertz and Abathur. This could be my last day of existence, she thinks. Better make it count.

"But we're not just here to revel in the past," she says. "We're here to have to a historically good time. So drink up, bid high, and let's make it one for the history books!"

This time Pearly lets the applause linger before going on. "I promise you, we have quite the lineup for you tonight—performances that will make you laugh, cry, and maybe even blush. As for the rest, well—you'll just have to wait and see, won't you? First up, we have a real treat for you. Please welcome the dazzling, the delightful, Professor Hannah Cohen-Jones!"

Pearly steps off the stage and sits in the front row next to Malcolm, who's fidgeting with his bow tie. "Where are they?" he whispers, as his leg bounces against his chair. "Have they moved?"

"Nope," she says. "Still standing there, just...waiting."

Hannah steps onto the stage in her flapper dress. The fringe sways with her movements, and the feathered headband adds the perfect touch of 1920s flair. She beams at the crowd. Out of all Pearly's charges, Hannah is most used to being on stage – though granted, not in fishnets.

"Good evening, everyone!" she begins. "Now, I know you're here for a good time, so I promise I'll keep the lecture short. Let's set the scene, shall we?" A blue spotlight hits the stage, along with the sound of a generic, jazzy trumpet. "The people of the 1920s were living in the aftermath of a world turned upside down—music, fashion, laws, labor, and just about everything else was all topsy-turvy. And smack dab in the middle of it all? Flappers. They didn't just raise their hemlines and chop off their hair. They broke the rules, they challenged social norms, and they had a hell of a time doing it." She winks at the crowd, getting a few chuckles. "But enough talk—let's bring a little of that spirit to life, shall we? If you know the words, I expect you to sing along."

The jazzy intro to "Minnie the Moocher" fills the room. Hannah launches into the song — not too shabby for a sociology professor. The audience joins in on the call-and-response, hi-de-hi-de-hi-ing and ho-de-ho-de-ho-ing.

Pearly steals another glance at Hertz and Abathur—they're still at the back, their expressions unreadable in the dim light. As the song builds to its final chorus, the crowd belts out the callbacks with gusto. When Hannah finishes, the room erupts in applause. Pearly wishes Theo could have seen this – he'd have loved it.

Hannah takes a bow and leaves the stage. Pearly gives her a quick hug as they pass. "Thank you, Professor Hannah, for taking us to the Cotton Club. Now, who's ready to keep this party going?"

The night continues with all kinds of performances, from a barbershop quartet to a local tap-dancing troupe to a comedian with a creepy ventriloquist dummy. The crowd eats it up.

After a few more acts come and go, Pearly steps back onstage. "And now, my darling-est little darlings—let's welcome to the stage the sensational, the stunning, the razzle and the dazzle, the one and only...Danielle!"

As the applause begins, Pearly catches Danielle's eye from the side of the stage. Pearly wishes she could beam all her feelings straight into Danielle's soul, all her apologies for pushing her too hard, all her confidence in how much she's gonna kill it. But she can't—well, at least not now. It'd be too distracting. But Danielle seems to understand anyway, and blows her guide a kiss. She looks stunning, but more than that—she looks ready.

Madonna starts to sing about fever. Danielle is *on* from the very first note, slinking down the stage, magnetic and playful and sultry, working the crowd with her eyes.

Malcolm leans in. "Hey, could you check on your, uh, your co-workers?" he whispers. "I don't want to risk being obvious, but I'm, like, kind of freaking out here."

Pearly casts the subtlest glance she can muster to the back of the room. Yup—they're both still standing there. For a moment, Abathur catches her eye—so she turns back to Malcolm. "They're clapping politely," she says. "But I can't tell if they mean it."

Time for the flashy part—the striptease. Danielle hesitates for the briefest moment, and Pearly silently urges her on. Then Danielle pulls off the jacket with a flourish, revealing the stunning burlesque costume underneath.

Yaaaaaas, girl!

Pearly catches a glimpse of Ruby floating nearby. She too looks proud, and excited, and a little bit wistful.

"Wow," Malcolm whispers. "She's really good. And her aura is glowing. Never imagined I'd see her doing anything like this, Pearly. You really stepped up."

Pearly smiles, feeling at least a little bit vindicated. "She did all the hard work."

Pearly feels the tension ease from her own shoulders as Danielle finishes, striking a final, bold pose. The room erupts into applause, with whistles and "bravos" and even a standing ovation. Hank claps the loudest. "That's my kid!" he shouts. "Wooooooo!"

Danielle catches Pearly's eye and subtly gestures to a young man near the front holding a bouquet of flowers. Must be Travis, the guy Danielle mentioned she'd been talking to. Pearly gives Danielle a thumbs up.

After the energy settles, the focus shifts to the auction. Pearly steps back from the stage, her attention now divided between the smooth-talking auctioneer and the collection of items up for sale – many of them finds from her basement digging with Sam. Guests raise their paddles and bidding wars ensue. As the final item is sold, the auctioneer steps back, and Charlie steps forward.

"Thank you all for your generous contributions," Charlie says. "Tonight's gala has been more than just a fundraiser—it's been a reminder of how much we all mean to each other. We've raised a significant amount of money to help keep this place—this community—alive. And that wouldn't have been possible without all of you—but...but..." Charlie tries to continue through the applause, but it's too loud. So they let themselves bask in it until it dies down. "But—there's one more person I'd like to thank."

The room quiets as Charlie scans the crowd. "Hannah," they say, "could you join me up here?"

Hannah looks surprised, but she gets up from her seat. Charlie meets her halfway, taking her hand as they guide her to the center of the stage.

"Tonight," says Charlie, "we've talked a lot about history—about preserving the past while building a future. And in doing so, I realized that there's someone who has been by my side through all of this – someone who's become my rock, my inspiration."

Charlie reaches into their pocket and pulls out the skeleton key. They hold it up for the audience to see, then turn back to Hannah.

"This key," says Charlie, "was once used to unlock the doors to a speakeasy that operated right here, in this very café. It's a piece of history that's been hidden away, just like so many parts of this place. It's a symbol of the doors we can only open together."

Hannah's eyes glisten as she listens.

Charlie steps closer, taking Hannah's hand and placing the key in her palm. "Hannah, you've already unlocked parts of my life I didn't even know were closed off. You know, back in high school, I always thought if I could just beat you at something—*anything*—I'd finally feel like I'd won. But standing here now, I realize that the real victory was finding someone who could challenge me, push me, and make me a better person. Even if you *did* steal that valedictorian title."

Laughter ripples through the audience.

"This key is just a small token," says Charlie, "but it represents everything we've started building together and everything I hope we'll continue to grow. Let's keep unlocking new doors—together."

Tears shimmer in Hannah's eyes as she looks at the key, then back at Charlie. "Thank you," she says. "You're opening parts of me too – parts I thought were locked forever."

Charlie leans in, their foreheads touching as they share a tender moment.

The audience breaks into applause. Charlie and Hannah exchange a soft, lingering kiss.

Of course, a part of Pearly wants to be the one on that stage, the one who makes the whole room go wild. But she's committed to putting the higher good above her own self-interest. And she has to admit – it doesn't feel terrible. Not great, but not terrible. As her chest expands and her grip loosens, she's actually happy that Thunder is finding love in this lifetime. She cares about him enough to want the best for him. Even if that doesn't include her.

"I don't know how you did it," Malcolm marvels, blowing his nose on a handkerchief. "I thought she'd never get past Theo." Pearly smiles, hoping Malcolm doesn't go bowling for a while.

As the evening winds down, the crowd quiets in anticipation for the final act. The stage is set for Sam's tribute. A large portrait of Ruby graces the backdrop. A single spotlight shines on Sam, who stands at the microphone in his top hat and vest, rouge concealing the pallor of his face. He glances at the portrait, then at Ruby herself, who "sits" in the front row.

"Knock 'em dead, handsome," she says, blowing him a kiss. He blushes, almost dropping the mic. After a quick recovery, he clears his throat.

"Good evening, everyone," he says. "Tonight, I want to a share a tribute to someone who's no longer with us, but whose spirit still resonates in this room. I know it seems strange to say, but this person means a lot to me. I'm talking about Ruby LaRue, the luminous star of the Moonshine Lounge."

A hush falls over the crowd. All Pearly can do is hope that Hertz and Abathur have the courtesy to wait for Sam to finish before they cart her away. *Please,* she prays, *just let him have this moment.*

Sam gestures to the portrait behind him. "Ruby poured every ounce of herself into her craft. She did it for the same reasons that so many artists do—but most of all, she performed because it made her feel alive. It made her feel like herself. And this is the place where her soul belonged."

He turns to the audience. "But Ruby wasn't just a burlesque star. She was a woman who faced the world head-on. Born into a time of segregation, where opportunities for a Black woman were painfully few, Ruby grew up in Chicago's South Side, surrounded by the struggles of her community. But she didn't let those struggles define her. She found joy in the jazz scene and strength in daydreams—dreams of being something more, of breaking free from the barriers around her."

Sam looks at Ruby, speaking as much to her as about her. "Ruby's childhood was difficult and lonely," he says. "But instead of letting that isolation break her, she used it to fuel her ambition. She taught herself to dance in the alleys of her neighborhood, and snuck into jazz clubs every chance she got. Eventually, she got noticed and her career took off. And though she became Ruby LaRue, the burlesque sensation—underneath, she was still Ruby Mae Davis, the little girl with the braids clutching the red paper fan. She was bold, yes, but also tender in her vulnerability, hoping to be seen beyond the glitz and the glamour."

Ruby's outline shimmers. The raw sincerity of Sam's words seems to reach through the veil, touching something deep within her. Hertz and Abathur haven't moved from their perch, waiting to do whatever they're going to do to flush Pearly's life down the drain. But even with her colleagues out to get her, everything feels worth it. Everything.

Malcolm smiles at Pearly. She hopes he can see that she gets it now – what it really means to be a guide.

"In her final days," says Sam, "Ruby battled not only illness but the deep ache of a dream unfulfilled. She never got to experience the recognition she deserved—not as a performer, but as a person. Yet even in her struggle, Ruby's resilience shone through." He swallows, as if he's unsure whether he wants to continue, but he does. "When I first came to Thunderbolt," he says, "I was struggling with my own sense of worth, unsure of the mark I'd leave behind. Ruby's story gave me the courage to face my own doubts – my own death – head-on. She taught me that we're more than just the roles we play, the expectations placed on us. We're all our flaws and complexities too. All our fucked-up experiences and the ways we push through them—that's what make us human. And Ruby is one of my favorite humans. So tonight, I want to honor her – not just as a star, but as the woman she was. Ruby LaRue may have been the name on the marquee, but Ruby Mae Davis was a real person. And that person deserves her place in history."

As Sam concludes his tribute, the room erupts in applause. Amid the clapping and cheering, Ruby floats onto the stage beside Sam, her hand touching his chest in an expression of gratitude, pride, and love. "Thank you for seeing me," she says, welling up with tears. "I feel so...complete."

Pearly watches Hertz and Abathur, finally breaking from the wall as the crowd disperses. They walk toward her with slow, deliberate steps.

This is it.

She stands her ground, heart racing. Abathur reaches her first, his angular face still set in a stern expression. "Pearly," he says, shaking his head. "I gotta admit, this isn't what I expected." He waves a hand at the room. "We came here to nail you for playing hooky, but it seems you've been playing a bigger game."

Pearly swallows hard, but before she can respond, Abathur's face softens, the sharp, fragmented lines relaxing into something more human. "And I've gotta say, you've done something beautiful here tonight."

Hertz steps up beside Abathur. His hat is pulled low, obscuring his face. Pearly's nerves spike again—he's been the wildcard all along. When Hertz finally lifts his head, he's still silent, and for a moment, the stern look remains. Then he pulls off his hat to reveal tear-streaked cheeks and red, puffy eyes.

"Geez, Pearly...that was...that was something," Hertz chokes. He quickly wipes at his face, embarrassed by his tears, but unable to stop them.

Pearly's jaw drops as she looks between the two of them. She did not expect this—not this emotional response from the two beings she was sure were here to write her final chapter. For the first time, she allows herself to hope.

"I've got some friends in high places," Abathur says, almost casually. "Old friends. I'll have a word with them. We haven't talked since the Ice Age, but I'm sure they'll remember me. Might be able to smooth things over for you if you're looking to change jobs."

Pearly can barely believe what she's hearing. "You'd do that for me?"

Abathur shrugs. "What can I say? I've weighed a lot of souls, Pearly. And you tipped the scales in your favor."

Before she can respond, Malcolm joins them, clearing his throat. "Does that mean you won't...?"

Abathur claps Malcolm on the back. "Relax, dude, you'll live longer." He chuckles at his own joke. "What happens in Eenob stays in Eenob."

Pearly lets out a breath she didn't realize she was holding. "Thank you," she says.

Abathur tips his hat. "See ya around, Pearly." He nods to Hertz, and the two turn to leave.

Now that she knows she isn't getting Recycled, the sparkle in Pearly's eye returns. "Well," she says, putting an arm around Malcolm, "I'd call that a success."

He loosens his bow tie, shakes his head. "I think I need another vacation."

FORTY-TWO

The speakeasy has all but disappeared as midnight magic transforms the carriage back into a pumpkin. That is, if "midnight magic" means "dish rags, a vacuum, and a little Nina Simone." The gala's over, and the café is quiet. Pearly's sprawled out at her favorite table as Charlie and Hannah take down the event banner. Sam sits across from her, too weak to help but enjoying the camaraderie and Ruby's graceful floating around the room. There's a lightness in her movements Pearly hasn't seen before, and the ghost's form looks more stable, with flecks of gold amidst the red in her aura.

Danielle emerges from the back room with a tray of champagne flutes. "Bubbly anyone?" she says, approaching the table. "This is the last of it, and I don't think any of us have had a chance to partake."

"Yaaassss!" Pearly sits up. "I think a celebratory toast is in order. Charlie, Hannah, get your booties over here."

The group gathers around the table, and Danielle distributes the flutes. Pearly looks into the fizz, remembering the last time she drank champagne—Thunder's award ceremony. That feels like forever ago. Is she still the same soul? Yes and no. She hasn't forgotten the past, but she no longer feels dragged down by it. And the ache in her heart is softening. It still hurts that Thunder cut the cord, but that hurt is giving way to a grounded spaciousness and contentment. Like she's clicked her heels and come home to herself.

"Pearly!" Charlie raises a glass. "I'd like to toast to you. None of this would have happened without your vision and determination. You annoyed the shit out of me sometimes, but I couldn't be more grateful. What you did for the café – for us – was, in your words, truly legendary. Thank you, sincerely, from the bottom of my heart. You really are a harvest wizard."

"To Pearly," says Hannah, raising her glass. "The harvest wizard." The others echo the toast, and Pearly gets all misty-eyed as she sips her champagne. Apparently, Malcolm was right—she's not some irredeemable failure. She's a good soul. *A good soul.* Whatever the Higher-Ups decide, this is enough for her. The thought gets her all choked up.

Sam clears his throat. His voice is low and raspy, forcing everyone to lean in. "I just want to say, these last couple of months have been...honestly, they've been the best I've ever had. Even with the cancer. I don't know, maybe because of it." He takes a long, labored breath. "But you were right, Pearly. If it hadn't been for you dragging me kicking and screaming out of my shell, none of it would've happened. I would've never gotten to know any of you. So I'm grateful, too. I was ready to throw away my life without ever realizing how precious it is. All of it. And even if the only things I leave behind are my questionable dance moves and the nightmares you had after watching *Invasion of the Body Snatchers* – it was worth it. Fuck, was it worth it."

A warmth blooms in Pearly's chest. Ruby hovers behind Sam, but something is different. The ghost glows with a luminosity so brilliant and pure, Pearly can only describe it as heavenly. It takes her breath away.

"That's not your only legacy," Ruby says, eyes shining. "Sam...you set me free. I'm not stuck anymore." He meets her gaze, and the look that passes between them melts Pearly into a puddle of goo.

"Oh my god," says Charlie, eyes bulging. "Ruby..."

Hannah picks up her jaw from the floor. "You can see her, too?"

Charlie nods, as Danielle gasps. "Oh Ruby," she says, "you're even more glorious than I imagined."

Ruby spins around, does a little curtsy. Then she clasps her hands together. "This was the best night of my afterlife. Thank you all for making it so special. I felt like I belonged somewhere for the first time. Somewhere with people who saw the real me." She turns to Charlie. "I'm so sorry for all the damage I've caused. I hope you can forgive me."

"Ask me again after I tally up the receipts." Charlie winks. "Gotta say, I don't know what we're going to do when you're gone. I've developed quite a skill-set in crisis management. I'm going to have to learn to knit tea cozies or something."

"You, knit?" says Hannah. "I would like to see that."

Charlie huffs. "Hey, it could happen..."

Pearly's brow furrows. "If you're free," she says to Ruby, "why you are still here?"

The ghost bows her head. "I'm waiting," she says softly.

"For what?" But even as the words come out of Pearly's mouth, she knows. A shiver runs up her spine, and she turns to look at Sam. His head leans against the wall, with eyes half-closed, barely breathing. Pearly's heart flutters. She exchanges a glance with Charlie, who nods, takes out their phone, and heads off to dial 9-1-1. But she knows. *This is it.* And the only way she could fail him in this moment is to not show up.

Hannah and Danielle step back so as not to overwhelm Sam as Pearly drags her chair next to him. She takes his hand. His skin is patchy and dry and almost translucent, exposing his veins. "Sam," she says. "I'm here. I've got you. There's nothing you need to do, or say, or be. I've got you." As she gently massages his palm and fingers, she feels him relaxing, soothed by her words and touch. "If it's time to let go, it's okay." She swallows a lump in her throat. "It's okay."

His palm pulses in hers, and she knows whatever part of him needed to hear that did. The old Pearly would have run from the scene or tried to fix it, using her powers as a guide to heal Sam just enough to keep Death away – to save him to make up for her failure to save Thunder, back when he was Andrew, in their Chicago life. But the new Pearly simply breathes with Sam, watching the subtle rise and fall of his chest, the tiny beads of sweat on his forehead, the way the light hits his enviable lashes.

A calm euphoria envelops her as she sits there, fully present. Pearly is no longer merely with Sam, but one with him. Her heart fills with love, but it's too much to hold. So she surrenders her grip and it spreads out of her body and into the café. The mirage of form disappears, exposing the energy underlying all existence. She's still Pearly, but she's also Sam and Hannah and Charlie and Ruby and Danielle and the table and the windows and the sidewalk and the sky and all of Eenob and the earth and the stars and the entire goddamn universe. It's so...peaceful. It registers somewhere in the back of her mind—this is it. This is what Abathur was trying to tell her. She always thought of God as some eccentric hermit holed up in Sector Zero, out of touch with the concerns of the little guy. But now, she feels like she can see God right there in front of her. God is a Loving Presence, and it's everywhere, swirling all around them. Hot damn. She wants to get naked and shout it from the rooftops.

As Sam takes his last breath, something happens to him. It's happened to Pearly hundreds of times, but it's never any less of a miracle. A pool of light-energy ripples through his chakras and gathers around the crown of his head, swirling like a galaxy. It bursts out of him in an ecstatic rush that even Pearly feels coursing through her. And just like that, Sam-the-Soul is standing next to his lifeless body. He blinks, disoriented, taking himself in.

Pearly calls out. "Sam..."

He turns to her, eyes widening as he pieces it together: he's dead. And yet, he still exists. A huge smile spreads across his face. "My god, Pearly," he marvels. "All the pain – it's gone. I feel so – so light."

"Yes," she says. "You're free now, too."

"Too?" He remembers. "Ruby..."

The ghost floats to his side. For the first time, they're on the same plane of existence. Shyness creeps in for a moment, like they're unsure if they can touch each other. Then they're in each other's arms for the first time, embracing with a kind of fierce tenderness that reminds Pearly of her early days with Thunder. These two have a long, shared journey ahead of them.

Sam takes Ruby's face in his hands. "May I?"

She grins. "You damn well better."

He brings his lips to hers, and as they kiss, their auras briefly merge, creating a rainbow current of crackling energy. But this time, no pipes burst and no windows shatter. The vibration of love is much higher than anger or fear.

As they pull apart, Sam looks up toward the ceiling. "Do you feel that? It's like a...tug."

"Yes," she says. "I think it's the Tunnel."

Pearly rises to her feet. "You're being called to complete your journey."

A white-gold shaft of light beckons above them, the Tunnel glowing faintly in its depths. Funny how beautiful it looks from this side, when you're not the one cleaning up the leaks.

Sam takes Ruby's hand, and together they float up toward the light, their forms becoming less and less visible until they shimmer out of existence. "Godspeed," whispers Pearly, as the Tunnel disappears. "Don't do anything I wouldn't do."

She can almost hear the universe laughing. Fat chance, babe. What wouldn't you do?

Forty-Three

Pearly's going to miss Eenob. As she approaches Thunderbolt for the last time, she feels nostalgia for everything
from the photo-op town square to the big-ass pothole she and
Seraphina always hit on their way into town. She pauses just
outside the café, taking in the old brick building with its wooden
sign swinging gently in the breeze. It's hard to believe all that's
happened since she pitched Malcolm her crazy idea. *What a
ride.*

Malcolm...Pearly wonders what he said in his report to the
Higher-Ups. She knows she did well with his charges, but she
also bent – OK, broke – a lot of rules. Is she getting that Recommendation? Or is she getting Recycled? It's some relief to feel
that it's out of her hands. She did her best, whatever happens.
Even if she has to work in Waste Management for the rest of her
afterlife – so be it. She'll put on that hazmat suit with her head
held high.

Thunderbolt is closed today, in honor of Sam's memorial. It
was small and bittersweet, but his mom seemed grateful to hear
that her estranged son had love and support in his final days.
Now the remaining Thunderbolt crew is gathering for one last

ritual to celebrate his life – and Ruby's. It was Hannah's idea
to plant the saplings. She remembered this as a Jewish tradition
she grew up with – when a family member died, they planted a
tree as a symbol of life, growth, and renewal.

Pearly walks around the café to the side that faces the cross
street. She finds Danielle, Hannah, and Charlie standing around
two potted red maples in the glittering outfits they wore to
the memorial. Sam made a request in his will that his friends
dress in the style of *Flash Gordon*, one of his favorite cult films
known for its over-the-top costumes. He must have known
Pearly would get a kick out of giving a eulogy in her interpretation of Ming the Merciless, with a red satin floor-length
tunic embellished with metallic gold cuffs, high collar, flared
shoulders, and of course, a scepter.

Two holes have been dug into the dirt, twice as wide and deep
as the trees. Charlie places the saplings in the holes and holds
them in place as Pearly, Hannah, and Danielle backfill with soil
and mulch, tapping it down to eliminate air pockets.

"I wonder if they can thrive here," says Charlie, eyeing the wall
behind them. "I hope they get enough light."

"You know," says Hannah, "I heard it helps to name them.
Makes them harder to kill."

Pearly smiles. "Exactly." She strikes her scepter into the earth.
"I hereby decree thee Sam and Ruby."

The sun shines brightly on each sapling's delicate red leaves.
It looks like they're reaching towards each other. But who
knows. Maybe it's just the breeze.

***

Back in the café, Pearly makes her way to her favorite table by the window. As she sits there, memories start to surface—dancing with Danielle to Chappell Roan, digging through the basement with Sam, making a dating profile for Hannah. Pearly has watched her charges grow, each in their own way, and now – as much as it hurts – it's time to say goodbye.

Hannah sits down beside her. She's wearing the key from Charlie around her neck. "Damn, girl," Pearly says. "You're glowing."

Hannah gives a casual shrug, fingers absently touching the chain. "It's the key."

Pearly quirks an eyebrow. "It's more than the key."

Hannah smiles, brushing a strand of hair behind her ear. "Maybe you're right." She glances at the counter, where Charlie is busy steaming a latte. They look up instinctively and give her a wink.

"So what's next?" says Pearly.

"Good question," says Hannah. "I'm trying to just stay open and trust in the unfolding." She leans back, crossing her legs. "I've got to say, one thing I didn't expect from my relationship with Charlie – and all of you – is how it's impacting my work. I'm already thinking about a new course I want to teach on the sociology of belonging. There's so much fear and hate in the world these days, and yet somehow we came together and created this little microcosm of connection and community. Maybe it's a small act of rebellion, but it feels important."

"Absolutely," says Pearly. "I think it's like the story of the turtle and the hare. Fear may take the lead, but love wins the race."

Hannah grins, but it fades a bit as she meets Pearly's gaze. "Pearly...about Charlie. Me and Charlie. Are you okay? Like, really okay?"

"I mean, as best as I know how to be." Pearly exhales. "You know, I bumped into Theo in the afterlife"—she probably doesn't need to disclose the bit about impersonating Malcolm—"and he said something about love being bigger than us as individuals. I couldn't really take it in at the time because I was holding onto so much fear. I didn't know who I was without Thunder, and I was afraid I wasn't worth anything on my own. It was like our bond became a crutch, and he was right – I stopped growing. But he didn't. This life – you and Charlie – it's good, Hannah. For both of you. And it's good for me, too."

She and Thunder weren't meant to be in this life – because it wasn't her life, and she wasn't alive to live it. But the next life, the afterlife – who knows?

Hannah sighs, looking more than a little relieved. "It's nice to hear that." She bites her lip. "Now it's just up to me not to screw it up."

"You won't." Pearly takes her hand. "That doesn't mean you might not stumble...a lot. But love isn't about getting everything right from the start; it's about learning how to pick each other up after you fall. You and Charlie—y'all are just at the beginning."

"You're right," says Hannah. "I just need to stop overthinking it."

"Now you're talkin' my language. But enough of this, I got some gifts for you." Pearly reaches into her cleavage. "First, a little something for our mutual friend." She pulls out a flopping fish cat toy.

Hannah cracks up. "How do you even fit that in there?"

Pearly winks. "You don't ask Mary Poppins for her secrets."

"Fair enough," says Hannah. She takes the cat toy. "Calypso will love this."

"And for you..." Pearly pulls out a pair of rainbow suede vintage platform boots, causing Hannah's eyes to widen. "Now you don't have to walk to campus in those beige monstrosities," Pearly says. "And every time you step into class looking fresh, you can think of me."

Hannah grins. "Thanks, Pearly." She traces the soles of the boots, eyes glistening. "You're leaving, aren't you?"

Pearly nods. "I was never meant to stay here. Malcolm's a good guide and a kind soul—you'll be in capable hands. And the truth is, if I stayed, I'd only be in the way."

Hannah hesitates, then nods. "I guess it would be complicated. But that doesn't change how grateful I am for everything you've done. I won't forget you."

"Neither will I," Pearly smiles. She stands up and gives Hannah a hug. "Now, before I lose my shit and start bawling like a telenovela star, go get caffeinated and bang out a lecture."

That was hard, but it felt good. As Pearly's about to settle back in her chair, she sees Danielle approaching with two steaming lattes in her hands.

"Praline pecan," Danielle says, placing a mug in front of Pearly. "My new fall favorite."

Pearly takes a sip. "Damn, girl. If I'm a harvest wizard, then you're a kitchen witch."

"I've been practicing my spells," says Danielle, as they both sit down. "Actually, I've been wanting to tell you...I got the apprenticeship in Copenhagen. I'm going to be working with Chef Hansen!"

Pearly's face lights up with pride. "Fuckin-A! Now that's what I like to hear! I knew you had it in you."

"Well, I'm glad one of us did," Danielle concedes. "You were right, you know—that performance gave me the confidence boost I needed to nail the interview." She pauses, glancing up at Pearly. "But it wasn't just about the skills or the job. Being up there, in front of everyone, embracing who I am... it was one of the first times I felt pure gender euphoria. Just being myself, without hiding, without fear. That moment gave me the strength to believe I could do this. And now, Copenhagen... it's really happening."

"It is," says Pearly. "I'm so proud of you."

"I have to say, I'm a little nervous leaving the States – I mean, I've barely been out of the Midwest – but it's an excited kind of nervous." She sips her drink, licking the foam off her lips. "And, uh, you remember that guy Travis I told you about? The one who came to the gala? Well...we've been hanging out more, and I think he's coming to visit."

Pearly smiles. "I love that." She motions for Danielle to sit down. "Come here, sweetheart. Let's have a little chat."

Danielle sits down. Pearly reaches into her cleavage once more, this time pulling out a recipe journal decorated with a delicate butterfly motif.

"This," Pearly says, handing it to Danielle, "is for you."

Danielle takes the journal, eyes widening as she traces the butterfly design with her fingers. "Pearly, it's beautiful... I don't know what to say." She carefully opens the front cover, where Pearly has written in elegant script: "For the fiercest chef in the Midwest. Always remember, transformation is your superpower!" Underneath, Pearly has signed with a flourish, adding a big, glittery heart.

Danielle's eyes well up as she reads the words. "This means so much to me. You've always known exactly what I needed, even when I didn't. I don't know if I'd be here without you."

Pearly waves a hand. "Oh, you would've found your way, one way or another. But I'm glad I could be part of the journey. Now, go out there and show Copenhagen what you're made of."

"Yes, ma'am." She stands up, ready to return to work, then pauses, turns back. "Hey Pearly – that card you gave me with your phone number? Will it still work? I mean, just in case I need you?"

"Sure," she grins. "But only for you, so don't be giving out referrals."

Danielle tucks the journal under her arm and gives Pearly one last smile before heading back to the counter.

There's only one person left. Pearly takes a deep breath as she finds Charlie at a corner table, squinting into their laptop in cute reading glasses she's never seen. Pearly's heart aches, knowing there's so much more she'll never see. Not in this lifetime, anyway.

"Hey..." she says, walking up to them. "Got a minute?"

They look up. "Sure." They nod to the screen. A spreadsheet reflects in their lenses. "Just so you know," they say, "the gala was officially a success. It's almost hard to believe, but we're in the black again. I mean, I'm still gonna have to watch the budget, but I'm confident we'll stay afloat."

"That's great, Charlie. I guess I can cross the Christmas Extravaganza off my list. Though I will be a little disappointed not to get to audition Eenob's aspiring Sexy Santas."

Charlie chuckles. "Never say never..."

Pearly smiles. "I trust that the rest of you can pull it off." It's inspiring to see Thunder take on entrepreneurial challenges in this life. The easy choice would've been to pursue nursing or therapy or something more aligned with his afterlife vocation. But a well-rounded soul seeks to develop themselves in as many areas as possible. "This place, these people—they're your legacy. You'll take good care of them." She reaches out, gently squeezing their arm. "Now, come with me. I want to show you something."

She leads Charlie out of the café and into the bookshop. There, warming up the reading nook in between two plush armchairs, is the electric fireplace Charlie pined for at Costco.

Charlie's jaw drops. "No freaking way. How did..."

"Danielle helped me."

"But—"

Pearly puts a hand up. "No buts. This is for all of you. So that you'll have a super-cozy spot to talk shit about me after I'm gone."

Charlie shakes their head. "Thank you, Pearly." They meet her gaze, and for a moment Pearly feels the old stirring of energy. But this time, she just lets it pass through her.

"All I ask," she says, "is that you keep loving Hannah. She's a good egg."

Charlie nods. "She is."

Pearly puts up a warning finger. "And don't you go breaking that egg, or I might just have to come back and scramble you."

They both laugh, and Pearly feels the last bits of clinginess letting go. She *is* okay. More than okay. She takes a deep breath, feeling freedom enter her lungs.

With her heart unburdened, she walks back through the café with a spring in her step. "Well, my loves," she declares, "my work here is done."

And with that, Pearly Gates sashays out, leaving behind a trail of glitter that will take the staff all damn day to clean up.

FORTY-FOUR

Pearly should be thrilled. She did some real good in the world, made amends with her charges, and hopefully avoided getting Recycled. But when she stands outside her home on Lightbody Lane, she can't help feeling a little lonely. In the past, the house would be filled with welcoming light and the mouth-watering scent of whatever Thunder was cooking. Tonight, it's dark and still.

With a deep breath, she opens the door and steps inside. "Dumb Pearly?" she calls out. Usually, her double is up at odd hours. She hasn't learned to manifest yet, but that hasn't stopped her from ordering pizzas and eating the furniture when she gets late-night munchies.

As Pearly enters the living room, her attention drifts to the mantelpiece. It's lined with mementos from her past—photos from that trip to the Grand Canyon, a seashell from a long-forgotten beach, a delicate lace glove from the Victorian era. She walks over and slips on the glove, one finger at a time. She knows she should probably put this stuff in storage, but she can't bring herself to do it.

She sighs, turning away from the mantel. That's when she notices a dim light coming from the kitchen. Dumb Pearly must have gotten the munchies after all. She heads over to investigate.

As soon as she steps inside, the room explodes with light and sound and sparkling confetti. The ceiling is lined with balloons, and rainbow-sprinkled cupcakes drift through the air like tiny comets. Pearly blinks, blinded by the sudden brightness, as her brain tries to process what's happening.

"Surprise!"

Pearly gasps. Her heart pounds as she takes in the sight of her friends and colleagues gathered in the kitchen with proud, goofy grins.

There's Malcolm, leaning against the counter in his white robe and a "belt" of blinking string lights. Dumb Pearly stands beside him, bouncing on the balls of her feet in her hazmat suit and a glittery party hat. Hertz and Abathur are there too. Hertz keeps looking around the room as if he's casing the joint while Abathur grins at Pearly and raises his beer all "good job, kid."

Pearly's shocked to even see Mr. Mustard, dumping whiskey into the punch bowl.

"Trust me," he says, "this bug juice'll give you one helluva brick in yer hat!"

Then there's Flaubert oozing down from the ceiling, tentacles waving in greeting. And at the counter, Diesel-the-bartender's mixing drinks.

Pearly looks around the room. "What is all this?"

"Girl," says Dumb Pearly, "it's a kiki!"

Pearly swallows. "For me?"

"Yes, for you," says Malcolm, passing around a tray of drinks. "To celebrate all you've accomplished."

Diesel steps forward, handing Pearly an iridescent cocktail. "This one's called a Death Drop," he says with a wink. "Designed it especially for you."

Pearly takes the drink, feeling a lump form in her throat. She did it. She really did it. "I'm honestly gagged," she says. "Thank you. Thank you all so much."

Flaubert tilts several eyestalks toward Pearly. "Got to hand it to you, Pearly," they say. "You actually pulled this thing off."

Pearly nods, blinking back tears. "Thanks for believing in me...or at least for not turning me in."

Malcolm raises his glass. "To Pearly!"

"To Pearly!" they echo, clinking their glasses together.

As the celebration continues, Pearly takes a moment to soak it all in. It's hard to believe this is actually happening. But it's real, and it's hers. She plucks a cupcake from the air, takes a bite, and closes her eyes as the white velvet melts on her tongue.

Just as Pearly is about to swallow the whole thing, the energy around them begins to shift. It's as if reality itself is bending and warping, creating a multidimensional ball of light in the middle of the living room.

In the center of the light, a figure begins to materialize—or at least, something resembling a figure. It's difficult to pin down, more an outline of presence than a fully formed being. The edges of its form blur and shift, constantly in motion, a kaleidoscope of light and shadow. *A fucking Higher-Up?* Pearly's eyes bulge. She wishes she'd dressed a little better for the occasion.

The room falls silent. Even Dumb Pearly seems to know to shut up.

When the being speaks, its voice bypasses the ears and goes straight to the mind. "Pearly Gates," it says. "You've taken a most...creative...approach in interpreting your duties these past few weeks—an approach that's included duplicity, risk, and a complete disregard for protocols put in place for the safety of both guides and charges."

Pearly's face falls. *That's it. I'm done. It was nice being a soul. Maybe someday they'll write a ballad about me.*

The being pulses, shifting colors as it continues. "And yet, every step you took – even the ones off the beaten path – led you exactly where you needed to go. You've shown us that your heart is bigger than your ego, and the good that you've done far outweighs your spiritual infractions. As such, congratulations are in order."

Pearly breathes a massive sigh of relief. "Thank you," she manages. She's glad there are witnesses because no way anyone would have believed her otherwise.

"You've proven," says the Higher-Up, "that you're more than ready for the responsibilities you've requested. So, it's with great satisfaction and honor that we officially promote you to the position of spirit guide."

Pearly's heart skips a beat. Is this real? She glances at her friends, at Malcolm's approving nod, at Dumb Pearly's stupid grin. This is it—she's made it.

As the words settle, a soft light begins to form in front of Pearly, growing brighter and more defined. The light materializes into a white robe, floating gently in the air before her. This is yours," says the being. "May you wear it well."

Pearly takes the robe. She glances at Malcolm. "Did you do this?"

He shakes his head. "I put in a recommendation, but that guy pulled some serious strings." He gestures to Abathur, who gives Pearly a nod. Pearly nods back, still trying to process it all.

"And you, Dumb Pearly," says the Higher-Up, turning its attention to her double. "You too have served well, despite the challenges of your limited form. We have decided it is time for you to step into your own light." The aura around the figure brightens. "You are hereby granted full soul-hood, with all the rights and responsibilities therein. And, if you wish, you shall inherit Pearly's old position in Waste Management – permanently."

Dumb Pearly's face lights up. "Werk, queen! Slay!"

Mr. Mustard tugs on his belt buckle. "Got my work cut out for me." He takes a long sip of punch.

Pearly can't help but smile. She gives her double a hug. "Looks like you're your own person now, kid. Which means you deserve your own name."

Dumb Pearly's eyes go wide. She starts spewing out possibilities. "Bubbles McFierce! Whiplash Wanda! Ginger Snap Dragon! Hoochie O'Hara!"

The Higher-Up's light begins to fade. "You have done well, Pearly Gates. Continue to serve with the same spirit, and rewards will follow. Now – go show these fools how to party."

You don't have to tell Pearly twice. The living room transforms in an instant. Glittering curtains materialize around a stage, with spotlights shining in the center. Pearly enters in a holographic bodysuit and a crystal-studded crown that gleams with regal brilliance. Her nails spell out "F-I-E-R-C-E" in rainbow crystals, completing the look.

The crowd cheers as she struts down the stage to RuPaul's "Supermodel." She sings. She dances. She flirts. She twerks. Pearly's every inch the diva, celebrating her triumph like the cosmic queen that she is.

Next up, Dumb Pearly bounces onto the stage in a hot pink vinyl mini-dress, knee-high go-go boots, a huge blonde wig, and a tiny toy purse. She channels her inner "Barbie Girl" and brings the house down.

Not to be outdone, Flaubert slithers onto the stage to perform Bowie's "Life on Mars?" Metallic scales and iridescent fabrics cling to their limbs, while bold, geometric patterns zigzag across their tentacles. Flaubert isn't much of dancer, but nobody cares. Everyone's having a great time. Even Mr. Mustard gets in on the action, lip-syncing a surprisingly enthusiastic rendition of "Save a Horse, Ride a Cowboy."

Eventually, the extravaganza winds down and Pearly slips outside for some air. The contrast between the raucous celebration and the quiet night is stark, and it puts Pearly in a reflective mood. The thought that's been hanging around the edges of her consciousness finally presents itself front and center.

Malcolm soon joins her. They stand together in silence for a bit before Pearly speaks. "There's something I need to do," she says, turning to him, "before I can fully step into this role." She hands him the white robe. "Hold onto this for me?"

He glances at her, nods. "I will."

She smiles. "Thanks, Malcolm."

Pearly heads to the garage. Seraphina is ready and waiting, as always. Pearly gets in, mentally preparing herself for what she's about to do. With a deep breath, she turns the key, and Seraphina roars to life. As they roll away from the house, laughter from the party echoes into the night. The road stretches out before them, filled with endless possibilities, but Seraphina seems to know where Pearly wants to go.

The landscape begins to change as Seraphina rounds a bend. Up ahead, the Cosmic Rebirth Center emerges from the darkness, its crystalline surface shimmering in the distance.

Seraphina slows to a stop in the parking lot as Pearly takes a moment to gather herself, staring up at the thing she's avoided for so long. For a moment, she considers turning back. Instead, she reaches out, giving the dashboard an affectionate pet.

"Thanks, old friend," she says. "Try not to pull any wild stunts while I'm gone—no drag racing without me!"

Seraphina rumbles an encouraging purr, making no promises. Pearly steps out of the truck, makes her way toward the entrance. Each facet of the structure reflects her own image—showing her glimpses from all her past lives. A lot of those glimpses feature Thunder, her partner in so many adventures.

But not this one. She wants to see what she can do on her own – what she can contribute as an incarnated human. And if she really wants to be a good guide – hell, a good partner – then she has to embrace the unknown, to stand on her own two platformed feet. There's no "end up together" when there's no end. But whatever happens, she has a feeling her story with Thunder isn't over.

The past life fractals fade, leaving Pearly to contemplate the image of her present self. Each reflection is a testament to everyone she's ever been. As she takes herself in, her breath catches in her throat.

"Well, I'll be damned…"

Instead of the emerald green aura she's gotten so accustomed to, Pearly's astral body is now framed by a sparkling sapphire blue.

She evolved. And she'll keep evolving, keep embracing what a new life has to offer. Reincarnation doesn't mean leaving herself behind. It means a chance to start fresh — to integrate everything she's learned, to bring her unique gifts into a world that welcomes her return.

Pearly takes a deep breath, and steps through the doors.

PREVIEW: PEARLY GATES AND THE MIDNIGHT CROISSANT

Set in the iconic City of Lights, *Pearly Gates and the Midnight Croissant* is a warm, witty romantic cozy fantasy about second chances, grand adventures, and the magic of showing up—fabulous, flawed, and fully yourself.

Preorder now: www.amazon.com/dp/B0FHVPZTG6

Read on for a sneak peek.

ONE

Pearly Gates is late—as in dead—but also late for a meeting. And not just a wee bit tardy. She is horrendously, spectacularly, ludicrously late. Pulling on her White Robe while trying not to ruin her still-wet manicure, she barges through frosted glass doors into the afterlife's Department of Human Relations. She considers the following excuses:

1. "I got stuck in one of those interdimensional potholes on the astral highway!"

2. "I realized I left my past-life altar candles burning and didn't want to start another reincarnation fire!"

3. "I had to handle an emergency involving a charge who got drunk and tried to astral project to Vegas!"

What she does not consider telling is the truth—she got caught up in conversation with her manicurist. But only because her department's new supervisor doesn't understand the important spiritual guidance a manicurist has to offer. Who better to ask about reaching out to her ex-soulmate Thunder, now that they're both back in the spirit world after their most recent incarnations?

As she barrels down a labyrinthine corridor lined in silver shag carpet, she passes floating orbs illuminating holo-portraits of each graduating class of guides. Pearly's not in any of them, of course. It would be easier if she was. Her situation is a bit more...unique. Instead of getting proper schooling, she convinced Malcolm—a burnt-out senior guide—to let her sub for him while he went on vacation. She broke a lot of rules along the way, but in the end, she managed to win over the Higher-Ups. Was it worth it? Absolutely. But the job has been, well...a little more challenging than she'd expected.

Pearly careens to a halt in front of Conference Room B, adjusting the blinking rainbow halo atop her cotton candy beehive before flinging open the door. Twenty-seven heads swivel to stare at her. None of them look thrilled to see her, and especially not the one belonging to her new boss.

Fuckety Fuckerton.

Mildreth Snaggs is not your typical soul—at least not in this corner of the afterlife. While most guides take on astral versions of their former human forms, Mildreth's incarnations played out on a fungal hivemind planet. And she still favors that aesthetic. She reminds Pearly of the Swamp Thing on magic mushrooms—a vaguely humanoid mass with moss-covered arms protruding from her White Robe, a portobello face, electric-blue eyes glowing like bioluminescent spores under a pair of black cat-eye glasses, and an unruly mop of lichen springing from the top of her head in all directions. A faint cloud of mildew lingers in her wake.

"Sorry, folks!" gulps Pearly, edging into the room. If only she could manage a low-key entrance! "Please do, uh, carry on."

"Well, if it isn't Pearly Gates." Mildreth quirks something that might be an eyebrow. "How kind of you to grace us with your presence. We trust the concept of time remains optional in your personal ethos?"

Pearly's tempted to bite back. Time doesn't *really* exist in the spirit world—at least, not in the way it does on Earth. But she doubts bringing that up is going to win her any points. So she just offers a vague set of prayer hands and heads for the empty seat at the far end of the conference table.

"Excuse me—*pardonnez-moi*—no, don't get up..." She squeezes past the other guides, clutching her scroll and a half-spilled latte. Her bejeweled chain belt snags on someone's robe, forcing an awkward dance of disentangling. Finally, she drops into her chair with flushed cheeks and a dramatic sigh of relief. Mildreth materializes a thick info-packet in front of her. Pearly tries not to groan at the title: *Karmic Rollover Period Compliance Manual (Version 7.3d)*.

"What page are we on?" she whispers to the guide next to her. Marty? Mitzvah? She should really make more of an attempt to befriend her colleagues. It's just... most of them are about as fun as an eye exam. And they seem to think she's more spectacle than substance. Maybe it's her past life as a drag queen. Or the fact that she skipped the line to become a White Robe. *Whatever.* She has Malcolm and her manicurist and her room-mate-slash-former-body-double, Dumb Pearly—a half-baked clone turned soul in her own right. She doesn't need a posse of sticks-in-the-mud.

The guide holds up his manual, and Pearly flips to page 322. Mildreth could've just sent the info to everyone's scrolls, but she loves to brag about being old school. Pearly suspects she just likes to use mountains of paperwork as a scare tactic.

"As we all know," says Mildreth, "the rollover period exists to ensure the proper soul-cycle closure before vibrational reallocation can occur, thereby reducing the risk of karmic residue contaminating the next incarnation's energetic template..."

Pearly's eyes glaze. Her thoughts drift back to Thunder. They were partners and soulmates for so many lives—playing out every possible combination of gender, sexuality, and culture the Earth had to offer. Nobody knows Pearly like Thunder. But she hasn't seen him since their breakup.

Well, not this version of him.

She spent time with his last incarnation—Charlie, the owner of the café where she guided her first set of charges. But Charlie never knew it was her—a rare feat of discretion on Pearly's part. Now that they're both back in the afterlife, she keeps meaning to message him. Or spontaneously "bump into him," how weird! She's just been dragging her heels. It makes sense—she *is* the dump-ee. And she doesn't know what his situation is these days. Is he still with Hannah? Not that it matters. She totally wouldn't care one way or the other.

Besides, she's been busy. Could "busy" be a way of avoiding her feelings? Maybe. Probably. Almost certainly. But she's not hurt anymore. She's proud she learned to be more independent, to source love within herself. If anything, she's just... curious.

"Failure to properly neutralize past life triggers," Mildreth drones on, "may result in erratic soulmate entanglement, which—as you know—is no longer covered by cosmic liability..."

Pearly considers sending Thunder a telepathic message. Maybe...

Pearly: *Thunder! Hi! Long time, no see*

Long time no see? Ugh, delete. Maybe...

Pearly: *Would you believe I had the craziest dream*

And you were in it???

No way. Too desperate. How about something simple?

Pearly: *sup bro*

No. Absolutely not.

Pearly sighs. If she can't think of the perfect thing to say, better to hold her tongue—er, thoughts. Instead, she opens a line to Malcolm.

Pearly: *I don't think my new supervisor likes me*

Three dots shimmer in the corner of her vision. A moment later:

Malcolm: *Mildreth Snaggs?*

Pearly: *Yeah*

Malcolm: *She's...tricky*

And I speak from experience

We went to soul school together, you know

Pearly: *Really? What was she like?*

Malcolm: *Exactly what you'd expect really*

Mostly kept to herself

Maybe it was the hive-mind thing but

I don't think she ever learned how to socialize

Not the way humans do, anyway

Pearly: *Huh*

Maybe I should invite her out for a pint

Give her a little Pearly Gates pizazz

Malcolm: *uhhhh yeahhhh*

I wouldn't

Pearly: *Why not? It worked with you*

Malcolm: *She's less gullible than me*

Remember, you can't charm a fungus

Pearly: *Maybe YOU can't. I can charm anyone*

Malcolm: *OK. Let me know how that goes*

"Pearly Gates, are you *telepathing* in the middle of a meeting?"

Pearly snaps back to the conference room to find Mildreth staring daggers at her. "What? No!" She sits up tall in her chair, flashes her best bullshitter's smile. "I was just reflecting on the importance of following protocols. I mean, where would we be without them? Flying blind in the throes of cosmic chaos, that's where." She gestures grandly to her packet. "I'm *thrilled* to know someone went to the trouble of creating a seven-hundred page guide for karmic rollover. I, for one, feel much safer knowing that unresolved grudges must be logged with a nine-step verification process and a laminated form." She leans in, all conspiratorial. "Do you know what they used to call me in soul school? *The Laminator.* Yup. Never met a sign I didn't...lacquer."

Silence. Mildreth is still staring. It's creepy how she never blinks, though that might be due to the whole "no eyelids" thing. Pearly shifts in her seat, suddenly hyper-aware of the other guides. One watches her like a zoo animal while sipping from a mug that says *Live. Laugh. Levitate.* Another types notes on her scroll while sneaking glances at Pearly. She can feel the attention closing in—twenty-six guides pretending not to listen, all thanking the cosmos that they're not the ones under Mildreth's scrutiny. Pearly's aura flickers. If someone doesn't say something soon, she might actually combust from secondhand judgment.

A mushroom cap unfurls from Mildreth's shoulder with a papery *pop*, like some weird fungal cuckoo clock. "Aura realignment break," she nods at the timer. "You may adjourn for ten minutes."

The guides begin collecting their scrolls and standing up. Pearly practically bolts out of her chair. She can't wait to get out.

Mildreth clears her throat. "Pearly Gates. A word please..."

Fuckingham McFuckerton the Fourth.

Pearly watches the room clear out with a rising sense of nausea. It's like that time she ate an astral gnat tartine—even without a digestive system, the idea was enough to make her dry-heave. With a sigh of resignation, she squares her shoulders and approaches Mildreth. In five-inch platform boots, Pearly still only reaches her boss's shoulder. But what she lacks in height, she'll make up for in confidence. Cool. Calm. Collected. Easy-peasy—

"These are your first officially assigned charges, are they not?" says Mildreth.

Pearly flashes a smile. She brushes a wispy pink bang off her face. "They are."

"You've had them long enough to know better."

Maybe. Technically, she'd been back from her last incarnation for ages—though it felt like a year, tops, given "astral time." But her old charges were temporary, and that assignment ended before she incarnated. These new ones were official. And apparently, under review.

Mildreth manifests another stack of papers—this one with Pearly's name on it.

Pearly freezes. It's thick. That could be good. But it's probably not. She clears her throat. "Long enough to generate a file, it seems."

"Yes, well…" Mildreth rifles through the papers, muttering indecipherable sounds. "We all have a learning curve—but at some point, one must ask whether the curve ever levels out."

Pearly's smile fades. "The Higher-Ups seemed to think I was cut out for this when they gave me my robe."

Mildreth's lips twitch upward. "And what do you imagine they'd think now if I showed them your file?" She flips a page. "I see multiple incidents of administrative negligence. Your case notes seem to be perpetually late and chronically underwritten. '*Mission served cunty realness. 10s across the board,*' is not a report. Nor is '*vibes were restored.*' And colorful as it might have been, a quarterly evaluation delivered via vision board does not meet departmental standards." She peers down at Pearly through her glasses. "What exactly were you thinking?"

Pearly was thinking that she'd rather get tossed into cosmic furnace for recycling than fill out one more goddamn spreadsheet—and honestly, what kind of spiritual potato sack doesn't appreciate an eye-catching vision board? Does no one appreciate rainbow glitter anymore? Or strategic use of decoupage? "Sorry," she says, swallowing her pride. "Guess I wasn't thinking."

"Clearly not." Mildreth nods. "Not only that, you've missed more department meetings than the rest of the department combined. You once took an emergency sick day due to—and I quote—'a bad hair day.' And you used your scroll to livestream a reality show recap during risk management training."

Pearly's throat constricts.

"And that's not even counting your protocol violations—need I remind you that you may not place a karaoke machine in the break room without express permission from management? But worst of all is your questionable guidance."

"Questionable guidance?" She's starting to spiral like a rhinestone in a blender. "Now hold up, I have to object to that one."

"On what grounds? Did you or did you not permit a charge to bypass a soul lesson by faking emotional growth on social media? Did you not give a struggling charge a 'gentle nudge' to pursue interpretative dance... during her grad school interview? Did you not 'help' a bitter divorcee by subtly reinforcing the idea that relationships are nothing but a trap for codependency and better off avoided altogether? Did you not suggest that a charge having a spiritual crisis binge a full season of *The Great British Baking Show* and wait for divine inspiration?"

"Hey, that one actually worked," says Pearly.

Mildreth shakes her head. "Even if I were to overlook these indulgences in poor judgment, it's clear you don't take your job here seriously, and that's of great concern to me as your supervisor. I have reports to file too, and the Higher-Ups hold me responsible for your success—or failure."

"But I love being a guide," says Pearly—and she means it. She's never felt more suited to anything, in life or the afterlife. And she cares about her charges. She really does. "I've just been a little overwhelmed. This is all—it's a lot of responsibility. And paperwork. I mean, come on, there's a form to request a form! But I promise, I do take it seriously."

"Do you now?" Mildreth eyes Pearly, who shifts her weight uncomfortably. One platform boot squeaks against the floor. "May I see your scroll?"

Pearly's jaw tightens. She considers shoving the scroll into her cleavage, or tossing it out the window. Except there is no window. So she reluctantly hands it over. Mildreth pauses on the lock screen, where Pearly has replaced the Department of Human Relations logo with a big, glittery middle finger.

Pearly gulps. She wants to say it was a joke, but she'd just be playing into Mildreth's hands. Or her appendages, or whatever.

Mildreth tosses the scroll back on the table like it's contagious. "Allow us to spell it out for you. You are not here to express yourself. You are here to serve the department. We don't care how you managed to slip by. We have no interest in flair, or drama, or 'turning it out.' Do we make ourselves clear?"

Pearly grits her teeth. "Crystal."

"Excellent. We'd hate to see you back in waste management," she says, sounding like she'd love nothing more. "If there's even an opening. But we're sure something will work out. We hear they're looking for recruits in astral pest control." She nods to the door. "Now—go realign that aura. It looks a little...flickery."

Pearly summons what's left of her dignity and sashays away. She wants to cry, but she refuses to let her new boss get the best of her. She was chosen for a reason, after all, and it sure as hell wasn't to blend in. She may not do things by the book, but she gets the job done. And if Mildreth Snaggs thinks Pearly's fashion choices disqualify her from guiding souls?

Well, buckle up, fungus.

She's just getting started.

Acknowledgments

This book would not exist without Josh Grapes. Well it would, but it wouldn't be nearly as sparkly. Josh is a brilliant editor (you should hire him). Deep gratitude also to Nora Bellot and John Crye for your developmental expertise.

To my stellar writing group, the Sixers—Barbara Boone, Mike Conboy, Ben Cooper, Sarah Griffin, Dave Melody, Krista Templeton, Rene Thomas (and my mini-group with Rene and Ronda Whaley)—I couldn't dream of better allies on this wild writing journey. A special shout-out to Tim Booth for those early critique sessions as we honed our craft.

To Chris Kuser, for being a wonderful champion of my work.

To my talented cover designer, Ryan Mulford—thank you for executing my vision so flawlessly. Special thanks to Outi Harma and Michael Conboy for additional design tweaks.

To my fantastic audiobook producer, Michael Nocny, for delivering a polished product so quickly and professionally.

To my early readers and supporters—Sue Lindgren, Gary Solomon, Sarah Greene, Flo Aliviado, all my Book Ambassadors, ARC reviewers and Kickstarter backers—thank you for believing in Pearly and helping to bring her to life.

To Elizabeth Gilbert, the Lovelets, and my Substack writer friends—especially Amy Gabrielle—your encouragement means everything. And to the spirit of Unconditional Love, which gives surprisingly good advice.

To the Deep Dance community and Council. What we've created together is so special, and I am eternally grateful.

To my LGBTQ+ community, for your bravery, perseverance, and commitment to queer joy. Thanks especially to Esther Loewen for your encouragement and insights.

And finally, to RuPaul— my biggest inspiration for this novel—and all the *Drag Race* queens. Thank you for bringing your artistry to the world.

About the Author

Bonnie Solomon has a passion for creating humorous, uplifting stories in magical settings. As a queer writer, she is committed to authentic and aspirational LGBTQ+ representation.

When she's not writing, you can find her cuddling the cat, shaking it loose on the dance floor, or finding the best latte in LA. *Pearly Gates* is her debut novel.

LEAVE A REVIEW

Thanks for reading *Pearly Gates*!

If Pearly's journey made you laugh, cry, or feel a little more seen, please consider leaving a review on Amazon or Goodreads. Reviews help readers discover the book – and they mean everything to indie authors.

www.ingramcontent.com/pod-product-compliance
Lightning Source LLC
Chambersburg PA
CBHW030348120726
47901CB00007B/1953